Also by Gail Godwin

The Perfectionists

Glass People

The Odd Woman

Dream Children

Violet Clay

Violet Clay

by Gail Godwin

 Alfred A. Knopf, New York, 1978

The author would like to thank the John Solomon Guggenheim Memorial Foundation for a grant which enabled her to write much of this novel.

THIS IS A BORZOI BOOK
PUBLISHED BY ALFRED A. KNOPF, INC.

Library of Congress Cataloging in Publication Data

Godwin, Gail. Violet Clay.

I.   Title.
PZ4.G576Vi   [PS3557.0315]   813'.5'4   77-12890
ISBN 0-394-49912-3

Manufactured in the United States of America

First Edition

To Robert Starer

TAMINO: *Wann wird das Licht mein*
Auge finden?

PRIESTS: *Bald, bald, Jüngling,*
oder nie.

(When will my eyes find the light?

Soon, soon, Youth, or never.)

The Magic Flute

Violet Clay

1
The Fate of
Fleeing Maidens

I am a painter. I like to listen to music while I work. On that hot August morning on which my story begins in earnest, I was listening to Schumann's *Carnaval* on WQXR and blacking the shrunken pupils of a pair of female eyes with my smallest-tipped sable brush. She had alert, astonished eyes. Her lips, full and inviting, were parted in confoundment. Her black hair was snow-blown and I had worked in a few gems of melting flakes. Behind her loomed a secretive-looking edifice of many devious proportions. In an upper mullioned window, a single lurid light shone. Even though I was doing hack work, I was in that rare-fied state of consciousness I like best: submerged to a sensuous degree in my subject, yet allowing my thoughts to roam free. Today they were striking out in many different directions, yet weaving a pattern, too. I was thinking of death and love and am-bition. I had begun by imagining Clara Schumann at her piano, playing this winsome music, thinking of her husband, who had finally succeeded at dying. I saw him hurl himself into the Rhine, in his early, unsuccessful attempt, and while the agile fingers of a late-twentieth-century pianist evoked him back to this earth again, I saw my young father disappear into a wartime sea that my adult imagination still painted red because I had come to consciousness calling it Coral. Down went my father. And on a stormy March night some ten months later, when I was still in my crib, my nineteen-year-old mother had walked out of the house in a fit of grief and up the street to the Charleston Yacht Club, stolen a sailboat belonging to a doctor, put up the mast and the sail all by herself, despite the fact she'd never sailed alone, and challenged the rainy winds as far as the cross-currents of the Ashley and Cooper rivers before capsizing. She couldn't swim either. The coroner's verdict: a reckless act in a moment of acute bereavement; she just hadn't weighed the dangers. He was our family's friend. The doctor's sailboat was returned intact, and my grandmother was spared the public acknowledgment of her daughter-in-law's suicide. Thus I joined the hallowed clan of The Orphan. I became accustomed merely to holding out my hand and receiving from others the currency of sympathy. But, at age thirty-two, I was discovering I couldn't buy so much with these earnings. This had been pointed out to me by my most recently departed lover, Jake.

"You'll never be a great painter," he had said in those final days when we were both going for the jugular (I had, at long last, called him "short"), "because basically, Violet, you *like* your crumbly old death ship of the past. How many times have you dragged your teen-age mother out of the sea in order to drown her again and get more sympathy? So she didn't find it worth hanging around to see what a wonderful little girl you were going to be. If she couldn't have her husband, she didn't want you either. At least she took some kind of plunge. Whereas you're scared silly as those gothic heroines you paint of taking any real voyages. You're afraid if you got really good at something people wouldn't pity you anymore, and you'd rather have the pity."

And with the exemplar's punctuation of his own sermon, he had packed up his oboes, his reeds, his jeans and his long-tailed tuxedo, and sailed away on a real voyage to Norway on an all-expense-paid "Baroque Music Cruise" with his group, leaving me behind to ponder my stagnation. Much of what he said hit uncomfortably close to the bone. What if Violet Clay wasn't to be one of the shining ones after all? But: no. I hadn't yet reached that point of resignation where I surrendered the image of my greatest self. If and when that day came, I might as well be dead.

But I was not dead yet. There was still time, I told myself, though not as much as there had been. I absorbed myself in my present heroine, soothing my alarms of failure with the comfort of Task. For economic reasons, I had agreed to give her life visual dimensions, and this I would do, down to the last detail of her foolish silver sandals, meant for neither walking in snowstorms nor running from a man in the best of weathers. That she wouldn't get very far was programmed into her script, so the shoes didn't matter. The Villain would show himself to be the Good Man All Along by the end of her night. She would be able to dry her hair at his fire. Artistically speaking, I had painted more contradictions into her face than her prescribed destiny warranted. But on the morning on which I invite you to enter my life, I was an illustrator, not an artist. I was still spending my skills on other people's visions.

When the phone rang, I was furious. Nobody I liked ever called me in the morning; they all knew better. And *Carnaval* was one of my favorite pieces of music. In the process of turning down the volume of the radio, I left a thumbprint of titanium white on the serrated knob, which would be the devil to remove. I was sure it was an enemy. It was: the new art director at Harrow House, the paperback firm I did covers for.

"Violet? Doris Kolb here."

"Hi, Doris," I said gingerly, repressing the "How are you?" which she always left hanging in a silence. She either could not or would not soften dialogues with the amenities I had been weaned on, such as: "Isn't August in the city awful?" or what every previous art director had automatically prefaced phone calls with: "Did I disturb you? Were you working?"

"Can you come into the office this afternoon? Anytime after four-thirty would be fine."

I resented the way she'd already assumed I had no choice. I'd been planning to take the afternoon off and see *Scenes from a Marriage*. Since Jake and I had split, I preferred afternoon movies, because I didn't have to stand in line with all those couples.

"I *could*," I said. "Is it anything urgent?"

She gave her splintery little laugh. In my mind's eye I could see the bared teeth, tiny and even, and the rather prominent expanse of gums. "I think it is," she said blandly.

"Okay. I'll come," I said. Then I added, "I'm working on the *Windrift Woman* art right now. I could rush it if you need it."

"No. I don't need it." She had a toneless, little-girl voice. From anyone else, this would have seemed an insulting remark. You would sense an innuendo. But with Doris, you soon got the feeling everything really *was* on the surface, like minimal art. I could visualize her at her uncluttered desk of aluminum and plastic, a white china jar full of unused pencils sharpened to vanishing point. Had she ever scribbled or doodled—or erased? Where on earth had she come from, this cool, static figure who had been hired to "reconceptualize" the Harrow House image? Our last director, once a well-known illustrator himself, back in the thirties, had been a sociable gothic enthusiast who could remember the plot details and heroines' names from such vintage works as *Necromancer of the Black Forest*, *Orphan of the Rhine*, and even Lathom's *Astonishment!!!*, in which the heroine discovers that her lover is her long-lost son. Not that the house printed such things; the genre had declined over the past century, he said, into the enfeebled "romantic suspense," as it was called in the trade—a booming business, for all its resolute avoidance of any real horror or sex. But, for one reason or another, the firm, which was part of a large conglomerate dominated by a certain food-packaging concern, had lost a little of its profits last year, and our congenial director had been put out to pasture, and a cool cookie called Doris Kolb had simply appeared one day behind her antiseptic desk. Since that time, several of the older illustrators had been let go. I had, in fact, taken over their assignments, including the one I was working on now.

I went back to my studio, switching up the volume on *Carnaval* as I went. She'd made me miss the wistful slow movement I loved best, the homage to Chopin.

I scrutinized my latest heroine. A small color photograph

was tacked to the wooden upright of my easel. When you've painted over two hundred women running away from houses, you begin to seek variations. Over my nine years of employment with Harrow House I had sponged off everyone from Giotto to Whistler, varying my medium between watercolor, gouache, or oils worked thin to dry by deadline time. It was my way of keeping my hand in, I told myself, my underground system of staying in touch with Art until the day when I had enough energy (and money) to pack in this job-beneath-my-talents and throw myself into full-time creation. On this particular morning I was painting from a small color photograph of myself. Actually, it was a photo of Jake and myself, taken last winter as we relaxed on the sofa after a dinner party. But I had folded away the half with Jake in it and all that was left was a disembodied hand curled possessively around my shoulder.

It was an interesting exercise, painting my own face. On the whole my face represents the person behind it. They say people make their faces after a certain age, but it is also true that before a certain age people's faces help to make them. My face was broad and shield-shaped, with a cleft chin that made me look bold and defined and rather combative. The black eyebrows looked like dark wings about to take off from the bridge of the nose; combined with the round dark eyes, they made me seem to stare when I was only looking normally at someone or something. The upper part of my face had often earned me the epithet "critical" or "sassy." My mouth, plump and wide and full, was my claim to being thought sensual and feminine. The top part of my nose was narrow and civilized, but the nostrils flared a little too savagely. I knew, even as I amused myself with the exercise, that I'd have to make last-minute modifications on this girl's face before she would ever be allowed on the cover of "romantic suspense" fiction. The mouth and eyes could stay—she was supposed to look feminine and astonished—but the stubborn square would have to be rounded, the alertness and flaring blended into something approaching acquiescence.

I worked till noon, then ate a sandwich standing up. I still missed Jake at mealtimes even though we had seldom lunched

together. He would go off to his studio at Carnegie Hall and I'd
stay home in mine. We'd meet in the late afternoon at our corner bar and compare the day. Much of his was spent making
reeds on a fancy French machine he had. He lived in terror of
running out of reeds during a concert. We frequently devoted
our first hour to a discussion of the music and art reviews in the
Times. What new young artist had been granted ill-deserved
praise simply because the paper had to fill up space. The reverse
sexism implicit in the music critic's covering a brass recital of
nude women while neglecting Jake's group's woodwind Baroque
concert. We achieved some of our best moments complaining
about the *Times*. By dinner we were usually quite high. Each
had unselfishly conspired to steer the other past the midday
knowledge of being unrecognized by the world at large. We
wafted home or to a restaurant in a gentle alcoholic dusk in
which the promise of more venturesome and profitable tomor-
rows already winked at us from the lights of passing planes or
shone down on us like squares of inspiration from the skyscraper
offices of moguls working late. After we ate, we drank more wine
or smoked pot, or good hash when we could afford it. On the
latter occasions we rolled around on the floor, friendly as pup-
pies, each distracted by his own private movie.

But when we drank we usually fought. We'd begin by analyz-
ing one another's psyches and then someone would go too far.
Our fights were "picturesque." Their borrowed quality of having
been seen somewhere before should have alerted us sooner that
we lacked any original passion. We just climbed into old frames
and played somebody else's scenes. "You *cow*," he shouted,
kicking me on the thigh and pouring sherry over my head. I
wept according to the battered-woman's script and cringed with
more pain than I felt, while my cool self watched, thinking:
There's nothing the least bit cowlike about me; I wonder who
he's confusing me with; thinking: I'm sure glad it's Taylor's and
not Harvey's Bristol Cream. "Get out of my life!" I once yelled,
and threw his clothes out the window, where they fell neatly
on top of a Cadillac coming out of a parking garage below and

were borne silently down the nighttime street and out of sight. We both stopped fighting and stood hip to hip at the window, chastened by the touch of genuine originality that Real Life had bestowed upon our hackneyed scene.

And now he was gone and all I could remember were bottles and bruises and shouted clichés, a few good moments, very few recollections of the unique person I'm sure he believed himself to be. He probably retained some cliché image of me as well. The truth was—and it shamed me to realize he must be thinking it, too—we had pretended feeling more than we'd felt for so long because it was better than being alone.

People should do better than this, I thought, brushing my teeth after the stand-up sandwich. I went back to the studio, to this poor heroine on whom I'd bestowed my face. *She* still had a way to go before her enlightenment. She was still in the Dark Ages, romantically speaking. She still believed Happy Endings were the end. Soon now, she'd be dragged screaming back to the warm house by the Villain, only to discover he'd been the Hero all along. The real Villain, disguised as the Kind Cousin cheated out of his heritage, had been waiting for her behind a snowy tree, blunt object in hand to "put her out of the way." How would her story end? Well, in *Windrift Woman* (the proofs of this masterpiece, smudged with fingerprints of dried pigment, lay on my worktable: I prided myself on being a cover artist who always read the books, who had never once given a heroine black hair when her author had given her blond, never given an edifice Romanesque proportions when its author had specified Norman) her destiny had been completed thus:

> I saw his dark eyes soften, his grim mouth relax into a smile. It was then I knew there would be no more black moods of indecipherable melancholy, for the real enemy to our happiness lay dead in the snow, dead by his own hand. Derek had sent Joseph for the constable and now we could do no more. When he bent over me, as I sat, still shivering, by the roaring fire, I felt the love in every line of his frame flow into mine, and I knew we would belong to each other now and always.

But what after the "and always"? Well, first she would redec-
orate Derek's drafty mansion. However well-to-do, bachelors
are notorious for making themselves uncomfortable. Then, that
feminine duty done, she would appropriate the tower room for
her own. She would lock herself in with the cumbersome antique key, and set out, in safety, to "discover herself." She might
paint. She would paint and paint and paint, losing track of whole
days. She would give herself over to the swirls and smells of art
all day and abandon herself to the swirls and smells of sex at
night. That sharp fault-finding little ego of hers would be left
outside like an orphan child. For a while. For a while she would,
therefore, be happy, and Derek, being a person who had always
had enough for himself, would be happy in her happiness. He
would bring friends home for dinner and she would cook magnif-
icent things, and, after dinner, she would show her paintings,
and a well-disposed friend or two would buy something. Then
she would create herself as a serious painter and become more
demanding of herself—and everybody else. A bad day in the
tower room would reverberate to the dining room—and the
bedroom! Ah, the bedroom! Now she lies staring at a patch of
peeling plaster on the high, fluted ceiling while Derek grinds
his teeth gently in sleep beside her and she sets herself the in-
somniac theme of why it is marriage kills passion, or is it only
her marriage? One really can't discuss these things with others,
for fear of having one's own shortcomings revealed. She remem-
bers back to earlier parts of her story, when, in his frequent
moods of indecipherable melancholy, Derek had only to glower
out at her from under shaggy black brows and her spine would
melt in delicious terror. Did she . . . was it possible that she
loved him better as the Villain? Did that make her a masochist,
then? Oh, what was the truth about all these things? Why oh
why had nobody prepared her for what came after the last page?
Well, it's a good life here in the mansion—especially since she
made him spend so much on the redecorating. Even when she
fights with him, all it takes is one look at those cream-and-gold
brocade curtains with the green fringe and tassels. How could

she bear to leave them behind, those curtains she designed and ordered herself? And even if she took them with her, which would be churlish, how ridiculous they would look hanging over some filthy window in a Soho loft, over somebody's warehouse. And she's not going to leave him—what is she thinking of? Oh, these night thoughts are perilous. They catch one at one's lowest ebb. She loves him. Of course she loves him. What exactly is love? Perhaps everybody else is only pretending to know. But . . . doesn't she worry about him when he goes out without his galoshes to oversee some improvement being made on his vast property? Isn't she genuinely fond of him when he raises his glass of claret to her at the beginning of a good dinner? Doesn't she adore the way her head fits nicely into the crook of his armpit when they walk through the fields at dusk? It's just that . . .

What is missing is that ecstatic sense of being dragged screaming toward one's destiny. But this *is* her destiny. Isn't it? Wasn't she dragged screaming toward it only . . . my God, was it only a year ago? Surely it's too soon to be tired of all this security. You can't expect to be dragged screaming to a higher destiny every year. Or is evolution speeding up or something? People getting through the successive growing stages of their lives quicker these days? But surely Derek is not just "a stage." That would mean she had been using him to climb on, like a ladder, to the next thing.

She makes him model for her. At first he is reluctant. A shade embarrassed. But he wants this marriage to work as much as she does, and besides, he is a good modern man who believes in the latest equipment; he believes a woman should have the latest in rights. The tower room is a little chilly, so she fixes up a small electric heater by his platform. It gives a ruddy glow to his pale, muscular legs. How nice men's rear ends are; they never seem to hang or get little dents in them. And how perfect their feet, as perfect as those Greek and Roman statues, not crumpled by a lot of stylish shoes. And the squarish way everything is built, like blocks fitted into one another: squares every place a woman has circles. And then that single vulnerable area, so purplish and poignant. It makes her shudder to think of boys carelessly sliding down banisters, as she paints her husband's genitals. What if those sacs should burst, like overpressed plums? What if . . . what if that thing got bent? For a long time she didn't even understand the joke told by her uncle, a war hero. A duchess was visiting an army hospital. She stopped beside the bed of a wounded soldier. "And what injury did you suffer, you poor man?" she asks. Blushing crimson, he replies that there has been an injury to his privates. "Oh, my goodness!" cries the duchess. "I do hope it didn't break the bone!" Whereupon the soldier bows and says, "My compliments to the duke, ma'am."

When she was a girl in boarding school, she attended tea dances at the nearby private school for boys. There were three brothers, the Iglesias boys from Cuba. All the girls dreaded dancing with these brothers, because, as one girl put it, "They get you in a death clench and then probe you with some sort of stick." But no girl dared refuse to dance with the Iglesias brothers, including herself.

No stick, this. It nestles against her husband's thigh, a hairless and shy creature. With that little opening like a mouth. She is suddenly seized with a prankster's urge to draw eyes on it, above the mouth. She laughs.

"What's so funny?" asks Derek, drawing himself up a little. His dignity is wounded.

She tells him she was laughing at her uncle's joke about the duchess. She tells him the joke. Privately she is thinking: Perhaps we should not have done this. Better perhaps to leave the whole thing shrouded in mystery. Let men go on walking softly and carrying their big sticks. Because this way, when they're exposed, when we have time to study their exposures and ponder them from all the angles, this way they become suddenly . . . like us. Just as perishable, just as naked, just as capable of being hurt.

From this point on, in the book of Old Plots, she has various alternatives. She can, for instance, attempt to "reconceptualize" his attraction, take steps to make him into "the other" again. One way to do this is to pick fights. Summon back those black moods. Force him to be the Villain again. And if she is really successful, he might become really terrifying: he might threaten to leave her, or ask her to leave the mansion. That will put the fear of God in her, make her grateful for what she has . . . for a few weeks at least. Imagining herself left, or without a nice home, she then sees freshly all the advantages of her present state. She is still and calm and gracious for a spell.

Or she might get pregnant. That way he surely becomes the agent of her fate again. The magician who taps her with his wand and transforms her irrevocably. Whoever heard of a mother continuing to be a gothic heroine? It is no secret that the Life Force adores transformations. It rewards its transformees accordingly. And so, as she abandons herself to biological metamorphosis, she is granted earth-shaking orgasms, even better than the ones she had as a bride, when Derek the Stranger became suddenly Derek the Groom. Ah, how we love those transformation scenes! But now the Groom has grown wan and weary, his powers grow familiar with use, and he must beget new life in order to revive these powers. And she is the vessel of these powers. She becomes elemental, mythical. She stands naked in the tower room, two electric heaters trained on her ripeness, a full-length mirror tilted so that it makes her seem a giant, and she fills canvases with huge, all-encompassing earth mothers—giantesses who look as if their taut abundance will split the canvas frames. Her creativity is metaphor for her bodily ripeness. Or is it vice versa? No matter. She has never felt or painted better.

But then, afterward, everything shrinks to human size again. Babies, on canvas, look suspiciously alike and children's faces are hard to draw. And the sex goes flat again. And what is to be done but repeat the whole process?

Or see all this ahead of time and reject it without doing it. Perhaps she is one of those persons who hasn't had enough of being a child herself yet. She decides to hold on to the wizening image of herself as perpetual maiden as long as she can, perpetually eligible for infinite rescues, infinite salvations, infinite new starts.

And there she is in town, after all, already idealizing what she has thrown away as she walks the unlovely streets looking for an apartment within her means. Gazing out of its sooty window (when she rushed out on him for good, it would have cheapened the scene to go back for the curtains), she summons the courage to do the minimum necessary for her survival. Where *has* all her energy gone? She must go out on the unfriendly pavements (everything so hard here; on Derek's estate, her feet touched only grass, Aubussons, soft earth, clean, crunchy snow) and, leaning her bare head into the armpit of no protector, she must go to the store where no one knows her and purchase orange juice, Tampax and some cheap kind of protein. Everything so difficult and mundane. Is this freedom? And the tower room was an oven compared to this freezing hole, for which she pays an outrageous sum. Or else it is overheated, drying out the last good years of her skin. She finds herself painting lots of angry things, just slapping thick slabs of clashing colors on canvas, wasting expensive paint. This is freedom? She switches to primed paper, it's cheaper, to assuage her guilt. She feels more of a pretender than ever, an artless drifter loose in the backwash of her "freedom," purchased with another person's pain. She makes a blazing, illegal, gesso-smelling fire in her fireplace and goes out after for a long walk in the rain. She catches a bad cold and ends up in bed with a strange man.

Derek, of course, remarries. He has allowed his pretty new bride to order new curtain material and make her own changes in the menus and flower beds of the mansion. After dinner, over brandy, they curl up together on his leather sofa by the fire and he tells her the story of how his last bride left him. It is a story his new wife loves to hear. She could listen to it over and over again. It is perhaps one of life's most piquant pleasures, she thinks (an imaginative person herself, who will later contribute her own variety of pain to his life), to be in a warm, well-appointed place, listening in comfort and security to the tale of the wild ungrateful woman fleeing into the outside world, toward some sharp, shivery destiny of her own.

I worked in a few waifish shadows on my heroine's cheeks. She would fatten on her marriage and grow thin again after her decampment. I decided to leave the apartment a little early and walk down Madison and see what my contemporaries were passing off as Art in the galleries, before presenting myself in Doris Kolb's antiseptic office to find out what her summons was all about.

2

Dreaming, Painting and Marrying

Nine years ago I had arrived in New York. It was spring and I had a few more months of being twenty-three. I had just left my husband. We had been married a year and a half. Toward the end of that year, I began having variations on a nightmare about a taxi. Lying next to the man I had vowed to stick with till one of us died, I would dream I had already left him. In the dream I was in New York City, holding on for dear life to the portfolio that had been my wedding gift, trying to flag a taxi. None of the nice ones would stop. Then along would come a battered, sinister old thing and hurtle to a stop. I'd get in and say, "The art galleries on Madison, please," or sometimes just, "Art," and away we'd go on the awful ride. In one version the taxi would drive and drive, the streets would get darker and scarier till I'd cry out, "Take me back!" only to discover there was no driver. In another version, I'd get to where I was going, the taxi would disappear, and I'd realize I'd left my portfolio in it. In another version, I would get in, complacently give Art's address, or think I had, and sink into a deep sleep. I'd wake and the taxi would be idling in exactly the same spot. "Where to, girlie?" the driver would ask. "But I told you!" I'd protest. "No you didn't," he'd say, "but you owe me eight hundred dollars already for just keeping still."

"But I don't have eight hundred dollars! Couldn't you take me and I could pay you later?"

"Nope, not a chance." Then he'd either make me get out, or sometimes come tumbling over into the back seat, where I waited for him, my legs already outspread—I waited for my consolation prize. If I couldn't have Art, I'd rut instead with this demeaning partner, who always revealed some nasty surprise—a greenish front tooth, a snake tattoo on his belly—the moment he entered me.

On such occasions I could not face my husband afterward at breakfast. After he left for his office, I would make another cup of coffee for myself and take it back to the bed where I had betrayed him in my sleep with a degenerate stranger and worry about what this dream was trying to tell me. I already knew, but most of my conscious energies, during those last months of our marriage, were spent trying to keep myself from admitting it.

I had sold out. I hadn't played square with my myth of The Young Woman as Artist. This myth had specified a certain order of events, a certain progression in the development of Self, and I had betrayed that order. I had snatched my security before I'd made a real try for my dream. And thus I was being forced by my undeceived and forthright unconscious, night after night, to seek out the confrontation I had avoided. "New York" in the dream represented this confrontation. That I never arrived at the galleries with my work intact, or that I settled in despair for sexual annihilation, was my dream life's metaphor and parody of my real situation. It was no good soothing myself with chronological particulars of Georgia O'Keeffe (one of my models). True, she'd had her first one-woman show at age twenty-nine—which gave me six more years. But she had found her style, she had found a way to put down on canvas what was in her head, she was an established painter when she married her Stieglitz eight years later, at the age of thirty-seven. She was light-years away from that young woman who won the Art Students League still-life prize for her traditional painting of a dead rabbit and a copper pan.

When I finished *my* art training, I took away that year's Senior Art Prize at my college. I felt I was exactly where I should be in my scheme of things, and therefore entitled to loaf a little after graduation. Since the age of sixteen I had worked during vacations as a camp counselor or lifeguard or waitress in a resort to help pay for my education. My grandmother acknowledged my right to a summer off, she who had banished me from permanent residency at the three-story house on Charleston's East Battery at the age of six. "Come on, if you want," she wrote to me, in my last month of college. "You have earned a respite. I don't know what you'll find to fascinate you among this rotting ancestral timber. I would have left years ago if it weren't for your Uncle Ambrose, who might one day take it into his head to abandon the Bohemian life in Greenwich Village and come home and play Southern Gentleman. Though his big war novel that's taking so long had better be a best seller if he plans to bail us out of all these mortgages. You'll find me scant entertainment. I seldom go out since your godmother moved away. What fun for a woman alone to go to the movies or the symphony? I don't even play anymore since I gave up teaching piano. But if you can stand the silence of all these old ghosts . . . not to mention *the heat* . . . come on. You say you'd like the boys' old room for your studio. Well, it's up to you. I know you painters have to have your light. I'll try to find a fan. But remember how *hot* it is on that third floor with no piazza to provide a cross-breeze!"

Not exactly an overwhelming welcome. But I was determined to have one last summer in that house of my lost girlhood before I embarked on my adult career as a serious artist. As for ghosts . . . well, as far as I was concerned, Charleston had always been a ghost town for me. From the age of six on, I had known it only in summer, when all the people *we* knew had fled to cooler places. Or for a few days at Christmas, on loan from my boarding school in the mountains of North Carolina. As my grandmother loathed society—except for my godmother's—it was usually just the three of us . . . and any ghosts (of drowned parents or dead husbands) that flitted in and out of the conversation.

A $19.95 window fan, still in its Sears box, awaited me in the third-floor room at the front of the house where my father and his brother Ambrose had slept as boys, and where Ambrose had later written his successful first (and so far only) novel in 1947. Outside my north window was a neighbor's garden in rampant bloom, sending a mixed aroma of magnolia, Cape jessamine, coral vine and oleander up to me three stories above. Outside the front window, facing east, was the Cooper River, with Fort Sumter a little to the left of our palmetto tree. But I was far less interested in national historical monuments than in personal ones. Down this river at night, right in front of this window, my mother had embarked on her fatal sail, when I was six months old.

I unpacked my new fan and plugged it in. I set up my easel to catch the north light. When I looked beyond my brand-new canvas, I saw the Cooper River aflutter with the moth-blue and peppermint-stripe sails. They were what I had planned to see. The composition they were going to inspire was to be my summer painting: the painting that would one day be hailed as "the first postgraduate work of Violet Clay." I had planned this picture all during my last semester in college. How could it be anything less than brilliant, suffused as it was with personal meaning! On one twenty-by-thirty-inch surface I was going to fix forever my feelings about my mother's death. All the omens pointed toward the success of this venture. My Uncle Ambrose had written his novel in this room. What is more, he'd been twenty-one at the time, the same age I still was for three more months. And what was even more, he, too, had taken my mother as his subject, the young widow who had spurned him when, at the tender age of seventeen, he had offered himself, Old Testament style, as his dead brother's replacement ten months after he went down with the *Lexington* in the Coral Sea. She had rejected us both, preferring to emulate my father's watery death almost outside our front door. Ambrose had been heartbroken, according to my grandmother, and lied his way into the army. But after the army he had returned to make art out of it. Now it was my turn. But where his refashioning of the event had been romantic and positive, mine was going to be symbolic and sinister. Unrequited lovers and unrequited daughters made things up to themselves each in their own style. He'd consoled himself first with war and returning a decorated hero. Bored with the inaction of local college on the GI Bill, he'd then consoled himself by writing a happier version of the true story. In *Looking for the Lora Lee*, he'd turned Liza Lee Clay from the bereaved young widow who drowns herself in a stolen sail-boat into a temperamental female Flying Dutchman, with her own yacht, who leads her ex-GI a merry chase down the Intracoastal Waterway. When he finally tracks her to an inaccessible cove, she confesses that she fled from him because of guilt. She felt guilty because she had already fallen in love with him through reading about him in her fiancé's letters. The fiancé was the narrator's best friend, whose Flying Fortress was shot down. A bit fanciful, but somebody must have believed it. When Hollywood took the option on my uncle's book, Ava Gardner wanted to play the part. My painting, to be called "Wasteful Sea," was to be both quintessential howl at my defecting parent and my first big work. The first week I made sketches. I had in mind the mood of Ryder's ghostly little boat in "Toilers of the Sea," with a sort of abstract figure in the foreground, reminiscent of O'Keeffe's "Black Cross." I felt very inspired as I sketched these derivations of others' works. I saw myself granting an interview to a well-known art magazine a few years hence.

—When did you first begin drawing?

—I have drawn ever since I could hold a pencil. I drew on the walls of my nursery, strange little animal-people to whom I gave names and whom I called my family. I was orphaned very early in life and spent my first six years in a big house on the waterfront with my grandmother. After the war, my uncle came back from the army and lived with us while he went to Charleston College. I adored him. He told these wonderful stories of how he parachuted down into Normandy and completed his mission in spite of a broken ankle. I followed him like a shadow till my grandmother told me to leave him in peace. But he felt sorry for me; he let me sneak up to his room every evening while he did his homework, providing I'd sit quietly and draw. I tried to draw things he would like. I copied his medals and the 101st Airborne insignia with its screaming eagle. I drew little sketches of people we knew that would make him laugh. This was my first bout with discipline and also trying to please a "public."

—Very interesting. Do you think of yourself as a Southern Painter?

—Well, I'm proud to share my birthplace with Allston. I was influenced by his "Moonlit Landscape" when I was a young painter. But I was also influenced by Ryder, Inness, the Swiss Fuseli. I like the way they have of catching the mundane off guard, getting out of the preconceived everyday vision. Perhaps Southerners aren't as ashamed of being dreamers. But these painters were all dreamers.

—You say when you were a "young painter," Miss Clay. You are hardly old.

—Oh, well . . . !

And suddenly I'd find the morning gone. Even over the hum of my Sears fan I would hear the mingled bells of St. Michael's and St. Philip's joining in on the quarter hour past noon, and I would clean my brushes and go quietly down, past my grandmother's closed boudoir, which she shared exclusively with her gin bottle, and lunch on whatever provisions I'd provided for myself the day before. And as soon as I sat down to my meal of chicken salad, Kool-Aid and butterscotch royal ice cream, I

would get very excited over the work I hadn't done today but
which I felt bound to do tomorrow. If only I didn't have to do
errands for Granny, I would tell myself, I could get a head start
on "the picture" this afternoon. But duty was duty, which was
to go upstairs after lunch but never before one, by which time
Granny was dressed and made up and regarded me with playful
nonchalance, as though I'd been another one of the ghosts who
inhabited her house. She would dole out some cash from a little
enameled box meant for playing cards, which contained our
weekly food and drink allowance. "Tell Mr. Dinwiddie we're expecting some people in, why don't you?" she would muse, on
the days I went for the quart of gin. (Which never left her room
and which, after I left it in the kitchen, I never laid eyes on
again.) At the liquor store I was obliged to purchase a "decoy,"
as well as the gin: some harmless liqueur a "guest" would drink,
so that Mr. Dinwiddie would not think my grandmother sat
alone swigging from her gin bottle. What had she done to save
face when I wasn't there? By the time she managed to be up and
dressed she was already her waggish, alcoholic self. Postponed
her first drinks till after she'd taxied to the bank and the liquor
store? At least I was earning my right to be here, I would think,
striking out into the hell heat of June Charleston. "How's Miz
Clay?" Mr. Dinwiddie would ask. "She hasn't been in to see me
lately." "Oh, fine," I'd say. "Busy with our company. We're having so much. Do you think this Hawaiian mix might be a refresh-
ing drink for them?" "They might find it tolerable," he'd say,
screwing up his finely chiseled raspberry nose, a by-product of
years of his choice bourbon. He would already have the gin
ready in the paper sack.

I had two beaus that summer. A trust officer from our bank
and a young decorator from Williamsburg who was interning
with the antique dealer who bought Granny's furniture and
silver whenever her funds dipped to the next notch. The trust
officer had a certain polished swagger born of his parochialism.
He was the sort of boy I might have married if I'd grown up on
the Battery, gone to Ashley Hall and come out at the St. Cecilia

Ball. That summer I was also flirting with Roads Not Taken. My closest childhood friend, with whom I'd roomed for years at the Pine Hollow School, Pequeña Bombal, had married her Argentine canning heir at seventeen. Our last term at boarding school, she had creamed her exquisite little face in front of the mirror and drawn endless sketches of her wedding gown, while I lay on my bed in our shared room, shaky and pimply from too much coffee and Dexedrine, cramming to maintain my A average so I could keep my scholarship to college. It miffed me that she gave not a single thought to the fact that she might be missing anything by choosing her Road. Just as I was miffed by the trust officer's fiancée (he dated me on the sly), who was having her premarital *Wanderjahr* with friends from Converse. While he mauled me with careless expertise among the dunes of Sullivan's Island, part of my mind was with Miss Pettigrew sashaying unseeingly past the treasures in the Prado, the Louvre and the Rijksmuseum, looking at herself in their frames and daydreaming of the pageantry of upper-class Southern wife-and-motherhood. The decorator beau was a bit on the effeminate side, but he took me to Perdita's for dinner and could get carried away under certain atmospheric conditioning in the darkness of Granny's former music room, among the portraits by Sully, the Georgian gilded mirrors, the ornamented cove ceiling and the Steinway grand, shut tight now and out of tune. I had told him I would one day inherit the Fortescue-Clay house, just to see how it felt. "How elegant it would be," he would ruminate in the darkness, growing bigger under the auspices of these lovely things, "to *entertain* in a room like this."

With the trust officer, who knew all about the double mortgage and the very strong probability of his bank's one day owning this house, I was wanton and rude, deriding his antebellum snobbery and mercantile compromises from the pedestal of my lofty art. I managed to wound his vanity severely several times; this had the contrary effect of increasing the pitch and duration of his ardor.

After these masquerades I would ascend our broad staircase

with the haughtiness of an untenured princess, wash off the lipstick ground into my face, and congratulate myself for having
achieved a modern girl's sexual rights without having to marry
and ruin my career.

I looked forward to the rare suppers with Granny. She'd
sometimes eat, provided I cook (though she ate little when
she dined), and we would have set a time, like a real date, when she
was to descend from her room in queenly languor, her perfumed
wrist brushing the banister, her cheeks flaming by now with
fast-circulating blood, and sit next to me at the Sheraton dining
table. The Empire Aubusson and the Regency sideboard had
disappeared since my last visit, and the room was a bit mournful
and spooky after sunset. The bare floors and empty walls made
our voices seem louder as I employed all my skill to elicit anything new pertaining to my dead parents or my baby self. If she
couldn't remember, who could? The fast-depleting rooms
around us (already this summer, my Williamsburg beau himself
had reluctantly carried out the old silver soup tureen and the
four matching Adam candlesticks) added an urgency to my research. I saw, like a speeded-up film, the winds of time and financial necessity whipping through this house and carrying off
tables, sofas, chairs, beds, family portraits, and finally my grandmother herself, robbing me of not only my heritage but even the
memories of my own history.

But it was a tricky business, getting her to talk. Oh, she
talked, all right, but her subject matter and her attitude toward
it varied according to the amount of gin she had put away upstairs and whatever effect it had had on the particular chemical
balances, or imbalances, in her body that day. Later, when I became friendlier with the bottle myself, I would learn how many
different varieties of drunkenness each person is capable of. As
well as the fact that each drunk has his own special routines. My
grandmother's routines included (*a*) a laconic recounting of how
she sacrificed a brilliant music career to marriage, (*b*) warnings
against men—especially lawyers—and all their tricks to lead you
into the trap, and (*c*) funny reminiscences about her long friend-

ship with my godmother, and their long war against Charlestonian snobbery. She was not the sort of mother who indulged in idealistic or nostalgic memories about her children.

"Granny, what was my father like?"

"Milledge was very serious. He lacked the light touch completely. Not like Ambrose. If he'd lived, he would have gone on to law school and become a judge."

"I wonder why he was attracted to my mother. You'd think he'd have fallen for someone serious like himself. Also their backgrounds were so different."

"That they were. But they had to get married, you know. I don't see why you shouldn't know that. You were conceived a little after Pearl Harbor, I think. They were married the following March. The first time he brought her home she wore an ankle bracelet. I had to ask her to take it off before we all went to church. Men are like that. The most serious ones will suddenly go gaga over some little powder puff. It's nature's revenge on them for taking themselves so seriously. You're small, like her, but you have a sunnier disposition. She cried a lot. She cried the entire time she lived in this house. Up and down the stairs she'd go, growing bigger and bigger with you, weeping into her hanky. She ate nothing but Jell-O and drank gallons of milk and listened to the news of the war on the radio. She and Ambrose would listen to the radio—he was dying to enlist, but was too young—or they would play records and dance. It was quite a sight, the two of them fox-trotting with that big belly between them like a chaperone. Violet and I used to laugh our heads off. It was your godmother, by the way, who first said: 'Watch out, Ambrose is sick as a puppy with love for his brother's teen-age bride.' Lord, I'm glad *that's* over. The war years, I mean. They were unsettling for everybody. Well, it doesn't look like Ambrose can make it down to see us. Working hard on his book, he says. But Violet will be joining us later in the summer, before you leave. What *are* your plans for the fall, dear?"

"Well, I haven't exactly made any. I'd like to finish a few

good paintings before I go. I don't have to leave by September, do I?"

"No, of course not. Just remember what I quoted to Ambrose recently in one of his slumps: 'A man of words and not of deeds is like a garden full of weeds.' "

"Yes'm, I will."

She excused herself early and wafted upstairs. As I went past her room later I heard her burning up the wire with the Big V., who had moved to Greenville because Charleston's sea air aggravated her arthritis. I could not bring myself to call my godmother "Violet." My whole lifetime had been spent trying to separate the sound of my name from hers, this big freckled woman who seemed always to be laughing raucously with my grandmother behind closed doors. I had heard the story till it ran out my ears of how the two women had met in the 1920s in the old Charleston Library on King Street, both of them "imported" new brides to the city. Georgette Clay had gone to the library for another novel to escape into. As she dawdled, sighing, trying to decide between two Ouidas, she soon became thrillingly aware that someone was doing the unthinkable: making a scene in Charleston, in the building still called by the old-timers "The Library Society." "Well, why don't you have *Uncle Tom's Cabin?*" demanded a husky female voice. "It is a national classic, you know. Well, can't you order it from another library, then?" My grandmother had moved closer, attracted to this large, Yankee-voiced, Titian-haired disturber of the local mores. She had offered the offender, *sotto voce*, of course, her own copy of Mrs. Stowe's masterpiece, and invited her to come back to the house for tea. Whereupon the large young woman burst into copious tears, crying, "You're the first white woman to speak to me decently in this inbred hothouse of a city!" My grandmother's feelings exactly about Charleston, only she hadn't dared put them into words. Together the two women put a lot into words over the following years. Violet Pardee was the ringleader. She had been in the National League for Woman's Service in World War I and repaired trucks and painted smokestacks in the Newark shipyard before coming South with Mr. Pardee, who directed cargo operations at Charleston Harbor. She taught my grandmother how to smoke. Barren herself, she suffered enthusiastically through both her friend's pregnancies. How many times I'd heard how she lay in bed with Georgette, right up to the end, and "shared" her labor pains. If it was a girl, my grandmother promised each time, she would find some way to insinuate her friend's name. It was not, however, till I lay helpless in my crib that she got a chance to honor her promise, convincing my mother, who was too busy mourning my father, that Violet was a beautiful name, feminine, shy—all that the Big V. was not. I was named Violet Isabel—Isabel after a drum majorette my mother had admired in high school. The Big V. was overjoyed. From my christening onward, she dedicated herself to reminding me of our shared name. She bought me little tin boxes of violet pastilles. She gave me dresses and hankies with violets on them. She sent regularly to the boarding school—for which she helped pay, so my grandmother would be free to take trips with her—expensive boxes of French soap, Roger & Gallet's Savon Violette, which I gave away to the teachers. I scrupulously called her Mrs. Pardee in the thank-you notes I was obliged to write, notwithstanding her frequent exhortations "just to call her Violet." I dreaded her power over me, the power of her bigness, of her money, of her influence over my grandmother, who after all had control of my life as long as I was a child. She had been able to buy my grandmother away from me. What if she one day took it into her head to buy me? My only hope was to re-create myself in my own image, till not even the shadow of the Big V. colored the image of Violet Clay.

"I have good news," said my grandmother at our next supper. "Violet is coming down from Greenville next week. Her nephew is driving her down."

"What nephew? Big V. doesn't have any nephews."

"Actually, he's a distant young cousin of the late Mr. Pardee. From the Georgia branch. But Violet has been so splendid about helping him ever since she discovered him. She's sent him through law school and now he's joined a firm in Greenville.

That's obliging of him, isn't it? Wants to keep an eye on that nest egg of hers, I'll bet. You'd better be nice to your godmother, Violet. You've got competition now. I must say, she has invested her money brilliantly. If she'd been a man, she would have been president of some multimillion-dollar corporation."

"Oh, I'll make out," I said, wondering exactly how I would earn my living after the summer. "Besides, he's her relative. He's got more claim anyway. How funny she never mentioned him in her letters. What's his name?" I could just see the toadying creep, the Big V.'s latest "purchase."

"She undoubtedly has mentioned him. You always did skim her letters; I've watched you. Lewis Lanier is his name. Rather nice. Sounds like the poet. Probably remotely descended or something. But better beware of lawyers, Violet. Look what happened to me." She cocked her head, gave me a searching look, then laughed deep in her throat.

"Don't worry. I have my own plans," I said.

"So did I. Ah, so did I, dear. That day in 1919 I sat down at my piano in Burnsville, North Carolina, and played the 'Valse Noble' from *Carnaval*, I was full of plans. A lawyer by the name of Charles Clay had come from South Carolina to see Father on a legal matter, and I was nineteen and wearing a dress of plum-colored satin that showed my statuesque proportions to advantage, and oh, I had plans! I had just returned from my triumphant recital in Raleigh and I was preparing my audition for the managers at Carnegie Hall that spring. Well, Father invited this lawyer to stay over, and after dinner he told Charles about how I'd made up my mind to abandon my old father and become America's famous woman virtuoso, and Charles removed his cigar from his mouth and asked politely if I would honor him with a selection from my repertoire. Not several selections: *a* selection. Now, I had just that morning satisfied myself with my own execution of Liszt's 'Campanella,' a very demanding piece technically. It was to be my bravura piece for the managers. Sweet young things who toyed at music just did not attempt such a strenuous work, whereas I was big and strong and very serious indeed. But I could tell from the way he asked me to play *a* selection that Charles was not a musical sophisticate and would probably expect a simple short waltz and would be bored if he got anything else. And somehow I couldn't bear the idea of being boring to this man. I knew, Father had told me some days before, that Charles had inherited a famous historical house from his mother and that he lived all alone in it, at thirty-two years of age, because so many belles had thrown themselves at him and his pedigree that he was put off by the whole thing. I didn't want this humorless cigar-sucking attorney, but I was certainly not going to risk his being 'put off' by me. So I decided on the 'Valse Noble.' It showed off my bustline and nice chin, because I could sit up straight when I played it. Not like in 'Campanella,' where I had to hunch and root for the double octaves and perspire all over the tremolandos. I was determined that nothing about me should indicate to this man I was making the least bit of effort.

"After I had played, Charles thanked me and said he was sure I would take New York by storm if those Yankees had any ears, and the two men retired to my father's study to settle their business. Charles left for South Carolina early next morning and the following week my father came into my practice room with a bemused smile on his face and a letter asking for my hand in marriage. 'Poor Clay,' I remember him saying, rocking back and forth on his heels, holding that letter between his thumb and index finger. 'Tell me, Georgie, whatever did you do to him?' It wasn't till I was a widow of twenty-six with two small boys to bring up and my fingers too stiff to do any of my bravura pieces anymore that I realized what had been done to me."

"But what I don't understand," I said, as I always did when she told this story, "is why you didn't go on up to New York and have your audition first. If you failed, then you could always come home and get married afterwards." Nevertheless, some deeply feminine side of me loved this story of how the talented young Georgette had succumbed to a blitzkrieg assault on her vanity.

"No," she said (as she always did). "He wouldn't have wanted me then. And besides, I already had my secret fears that I might

not succeed. And even if I got past the managers and had my
Carnegie Hall recital, what then? Father was not rich. How
would I support myself till I became famous? Then a subversive,
tempting picture flashed through my brain, even as I was reading through Charles's letter to my father. The picture was of that
lady so feted in our day—her praises were sung in every
women's magazine—the accomplished wife and mother who
turns her gifts to the enhancement of Home. I saw myself, safe
and rich and beautiful, seated at a nine-foot grand in Charles's
ancestral home, playing the G Minor Ballade by Chopin, followed by Mozart's sonata with the Turkish Rondo, to a select
cultural gathering, after which my two beautiful children would
be led in by the servants to say good night, during which time
several guests would whisper, 'She could have become America's Clara Schumann, you know. . . .' And this picture was later
realized in most particulars. I did play the G Minor Ballade and
the Turkish Rondo—on a *seven*-foot grand—before some of our
cultured friends on several occasions after the birth of Milledge,
your father, who would be carried downstairs by Charles, as we
had no servants. All our money went on the upkeep of this old
monstrosity: we were antique-poor the way some people are
land-poor. By the time Ambrose was born, four years later, I was
too stiff for either the Rondo or the Ballade. And then Charles
had no sooner fathered these two boys than he ups and dies. But
you know, years later, years after he was gone, I remember one
of his friends introducing me as the lady who had brought the
house down at Carnegie Hall, then given up her career and
come home to marry Charles. Do you think Charles made that
little modification himself? I think so. People often make
after-the-fact variations on their love stories to make the property seem more valuable. Ambrose, for instance, making your
poor mother into an aristocratic *femme fatale* with her own
yacht. I'll never forget the time I asked Liza, just before she and
Milledge married, whether she'd chosen her pattern yet. And
she said, 'Oh I'm not going to make my dress, I'm going to buy
it.' Poor girl, the first time I served broccoli, she ate only the
stems and very carefully pushed the florets to one side of her

plate. You haven't done so badly, Violet. Imagine if I'd let you go and live with your other grandparents. You'd be married by now, with at least three squalling babies, probably working in a mill. There would have been no college, no art. . . . By the way, when am I going to get to see what you've been up to?"

"Give me a few more weeks," I said. The truth was, my "Wasteful Sea" had become hopelessly becalmed. I had reached that sickening point on the canvas where I had messed up whatever was promising and didn't yet have the heart to gesso it over and start again. Already it was July and I had nothing to show. I still couldn't understand how a subject so loaded with emotional content for me could look so flat in paint.

"Well. I hope you'll invite your godmother up to your studio. She has taken an interest in your development from the very beginning. And don't go falling in love with her nephew. God knows I won't be leaving you any nest egg, though I have willed you my pearls, but you can at least profit from my example. Beware of lawyers."

"Don't worry about me," I said.

After Lewis and I were married in October, I did not paint for a while. Not that he discouraged me: on the contrary. His marriage gift to me was a full-sized black leather portfolio, with my new initials stamped in gold. I had made a big thing about my art from the minute he entered the house on the Battery. I worked especially well that week and a half he stayed with us. (It turned out he had planned his vacation that way.) Every morning I was in my studio by nine. It was the hottest time of the whole summer and I dripped sweat and kept the fan on High. I painted abstracts; they were quicker. And I didn't want him to be able to judge me. I was not going to "paint down" to him, as Georgette Rogers had "played down" to Charles Clay. Then, just before I invited him and Big V. and Granny up for "the show," I lost my nerve and got out my old best things and mingled them with the wet new ones. "These aren't finished, are they Violet?" boomed the Big V., blowing smoke toward the

new abstracts. "I was experimenting with field constancies," I
replied coolly. "An artist has to experiment, Aunt," Lewis said.
"I know so little about the technical side of painting, but personally, I find this soft green as suggestive as if you'd painted a
scene. It reminds me of the mountains in spring up around Flat
Rock, where I've just bought myself a little cottage." He spoke
decorously, with the soft *r*'s of Georgia. He was tall and bony,
with ashy hair and kind, reflective eyes. Not at all the lackey I
had expected. He seemed really to be fond of the Big V., to find
her interesting company, but he didn't toady to her. In the afternoons, after I had "worked," he and I would pack a picnic lunch
and drive over to Sullivan's Island, to the beach, leaving the two
old friends shut happily in my grandmother's air-conditioned
bedroom. She drank much less when her friend was there. (Now
it seems obvious to me that they were planning our wedding.)
Lewis and I sat on the beach, and exchanged autobiographies.
He came from a family always short of money but long on love,
he said. He exuded an air of authority and never got flustered.
Life seemed to be going along exactly as he wanted. He told me,
as we sat practically naked in our bathing suits, that I had striking eyes.

When we honeymooned at his cabin in Flat Rock, he kept
expecting me to dash out on the deck with easel and paints and
capture the fall foliage. But I had gone all funny and languorous.
There was something delicious and sensual about my abdication.
I had walked willingly into the trap of those tough and cunning
old friends, playing us off like their pet summer puppets. How
long had they had it planned? Lewis and I lay together and tried
to reconstruct it. He had been told about me, the orphan of War
and a Romantic Suicide. He had had, he said, a frequent dream
of "saving" me long before we met. "You were nine, and you
were walking into the ocean. I knew I had to get to you before
you went in over your head and drowned." He attributed my
age in the dream to his having once been shown a photograph
of me in my braids and boarder's uniform at the Pine Hollow
School for Girls. Often when he made love to me he would

murmur almost angrily in my ear, "Poor little girl, I'll take care of you now," and this never failed to send me over the edge.

There was something sexy about having been captured, having been forced by the machinations of those two old Eumenides to lie down in the sweet juices of traditional womanhood and abandon the hubris of an edgy, lonely struggle. I didn't touch a paintbrush those first months of captivity. What for? The colors of satisfaction oozed out of my very pores. I posed for myself in front of the mirror, turning this way and that, thinking: I am now a wife. I breathed the odor of flowers, arranged them in vases, but was not tempted to turn them into still lifes. I lapsed, I gave myself up to my senses, to Womanhood. Lewis was the agent of it, therefore I assumed I loved him. There had been others before him, but our nervous scramblings had been egotistical, "experimental," done for the sake of doing it, like the abstracts. I stood in my closet and fingered my wedding dress. "And thereto I give thee my troth," I had promised him, before all, in church. When we made love, I was also swept repeatedly to pleasure by chanting, "Who are you?" "Your *husband*," he would answer, with the penultimate thrust of his manhood. But one time, carried away, he cried, "Your *wife*," and then revised himself when it was too late. This still embarrasses me whenever I think of it.

By the following spring the honeymoon was over. The nesting instinct that had flared up briefly had subsided. I had hung the curtains of my choice and changed the colors of his walls in the duplex in Greenville. I had tried my difficult recipes and weaned him away from white, button-down-collared shirts. There was nothing for it but to begin sketching again. I was not pleased with my sketches. They seemed just the kind of thing you'd expect a young-wife-who-had-once-wanted-to-paint to do. My grandmother's tale about how her fingers stiffened after marriage began to haunt me. Was history repeating itself? Had she wanted it to? Lewis had told me it was the old lawyers who refused to abolish the dreaded bar exam. The oldest partner in his firm had said, "I lost forty pounds and all my hair fell out when I was studying for the bar, and I'll be goddamned if these young twerps are going to have it easy!" Because Georgette hadn't made it to New York, had she conspired to prevent her granddaughter from getting there? I began to brood. I took out books from the library about artists, subtracting their birth dates from the dates of their first successes. Matisse had finished law school, switched vocations, and painted his first important picture at twenty-one! Ambrose and Matisse at twenty-one, damn it, had made their mark, and here was I going on twenty-three! Ambrose, the bastard, hadn't been able to make my wedding. He sent a slim silver vase from Tiffany's.

I persuaded Lewis to pose nude for me. "I've got to draw from life or I won't develop," I said. "I need inspiration. If you can't give it to me, who can? All during college they made the male models wear straps when they posed for us. I think what's holding me back is, I haven't been allowed to look on the mystery of Man. If men artists through the ages have taken their inspiration from Woman, then surely it works the other way round." Lewis agreed reluctantly, provided I'd let him smoke his pipe.

He refused to stand up in the posing sessions. We compromised on a straight-backed chair. Between puffs on his pipe, his face tried to assume that masterful, authoritative look that had pleased me at first. But when this look sat atop his bony clavicle and rather skinny chest, he became a boy trying to look like a man. Every time I suggested any position other than the habitual one in which he sat while dressed, always slumped back, his legs crossed at the thighs, he would complain with dry amusement that the canework on the chair bottom pinched his balls. But I detected the alarm of threatened modesty behind that mocking tone. Then he started suggesting I take off my clothes. It would be more equal, he said. Then he'd start breathing heavily between the puffs on his pipe and just when there was beginning to be something to paint down there, we'd end up in bed. I would pretend to have been swept away from my easel by these greater urges, while inwardly I spiraled toward despair. I seemed to have lost my art through marrying Lewis and lost Lewis through practicing my art on him. For though I finally did get my portrait in oils of him sitting back, naked, with that pipe, I had lost somewhere in the bargain his mystery for me. Now when he whispered in my ear, "I'll take care of you now," those fierce words no longer did their magic. I had looked upon his vulnerability. He needed reassurance, he needed taking care of, just as much as I did. It was about this time that I began dreaming the taxi dream.

Shortly after our first anniversary my grandmother died. Mr. Dinwiddie found her. When she hadn't been in for three days to pick up the quart of gin and the "decoy" bottle, he went to the house and climbed in a window. She was fully dressed, lying on her bed. Both bottle and glass were concealed in the flowered slop jar of an eighteenth-century commode beside the bed. Her face wore a mocking, triumphant little smile.

Ambrose flew down. Lewis and I met him at the Charleston airport. He looked robust and glamorous even in his grief. I fancied I could smell New York on him. Beside Ambrose, Lewis suddenly seemed young and too angular. The two men took over all the arrangements. I stayed at the house with the Big V., who shut herself in my grandmother's room and wept loudly. Ambrose went alone to the bank and came back and explained to me that the house was no longer ours. The morning he left, he went into his mother's room and stayed for some time. On the way to the airport he told us he'd taken his letters to her, which he'd found in her drawer. "Couldn't you come back to Greenville and stay with us a few days?" I begged. "We have a guest room." I was already planning which patterned sheets to put on his bed. "I want to hear about New York. As soon as I can get a body of work together, I want to go up there and see if I can find myself a gallery." Lewis repeated the invitation. "Sorry, kids. I would love nothing more," said my uncle, "but I got to get back to my book. It's getting later than I realized." He blew his nose, and Lewis tactfully asked him if he had a title yet.

"Well, I was going to call it *The Last Hero*," said Ambrose. "But now it's turning out to be less of the traditional war novel and more of a novel about the uncertainties of peacetime and how they affect the adventurous personality. I've decided to call it *No More at Ease*." He folded his large monogrammed handkerchief and gazed out the window as though he were already in New York. "But," I said, "you're still going to keep that part about meeting the German soldier on the dark beach and one of you has to shoot." "Oh, yes, can't leave that out, can I? When it was the original inspiration for the book." He sighed and looked weary. "The war was so damned long ago," he said. At the departure gate, he suddenly cheered up. He kissed me, pumped Lewis's hand and hit him on the shoulder. "You two take care of one another, hear?"

Lewis and I drove the Big V. back to Greenville. She was heavily sedated and wept quietly in the back seat. It was after midnight when we let ourselves into our duplex. I felt awkward. Why was I standing here with this stranger in this young-married setting? Our rooms seemed suddenly so bourgeois, so arranged to please everyone but ourselves. Whom *had* I been trying to please? I turned to Lewis and saw him regarding the rooms in a similar way. He looked as if he had lost his way. This frightened me. I began whimpering, "Now I have no one but you. You'll take care of me, won't you?"

"I'll take care of you, I'll take care of you," he chanted like a dervish above me in bed, night after night, into the winter that would be our last together.

"Perhaps we should have a child," I began whispering, as our life together drew to a close and the taxi dream gained relentlessly on me night after night.

"Would you like a baby, would you like me to give you a baby?" he'd chant back.

"Oh yes, oh yes." But as soon as I'd used this to get me where I wanted to go, I'd hurry into the bathroom and douche. Which version of the taxi dream would it be tonight, I'd wonder cynically, sitting on the toilet.

In mid-April of 1966, when azalea time had come and gone in the mountains around our cottage, but when the air was still raw in the north, I arrived alone via United Airlines at the old Newark air terminal. I had one suitcase and my wedding gift portfolio. I took a Carey bus into Manhattan. On the bus ride I held myself very straight and gingerly, as if there might be a bomb concealed someplace inside me. I was still a little shocked at my quick decision to pull up my security by the roots and confront that scary metaphor for success: New York. In a last-ditch attempt to dissuade me, the Big V. threatened to take me out of her will, and did. She died within a year of my grandmother.

From the East Side terminal I took a taxi to my destination. It was a legitimate Yellow Cab, driven by a respectable-looking man with no rotting green teeth or lewd designs on me. The fare nowhere near approximated the impossible eight hundred dollars. But then, my destination was not yet Art. It was the Martha Washington Hotel for women. In a last ritual gesture of "taking care," Lewis had called ahead to book a room.

3
Still Life with Taxi

As I walked down Madison, past the galleries, nine years later, on my way to the offices of Harrow House Gothics, to comply with the inscrutable summons of my new boss, Doris Kolb, my mood was not too pleasant. I doubted Doris was up to anything good concerning my fate. My bad planets were starting to gang up on me lately. Losing a boyfriend, even after you've decided you didn't love him, always brings on a lowering of self-esteem. In addition, his departure had spawned financial problems, as he had paid half the rent, food and alcohol. But these real-life uncertainties were only at the edge, not at the center, of the increasing discomfort that dogged my steps as I passed the windows exhibiting the efforts of my more successful contemporaries. The discomfort came from the memories of a younger me who'd had better hopes for herself.

I looked at my reflection in each plate-glass window I passed and recalled every detail of that younger version, getting dressed in a room by herself in the Martha Washington Hotel. It was morning. It was spring. The room was muggy and beads of sweat erupted on her forehead almost as soon as she had finished covering it with a smooth liquid mask of Touch & Glow. Or was the sweat partly from terror? For she was on her way up this same avenue which I now walked down, to present her fledgling credentials to the keepers of the gate. Will they admit her to Art's inner sanctum?

She sprays herself with a precarious dose of underarm deodorant. She inspects her brassiere, garter belt and stockings for loose hooks or snags before putting them on. She still wears a slip in those days; she puts it on. Then the dress, an Anne Fogarty linen sheath of harvest gold, and a single strand of real pearls belonging to her late grandmother, and then slips her long, narrow feet into the black I. Miller pumps shaped like twin rowboats, and she's ready for the perfume (Chant d'Arômes, which, for many years after, will connect her to this day, when she even so much as sniffs it, hurrying quickly through a store) and the lipstick, which has not yet gone out of fashion—but only just not. She blots the lipstick on two folded squares of toilet paper, and peruses herself from the neck up in the stifling bathroom of the hotel. It is important to her that she become a success while she is still young and attractive. That has always been part of the dream. So it is perhaps understandable—it is in keeping with her ideas of how success happens—that only after her person is thoroughly approved by her (as far as is possible in a bathroom mirror) does she think to sit down and take a quick retro-spective tour through her portfolio, which she will soon open for the Powers That Be.

Those lonely Southern winters at an all-girls' college, in charcoal: some haunting shadows there, eked out of an unprom-ising landscape of flat fields and scrub pines by a longing eye hungry for a crumb of romance, of moors and wild gloom. Any-one can see the artist has a steady hand, patient for the close de-tail; no one has to know that there was nothing much else to do.

While the pastel and watercolor "Studies for Three Graces" do not exactly break with eighteenth-century subject matter, the figures defy gravity with a true Blakean abandon, and a sub-tle manipulation of tonal values hints that the young artist is on the way to discovering how color must be used if it is to "catch the mundane off guard."

The lithograph series, "Dark Angels Fly at Night," deserved the 1964 Senior Art Prize at her college. What started off as a lucky accident between grease and water was compounded by her imagination and made deliberate by the discipline of her hand. The feathering of the angels' spread wings, taken to an al-most grotesque naturalism, heightens the intended ominous tone, for the angels resemble birds of prey.

A budding portraitist makes her debut in the color slide of the oil painting "Nude Husband Smoking Pipe." The contrapo-sition of the model's sedate facial expression against the unpro-tected contours of the body makes a wry statement (unintended by the artist) about the divisions in civilized man. It also gives the young woman bowed over her portfolio in the hotel room a momentary pang of remorse. She thinks of all the trouble she has caused the decent man in whose basement this painting now awaits its triumphant summons for crating and shipping, along with her other works which were too large to bring. Then she forgets her guilt in a moment of panic: What if the triumphant summons never arrives for these works?

But then she comes to "Still Life with Violets," which re-vives her. This small canvas she brought with her; it is her talis-man. She did it just this spring. Spring comes earlier in the

South, and she had been walking one weekend in the woods behind their mountain cottage while her husband played golf with their houseguests. Her hopes for this marriage, based entirely on boarding school fantasies and her self-delusions concerning her reasons for marrying, had fallen like petals round the indestructible base of her ego. What was to be done with such a realization? Bury it here in the woods and come back next spring and hope something else had flowered? Or come back to find some worse realization had blossomed in its place, and bury that, until, after succeeding springs, it would take the length and width of her own grave to come to terms with all her evasions? As a compensatory gesture, she stooped down and began plucking violets, close to the ground, to preserve as much stem as she could, gathering herself back to herself. Then her painterly eye for contrasts began seeking other plants as well. She was drawn to some comical spiky things, some sort of burs. The violets by themselves were too sentimental, much as her nostalgic, symbol-seeking self loved them. She hurried back to the cottage and took out her paints. A few of the tubes were dried. Never mind. She had a few good hours before the early spring dusk to paint a little still life. In went the violets and burdocks to the slim silver vase from Tiffany's, Ambrose's gift. Onto a table in front of a window facing the encroaching forest, burgeoning with new spring growth. For the first time in months, her mouth watered as she seized on her composition: three areas, three shifts in plane. The forest, broken up into many tiny strokes, suggesting the rhythm of growing plants; the chosen violets and burs, plucked and arranged by conscious choice in the solid vertical container; and, underscoring, giving depth, to the whole composition, the quality of light in the patches of sky she was lucky enough to catch, at that soon-or-never time of day just after the sun goes down.

She was immensely satisfied with the little painting. Her husband and their friends came back from golf and pronounced it charming. "I like it," she told them, "because it goes beyond a mere accurate representation of things. It combines them in such a way they make a statement about relationships and priorities . . . in the universe at large as well as my own universe. I see this painting as a sort of personal statement, a representation of myself, as well as a still life." They were impressed with this soupçon of painterly philosophy, especially as it graced a good dinner. She hugged her triumph to herself that night, in bed with her husband, where she generously feigned an ecstasy she no longer felt. Perhaps it was all going to happen after all! She would become an acclaimed painter without ever having to suffer and starve in New York. Perhaps she would end up with the kind of marriage O'Keeffe had: six months at home with Alfred; six months in the desert alone. Only, she, Violet, might not go to the desert. Perhaps she and Lewis could arrange things so she could spend six months with him at home, and six months in New York . . . supported by him?

It is to her credit that upon waking the next morning, she understood this plan would be unfair. She had dreamed the taxi dream again.

I was turned away unceremoniously at the first two galleries. So promptly it was hard to take it personally. Sorry, we have all the artists we need. There's no one free to look at portfolios today. At the third—or was it the fourth?—I was begrudgingly told I could come back next week, when the boss was in. In the next, a woman wearing a wide-brimmed red felt hat paused from her conversation into a matching red telephone, held a few of my slides up to the light, squinted, and shook her head. "Sorry," she said. "Anyone can see you've learned your stuff, but we're just not hanging this kind of thing anymore." "Well, thank you," I said, "thanks for your time." "Not at all! Better luck elsewhere!" And she even smiled at me before resuming her narrative into the red telephone. "He was just one of those people who *forces* you to be cruel, if you know what I mean," I heard her explain as I went out the door.

"What does it mean," I asked the kindly old man, wearing a bachelor's-button in his lapel, "when someone says, 'We're not hanging this kind of thing anymore'? I mean, she said it was good, but what did she mean by 'this kind of thing'?"

The old man's name was Samuel Green. He had been all alone in the Green Gallery, one of the less showy ones, when I came puffing up the two flights of stairs. He had introduced himself at once, just as nice older people always did at home. The paintings that hung in his gallery were awful, nothing but flat stripes in circus colors painted so close together they hurt your eyes if you looked too long. But he himself, Mr. Green, was a gentleman. He inquired whether I was from the South; he was sure he recognized the accent. He loved Southerners, he said. His own mother hailed from Biloxi, Mississippi. After he had looked through my slides, making little exclamations of approval, I had regained enough self-confidence to tell him what the lady in the red hat had said.

"What she means," he said with a sigh. "Yes, I suppose it's only fair that someone put you right. You look like a sweet, earnest girl. Anyone can tell, from the way you dress and carry yourself, that you're a lady. You should see what some of these young people wear when they come in to show their work. Makes you wonder what the world is coming to, not to mention *art*. Would you have time to sip a cup of coffee with me, Miss Clay? We're not very busy here today, as you can see. And I shall try to explain to you about these things."

I consented and he looked very happy, almost reprieved. He bustled off into a little side room, where I heard the telltale clink of a spoon in a jar and the usual sounds of instant coffee in progress. I looked round once more at the awful stripy pictures. Mine were certainly an improvement over anything here. But would it damage my reputation to hang my first show in a gallery that didn't even have windows looking out on Madison Avenue? It was clear that Mr. Green liked some of the slides. He had exclaimed quite believably over my "Nude Husband Smoking Pipe," saying, "I do so like a picture that has a person or two in it . . . and the nudity is in very good taste; not offensive at all, my dear." But I must go slowly. I must guard against letting

him charm me into an exhibition with a cup of coffee. But then
—on the other hand—Stieglitz had bulldozed O'Keeffe, against
her better judgment, into leaving her paintings at the "291."

Mr. Green came back with the coffee. He sat down beside
me on the sofa. In a concerned, fatherly voice, he explained
"these things" I should know.

The first was, he said, it was 1966 and representational art
had been dead for some time now.

The second was that frankly he didn't understand why this
was so—he himself preferred things to look like what they were.
But then, it wasn't his line of business. This was his son's business. He was only "sitting" with the paintings till his son came
back from visiting a painter's studio downtown.

My face must have fallen alarmingly. Mr. Green set down
his coffee mug and said, nodding toward my portfolio, "Can we
take a look at what else is in there? Do you have anything a bit
more abstract? Not for me, you understand, but I might be able
to put in a word with my son. He sometimes listens to me . . .
or pretends to, anyhow. What are these lithographs? *Very fine*.
The draftsmanship on those angels' wings puts me a little in
mind of Dürer. . . . What a pity we live in the times we do,
Miss Clay, all this slashing and splashing around of paint and
calling it art. . . . Oh, oh, oh! Are those burdocks in that vase,
with the violets? I declare, they are! I haven't seen burdocks in
years. And you've done them so well! Every little bristle. They
do seem, almost, to be laughing at us, don't they? Oh, I like to
see something painted to look like what it is. And yet with a certain style of your own. Yes, certainly with a style of your own.
I love this little painting."

"But . . . what do you think I should do, then?"

"Do? Oh, you mean about your career and all. Pity life has
got so complicated. Otherwise I'd say go home and paint more
of these lovely things. Paint for your own pleasure! But you want
to have a show, you want to be recognized. Oh, dear. You see,
what my son likes, just at the moment—his tastes change frequently—is this sort of thing," and he waved his hand at the

stripes on the walls. "These were done by a new artist, a young man recommended by Frank Stella."

"Ah, Frank Stella," I murmured. Who the hell was Frank Stella? None of my teachers had mentioned him.

"Have you really left the South for good? All the lovely flowers down there?"

I assured him I had.

"I suppose you'll be wanting one of those uncomfortable lofts for yourself, down in the Village." He sighed. "You'll give up burdocks and start going through ever so many phases, like they all do, until soon nothing will be recognizable and then my son will get interested. Who am I to stand in the way? But, Miss Clay, I have taken an interest in you and I'm going to tell you what I think you should do. Would you like to hear wherein I think your best course lies?"

I assured him I would.

"Greeting cards," he confided, as though he'd given me the essential push in the right direction. "The things they are doing with greeting cards nowadays . . . it's where much of the *old* art has gone. The greeting-card industry is a sort of underground art museum for those of us who have not lost touch with human values, the things that touch the human heart: trees, flowers, young people in love, animals and sunsets, your wonderful burdocks! Which"—he inclined his head toward mine—"just between you and me, I prefer to anything in this room!" He beamed at me, as though he'd just bestowed a prize, and stood up.

I thanked him and zipped up my portfolio. My things seemed suddenly unworthy of the price Lewis had paid for it. A genuine leather portfolio. Mr. Green insisted on walking me down the two flights of stairs. At the entrance to the street, he looked wistfully up and down at all the traffic. "It gets lonely upstairs," he said, handing me his card. *National Grange Mutual Insurance Company* had been crossed out, and a telephone number carefully inked in. "Perhaps you'll call me sometime. I'm retired, I have a little place near here. I'll take you for a nice steak. Nothing in poor taste, you understand. Just a good meal and some interesting conversation."

Somewhere around Fortieth Street I came to myself. Mr. Green's card was crumpled damply in my palm. There was something wrong, something sticky and unpleasant inside my legs, making it difficult for me to walk. I went into the recess of a bank building front, surreptitiously lifted my dress, as though inspecting a high run in my stocking, and saw blood all over the insides of my thighs. If it hadn't been for the stockings, it would have come dripping to the pavement by now. I put down my portfolio and searched through my purse. Not even a handkerchief or a piece of Kleenex. I panicked. How could it be my period? It was too early. Whatever it was, what was I going to do about this blood? I would have to do something very soon. The final humiliation would be to go dripping down the streets of the city that had rejected me. For all I knew, I could be arrested. This was much worse than any nightmare about taxis. I afterward wondered what O'Keeffe would have done. Not what I did, I am sure. I unzipped my portfolio and went searching for the thinnest consistency. The "Studies for Three Graces" I valued least, but watercolor paper was out of the question. One of the Senior Art Prize lithographs lost the lottery. Feeling as though I'd come to the end of some good and simple part of my life, I sacrificed art to necessity, folding Part II of "Dark Angels Fly at Night" into the shape of a long Kotex. In a furtive contortionist's flash, I plunged it beneath my panties, between the garter belt stays.

The first few steps were awkward. I crackled as I walked. I could feel the warm fluid seeping relentlessly out of me. I somehow made it back without disgrace to the hotel. The Anne Fogarty sheath had just begun to spot in the back. Had Mr. Green seen anything when he accompanied me to the door? I took off everything and while my hot bath was running, I tore the blood-soaked lithograph into manageable pieces and wrapped it in a thick bandage of toilet paper before putting it in the wastebasket. Didn't want to offend the maid. I lay in the tub till the water was cold and had turned the color of a ripe watermelon. I counted back to the day of my last period. No, I wasn't all that early. Shock could have brought it on. The shock of reality meeting the dream. I began to cry, halfway through my fantasy of being rescued from all this by Lewis, before I realized what a dirty double-crosser the subconscious was: driving me out of my warm marriage bed with the taxi dream, but at the same time planting a pernicious little escape clause. "Perhaps we should have a child?" I had whispered to Lewis, then fled to the North to eke out my brave, lonely destiny. One foot in the door of the Unknown, the other still holding open its place in the Book of Old Plots. For what if the blood had not come? The tearful phone calls (collect, of course). The frightened, relieved capitulation. The return of the prodigal wife. Or would he have come for me? (That had been my fantasy in the bathtub.) Safe again within the bounds of just enough approval, I would have painted my way complacently through all the violets, then the roses and the lilacs, and finally become my very own Still Life with Lilies. My grandchildren would fight over my best paintings after the funeral. They would hang them in their homes and get busy tending the Legend. How She of the Untamed Spirit had once flown the coop but returned in plenty of time to cultivate her own garden—and make their lives possible.

Now here I was, in a run-down women's residence hotel, trapped in the chilly pink waters of my new freedom. And with no prospects—not even a biological one—of any legend to commemorate the fact that I had walked the earth, that I had once been special.

Much had changed on Madison Avenue since that day of reckoning nine years ago. Clothes styles, for instance. Skirts cut on the bias, swaying bell-like from nipped-in waist to lower calf, had obliterated the old knee-length tubes of sheaths. Garter belts had been rendered obsolete by panty hose. No young woman in her right mind sprayed herself with poison clouds of underarm deodorant. Many beauty aids had become downright menaces.

But a certain number of menaces had become beautiful

again, I couldn't help noticing, as I loitered outside a few galleries. Menaces like representational art. (I wondered whether old Mr. Green had lived to see the change, this triumphant arrival of greeting-card art onto the gallery walls.) Not only were artists painting things to look like themselves again; they were painting them to look like photographs of themselves. Nine years ago, my violets and burdocks had been too real; now they were too much like painting.

So. I couldn't have won either way, I said to myself, with maudlin self-vindication. The times were out of joint for Violet Clay. I couldn't have made it however hard I tried.

But then I saw something that made me swallow my sour grape, seed and all. In the gallery I now stood in front of, I saw a painting I wished I had done. It was exactly my line of thing . . . or what my line of thing might have evolved into, had I gone on following it.

I went in. I looked around the walls. All my worst fears were confirmed. My alter ego, my better self, was having a one-woman show. I took a brochure from the pile stacked on a low teak table beside a green ceramic jar of dried grasses. She was even, according to the biographical sketch, born in the same year, 1942, but her name was Hope Sullivan, not Violet Clay.

"I spent a solitary but far from lonely childhood, just outside Cedar Rapids, Iowa," the sketch quoted. "My earliest memories are of roaming around by myself, looking at clouds, or the way the sun hit old bottles in the window of my aunt's farmhouse. The light would change a thousand times in a single summer day. The possibilities of what a certain kind of light could do to the white petal of an iris, as I lay underneath that flower and looked up, could send me into a trance. Now, although I have lived in New York City most of my adult life, I find my visual memory of certain of these moments of light still triggers an emotional response so powerful that I can translate its essence (without the figurative trappings of the memory, of course) immediately into paint."

I stayed for quite some time in that gallery, paying my begrudging but sincere homage to each of Hope Sullivan's "moments of light." I could recognize many of the processes that had gone into her "translations." For I could translate them back into similar raw experiences of my own. The painting she called "Gravity," for instance. I, too, had felt the sheer weight of the sky on some days, the way it rests ponderously on the earth, so ponderously that it might roll away and form its own globe. Hope Sullivan had caught that moment when the eye says to the sky: "Go on then, break away if you must: lift off, roll!" And the reproach of a certain color, whether it was once an amber bottle or not, perched crookedly against the waning light on a day when nothing has happened: I, too, had reflected on the sadness of such juxtapositions. But she had painted it and titled it "Reflections."

The big one I had seen through the window was called "Energy." A golden disk, pulsating with light. But what made it pulsate, how had she achieved those vibrating effects? Come closer. See the figures inside the disk. The circle is crammed with figures, merging, pushing, dancing, jumping, moving toward and against one another—on one plane of color. On another plane: each lonely figure moves in several light-years of his own space. That was what my "Studies for Three Graces" were all about, what they were working toward. So simple to see what you had planned to do—after the person who did it taught you how to look.

According to the black-and-white photo on the brochure, she was pretty, too.

And a bit of a liar, as well, in the first glib spotlight of recognition. She hadn't translated those moments of light "immediately into paint" any more than this was now my show. She had painted herself into and out of who knew how many dark alleys and cul-de-sacs before coming out with these luminary pieces. But: she had been painting, these nine years, following the gloom as well as the gleam, while I . . . had been sitting stock still in the idling taxi, running up the bill.

Well, at least, I consoled myself (one art which I had not neglected!) as I hurried down the remaining blocks to keep my appointment with Doris Kolb, at least my day has reached its darkest point.

But the day was not over yet.

Obsolete Heroines

Harrow House Gothics was on the twenty-first floor of a modern office building. But the décor of its labyrinthine corridors—once you got past the receptionist who guarded the massive, phony "oak-carved" door just beyond the elevator—matched the mood of its staple product.

I rather liked that mood. I felt at home in it. The walls were papered in a dark rose color, with fake wainscoting. Deep brown carpeting muffled the sound of your step. Unless you happened to meet the rare assistant, rushing through the gloom with a batch of proofs or contact sheets, you might easily convince yourself you were an orphaned relative, wandering through the eccentric picture gallery of a Victorian aunt. The "paintings," enormous blowups of cover illustrations, were framed in ornate gold leaf and illumined kindly by Tiffany "gas lamps" with 25-watt pink-tinted bulbs. All those young women running away from all those houses! One of my own illustrations hung here. I had painted it some time ago. I could remember the name of the book, *The Solitary Cry*, and even the plot (a cast-out wife who returns to utter threatening warnings to her successor through a complicated apparatus connected from the gazebo to the main house), but today, as I stood before my own work, a

painting I had spent time upon, I couldn't for the life of me remember applying a single stroke of the brush.

In the old days, when Williamson, the nice art director, had
been in charge, I had looked forward to dropping down to the
office, to deliver or pick up an assignment—or often just to chat.
He had made his office atmosphere as rose-colored as the soft,
flattering light that fell on our illustrations in the corridors.
There, among his nostalgic clutter of bric-a-brac, he offered his
illustrators Chinese tea in paper-thin cups and made us feel
comfortable with what we were doing. He liked to banter, with
an easy, knowledgeable irony, about "books and pictures" as he
called them. He made it all seem relative when he told you to
make your next girl's cloak a velvet one, "with that nice, rich van
Eyck-y quality you do so well, Violet," and you sipped your
smoky tea and gazed up in smug horror at some melodramatic
print he'd torn out of an old book and pinned on his wall. A
woman sunk in prostration at the feet of a stern man, her faulty
drapery stacked in unconvincing folds about her ankles . . . van
Eyck would turn over in his grave. You left Williamson's office
feeling that what you were going to do wasn't so bad when you
considered how what had been done already wasn't all that
good.

Doris Kolb had removed every trace of her predecessor's
bric-a-brac and had the walls painted white. She had aired him
out completely, poor Williamson. Gone were the soft-glowing
turn-of-the-century student lamps; she preferred overhead fluorescent. After the rose-and-brown-tinted corridors, her stark office assaulted your eyes with the unfriendly glare of a police
line-up.

Her door was open and she had her back to me. She was
tacking up some photographs on her wall. Well, well, so old
Doris of the bare desk and blank walls was going to let us in on her
tastes, at last.

I knocked on the molding of the door, for form's sake.

She did not turn; she just went on with what she was doing.
It was as if, I had noticed in my few meetings with her, her stim-

ulus-response equipment worked more slowly than most people's. That or something more sinister: that her simplest act was calculated to produce a certain desired employee reaction, and she had no time to waste on the superfluities of ordinary human intercourse. All the artists disliked her, or were a little afraid of her. Several rumors had developed about her flatness and inscrutability, the most appealing being the one put forward by one of the fired artists, which was that she was some kind of robot, an expensive, computerized mass of wires and electrical responses purchased for greater efficiency by the great conglomerate that controlled us all. Another artist said she was the niece of one of the directors, that her background was in neither art nor design, but in marketing research. Someone else was sure they had seen her working formerly in the accounts department at a department store.

She decided to turn around. "Hello," she said.

She was not a bad-looking woman. She had a round, smooth, precisely made up face, two spots of color in the cheeks, like a doll's, and clear, flat brown eyes that didn't blink very often. Her nose was long and narrow, turned up a little at the end, like those illustrations of Mary Poppins, and it occurred to me as I sauntered over to look at her photographs (since she was not, apparently, going to ask me to come in) that her nostrils were too narrow to allow for even the most minimal nose-picking. You thought things like that, with Doris. They surfaced, as crude jokes will in repressive surroundings. She always wore the same thing. A white blouse and dark pants. Was she a unisex adherent or was there something ugly about her legs? It was hard to guess her age from the expressionless face. It reminded me a little of those plaster casts I had drawn from in art classes. She was roughly between twenty-nine and forty, as far as I could tell.

"I see you're putting up some photos," I said, drawn as usual into fake cheerfulness by her silence. "They look interesting— what on earth are they? Photographs of women screaming?"

"I'm so excited about these," she said flatly, tearing her eyes away from the one she had just tacked up and looking at me for the first time. I seemed to remind her of an unpleasant duty, for she looked at once away again, back at her pictures.

So I looked, too. All of them—there were about ten—were close-ups of women screaming. Just their faces. The backgrounds and the bodies had been taken out by a vignetter.

"How . . . unusual," I said, walking up and down the row of them. The more I looked, the more uneasy they made me. It took me a few minutes to figure out why.

Doris just stood quietly, waiting. It seemed to please her when I said at last, "But . . . aren't these photographs of real screams? I mean, these women seem to be in real trouble!"

"Oh, yes, they're in real trouble, all right. These are real screams. Not painted ones."

"But . . . how . . . ?" I kept coming back to one photo. A female face contorted with such emergency that there was no question of pose. The hair lay back at an odd angle for an upright head. As if this photo had been made of someone lying down, and then turned around. There was a highlight of spittle at one corner of the mouth. The eyes were no joke either. I had never painted terror like this into the shrunken pupils of my heroines.

And the whole thing haloed in the simple, cameo-like vignette.

"These were done by a talented young woman named Vicki Valus," said Doris. "The one you keep looking at . . . the girl in that picture was actually being raped at the time that was taken."

"But *how* . . . ?"

"Telephoto lens."

I had been about to ask: How could someone stand by and take a picture when another woman was being raped?

"It was right outside her apartment," added Doris. "It was already happening. There was nothing anyone could do."

"Except take a photo," I said dryly. I kept staring at the screamer, fascinated in spite of myself. So this is how you would look if it happened to you.

"What do you think of the vignette technique?" asked Doris.

"Well, it sets it off," I admitted. "And gives it a certain ironic distance . . . and a certain shock value at the same time."

This time she gave me her full smile, baring her small teeth and the healthy, shiny gums. "I thought so, too. A whole series. Each of these women, just a sepia-toned vignette, sort of old-fashioned-looking from a distance, a trademark that will come to be known as a distinctive Harrow House imprint. I was thinking of *this* one"—with something close to deference, she led me to a woman with a different kind of scream—"for the cover of *Windrift Woman*. Vicki was working as a news photographer when she shot this. The woman's husband was a line repairman for the telephone company. He was working in his own neighborhood when he was electrocuted. The woman was coming back from the laundromat when she saw a crowd gathered around the pole. Vicki was able to catch the woman's expression at the moment when she first realized it was her husband."

"How enterprising," I said. In case you're worrying, I had not missed the *Windrift Woman* reference. So that was how it was to be done, with me. With the others, the ones who got the ax before me, the excuse had been a "payroll reduction due to rising costs, etc." That must have been before Doris had discovered the resourceful Vicki Valus and decided to wipe out altogether the old image of girls in costumes running away into their painted nights.

I was remarkably calm, considering. The cool photographer who lived inside me was waiting, with bated lens, to see how I would take this latest setback. I remembered Schumann and suddenly saw our meeting, mine and Doris's, as a typical one between a David and a Philistine. No wonder the composer had found it necessary to create his own *Davidsbund* against this ob-tuse enemy.

"But, Doris," I said, "there's one thing you might not have taken into consideration. The type of reader who buys our books just doesn't expect the kind of violence promised by these screams. And the people who bought the books *because* of these violent covers would be furious when they found nothing but 'romantic suspense' inside. I mean, well, as Williamson used to say, the subject of the modern gothic isn't real terror. It's terror as an erotic metaphor."

"All I know about Mr. Williamson," said Doris, "is he failed. And gothics are popular, but not so popular as they were. Our profits last year declined . . . but you artists don't want to know anything about dirty business. My job is to get more people to pick our books out of the racks at the drugstores and airports and bus stations and take them over to the cash registers and part with a dollar fifty. I don't care what they do with the books after that. The stuff inside deserves the trash can, if you want my opinion. But our covers don't have to be insipid imitations of all the other gothic covers in the trade. I mean, look at these. . . ." She opened a drawer of her desk and flung down across its tidy surface a handful of Harrow House titles.

She was, for the first time I'd ever seen her, aroused. She cared about something, after all. What exactly was it? Making an insipid product look inviting enough to sell? Her image of herself as a person who knew how to make something sell? In a different situation I might have asked her, but—in spite of the presence of my "cool photographer" who registered the details of the scene—I was battling furiously with hurt pride. One of *my* covers had been slung on the desk, with all those others. And it was no more memorable than its companions.

"You'll be paid for the *Windrift Woman* work, of course." She opened the middle drawer of her desk and took out a white envelope. My name had been written on it in red felt-tipped pen. "There's a bonus, as well," said Doris. "You've been working here quite a while, I believe. Too bad we don't pay unemployment benefits for our free-lance people. But you shouldn't have any trouble getting on with one of the other houses."

I took the envelope, noticing her perfect manicure. Each nail must have had at least four coats of shiny red varnish on it. I wondered if she had written my name in red on the envelope. So she had perfected the art of firing someone without even asking them to sit down.

All of a sudden I was six years old again. My grandmother

was sewing name tapes into all my underclothes. I was being sent off to a place in the mountains of North Carolina called Pine Hollow School for Girls. Even the vowel sounds were ominous, gloomy and lonely. My grandmother was telling me what fun it was to board, and how I would make close friends, some of them for life. Look at her friendship with Violet Pardee. How nice it would have been if they could have met earlier and had their whole girlhoods together. She was allowing me to "help" her by holding the thick roll of name tapes and cutting each one off when she was ready. I had been staring down at my name, printed over and over again in the same upright red letters (just like the red on the envelope Doris handed me). I understood somehow that my grandmother was saying one thing and thinking another. Then there was an awful moment when VIOLET CLAY had become just a bunch of letters. I stared at the tapes frantically: where had my name gone? The letters danced mockingly, refusing to have anything to do with me. They were merely letters. There was no Violet Clay.

I knew I had to get out of Doris's office if I was to preserve my cool. Otherwise I would break into sobs. I'd hate myself worse than ever if I started crying in front of her.

"Do you want a tissue?" She was offering me a small packet of Kleenex.

"Oh, shit," I said, just before my face collapsed with a strange muffled bark into the Kleenex.

Doris said, "You'd better sit down." She went to the door and closed it. I saw her glance at her watch.

I sat bawling for some five or ten minutes. It was really very weird. My mind went on with its own thoughts while my body demanded this undignified outpouring. I was thinking how much money I had left in the bank, whether I could afford to stay in my apartment for the coming winter, what it would have been like, my life, if I had stayed on with Lewis and painted and cooked in the absence of great art or passion. At least I would not have to worry about a roof over my head. The roof, at the moment, seemed infinitely attractive. But it was too late to ask him to take me back, because life had not stopped for him when

I left. He was remarried, with twin boys. So this is what I had made of my "freedom," all nine years of it. And I thought of my Uncle Ambrose when I had seen him this past spring looking so much older, cradling his swollen jaw with his hand (he'd just had a tooth pulled and was very depressed about it) and saying in a baffled singsong concerning his seven years out of the country, "Where all that time went I just don't know." He'd been in Mexico, first in the mountains, then near the sea. Now he'd come back, to see to his teeth and "see that goddamned albatross of a book through to the finish." He kept shaking his head, as if someone had told a joke and he couldn't quite catch the punch line. "Where all that time went I just don't know," he repeated, like a litany. I saw his tongue go repeatedly to the roof of his mouth, where the new hole was packed with cotton. Now he was up in the Adirondacks, in a rented cabin with his albatross. I didn't even have an albatross, just some promising canvas, neglected for years in a corner, that I could dust off and see through to the finish, thus making good my nine fallow years in this city.

Doris was scribbling notes on a memo pad. At least I had made her sit down. Finally she looked pointedly at her watch. "I have to lock up now. I'm meeting someone. We're going to have a quick bite and catch Bergman's new film. Have you seen it?"

I laughed bitterly. "I was planning to go this afternoon. Before you called."

"Well, there is still time. See a later show. Don't forget this." She rose and handed me my check for the second time.

I stood up and put on my sunglasses. "Good luck with your violent vignettes. I hope they go." I hoped they fell flat on their faces.

"If they don't go"—she smiled broadly, showing the gums—"*I* will." With a sharp red nail she traced a dagger path across her neck. I wondered who the "someone" was that she was meeting. "That's the law of the jungle," she said. "You can keep those if you want. I don't need them."

She meant the Kleenex.

5

Cocktail Time

The first thing I did when I got home was fix myself a drink. It was going to be a lethal one. I switched on the radio, en route to the kitchen, and there was Duncan Pirnie, chiding me in his mellifluous older-brother voice that it was already forty-five minutes past cocktail time. A lot of happy alcoholics must listen to WQXR in the late afternoon. How nice, beginning at a quarter to five each day, to be *told* it's time to polish up the pretzels. I crushed ice with the ritual of a true devotee and packed it into a tall glass. I sliced my lime. I took the bottle of Stolichnaya from the freezer and poured the glass three-quarters full. I added a dollop of tonic, for taste. Pirnie announced convivially that the last two works I had just heard were by . . . two names I immediately forgot. "They were contemporaries of Beethoven and wrote much useful music for the piano."

I took a deep swig of the icy vodka, thinking of Jake because it was he who taught me to keep it in the freezer. Like antifreeze, it had an alcohol content so high it couldn't freeze. By such trivia do our old lovers return to haunt us.

What contemporaries of mine would be the "Beethovens of Visual Art" as seen by art lovers in 150 years? Would Hope Sullivan make it? Hard to say. But at worst she had the hope of being dug out of storage to prove "useful" to some historian, to illustrate some point he'd already made up his mind about. Whereas I wouldn't even be in storage, except maybe in some half-rotted box of books in some antique store. "Oh, look, honey," some lady might call to her husband. "Come over here and look at these silly illustrations people used on their books. Whatever is that girl running from? It looks a perfectly good house to me!"

I went to my studio and switched on the fluorescent lamp over my drawing board. I drank more vodka, picked up my biggest flat hog's bristle and swilled it around in a puddle of lamp black. With strokes worthy of Franz Kline, I obliterated every wall, every tower, every window of my heroine's background. "There goes your house," I said murderously. "If I don't have one, why should you? No ancestral home across the street from the sea, no duplex or weekend cottage in the mountains, not even a two-hundred-dollar-a-month apartment in a dirty old building with someone sharing the rent. Come on out in the cold with me!"

Then I had to laugh, because the August heat was stifling in this room, a studio I'd never really liked. I had wanted the room Jake and I had used for our bedroom. It was larger and the light was better. One more of the many concessions to companionship at the expense of art, I thought, feeling more furious by the minute.

I took a smaller brush, mixed a bit of purplish gray, and set to work on my heroine's face. I painted shadows of weariness (and last night's drink) under her eyes. With these telltale smudges I disqualified her from the ranks of the perpetually fresh maidens, perpetually eligible for fresh starts, rescues and salvations. "You are over thirty," I said mercilessly, downing the remainder of my drink, sucking the last of it through the ice. "Mrs. Rochester has burned down your house, and Mr. Rochester has been dead for a century. You can't stick with your derivative Derek for two years, even if you did go back, and now I've made it impossible for you."

I made myself another drink and came back. Anger bubbled into my throat, surging up black and boiling from the depths. I set to work with real energy, canceling all her alternatives. I took away her youthful, pert little jawline and weighed it down with cynicism, disappointment and the plain old passing of the years between arrogant youthfulness and young middle age. "So," I said, painting fast and drinking faster. "You're no longer young and you're not so pretty. No man is going to save you from yourself because you appeal to his eye. Now what?"

I devoted my attention to her body. But here she eluded me. Where was it? At what point in my nine years of laziness, of professionally avoiding my profession, had I abandoned anatomy for drapery? She was a mere head perched on top of a floating cloak, the whole being borne unconvincingly along on the twinkletoe silver sandals. "Okay," I said. "You can brazen it out a while longer under there. The right cloak can cover your sins for a few more years. Eat, drink, and weep for the person you might have been. For the rich, full life you once dreamed of making for yourself."

In a childish fit of pique, I picked up the wet black hog's bristle and crossed out her "body" with two clean strokes. I felt as though someone had canceled out all my own hope as well, taken away everything: my man, my livelihood, my youth, my promise, what looks I had, the roof over my head. For I would have to move out now. Harrow House paid me $250 a cover. Usually I managed two covers a month. With Jake paying half of everything, this was ample. After he left, I planned to cut down on food and clothes, dip into my savings a little and hope for a miracle (or another lover to move in?). But this could continue only if my job with Harrow House continued. Which it didn't now.

As any of you know who have been there, there is a certain point on the road downward from your hopes where you find yourself deriving more comfort from imagining the worst than imagining what steps you would have to take to make things better.

I was now at this point. I had looked at my severance check from Harrow House on the way home. It was rather generous: $500. In addition to this, I still had about $1,200 in the savings bank. Clearly, I was not going to starve in the next few weeks. But already (aided by the vodka, I'll admit) I was entertaining visions of myself at the Bottom. I saw myself among those derelicts who lie on the sidewalks next to the grills where the warm air comes up from the heating systems of buildings; I saw myself as one of those muttering old ladies who hurry through the pub-

lic library carrying ancient shopping bags and blaming some invisible person for having wronged them. I saw myself walking
down Forty-second Street in crotch-tight shorts and platform
shoes, soliciting sailors.

The grooves of my mind were more accustomed to the con-
cept of Violet Clay as victim than as victress.

In someone else's story, the heroine would have embraced
her setback, welcomed it as a prod to catapult her out of her
slough. She would have seen her dismissal from a job that had
kept her on the side road of art for too long as a blessing in disguise. She would have read into the good fortune of Hope Sullivan both a push and a promise for her own eventual emergence
—if she began this moment and worked for it. *Okay, Violet,
you've wasted enough precious time! Sober up and let's clear up
the mess!* And off she'd go to the kitchen, not for a third drink—
as I was doing now—but to brew a pot of strong coffee, put
something solid in her stomach, and then sit down with her account book, figuratively *and* literally, and take stock.

Somewhere during my third Stolichnaya (by this time I'd
dispensed with all pretexts of lime and tonic) I gave myself over
totally to what Jake used to call "your Poor Little Me jags." Set-
backs of any sort whetted them and alcohol abetted them. First
I catalogued in my mind, like a child's unedited Christmas list,
all the things I had wanted. Then I evoked the names and faces
of those who had accidentally or willfully blocked my roads to
achievement and fulfillment. With the names and faces bobbed
up phrases, fully formed and with an incontestable rhythm, like
certain worn-smooth sentences that recurred predictably in the
gothics I had illustrated: "And then I knew that someone in that
house wanted me dead." Sentences like that.

"*Other men got off that ship alive,*" as *my father's stern
young face sank once more into a bright-pink sea.*

"*Other women lost their husbands and still managed to bring
up their daughters.*" *My mother.*

"*If she couldn't have Carnegie Hall, she wasn't about to let
me have Madison Avenue.*" *My grandmother.*

And so on. And like a drunk trying to walk a straight line, my logic wove its own weird patterns of cause and effect. My uncle's failure to finish his big novel I saw as a breach of promise to *me*. Nine years ago, we had clinked our glasses to mutual success. On my second night in New York, we had stood beaming at each other in his apartment and sworn to be true to our dreams. It now seemed perfectly logical that if he had kept up his side, I would have kept up mine, and today it could have been my show in the gallery and not just Hope Sullivan's.

Ah, that spring! Nine years ago! Why couldn't we go back and start over? (And I checked my glass and hurried to the kitchen for a refill so I wouldn't run out in the middle of a memory guaranteed to render its saturation point in remorse; it was a presageful memory also, in light of what I would learn later this evening.)

Nine years ago.

I had phoned him on my very first morning in the city, forcing myself to wait until the civilized hour of ten before I gave his number to the Martha Washington switchboard. His phone rang eight times and I was reluctantly preparing to hang up when he answered. His voice sounded guarded, as though he was expecting someone he would rather not talk to.

"I hope you weren't working on your novel and I've interrupted you in the middle of some important scene," I said.

"Hey, who is this?" He sounded a bit more approachable, almost flirtatious.

"It's Violet. Who do you wish it had been?"

"Violet? Sure enough, is it you, honey? How nice of you to call." His voice metamorphosed a third time, into the avuncular one I was familiar with. "How's everything down there?" he asked.

"I'm *up here*," I said. "I . . . I've left Lewis."

"Whoa, now. You've what?"

"Lewis and I are finished. I've come here to live. And to paint. I'm staying at this place called the Martha Washington till I get settled."

"Well, I'll be damned. This *is* a surprise. How did you know about the Martha Washington?"

"Lewis found it in some book at his travel agent's. He thought it would be safer, for a start."

He laughed, "It sure is. Safe as a henhouse. Poor old Lewis —I feel right sorry for him. I take it it was you who wanted to leave."

"Yes." I tried to sound suitably serious. "It was a mistake for me to marry."

"Mmm . . . mmh!" he echoed solemnly. And then, switching back to the gallant upbeat: "But won't it be a treat for me, to have some real kin in this town. Are you free for dinner this evening?"

"It just so happens I am. But I don't want to tear you away from your schedule. You weren't planning to work on your book or anything tonight?"

"That's Mr. Trollope you're thinking of. I have to get my 'one true sentence' before lunch, like Hemingway, if I'm going to get it at all."

"Oh, I'm sure you'll get it! Do you know where my hotel is?"

"I seem to recollect having been there a time or two before," he said playfully "Now, can you be down in the lobby at six sharp? 'Cause I've got something special I want to show you. And it won't wait."

I was waiting in the lobby at ten to six, having begun to dress and make up my face at four-thirty. I had paced myself deliciously through the whole of the day, knowing I had something to look forward to. Now I sat in a faded high-backed chair in full view of the entrance, confident of being picked up and therefore able to observe others unselfconsciously. Most of the residents who came briskly in, or loitered by the blind man's magazine stand, were girls my own age—some a little older. I took in their faces, their clothes, their strides and poses, the names of the stores on the shopping bags they carried. It excited me to think how many of us had come here to realize our childhood dreams of various sorts of stardom. That all of us would not make it, that

some of us (I secretly thought "some of them") were destined
to fail, only made the venture more thrilling.

On the dot of six, he veered through the entrance with his
tall man's loping gait. He had the carriage of the easy winner,
the look of one who knows he is eagerly anticipated. He wore
impeccably pressed cavalry twills, his habitual heavy wing-
tipped cordovans that gave both swing and substance to his long
stride, and my very favorite jacket: a red-black-and-white
hound's-tooth that he'd bought in England when he was stationed at Newbury with the 101st. It played up the blackness
of his hair and the boyish high color in his cheeks. He saw me
at once and came over.

"You're looking great!" he said. He bent to kiss me, pucker-
ing his lips en route.

"You are, too. I've always loved that jacket. It connects me
to the past." I was aware that other girls in the shabby lobby
were eyeing us hungrily, as if we were a color illustration of what
could happen to them.

"Thank you. Maybe that's why I like it, too. Come on, now,
the sun will be setting soon." He took me by the elbow and pro-
pelled me into the sweet lemon-colored air of spring. He held
up his hand and a taxi shuddered to a stop. I felt as though we
were on a movie set. He got in first (the only man I've ever
known to practice this fine art of taxi etiquette which keeps a
woman from having to slide across the seat, ruin her dignity and
maybe tear her stockings) and gave the driver an address.

"What does it matter," I said, "when the sun sets? We won't
turn into pumpkins."

"No, but we'd miss out on my spectacle."

The taxi took us to a large office building and we hurried
through a sort of arcade. We took the fast elevator to the top
floor. My ears popped. Ambrose smelled of something musky
and sophisticated.

It was a rooftop cocktail lounge, already filled with the soft
murmur of many dialogues. The minute the headwaiter saw Ambrose, he came over. The two men shook hands.

"I've got your table by the window," said the man. He looked at me appreciatively. He probably thought I was a new girlfriend.

"How've you been, Alfred? We made it just in time, didn't we? Oh boy, it's going to be a beautiful one. This is Violet, my niece. She's going to live in New York and I want her to see it at its enchanting best."

"How do you do?" said Alfred, seating us. "What would you like to drink?"

"I don't know. What are you having, Ambrose?" These were my pre-vodka days, when the thought of alcohol held little charm for me.

"I'll have my usual, Alfred. Bourbon and branch water. What can you suggest for the lady?"

"How about a Manhattan," said Alfred, "seeing as you're going to live here."

"I'd love one," I said, having no idea what it was.

After Alfred had departed, I said, "You seem to be a preferred customer."

"Oh, I did a little feature article on this place for *Esquire*. I do that kind of thing, you know, to keep something in the till while I plod away at my opus. Why are you smiling? Did I say something funny?"

I was smiling from pleasure. The pleasure of being at home. After all these years in New York, he still spoke like a confident Southern schoolboy reciting poems he knew by heart. "How've you managed to keep your Southern accent after living in the North almost twenty years?"

"Oh, I polish it up once a month or so, like the family silver. Yankees love family silver—look how much they stole from us." He winked at me and picked up one of my hands. "So you're going to be an artist, huh?"

"I'm going to try. I'm going to take my stuff around to the galleries. Maybe tomorrow."

"Don't go shotgunning for the first gallery that makes you an offer. Let them know you're looking them over, too."

"Okay." I thought this was excellent advice.

Our drinks came. The two men checked their watches as the sun disappeared behind a tall building with an ornate top. "If we were in Charleston, Alfred," Ambrose said, "the sun would have set fourteen minutes ago. Now, Violet, I want you to watch a truly enchanting spectacle."

I did. There below was the city I had come to conquer, spread out for me like a napkin in my lap. Minute by minute it grew more chimerical. Slowly the island of Manhattan turned pink, then gray, then blue. I gulped my Manhattan and ate the cherry and heard Ambrose's amused voice order another round.

The lights began to go on. One here, a whole string there, as an entire floor of a skyscraper suddenly came ablaze, or a suspension bridge outlined itself. I was feeling light-headed. I would stare hard at a certain building, willing a light to come on in a certain place . . . and it would! The nearer I got to the end of my second Manhattan, the easier this trick became.

"Good God, I love this place," I said. "For the first time, I feel something has lived up to its promises."

"I feel the same," said Ambrose. "No other city in the world can hold a dead match to this one."

"Now if I can only live up to *my* promise," I said.

"Ah, that's the trick. You've got to keep your eagle's-eye view. That's why I brought you here. Just keep looking down, honey. Look down from the heights at the streets. Don't they look tiny? See that little bitty car moving through that cavern? All the publishers are down there. All the art dealers, too. We have to make our impression down there, but the real thing is the bird's-eye view. Hey, see that ship down there moving out of its berth? Do you know what the name of the channel is that lets ships into New York Harbor? Ambrose Channel. How about that?" He flashed me his dynamic handsome-man's smile. "You got to go through me, kid. Are you getting hungry? We're going back to my place when you are, and cook steaks."

In the taxi, we settled back for the ride to the Village and grinned at each other. "Boy, I feel good," said Ambrose. "Are you going to try to get some kind of work till you establish yourself?"

"I'll have to, if I want to eat. That's one of the things I wanted to ask your advice about. What's the chance of me doing work for magazines? I have a good eye. I can make things look like themselves with a few lines."

"Don't I know it. In the old days you like to broke me up with those cartoon figures you drew of the kids who came to the house to take piano. And that dilly you did of Aunt Violet Pardee, with her quarterback's shoulders and that pair of foxes she wore. You had the foxes about to bite off her ears, remember? I tell you what. I know this lady at *Vogue*. I'll ask her to be on the lookout for something for you."

"*Would* you?"

"I'd be happy to. She's a real nice woman. You'd like her."

We got out a few blocks from his place on Waverly, as he wanted me to see the Village. "It's got a certain atmosphere," he said, leading me down attractive narrow streets of row houses with interesting paintings and plants in the lamplit interiors. We passed pubs and coffeehouses full of people, and shops smelling of incense and leather and old books, still open at night. Ambrose explained that many people now considered the Village what the Left Bank in Paris had been to writers and artists in the twenties and thirties. "Here comes an artist now," he said. A woman in her forties with sibylline eyes and long gray witchy hair was coming toward us, walking a small fussy-looking dog with a plume tail and a face like a hairy chrysanthemum.

"Hi, neighbor," called Ambrose.

"Hello, Fitz," she replied in a husky voice. She passed, giving Ambrose an arch look and me a knowing smile.

"Why did she call you that?" I asked.

"Oh, she says I remind her of Scott Fitzgerald." He smiled to himself. "My clothes, the way I part my hair, or something."

"What kind of paintings does she do?"

"Well, I'm not sure she's still painting. She used to have shows; she was pretty well known for a while there. But now she does these drawings . . . well, she's a lady pornographer, Violet, to tell the truth. She does illustrations for a certain kind of book. But they're high-quality—she's shown me some of her work. Pornography is a very old art. She's been to Japan to study their ancient techniques, and to China. She has more commissions than she can handle. She does work for West Germany and all the Scandinavian countries and rakes herself in quite a pile. That little piece of fluff on legs you saw her walking—you know, she paid over a thousand dollars for that damn thing." He threw back his head and laughed. "Can you imagine anybody paying that much for a dog?"

"Do you know her well, then?"

"We're good buddies. Folks are friendly down here. It's like a small town. You may want to locate here yourself. Ellie has her studio not far away. Her real name's Elvira, but whoever heard of a pornographer named Elvira? Here we are, honey. This is my roost." He held open the door of an old gray building. Inside, there was a foyer with a row of metal mailboxes. His was the only one that had a genuine calling card in the slot. "It's five flights up," he warned. "Better get your breath."

I had to stop after the second flight, my heart was pounding so. "You aren't even breathing hard," I accused.

"That's 'cause I'm used to it. Keeps me in shape. I'm getting old, you know. I turned forty in February."

"Forty's nothing to a man," I said, going up the next flight.

"In some ways it is," he remarked pensively from behind.

My expectations were sinking at the sight of the shabby doors on each landing and at some of the smells coming through these doors. I was new to New York and didn't yet know that quite nice people paid quite large sums to live behind shabbier doors with worse smells.

But once inside Ambrose's apartment, I was reassured. It was just the sort of place a writer should live in, crammed with books on shelves all the way to the ceiling, and with the latest newspapers and magazines on every surface. There was nice hi-fi equipment and there were loads of records, and healthy hanging plants in the windows, and bright pillows in the corners of the window seats. And there was his working space, a massive old office desk, with his typewriter on it, and even a sheet of yellow paper rolled in the typewriter.

"Did you get your one true sentence before lunch?" I asked, going over to snoop. Something in the arrangement of the things on the desk indicated to me that he was prepared for my inspection.

"As a matter of fact, I got a whole page," he said, coming up behind me. "You inspired me."

I noticed his shelves contained multiple copies of *Looking for the Lora Lee*. Above his desk was a corkboard on which he had stuck various things. A laminated review from the *New York Herald Tribune*, with a small photo of him looking ridiculously young. "Clay's Modern Lorelei Sets Hero a Tricky Course," said the headline. The last few lines—"an appealing first novel with fast-paced action and a venturesome love story"—had been underlined. A publicity photo of Ava Gardner in her prime, with "To Ambrose Clay, Love and Kisses" written in green ink. And a note card on which had been typed:

> The difficult thing is inventing
> when you are encumbered by memory.
> —André Gide

A stack of yellow pages in a Manila folder reposed beside the portable typewriter.

NO MORE AT EASE

a novel

by Ambrose Clay

was typed neatly on the cover. In the typewriter was a fresh yellow sheet with the number 75 at the top.

"Well," said I, "I've got what I came for." I snatched up the folder and made as if I were going to abscond with his novel.

"Hey, give me that!" But his tone was playful.

"No," I called, striding away toward the big brass bed I'd glimpsed round the corner. "I'm going to settle in and have a good read while you cook our steaks. Maybe you could bring me a glass of wine."

I plopped down on the bed. "Mmm. Just right for reading the novel the world is waiting for." I wanted to see how far he'd let me go.

He followed me and playfully retrieved the folder. "You don't want to take up our whole evening with that," he said. "Tell you what I'll do: I'll let you read a little bit of what I wrote today. Will that abate the voracious bookworm's appetite?"

"Well, I suppose a crumb is better than nothing," I teased.

He was already going through the pages. There was an earnest look about him that was new to me. "Tell you what. I'll let you read the whole page I did today, after you called. Okay?"

He handed me the page and wandered over to a pipe rack that stood out on a low bureau beneath a large gilt-framed mirror. He took out his handkerchief and began dusting the pipes methodically. I could look up and see his face in the mirror, the features very still, the dark-lashed eyes cast down on the pipes.

I was not prepared for the serious tone of what he'd written and had to read each sentence several times. I also had trouble concentrating because I was trying to prepare something fascinating to say about it before I'd even read it. It appeared to be an interior monologue in which the hero was assessing his own character. There was a passage on "charm" that particularly impressed me. It went something like this:

> *Charm* (thinks the hero) *was when people automatically said yes to you without your doing anything. He supposed he must have this quality because people had been saying yes to him without his doing very much of anything all his life. There was nothing wrong with that. It was a pleasant feeling; he'd be the first to say he liked seeing yes in the eyes of his people rather than no. But what if a man got charmed by his own charm? What would he do then?*

After reading this, I looked up, perhaps to voice some prefatory praise on this passage alone. I caught Ambrose regarding himself in the mirror in a way I knew I hadn't been meant to see. I looked down again at once and read through the remainder of the page, not registering a word more. I was still too young to have looked at myself that way in a mirror, but old enough to recognize the look. It was the look of one who has recognized the enemy in the glass.

"This is very deep," I said. "You have drawn a very complex, appealing portrait just in these few lines. I'm flattered that you'd let me read it."

"You weren't bored?" he asked, turning away from the mirror. "It's not too philosophical then?"

"That's part of its charm," I said. "That someone who *is* obviously appealing to others without trying could be so self-searching at the same time. It gives him an added depth."

"You think so? Really?"

"I really do. I'm dying to read more. I hope you'll let me."

"I will as soon as I have it. You're not bluffing me, sport?" He hadn't called me that in years. I looked up at him flashing his old radiance in the colorful hound's-tooth jacket. Already the mirror glimpse was fading fast from my memory.

"I'm not bluffing you. I think it's going to be a great book, based on this and what you've said about it."

"What I've said about it . . . ?" he coaxed.

"You know, the adventurous personality living in a time without dramatic challenges. No big wars or anything. Maybe you'll be the first to write about a new kind of man living in our time. The kind who has to create his own inner challenges because the outer ones have all been dealt with."

"The existential hero, you mean?"

"Well, yes, but 'existential hero' has become such a dull, passive image. Your man will still have the old Byronic verve. He'll be a sort of charming mutant bridging the old and the new."

"Damned if you don't put things well, honey. I declare if you aren't just the fortuitous omen I was needing. I like what you said about the portrait, too. A complex portrait of a new kind of man with some of the old left in him, too. I believe that's just what I have been trying to do. Only I was still so tied up in all these old notions of plot and action that I lost myself in the woods for a while. Come on now, I've got a nice bottle of wine. You and I are going to drink to our respective successes."

That's just what we did. Standing ceremoniously in the midst of his big room. "To your first show and my big book," he said. We clinked our glasses and drank. His cheeks were flushed and his dark eyes shone with confidence. He was the very picture of the man who had already accomplished what he now set out to do. "And to the first of our many evenings together," he proposed, raising his glass for a second toast. "I think you and I are going to be good for one another."

"I'll drink to that," I said happily, never dreaming how many things would happen to us both and how many months would pass before I laid eyes on my uncle again.

Each age brings with it its own light, said Matisse, adding that the only light that really exists is in the artist's brain. I believe that certain periods of one's life also bring with them characteristic colors: auras, or mental hues, meaningful to the soul's eye. The spring I arrived in New York was, for the most part, blue. Blue is the color of dreaming and of infinite time and space. It is the color of young nights, of enchantments. The evening I spent with Ambrose was blue.

Whereas the August evening nine years later where you left me swilling vodka and stewing myself in a lethal brew of self-hatred and remorse was a garish, sickening pink. My studio was swathed in the pink of the sun gone down, the color with which vain old women light their rooms. My canceled-out gothic heroine gazed up at me with her frightened eyes through the pinkish gloom. My studio was the color of dreams that had lain around too long and were starting to smell at the edges.

I went to the kitchen and got the bottle of vodka, stumbling through the dimness, carrying it like a stillborn baby, till I found the general direction of the bedroom. I shut the blinds against the last tincture of day emanating from the sky outside. "Die, light," I said. I lay comatose, listening to the radio. "Symphony Hall" was doing excerpts from Prokofiev's *Romeo and Juliet.* The whole idea of fresh young love seemed obscene. I looked around for my glass. I had left it behind in the studio. Then, with the alcoholic's cunning lift of heart, I groped triumphantly beneath the bed till I found last night's glass. I hefted it up bearing fingerprints and dustballs, and topped it with my 90-proof poison. I believe that if it had been real poison I would have quaffed it with joy. I passed out before I remembered to take a sip.

Sometime later the phone woke me. It took me a minute to recollect who and where I was. The conductor of the Cleveland Orchestra was being interviewed on the radio. I groped in darkness for the lamp switch and picked up the telephone, but must have neglected to say hello because the voice on the other end kept saying it over and over urgently. It was a woman's voice I was sure I'd never heard before, oddly high and ethereal. I felt quite nauseated.

"Hello? Hello, please! I'm trying to locate Violet Clay," the high-pitched voice went on.

"I'm she," I finally got out, suppressing a heave at the sight and smell of the dirty glass full of pure vodka.

"Oh, thank goodness. My name is Minerva Means. This *is* Violet Clay? Ambrose Clay's niece?"

"Yes, but I'm afraid I can't put you in touch with my uncle. He's living in the Adirondacks and doesn't have a telephone." Over the years, I had more than once received calls from strange women trying to get through to Ambrose.

"Oh, dear. I'm afraid you don't understand. I'm calling from the Adirondacks, you see. It's about your uncle I'm calling *you.*"

"What about him?"

"Well, dear, I'm afraid this is very bad news. Your uncle took his life this evening."

"Took his life?" I could only repeat blankly.

"Early this evening. This is the first chance I've had to call you. A neighbor's little girl found him and by the time we called the troopers and the coroner came . . . He left everything very orderly, his wallet and car keys and registration papers all laid out on his table, and a note in his typewriter, and then a note for you in a sealed envelope, with your address on it. As a matter of fact, dear, the trooper is here with me now. He wants to know if we can open the note. I could read it over the phone to you."

"Yes, please." I could already hear the crackling of paper at the other end. "But I don't even know how he killed himself," I said.

"It was with a German Luger," she said. "The coroner says he lay down on the floor first, so he wouldn't fall, you know. I'm afraid it's a very short note."

"Please read it." I was remembering Ambrose playing stunt man at my fifth-birthday party, leaping from the top of my swing to demonstrate to a bunch of rapt little girls how a paratrooper fell safely to the ground. And afterward how we'd all crowded round to see the strangely shaped weapon taken from the body of the dangerous Nazi who had almost killed my uncle.

" 'Violet honey,' " she read aloud in the high, ethereal voice. " 'I'm sorry, there's nothing left.' "

"Is that all?"

"I'm afraid so, dear. The other note was brief, too. It said, 'I have decided to take my life.' With a signature. Mr. O'Halloran, that's our coroner, says it was what he calls a *thoughtful* suicide."

"Who are you?" I sounded very rude. "I mean, why are you the one to call?"

"I rented him the cabin, dear. Oh, this is so upsetting. I never dreamed anything like this would happen. He always seemed so relaxed and cordial. Excuse me . . ." I heard her speaking with a man. "Lieutenant Quentin says for me to tell you they will need the note for fingerprinting and such, but you will get it back."

"Why do they need it for fingerprinting if they already know it's a suicide?" In fact, by this time, I was pretty sure it was, myself. I felt I had carried this knowledge somewhere inside me for years.

"It's their routine, dear. They're so very thorough. You should have seen them up there at the cabin, dusting and taking photographs. When do you think you can come up? Do you drive? If not, I have the bus schedule for you."

"I'll come tomorrow as early as I can," I told her, already planning on what measures I'd have to take to sober up. Thinking of them, I retched again. "Can you give me an early bus?"

"There's an eight a.m. that gets here at two. Adirondack Trailways. It's the one to Massena. Tell the driver to let you off at the Old Coach Inn at Plommet Falls. It's not a scheduled stop. I'll meet you there and we'll go over to Mr. O'Halloran's. He also has a funeral home. That's where they are taking your uncle. I'm very sorry about this, dear. As I said, I had no idea anything like this was going to happen. If I had, I would have done more to cheer him up. But he had another neighbor, much nearer his own age—that's Samantha, the mother of the little girl who found him—and even she didn't have an inkling he might do anything like this. We were speaking about it just a few minutes ago, with the troopers."

"Oh, God . . ." It was just beginning to be irrevocable to me. All these official facts, all these new people. Any minute now I was going to have to face overwhelming implications.

"I would try and rest now, if I were you," said my caller. "There's nothing more any of us can do tonight. I will tell you one thing, for what comfort it's worth. It was a neat suicide. Mr. O'Halloran said he certainly knew what he was about. So you'll be able to say your goodbyes to him without averting your eyes. If you're anything like me, you tend to imagine the worst. Now I'm going to give you some advice, dear. Set your alarm clock so you'll make your bus and then . . . I don't know what your morals are but if you keep anything strong in the house, it might be a good idea to take a little drink. Just enough to take the edge off this terrible news so you can get some sleep."

I thanked her and hung up and walked an unsteady path to the bathroom. There I knelt on the cold tiles and, professionally as an old Roman, inserted two fingers deep into my throat. The nausea and ensuing nastiness which tore from my guts was a welcome relief. I applied myself single-mindedly to the task at hand. As if, in the process, I might succeed in spewing this sick bad dream of a day from my life.

6

Milo's House

I washed the taste of vomit carefully from my mouth, but not all the mint-flavored toothpaste and dental floss and Water Piks in the world could quite wash out that remaining little taste of shame. "Die, light," I'd said, cocooned like the coward I was in pillows and sentimental music and alcohol. But at dusk, in that cabin in the Adirondacks, the person who meant business had gone ahead and pulled the trigger.

I packed a small suitcase for the next morning. What would I need for what I had to do in Plommet Falls? I put in a dark cotton dress, just in case the funeral would be there. But it had to be somewhere. And I would be the one who would have to decide. I packed slowly, devoting meticulous care to the placing and folding of each item, as though this orderly activity on my part could straighten out the mess at large.

Then, in search of more housekeeping to put between me and the night ahead, I went from room to room collecting empty glasses. I must wash all these glasses and file them neatly away on the shelf. Already I saw the woman who had drunk from them from a critical distance, like a corrupt friend one knows will soon have to be dropped.

I turned on the overhead light in my studio, while I rounded

up glasses—from how many days? The small children of the previous tenants had slept in this room. When Jake and I moved
in and I had turned it into my studio, I had scrubbed their pencil
marks from the walls and used a whole can of Lysol spray to rid
the room of a faint urine smell. Now I fancied the smell had
come back. And why not? The emanations of childish rage were
thick in the small room. My x-ed out gothic heroine reproached
me forlornly from her black night. I turned her face down.
Somehow I could not envision ever painting anything else in this
room.

In the kitchen I washed the glasses in hot sudsy water, dried
each scrupulously and put it away. It was not yet ten o'clock.
Ten more hours to get through till bus time. I decided to clean
the kitchen, beginning with a basket on the counter that served
as a catchall for unanswered mail, felt-tip pens that had run
out of ink, bank deposit and withdrawal slips, and buttons that
needed to be sewn back on things. In the basket I found—perhaps I had been searching for it unconsciously—the one postcard Ambrose had sent me from Plommet Falls, a doe and a
buck drinking together from a stream, postmarked June 15,
with the following message: *Greetings from Fenimore Cooper
land. On the whole very peaceful here. Lots of beautiful scenery
to paint, or to write about, for that matter, if you're Thoreau.
Hope you are taking good care of yourself. Meanwhile, as the
British say, we must press on. Love, Ambrose.*

Now I stood holding this postcard—there was no place to sit
down in the tiny rectangular kitchen; you had to close the door
every time you opened the refrigerator—and dredging up memories as well as guilt. Why hadn't I answered it? It even had
a box number inked in above the message. But did postcards call
for an answer, especially when their "meanwhile" held every
promise of a follow-up letter, or meeting? I had always answered
Ambrose's *letters*, few and far between as they had been during
those years in Mexico. He had revealed little of himself in his
letters, penned on the stationery of various hotels—and once or
twice on the kind of stationery only a woman would buy. He

seemed to exist in a peopleless vacuum in these letters: there was weather (always weather), there were thoughts (about books, about the progress or nonprogress of his) or a mention of a painting he had seen in "a studio" in Oaxaca; and there was scenery and there were sometimes descriptions of exotic flowers or the food in a restaurant. But no persons were mentioned. The studio might have existed in thin air, or the restaurant (in which he ate all alone, as in a surrealist dream?). Actually, my letters to him were not very peopled either. I told him things that were happening in this country that he could read for himself in the airmail edition of *Time*. I waxed safely ambitious, sticking to the whimsical "One of these days when we've both accomplished our *opuses* . . ." To the relief of us both, my poor Latin gave us an occasion for one of our few lively exchanges. "Sport, don't you know *opuses* ain't no plural? It's *opera*. At least we ancients were properly educated." Then I wrote back how if the average person heard us discussing our *opera* he'd just think we were writing an opera together. And so on. Never did the mention of a current passion besmirch our dutiful if sporadic exchanges. I took it for granted it was decorous of me to withhold Ivor or Jake and the in-betweens from my uncle. I was shocked when, late one night (Ambrose had been in Mexico about four years), my phone rang and some woman started weeping loudly over long distance about what a cad Ambrose Clay was. She had found a letter from me and assumed I was his wife. "He may think of himself as Casanova," she cried, "but the world has other names for men who live off women!" I had repressed this at once and only now remembered it.

The drawn, yellow-complexioned man I had met for lunch this past spring did not seem to think of himself as Casanova. His clothes were good as always, but a bewildered look had replaced the easy smile. And he seemed upset out of all proportion about losing a tooth, even though it wasn't near the front.

"I thought for damn sure old Norris could save that tooth," he kept saying. "He was doing root canals before anyone else, when I first came to New York. I couldn't believe my eyes when he picked up those pliers today and said it was too late. 'But, Doc Norris, you're the Miracle Man,' I told him. 'I may be the Miracle Man,' he said, 'but even miracles have their deadlines, and there's poison all over your jaw. You're lucky we don't have to pull more.'" He wore his hair longer, curling down the back of his neck. There was a lot of gray in his sideburns. But he still spoke in his buoyant singsong, making an entertaining story out of the things that disturbed him. "Well, I expect they'll all fall out soon enough. Have yourself a cocktail, baby. I can't join you because of that bout with hepatitis I was telling you about. Lord, when the body goes, it goes. Pretty soon I'll look like these old guys at the Y where I'm staying. The damnedest thing. There I was, sitting on the can, and this old toothless face suddenly peers up at me from underneath the door. Do you think it was my future self?" And Ambrose laughed, as though imagining the worst had made the present moment not so bad after all.

"You're staying at the Y?" I said in dismay. Then realized my tactlessness. Perhaps he was short of money.

But he smoothed it for me. "I thought it would be a good way to reorient myself into American life. It used to be a right pleasant place when I played squash or swam there. Now there isn't much to connect it with its name. The young aren't young, the men aren't men, and the Christians . . . well, they got lost a long time ago. But I may as well stay a few more days, as I'm settled in."

"Of course!" I agreed heartily. I took a large sip of my vodka martini. "And what . . . will you do after that?" Guiltily, I found myself looking forward to the end of this lunch. I had come in hopes that my long-lost uncle, returned from his secret life south of the border, would cheer me up and rekindle my own low-burning hopes. Now I was glad I had already explained I had to meet "a friend," whose woodwind group was giving an afternoon concert.

Ambrose said he wasn't sure whether he'd relocate in the city. "What I have been toying with, you know, is renting myself a little cabin way up in the woods somewhere and finishing my book. If I don't finish it soon, *I'll* be finished." He winked at me and took a spoonful of hot soup. I saw him wince when it touched the hole where his tooth had been.

"That's great. Is it . . . is it still called *No More at Ease?* I like that title. It implies so many things."

"Yes, well, it's been through a few sea changes since I last saw you. So much has happened. So much has changed. I'm not the same man who was writing *No More at Ease*. That's something I was meaning to talk to you about. Do unfinished paintings shape-shift as much as unfinished novels do? Do they seem to take on a life of their own, the longer you live with them? I was lying in my room at the Y last night—me and my throbbing ex-tooth—thinking about how a novel long in the writing is like some strange amoeba-like creature. Just when you think you've got your mind around it, it sprouts another protrusion. You devote your attention to the new protrusion, but meanwhile some other part you thought you had under control changes its shape . . . or disappears altogether. Have you found that, with painting?"

"Well, of course, I've been doing mostly illustration work these past few years. But I don't think painters spend years on one single painting, planning it out and such. They tend to paint lots of paintings, working toward that final realization. That's why you'll often go to a painter's studio and find the walls lined with fifty or sixty versions of a single idea."

"You mean like drafts?"

"Yes, a little."

He sucked at his tooth socket. "Maybe I'd have done better to write out the successive drafts. At least I'd have something to show for all this time." The look he was giving me was as near as he'd ever come to admitting failure in my presence. On the strength of it I ordered a second martini. I'd completely lost interest in my spinach omelet. I wanted both to reassure him and be gone. To set him back on the road ahead of me in order to give myself a little more time. "I've got to see that goddamned albatross of a book through to the finish," he announced gloomily. "That's mainly the reason I've come back."

"You know what Rodin said," I told him. "You don't ever finish works. You just decide, at a certain point, to abandon them. I think you should set yourself a deadline, go somewhere beautiful where you won't be disturbed, and go flat out on your book. And then, when the day comes when you feel you can't do any more, write 'The End' and abandon it. Type *No More at Ease* on a clean title page and send it off to the publisher. That's what I think you should do."

He was listening to me as though I were giving him the recipe for salvation. "You think I should, huh? Just go flat out, as long as I can, and then 'abandon' it. Ha, I like that. Abandon it. You know, I just might do that, Violet. I was thinking about calling it something else, actually. I was toying with *Capriccio*— the caprices of fate as well as the hero, you know. The form would be looser-knit than originally planned. Maybe in movements, like a piece of music. Or mosaic-like. I want to have the freedom to skip around if I want. After all, it would better suit the material of the book, which is that of a modern man awash in the flux of too many complexities and possibilities."

"But it sounds wonderful!" I exclaimed. My head, at long last, was beginning to buzz with the vodka. "What are you waiting for? I love the mosaic idea. Little pieces, in many different moods. Then you'd never get bored."

"I think you're right," he said. Then his hand went to his jaw, which was still numb from the Novocaine. "Where all that time went I just don't know," he said in the schoolboy singsong. The baffled look was in his dark eyes.

"There's still time!" I said, beginning to sound like Little Miss Sunshine.

But he didn't seem to notice. "You think so?" he said, looking happier.

At some point during my third martini and his cup of custard, we decided he should get going at once, find his rugged paradise of pure intentions, and set an end-of-the-summer deadline.

"If you did, say, ten pages a day, you'd be finished in forty days," I said. "You weren't planning over a four-hundred-page book, were you?"

"Forty days," he said. "Nice symbolic number. Jesus in the desert."

"Then you ride triumphantly back into the city on your donkey and wait for the reviews," I said.

He threw back his head and laughed, really laughed, for the first time during our lunch. I saw the poor tooth socket on the upper-left-hand side, packed with bloody cotton. "You know, Violet, you always have been able to put fire into me," he said.

Several days later my phone rang. I heard coins jangling into a metal box. It was Ambrose, calling at the worst time imaginable. Jake had just "moved out"—he was to move out and in again several times before the final July break—and I was left alone, in rage and hysterics, to sort out all his latest accusations and debit new evidence to my account as a failed human being. Ambrose, on the contrary, sounded vital and euphoric, his old robust self. The recent memory of his yellow cheeks and baffled eyes fell away as he talked. He was calling from a country store in a tiny village in the Adirondacks called Plommet Falls. He had taken my advice and had just that morning rented himself a cabin in the woods. "I'm on my way up there now, with my typewriter and supplies," he announced happily. "And I've already bought my donkey for my triumphal ride back into town. It's a 1968 Pontiac donkey, a little rusty on her flanks, but she'll get me where I'm going." He reiterated what a good influence I was and asked me was the day as pretty down there as it was where he was. I bravely said yes, I could see little green shoots on the new trees which had recently been planted along my street and after he hung up, I thought: Well, *he's* all right again, and collapsed on the unmade bed and had a good cry for myself.

Now, as my first tears fell on the deer postcard, I tried to distill my grief, to make it purely for the loss of his hope. As of June 15, he had still been pressing on. The summer doe and buck drank innocently from the stream, impervious to autumn's gunfire. The juxtaposition between then and now seemed unutterably sad. I swung back and forth, between those old robust

illusions and the new depleted reality, until I discovered—with
no little disgust—that I was weeping for my own interests again.
From whom in the world could I now demand the uncritical ac-
ceptance and well-disposed expectations that go with kinship?
Whom now could I count on to think well of me, to think of me
in my absence at all?

At this point I remembered my friend Milo. Deeper down
in the basket, in fact, were two of his postcards to me from
Greece. Was he back from his island in the Aegean? Had he finished gathering material for his new book?

Oh, please let him be back, I prayed, already heading for the
phone.

When I began living with Jake, Milo had become one of
those casualties of platonic friendship that have to be sacrificed
for the good of the other, sexual, relationship. Jake was suspi-
cious of Milo's disinterested affections. He made jokes about his
pen name and said there was something fishy about a man who
took women to plays and concerts but never to bed afterward.
"Where would you be if Milo hadn't taken me to *your* concert?"
I would counter, but only in the earlier days, when I knew he
would not reply, "A hell of a lot better off!"

For it had been at Milo's invitation that I first laid eyes on
Jake. He was the soloist in the Marcello oboe concerto. Sitting
next to cool Milo, who smelled faintly of sandalwood, I was attracted to some petulant, bad-boy quality in the small, dark-
haired oboist. The way he played his instrument brought out its
medieval qualities, sending visions of goat-footed pipers through
my head. There was a reedy-sensual poignance to his sounds.
His black hair kept falling in his eyes. His pixie face went beet
red from sustaining long breaths as he went searching up and
down the scale—looking for an entrance into somebody's heart,
I'd thought, feeling a slow lust born of sentimentality beginning
to uncoil in my womb. Milo, who knew one of the violinists,
asked would I like to go backstage after the performance. I said
I would. I was between lovers, but not for long. When I shook
hands with the dark little oboist, welcoming two years of physi-

cal and mental turbulence into my life, gentle Milo receded, seemed to float away, almost, until I should need platonic empathy again.

Milo had saved me from my worst instincts some six years ago. Or rather, the influence of one of his novels saved me, as I didn't know him yet. At the time, I was under the enchantment—that is the only way I can describe it—of a Hungarian, a refugee and ex-painter named Ivor Sedge (anglicized from Istvan Szegedyi). We had been involved for eighteen months in an obsessive physical union which had literally shut out the world, and now Ivor had asked me to leave New York and follow him. There was to be no further question of my art, as Ivor, once a celebrated artist in his own country, had given up art himself. At this crucial juncture, Harrow House assigned me a new gothic to illustrate. It was called *The Secret of Seven Towers,* by a writer well known in the trade named Arabella Stone. I was flattered initially, because only the better-established artists ever got to illustrate her books, which sold widely and were, both in craft and content, a cut above the average. I figured I had time to do one more cover before I abandoned it all and went on the road with Ivor, so I took the proofs home to skim, so I'd get the details right, and ended up reading the book slowly from beginning to end. It had the staple "romantic suspense" plot, but some books, of whatever genre, have the power to make you want to change your life and this was one of them. The two main characters, a man and a woman eventually destined for each other, though they didn't know it yet, were so bright and bold, with a true elegance of mind and each with an innate wideness of heart that only required a bit of growth, that they put my self-pitying, self-destructive inclinations (temporarily) to shame. Of course I could not give up my painting—or, for that matter, my hopes for a love relation such as these two won for themselves—and go with Ivor out of cowardice and sheer physical greed. I did a lovely cover painting instead. When Arabella Stone received the proof, she wrote me a generous note via our mutual publishing company, telling me that it was not only the best illustration of any of her books, but she felt it gave added visual interpretation to "movements of the soul I only hinted at." She asked if she might buy my painting and invited me to lunch. I accepted, also via Harrow House, as she had given no other address, and went expecting to meet a well-bred older woman, a sort of fairy godmother with a romantic turn of mind. I was even rehearsing the confidences I planned to make to her, about how her elevated love story had saved me from Ivor; perhaps she would be very rich (her books went through many reprintings) and offer to sponsor me for a year while I devoted myself to serious painting. I was quite ready to give myself over to an ennobling relation with an older, wiser woman and swear off men and all the reductiveness of their demands for at least a year.

You can imagine my confusion and adroit shifting of expectations when the waiter led me to the "Stone" table and a tall, slim golden man wearing a three-piece suit stood up and flushed pink with apology for his "joke," and took my hand in his firm cool one and introduced himself as Milo Hamilton, alias Arabella Stone. "But I love it," I protested. "I love things like this. It gives a little shot of adrenaline to the imagination. I was prepared to like Miss Stone. But I'm sure I'll like you just as well. Maybe even better." Then it was my turn to flush. The two of us sat down shyly to the prospect of our lunch. Which turned out to be progressively stimulating, always nourishing, without ever once threatening to glut. What a civilized change from Ivor! Our single-minded excesses now seemed sickening to me. Had fate been kind to me at last, dropping this golden dream of a suitor into my lap? Milo Hamilton was handsome, intelligent, subtle. He radiated empathy for everything and everybody in his surroundings. All subjects seemed to hold interest for him. Like his books, he made you want to be a better person. By the end of the lunch, I was speculating whether our destinies would resemble those of the two lovers in *The Secret of Seven Towers*. But as we continued to meet, he gave no sign of anything more than genuine delight in my company, and at some indefinable point we became friends and I stopped—honestly stopped—wanting anything else.

"Please be home, dear friend," I said, counting one, two, three rings of his phone across the river. "I need you to be." And he was.

"Violet! What a nice surprise. I was just thinking of you earlier this evening."

"You were? What were you thinking?"

"Oh, I was out working in my garden, watering things—it's been so dry—and I was working up a new book in my mind, and then I thought of an idea, something I'd like to try for a change. And I imagined myself telling you about it. I've missed seeing you, Violet."

"I've missed you, too, Milo. Our talks and everything."

"And how is . . . Jake?" This was as near as he would come to saying why we'd had to miss our talks.

"He's in Norway at the moment. But he won't be coming back to this address."

"Mmm. That is a change," said Milo thoughtfully. "You're okay, though?"

"I'm certainly not pining about *that*. . . ." I paused. I couldn't quite bring myself to dump my bad news into this gentle conversation. "Thank you for your cards. How was Greece? Did you get lots of good material for your next novel?"

"I can't say I did, actually. I found the atmosphere uncongenial to the sort of thing I write. What I did do"—and he gave a strange little laugh—"was deliver a baby."

"Deliver a baby!"

"Yes. There was a woman I'd hired from the village to come and do cooking and a bit of cleaning. I didn't even know . . . she seemed much too old . . . I just thought she was very fat. One morning she hadn't brought my breakfast to the porch, so I went to the kitchen and there she was writhing on the floor. She'd thought she could make it through the morning, apparently, go home and have the baby and be back for work the next day without my ever knowing, but her timing was off."

"But what happened? Did you really . . . ?" I somehow could not picture clean, cool Milo plunging into such a task.

"I did. There wasn't very much to do. It had started coming already. It was like a dream. I boiled water. We . . . the two of us got through it. . . . It was a baby boy."

"God, Milo, what an experience."

"Yes. Well, that's my news. I want to hear about you."

"Ah, Milo. My news is not so good." As if they'd been given their cue, the tears streamed down my face. I couldn't speak for a minute.

"Violet, what is it? Has something happened to you?"

"Not to me. To Ambrose. My uncle just committed suicide. You know I told you he rented a cabin up in the Adirondacks. He went up there for the summer to finish his book. This lady just called—the one who rented him the cabin—and he shot himself. Just this evening."

"Oh, Violet, how awful. How perfectly awful. Where are you now?"

"At my place. I'm taking the bus up there tomorrow morning. I just wanted to speak to a friend. I thought of you."

"And I'm glad you did. Look, Violet, would you like me to come uptown to you? Or better yet, why don't you stay at my house tonight? Get clean away. We'll get you to the bus in plenty of time. Tomorrow's Saturday. There won't be any traffic."

"You know, I think I'd like to come to you. I'm already packed for tomorrow. I could get in a cab and be in Brooklyn Heights in less than a half hour. If you really mean it."

"Of course I really mean it. Come as soon as you can. I'll be waiting. Oh, poor Violet. I am sorry. I know how much you liked Ambrose. He was your hero in a lot of ways, wasn't he?"

"In some ways, yes."

I got out of my apartment as quickly as I could, glad to flee the ugly demons I had been breeding there for the past few weeks. There was a Checker cab cruising right outside my building with its light on. We took the East River Drive. The lights on the bridges dazzled their faerie promises, as always. They had not received any news of Ambrose's death. "No other city in the world can hold a dead match to this one!" I heard him say, with the singsongy incantation he always used on hyperbole. How was it possible his voice was so alive in this cab with me when he had ceased to be? How long could I hold it, the exact memory of the voice? Already his appearance was fading. Wasn't that backward if I was supposed to be an artist, a visual person?

Milo was waiting on the steps of his brownstone. He paid off the taxi driver in spite of my protests. He had grown a neat blond beard since I'd last seen him. It made him look nearer to his thirty-five years. Previously he had looked rather seraphic; now he resembled a dignified prince of a country that no longer existed. He kissed me. The beard felt rough and masculine; the kiss itself was the dry, quick graze of a polite child. Oh, well, you couldn't have everything. At least he wouldn't feel duty bound to whisk me off to bed to assuage my grief. We could just be quiet and talk.

"I like your beard," I said, feeling guilty, as always, for thinking about sex around Milo. We stood in the mellow street light of Joralemon Street. This was another world from Manhattan. It was like a safe, quiet neighborhood out of the 1930s.

"Thank you. I thought I needed a change. Now look here, Violet, how can we get you to the end of this awful day? Would you like to walk down to the promenade, or would you like to eat something first? I made a salmon mousse for supper. There's lots left."

"I wouldn't mind some food. I feel sort of queasy. I drank my supper tonight. In addition to everything else, I was fired today. By that cold-fish new art director, Doris Kolb."

"But you're the best illustrator they have!"

"Illustration has become obsolete. Doris wants photographs. She's going to use real photos of real women screaming real screams. She showed me some of them. One of the women is really being raped by a real rapist at the time the picture was taken."

"You must be joking," he said, carrying my bag up the steps
into his lovely house. "I can assure you she won't put any raped,
screaming women on the covers of *my* books. I'll go to another
publisher. I'll just quickly take your bag up to your room. Make
yourself at home. There's an open bottle of wine in the refrigerator."

"I think I can wait for a while on the wine," I said. I watched
him lightfoot it up the stairs, carrying my suitcase. I felt better
already. Thank God for the Milos of the world. They made you
believe in the possibility of surrogate families. I went into the
room to the left. Milo's house was one of those narrow ones
which startle you with their depth once you get inside. He had
knocked out the walls between what had once been three small
rooms, "railroad style," a living room, dining room and kitchen,
and made of the space one sweeping, open area with French
windows at the kitchen end, overlooking his splendid garden.
Milo was half English, on his mother's side, and his Englishness
showed in his manners and his flowers. The house was rather
bare by ordinary upper-middle-income standards, but everything present had both a functional as well as an aesthetic purpose. The beautiful faded rug of mellowed gold and orange was
a floor covering, but it also happened to be a Tabriz animal rug.
I had absorbed a bit of knowledge about rugs from the ones
Granny had sold over the years to pay our debts. We once sold
a Tabriz, in better condition than Milo's, as well as a seven-
teenth-century Oushak. Had part of the proceeds been sent to
Ambrose? I suddenly wondered. There were just enough, but
not too many, places to sit: two modern beige chairs of Danish
design and two old ones which wore summer white covers. On
the tables next to the chairs and on the mantel were bowls filled
with whatever flowers Milo's garden produced at the moment;
tonight there were two black bowls, on either side of the framed
Demuth reproductions above the mantel, filled with tiger lilies,
purple phlox, yellow daisies and babies'-breath. The phlox
scented the large room with its warm fragrance. On the long,
dark refectory table at the other end of the room, where a woven
mat of indigo had been set with plate, silver and wineglass, there

was a silver bowl swimming with half-open roses in a lovely peach color. I could visualize Milo cutting these flowers in his garden, then giving a great deal of care to their arrangement.

I went over to admire the Demuths, which Milo had arranged in chronological order above the mantel. They were his pride and joy, these extremely good reproductions of the artist's watercolors for *The Turn of the Screw*. Several of the originals were in a seldom-lent private collection in New England, but the lady who owned them had written a fan letter to "Arabella Stone" about one of "her" books, and the two had struck up a correspondence; and the lady, learning of Milo's fascination with Demuth, had the reproductions made and presented them to him as a gift.

Milo came down again and joined me in front of his treasures.

"If you ever get tired of these," I said, "I think I know where I can find a good home for them."

"I'll keep that in mind."

We stood together looking up at the pictures. Ambrose's death was warm in the room with us as the scent of the phlox. We moved tacitly toward its gravity by discussing other things first.

"That," I said, touching the illustration in which the governess looks up at a tower we cannot see, and we see only her face as she is seeing Quint's ghost, "is to me the greatest portrait of a gothic heroine ever done. Look at her face, the way she has her arms crossed down in front of her black skirts. Demuth saw exactly what Henry James wrote: that what was going on in her own mind was the real horror. He caught the writer's intention, which is what a good illustrator can do."

"I know of another illustrator who once did that, to a lesser effort of mine," said Milo, putting his hand lightly on my shoulder. "You know, I've just discovered the oddest thing. Look at her hat"—he pointed to the first illustration, in which the governess is being interviewed by her prospective employer—"and then look at his face. Now, I've just finished this biography of

Demuth—if I had known I was going to see you, I wouldn't have returned it to the library—and there are photographs of his mother wearing a hat exactly like the one the governess is wearing. And the employer looks exactly like Demuth himself! The mustache, the shape of the face, and even the dark suit and the way he's standing. It's a self-portrait of Demuth himself!" Milo seemed very excited with his find. "But what I'm wondering is, did he know it when he illustrated James's story? Was he conscious of what he was doing? Did he say, 'My governess must wear a hat. Let's see, a hat. I know, I'll give her that one of Mother's, with the bird on top'? That seems pretty plausible to me, copying a familiar hat. But did he know he was painting himself at the time he was doing this? It would interest me to know."

"As a matter of fact, I was painting my own face into a cover today. God, that seems weeks ago. And it was only this morning. But in my case, I knew I was doing it. It was the only way I could work up any interest in my hack assignment."

"You know, Violet—come to the table and eat—I was thinking upstairs . . . I know this is not the evening for looking on the bright side of things, what with this tragic news you've just learned, but as far as your leaving Harrow House is concerned, I think it might turn out to be a blessing in disguise. For so long you've wanted to paint your own things. I've seen how unhappy it's made you, always having to dilute your energies with these covers. Maybe what happened today was fate's way of saying it's time to take the plunge. Maybe it's time for both of us to do something different. A bit more challenging to the old imagination." From his refrigerator he took out dark bread, butter, a platter of salmon mousse, a wedge of Brie and a half-full bottle of Pouilly-Fuissé, and managed to convey these expertly in one trip to where I sat feeling coddled and a bit ashamed of this mounting glow of well-being at such a time.

"You're right," I said, thinking it would be churlish to bring up the subject of money, of how I was going to make a living, when, after all, I was still alive. And relatively young and healthy to boot. "When you said on the phone you'd had an idea for the new book, is that the something different for yourself you had in mind?"

"Yes. I haven't actually thought it through enough. We can talk about it sometime. After you've been to the Adirondacks. Violet, do you know why he did it?"

"I think I do. I mean, he left me a very short note; she read it over the phone to me. It said: 'I'm sorry, there's nothing left.' A stranger reading that note might think he meant money. But I think he was referring to the last conversation we had about his plans to finish the book. I think he meant *that* kind of nothing left. Of course, it was quite possible there was no money left either. I mean, we have never had any money in our family, and all he could have had would have been savings. But I don't think Ambrose would kill himself just because he was broke. If he needed money, he would have found a way to make some. He always did before. I think something inside him just ran down like an engine . . . and he didn't have the necessary will or desire to rev it up again. I think I saw this happening this past spring, but I didn't want to admit it to myself, so I gave him a big pep talk about 'You can do it!' and sent him off . . . to his death." I put down the black bread on which I had heaped a greedy portion of salmon mousse and burst into tears.

"Come on, Violet, that's just guilt. From what you say, he was pretty low last spring. If anything, you may have talked him into an extra summer."

"I don't want to mess up this elegant handkerchief, Milo."

"There are dozens more upstairs. I have a weakness for Indian handkerchiefs."

"In that case . . ." I blew my nose into its cool lemon-scented silk.

"You're bound to feel this deeply, Violet. He was more than just an ordinary uncle. He was the nearest thing you had to a father. I never met him, but from all you've said he was a delightful man. You looked up to him for all these years. Go ahead and cry. He's worth your tears. And then please taste that mousse. I'm rather proud of it."

"Aren't you going to drink some wine with me?"

"Well, maybe just a little. I haven't been sleeping well since I came back from Greece and my doctor gave me a mild prescription. I'm not supposed to take it right on top of alcohol, but it will be a while before we turn in. In fact, I may even skip the pill tonight. Having you in the house may be all the calming influence I need." He fetched himself a wine goblet to match mine and poured it full.

"But you've never had trouble sleeping before, have you?" I was surprised that calm Milo would ever look to me for a calming influence.

"No. This is nothing. When I get started on something new, it will go away." He smiled at me warmly and raised his glass. "Let's drink to the memory of Ambrose."

"And to friends who are there when you need them to be," I said.

For someone in grief, I managed to eat an awful lot. Why, I wondered, didn't death take away my appetite? Would it have if I had loved him more? Or was it that he was still so alive to me?

"I'll never forget the time he came to speak at our school," I told Milo. "You say I looked up to him all these years. . . . Well, that day was just about the pinnacle of my admiration. It started off terribly, but . . . Did I ever tell you about that time?"

"No, but I wish you would now."

"Well, when I was in the fourth grade at the Pine Hollow School, Ambrose was invited officially, with an honorarium and everything, to come and talk to the girls about being a writer— at his own convenience. He always visited me at least once a year, on his way south to see Granny or on his way back to New York. These visits were unannounced and usually late in the evening so that a teacher often had to get me out of bed and I wouldn't even have time to dress, I'd just go down to the parlor in my robe and slippers. But this was an official invitation, arranged by the English teacher, an unmarried woman who lived at the school—her name was Inez Raper. I think she was a little in love with my uncle; she was the one who always got me out of bed when he made his impromptu visits. She was a shy, wistful woman, probably even pretty if it weren't for the fact she seemed very old to us. She was about twenty-eight at the time. She worshipped artists of any kind; she thought they were a different breed of human being entitled to special privileges. After she'd met Ambrose and learned he was a writer—I remember him telling her about how he'd just been out to Hollywood: that was when they'd optioned his novel and he was supposed to write a screenplay—she got his book and read it and somehow wangled this invitation for him to come, at some time when he'd be passing through anyway.

"It was arranged for him to come on our Assembly Day, which was the first Tuesday of every month, beginning at two: we'd have a senator speaking about current events; one time we had Nathan Milstein and he stopped in the middle of a piece because a second-grader was talking. . . . Well, anyway, the famous Tuesday came, two o'clock came, and there was the entire school gathered in the big music room where these assemblies always took place, and the punch and cookies had already been set out on the long table for the reception afterward. Two-fifteen came, and two-thirty, and there we all were waiting and I could sense the teachers looking anxiously at one another and then looking more and more annoyed with Miss Raper, and with me, so I fancied. The music teacher started a round song, 'White Coral Bells upon a Slender Stalk,' which I can't hum even now without starting to feel nervous, and we got through that a few times, all the girls liked it, and then we went on to 'Plant a Little Watermelon on My Grave,' and 'My Name is Jan Jansen, I come from Wisconsin,' and we were just getting warmed up with 'The Noble Duke of York' when suddenly everybody started shushing everybody else and Miss Raper walks forward with our eagerly awaited speaker as proudly as if she produced him out of a hat. His tardiness was instantly forgotten as he made his way to the front of the room, where a lectern with a pitcher of water and a glass had been set up for him between the two enormous grand pianos that stood back to back and were never moved. In my memory Ambrose was wearing a white suit, but that can't be possible because this was in November. He stood collecting his thoughts for a minute, looked over the audience till he found me, raised his finger in a little hello, and then swung right into his talk about writers and writing.

"He talked easily, without a single note, though often he'd look up at the ceiling as if selecting his next idea from there. He talked in an anecdotal, pictorial way, the perfect tone for children, so we could all see tall Tom Wolfe scribbling feverishly on top of the refrigerator, and Ernest Hemingway chewing his pencil tip in a sidewalk café and Dickens cringing as he dredged up memories of himself as a child in a blacking factory as Dickens the grown man with the black beard wrote *David Copperfield.* 'The nice thing about being a writer,' he told us, 'is you can write anywhere: sitting in a train, perched in a treetop, or even in back of a room where nobody's paying any attention to you, or where something's going on that bores you.' The teachers laughed nervously, thinking, I guess, of a whole wave of scribbling going on in the backs of the uninteresting classes. Then Ambrose said that a writer should always carry a small notebook, and be ready to whip it out anytime during the night or day if you saw or heard or felt anything interesting. During the question-and-answer period, one eighth-grader cast a sly look over at the teachers' row and asked what you should do if you saw or heard anything interesting after lights out. Ambrose laughed and I could see him tactfully preparing to walk the fence. 'Well,' he said to the girl, 'in my day, there was something called a flashlight, but'—and then he transferred his gaze to where the teachers sat—'a really dedicated writer often has to learn to write in the dark, literally *and* figuratively.' Several teachers nodded knowingly. Then he said, 'Now, you've all been told, I'm sure, to write about what you know. And I'm not debunking that advice. But it's also fun to write about what you don't know; don't be afraid to imagine it. If monsters interest you, write about them. If you wish you knew what an enchanted princess did in her castle all day long, go there and find out.

Your only duty is to make it believable for the next fellow, so that he can reach out and *touch* the knobbly skin of the monster . . . or maybe the monster has nice silky skin as soft as the princess's hair. And you should brush the princess's hair from the *princess's* point of view. You have to get inside her scalp as well as her castle.' The good writer, he told us, gets inside the head of whoever he's writing about. There was no castle with a moat wide enough, or an iron gate thick enough, to keep the writer with imagination out. He said a lot more, but I don't remember it. I missed some at the beginning, because, being related to him, I was nervous about him making a good impression. And then, when I saw he *had* made a good impression, I missed some more because I was already imagining how I would benefit from it after he was gone: my popularity rating would soar.

    "Then he asked us each to describe something so that someone else could really see it, in a special new way. He said to take something we knew, something in nature or in the classroom or in our daily lives, and make a word picture so that somebody else could see exactly what we had in mind. He said if hills looked like white elephants, then say so, and by saying so other people might really see the way those particular hills looked. Then Miss Raper passed out pencils and paper and we were given five minutes. A lot of girls got so nervous they couldn't write anything. You never heard so much sighing and scratching out. My own mind went completely blank and so I drew a cartoon of my uncle standing behind the lectern, with a friendly white elephant looking over his shoulder. At the end of the five minutes, everyone passed her paper to the end of the row and then the teachers delivered the stack of papers to Ambrose, and he went through and read the good ones or the striking ones aloud. The eighth-grader who had asked the rebellious question had a good one, something like: 'A thought like a slow dark fish.' He said, 'Who wrote this?' and the girl raised her hand. 'Very unusual,' he said. The dark fish girl was a sort of dark customer herself, with straight black bangs and a slight mustache.

"Then he came to my roommate Pequeña Bombal's description; she had written: 'The new moon was like a fingernail cutting.' He almost passed this one over, then decided to read it aloud after all. You could tell he didn't think it was one of the best, but he thought he ought to read as many as possible. 'Who wrote this one?' he asked politely. Pequẽna sprang up from her seat and cried out, '*I* deed, *I* deed!' She was already a beautiful woman in miniature. When Ambrose saw her he perked up and grinned delightedly and said, '*Very* striking simile indeed.' '*Gracias, señor,*' she replied, with a curtsy. I think I've told you before about my mixed feelings for Pequeña. I still dream about her. I guess there's a person in everyone's life that you just can't outgrow subconsciously, even though when you're awake you know you don't want to be them, that their life would be much too narrow a fit for you. Pequeña was our most exotic little boarder. I think they had put her with me because we would support each other. I was an orphan and Pequeña was a half orphan. When her mother had died in Argentina, her father, who was in the diplomatic service, brought her back with him and enrolled her in a plush nuns' school in Washington. But she was expelled for singing the 'Internationale'—one of her black-sheep uncles, a Communist in Buenos Aires, had taught it to her for a joke. So she was sent to Pine Hollow. At the reception after Ambrose's talk, she asked him to sign her autograph book. I saw him studying her elfish little face, the diamonds in the little pink ear lobes. Then he wrote: 'To a charming young lady. I wish I had been born later.' When she showed this to me, I thought: Can't he see through her? She acts like that with every man, even Harold our gardener at the school. I was a little annoyed with him. Oh, I remember one other thing Ambrose said in his talk. He said to warm your imagination up you should write about something you wanted to happen. Then on an impulse he added: 'Or something you don't want to happen.' Then he realized he was talking to children. He looked embarrassed and quickly amended that we shouldn't try this second thing. When you were young you should stick with what you *did* want.

That was the one uneasy note of the whole affair. Besides his being so late, of course. At the reception afterwards, I overheard one of the teachers saying, 'Mr. Clay certainly does smell redolently of cloves. Is that why he was so unprompt?' And Miss Raper came hotly to his defense: 'What is wrong with being a bit unprompt, or, for that matter, with the smell of cloves if it makes you as eloquent as Mr. Clay?' Miss Raper later married a blind lawyer in town and was apparently very happy. Pequeña wrote to Ambrose and asked for a photograph. He sent her one —a later one than even I had. She put it on her dresser and burned candles to it when she wanted anything. She said you shouldn't bother the saints with certain earthly requests. She called Ambrose 'El Primer Caballero.' When she fell in love with the canning heir she had been groomed to marry, she burned candles to Ambrose for the heir, whose name was Enrique, to propose her senior year so she wouldn't have to go to college. He did. She wrote me several times after her marriage. But I was in college and busy and I never got around to answering. I think her husband is in the diplomatic service now. For a long time I wondered what she did with Ambrose's picture after she married. Did she burn it or hide it somewhere and take it out whenever her marriage didn't come up to her expectations, and sigh for 'El Primer Caballero'? Anyway, that's the story of how he came to our school in all his splendor and captivated everyone from eight to twenty-eight. Well, *almost* everyone from eight to twenty-eight."

I had completely transported myself back to that day. I also felt strangely as if I had conjured up Ambrose replete with his former glories and promises of more.

"I can just see him dazzling those little girls," said Milo. "I can even"—he laughed—"smell those cloves. And what a vivid imagination. A monster with skin as soft as the hair of the princess. And how eerie, that remark he let slip out, about writing about something you don't want to happen. I was just thinking, down in the garden tonight—" He frowned, stopped himself. "No, your uncle was quite a guy. A splendid figure. Everyone should have at least one such figure in his life."

"Yes," I said, feeling we were doing some delicate balancing act between us, Milo and I, to keep Ambrose alive through this night while his freshly dead spirit perhaps hovered in some transition ether. "Even when I didn't see him for months . . . years when he was in Mexico . . . I felt he was there for me to refer to, living his life a little ahead of mine, wanting the things I wanted. Even his flaws and mistakes have given me a certain comfort. I could sort of measure myself, judge myself, by him. I can't imagine not having someone between me and . . . I'm not sure what. Darkness? Hopelessness? Where he has been for so long is it going to be just dark, hopeless space? I mean, you can't refer to a void, can you?"

"Well, Violet, I don't know. Are you so sure it's going to be a void? He has left a space, yes. But why does it have to be dark and hopeless? And I'm not sure you could make it empty even if you wanted it to be. Something remains. There are ways to refer, as you put it, to people we love who have died. I don't mean séances. Though maybe they're a crude way of expressing the interchange that takes place between the dead and the living. The dead and the *loving*, one might even say. The feeling that persists is what matters. These things are different for each of us, but I've experienced it with someone I love who is, whatever the word means, dead. But she isn't, you see, as long as I live. I'm speaking of my mother. Our interchange is still very much alive. It's still changing, even. It's not a static thing, like . . . like rose petals pressed under glass or anything. It's still growing. As I move through my life and experience new things, understand new things, my dialogue with her shifts. I ask new questions of her. And she asks new questions of me."

"Do you mean she still wants to know things?" Milo's words had given me the shivers, but somehow they were shivers I wanted to explore. Especially since I didn't have to do it alone. He'd be there with me so I wouldn't scare myself too much.

"Yes. Oh, yes."

"What kind of things?"

"All kinds. How things work. Things that weren't invented in her lifetime. For instance, my new typewriter, with its car-

tridges for correcting mistakes . . . the inside of the 747 that
flew me to Greece . . ." He glanced up at me and flushed
slightly, as though he knew he had invited ridicule. But seeing
none in my face, he looked relieved and continued. "I often hear
her voice, the exact pitch and mood of it. 'How clever,' she says.
'So that's how they do it now!' I often . . . I often find myself
moving more slowly through some event of my life than I normally would, so that she can be sure to follow. . . ." Then he
really did turn pink and looked away uncomfortably. "In
Greece, during that . . . emergency I told you about . . . with
the baby, I don't think I could have come through if I hadn't had
her there with me, while that woman rolled on the floor and
cried out to me in a language I didn't understand. 'Now Milo,'
I could hear her saying, in a sort of arch, amused tone she often
used—she never lost her British diction—'this is nothing extraordinary. Women had babies unassisted for centuries. This
one was rather unfortunately timed to meet the plans of your
day, but let's put on a pot of water, that's always a good idea,
and help nature see this poor embarrassed soul through her
crisis. . . .' "

"And you did," I said enthusiastically, for now he'd gone
quite pale.

"Yes. Or we did."

"I wonder what Ambrose might still want of me. I was always
so intent on what he was to me, I never really considered what
I was to him. Do you think he wanted something from me,
Milo? Something I could have given him when he was alive, and
didn't?" Overwrought with all these rarefied metaphysics, I began to weep and shake and would have worked myself into a
hysterical state if Milo hadn't quashed it by saying quietly:

"Remorse is useless in the interchange, Violet. Believe me.
If you loved somebody—as I'm sure he loved you—would you
like to imagine that person desolated with guilt and remorse after your death over whatever he might have done for you? Not
if you really loved, you wouldn't. It would make *you* feel guilty
and awful. You'd rather imagine him missing you positively, re-

membering you, referring to you, as he moved on through his days, rather than connecting your memory with such pain he almost dreaded thinking about you. Wouldn't you?"

"Of course I would." I sobbed, imagining Ambrose wincing with pain every time he remembered me after I was dead. "Oh, Milo, what a special person you are. What would I have done if you hadn't been in the world tonight? It's helped me, talking like this."

"Come," he said, standing up. "Let's walk down to the promenade and see if any interesting ships have come in. What you may not have realized is you help me, too. I have missed seeing you, the special way you respond to things. It works both ways, you know."

"How funny," I said, blowing into his lemon-scented hand-kerchief some more. "I never considered that."

We went out into the late-summer night and walked slowly down Joralemon and over to Montague and onto the promenade. The lights of the Battery winked from across the dark river. There was an enormous oil tanker resting on the berth. Its empty decks were freshly painted orange and shone from the light of the street lamps. I wondered if this tanker had passed through Ambrose Channel. I had lived in the city for nine years and still did not know exactly where Ambrose Channel was. Now I resolved to take closer note of the world I lived in and the other people in it.

"What made you start writing gothics, Milo? I don't believe you ever told me."

He laughed softly. "I don't believe you ever asked. Odd you should ask tonight, after what we've been talking about. It was something I started when I was sixteen, when my mother became ill. I think I told you she was an invalid the last three years of her life, when we lived up on Lake Ontario. She was fond of reading; it occupied most of her waking hours. The village we lived in was too small to have its own library, but the bookmobile came every two weeks and I'd go and select books for her.

When the drug she used to control her disease began to affect her eyes so that she couldn't focus, I began reading aloud to her. She liked . . . I didn't think of them as gothic romances then. They were . . . oh, stories that took place in the English countryside. She never got over her homesickness for England. Not that she complained about it. We had had to come to America after the war in order for my father to get the proper medical treatment. He'd been badly damaged, in his mind, during the war, and there just weren't the facilities—or the money to pay for them—if we had stayed in England. Even he would have preferred to stay there; he'd fallen in love with the country while he was studying at Oxford and married my mother, and they'd bought a little farm with their combined inheritances. First we went to live with his parents, in Rochester, and then when I was twelve my father died and my mother had some difference with my grandparents, who were very old, and so she and I struck out for ourselves. She worked for the florist in our village until she got ill, and then there were the operations and the drugs and the failing eyesight, which brings me to why I started writing stories. One day, you see, the bookmobile's reading matter—the kind she liked—gave out. I remember walking home empty-handed, thinking how disappointed she would be. If only I could somehow miraculously discover a volume, hidden away in our house, I thought. When I got home she was asleep. I went to my room and it suddenly came to me. I would write a story for her. I knew the things she liked. Lots of description of a stately house, a bit isolated but with beautiful trees and gardens. Some mystery or trouble going on in the house. And always a young woman, who would be about my mother's age around the time she met my father. And a love ending, after the mystery was cleared up or the ordeal gone through. That's what she liked. . . ."

"That's what we all like. That's why Arabella Stone's books sell into the millions," I said. "But go on. Do you really mean to tell me that as a boy of sixteen you just went to your room and tossed off a gothic?"

"No, of course not. But I got a fair way into a chapter. She usually fell asleep halfway through a chapter anyway."

"Oh, God, Milo, I love this story. And then you went down and read it to her?"

"I did. But I pretended I was reading it from a real book. I camouflaged my pages inside my copy of *The Wind in the Willows*. I always sat at the foot of the bed, because she liked to see my face as I read, and the book was always hidden by the bed anyway."

"And did you fool her? Or did she guess?"

"Do you know, Violet, that's one of those mysterious things. I'll never really be sure. That first time, I remember her being very attentive, and afterwards she said something like, 'Milo, this is the best book you could possibly have selected for me.' Which could mean . . . either thing, you see. And then as the months went on and it became as natural to me, that writing the daily chapter, or half a chapter, as making the meat loaf or the shepherd's pie in the evening, I believe I stopped thinking about it. Oh, I just remembered something else. She sometimes put in her order for what was to happen next. She'd say, just as she was getting drowsy, 'Oh, I do hope that Cousin Giles won't turn out to be all bad. I've grown rather fond of him.' And I'd abandon my plans for making him evil and bestow on him some late-blooming virtues so he could be worthy of the heroine. I felt . . . you know, I felt at times I was giving her back her lost girlhood, her lost marriage with my father. They had so little time together before the war ruined his mind and he became so violent and depressed and . . . but anyway. And you know, Violet, I can't take all the credit for Arabella Stone's success. Even after my mother died and I went to college and continued to write these things just to keep myself company, it was she who always dictated to me what she hoped would happen next. It has been a partnership, don't you see."

"How did you come to publish them, though?"

"I was a senior . . . I majored in chemistry because it seemed the pragmatic thing to do—I planned to be a research chemist—and then I realized I was bored by chemistry. But I have to make a living, I thought. Then I wondered if I might possibly sell my romances, as I called them, since I seemed to be writing them anyway. I gave a great deal of thought to the pen name—I knew they'd stand a better chance if a man didn't send them in—and chose my mother's maiden name, Stone. Arabella I found in a book of names. It means 'beautiful eagle.' I liked that. Also, it sounds like 'arable.' Arable stone."

"Bringing Stone back to life!"

"Why, yes. Bless you, Violet. Don't you dare stay away so long again. It will be a long time before I take you backstage after a concert again. I'm not giving up your friendship so easily next time."

"You don't have to. It was a needless division."

"Never mind." He brushed it off. "Look up there! The upstairs bay window of that old house. Have you ever seen anything so quaint?"

I looked up. There, glitteringly lit by a chandelier, in the large bay window of an old waterfront mansion, were three old ladies having dinner at a long table. One sat at the head, flanked by her two companions. All three were dressed in jewels and evening gowns. They ate decorously. The hostess took a sip of wine from her goblet. Milo and I stood arm in arm, entranced.

"What a scene!" I said. "Remedios Varo might have painted it, only there's nothing sinister about these three at all. Imagine! Three elegant old ladies having a midnight supper in full view of the world. It's almost indecent, spying on them like this."

"Oh, they don't care," said Milo, with the facility for instantly drawn characters that had made Arabella rich. "They are completely involved in themselves. We are only part of their backdrop, two figures in the darkness of the promenade to enhance their supper. They've left their curtains open to catch *us*, not the other way round."

7
A Reverie

Milo took me upstairs to my room, where I'd slept twice before during our friendship, once when the heat went off in another of my apartments, once when a lover (pre-Jake) had refused to leave and threatened to beat me up if I left. I had feigned sudden docility, made us both some food, then had gone innocently down the hall alone to "empty the garbage," and took a cab and fled to Milo's. What a relief, now, to be shown into the narrow, monastic little guest room at the front of the house with its dark-blue walls and neat white bedspread turned back on fresh sheets with the creases from the laundry still in them. Everything so chaste and sane. I felt as if I'd left the strife and confusion of the emotional life and gone on a spiritual retreat to Milo's guest room.

"Everything feels and looks just the same," I said. "Yet it's been ages since I last slept here."

"Three years," he said, surprising me by remembering better than I. "And your painting still hangs in my workroom in the same old place, too."

"Oh, can I look at it?" I suddenly wanted to see it very much.

"Of course."

His workroom was at the back of the house, overlooking the garden. He went in first and switched on an arc lamp. When I saw his desk I experienced my usual pang of jealousy for his assured and organized creative life. The way everything waited for him there, his books, his jars of pencils, the pristine squared stack of student's loose-leaf notebook paper, you had every confidence that within three or four months of steady, almost automatic, application on his part—looking down from time to time

103

to admire whatever was growing or promising to grow in his garden; looking up an architectural detail or a date in English history in one of his reference books—another novel would emerge and duly be typed up and sent across the river and printed and bound between paper covers and placed in the racks to be eagerly plucked out again by the multitudes of lonely readers who wanted fresh reassurance that the shapely, enduring romantic conclusion was still possible.

And there on the white wall above his worktable was my painting, the illustration for *The Secret of Seven Towers*, matted in light gray and framed in thin silver.

"God, did I paint that?" It was truly a lovely painting. I could say it objectively, coming on it after three years. I could look at it as if a stranger had done it. It was drenched with an inner glowing. The forms were right. The colors were right. Everything for once had come together.

"The only painting I ever sold," I said wryly. "Except once, when I first came to New York, I sold a pen-and-ink drawing of a house. But I have to be honest. It was of our old house in Charleston and I sold it to one of Ambrose's girlfriends. But you know, Milo—I hope you don't think I'm being conceited—I can really see how anybody would want to buy this painting."

"That's my girl," he said, seeming to include both me and the girl in the painting. She sat erect upon a barely penciled-in settee, with a scroll-like back, her hands folded on her lap, looking out very solemnly from a warm rose-brown interior. To her left, on another plane suggesting the outdoors at night, a man stands enfolded in the color that surrounds him, a deep blue-green. He is looking toward her, but of course can't see her. She's in another dimension. And yet there they are, within inches of each other. It made you feel good to look at them. You felt you knew more than they did, even about their own eventual happiness. I had used watercolors because I had felt inspired and wasn't afraid of making a mistake. I had worked on very wet paper—it all came back to me now—quickly and intuitively creating the figures by daubing Kleenex against the wet colors. Later, when the whole thing was dry, I went back and penciled in the barest facial and clothing outlines. I wanted them to be able to pass for a couple anywhere, anytime. Williamson, who was still reigning as art director at Harrow House, had suggested I take it home again and put "a wee bit more period detail in the furniture and the clothes; and perhaps make their faces a bit more distinctive." But I had known this illustration was right as it was. "Look," I had argued, "this way, when people finish reading the story, they can flip back to the cover and say, 'Hey, that could be me! This story may have been set in nineteenth-century England, but it can still happen to the likes of me.' " And Williamson had laughed and said, "Okay, you win. If you feel that strongly about it. We'll have to get the author's okay on the proof, though." We did. And I also got a raise.

"It's light and rich and says something important about balance," said Milo. "Speaking of balance, I've decided to set my new book on this side of the Atlantic for once. And down in the garden this evening it occurred to me that I might write this one from a different point of view. It's always the woman who is the innocent, who comes to the house and battles the dark forces. Why not have the innocent be a man for a change?"

"You mean a sort of male Jane Eyre?"

"Something like that."

"But won't that turn things around romantically? The man will be passive and the woman will be the aggressor. I mean, if you have him coming to her house." But then I added quickly, knowing how tender writers are about their projected works, "It sounds great. It'll certainly be *different.*"

"A change," muttered Milo, turning off the lamp in the study, "a new balance, perhaps." He walked me back to my room. "I'm afraid you've only got about four hours for sleeping. I'll wake you in time to make your bus. I'll set my alarm. I may even sleep a bit myself, with you in the house."

"Why *have* you been having trouble sleeping, Milo?"

"Oh, it's silly. Since that episode in Greece, you know, about

the baby, I've been having a recurring dream. I dread it so much
I keep waking myself up before I have it. In it, I'm delivering
that baby again. I'm trying to get a grip on his head, but it keeps
going beneath the water. In the dream I'm pulling him out of
a body of water. The mother, a grotesquely fat woman, is standing beside me and somehow I understand that if I do succeed
in bringing him out of the water she will kill us. So I'm trying
to get a grip on his head, at the same time wondering how I can
run with him once I do get him out . . . if I do."

"Oh God, Milo . . . how awful. And how unfair! Because
you succeeded in delivering him in real life! That sounds a little
like my math dream I had for years. I was always too late for a
math exam, in dream after dream. And I'd always cry and cry
and wake up sweating. Then one night I got disgusted during
the dream. I decided to go up to the teacher and say, 'Look, I
missed the exam because I couldn't find the right building. Will
you let me make it up?' And she smiled and said, 'Of course!'
and that was the end of that silly dream. Maybe you should turn
around and ask your woman why she wants to kill you."

Milo laughed. "Violet, you're incomparable. Perhaps I'll do
just that."

There was something so safe and schoolgirlish about lying in
the dark at Milo's house. With the clean-smelling sheet tucked
chastely up to my chin, I felt I'd shed all the disillusioned years
leading up to tonight. Milo's well-set-up workroom had inspired
me, the story about his mother had intrigued me: if only I had
had some productive influence in my life. Some doting person
demanding a new painting or drawing from me every day. You
needed to believe someone was waiting for what you could do;
it spurred you on. The perverse thing was that I felt more
spurred on right now than in months. I felt: If only this tragic
thing had not occurred, if only I didn't have to take the eight
a.m. bus to Plommet Falls in less than six hours, I would go
home and paint like a demon as soon as it gets light. But would
I have felt that way if the call had not come? I would still be

passed out cold in a stupor of vodka and despair, the radio by now popping static to my unconscious ears, the sound perhaps influencing some vile dream. Poor Milo; I didn't envy him his dream. One's days posed enough difficulties without having to fail or be frustrated all night in a dream. I tried to visualize Plommet Falls, the cabin where Ambrose had faced his dark realization. Then my thought veered back toward Milo's workroom, everything set up for the work that would come next, and blessing the whole endeavor, on the wall above: my lovely painting. I had been struck with the mergence of the two planes, the close-valued rose-brown interior (like the interior of a human heart) and the airier, diaphanous outdoor blue. There was something immensely satisfying about the union of those two planes. I wanted to paint something like that again. Like it, yet different. Another version. Seeing it had reactivated some emotional impetus I had not followed through. Then I dozed and woke again to footsteps and low voices passing beneath the open window. A man and a woman going home together in the early hours. Windows, I thought, still partly asleep. Other people's lives through those windows. All these people moving through their blue dusks and dawns. And suddenly I was back in my room at the Martha Washington, all those dusks and dawns ago, waiting for it to happen, waiting for my fate to begin shaping itself. I waited mostly for the phone to ring, for Ambrose to call and ask me out again, for the lady from *Vogue* to call and offer me a job, for some outside voice to explain to me what I was doing there and where I was to go next.

The evenings went by. I would hurry back from supper, usually at a little Japanese place next door to my hotel where I'd eat early before the couples came, and sit on my bed (there was no chair) and wait for the call from the one person I knew in this city. Each evening the spring light lengthened just that bit more, and I would tell myself as long as there was any light in the sky there was still a chance he'd call. While I waited, I took out my sketchbook, and with a particularly nice ballpoint pen I had at the time, evoked the view from my sooty unscreened window, practicing my control over light and shadow with loose and tight crosshatchings. I had the proverbial poor girl's room that faced out over the air shaft, and I could see into the windows of other girls with similar rooms. There were lights on already in some of these rooms, but I strained my eyes in the bluish gloom because I was afraid to risk breaking the spell of my own shadows. These neighboring windows were like squares painted into the indigo of the spring dusk, squares containing the secrets of other people's lives. Girls lived there, girls like myself, who were biding their time in rooms that cramped their style till they could become something better. I saw a set of bikini panties and bra, in a leopard-skin print, drying on an octagonal wooden clothesline; a window full of paperback books; a windowsill that looked like a cosmetics counter. In one window, catty-cornered to mine and a floor above, a green portable radio pealed out a sound bravely disproportionate to its small size and filled our enclosure with music. It was a song I liked, one that had a significance for me. Still debating the merits of perilous freedom versus stifling security, I had contemplated its tempting lyrics over the last few months whenever I'd heard them. It was called "Downtown"; perhaps you remember it, too.

Suddenly, on one of these blue evenings, a head of the most amazing hair began unfurling itself from this window. It was a rippling, wavy blond, the exact color and texture of a fairy princess's. Its owner was apparently hanging it out to dry. But it kept coming! It must have been down to her waist, or longer. She bent deeply forward until the hair finally reached the window directly below. "Mary Anne!" called a muffled voice under the hair. "Mary A-anne!" "Yeah?" replied a burly voice. "Are ya using your big rollers?" called the hair. "Nah, ya want 'em? Wait a sec. I'll send 'em up." I watched, enthralled, as Mary Anne produced a clear plastic bag filled with pink metal rollers, deftly knotted a strand of her upstairs neighbor's wet hair around the bag, and tugged twice. "Thanks!" called the muffled voice, and the hair, bearing the attached cargo, was borne upward and withdrawn into the window above.

And I had put down my pen and my pad, enchanted by what I had seen. Reality had outstripped my ability to render it. For how could I possibly convey, through mere shape or line, all that this scene meant to me?

But now, looking across the space of nine years at that evening, I understood its essence. There I had crouched in the shadows of my own potential. I had my feelings and I had my materials, but I didn't know how to make one work for the other. There I sat, waiting for something to happen, for the phone to ring, for help to come from outside. That something was happening inside, I never considered. That certain equations were being made, certain colors and tonal values being locked away in my visual memory which could later be opened by the right combination of accumulated experience, I never dreamed. And if I had been told, I would have replied impatiently, "But I want something tonight!"

Now I saw the painting that might come out of all this. It would come out of that evening, but balanced by this one. "Violet in Blue" was how I thought of it. Of course, it wouldn't have windows filled with books or lipsticks or panties hanging out to dry. It wouldn't even have that marvelous Rapunzel moment when she let down her hair and brought up not the prince, but curlers to get the prince. All the outward indications of the theme, which had served to keep the memory full of energy for me, would be effaced. The literalness of the experience would be translated into paint. So, though I might know that "Violet" had originally stood for me (and for all those lives like mine, trying to make a place for themselves in the ongoing blue), the painting would have only the color violet, costumed in many tones, a color sometimes greedy with impasto, trying to steal center stage with the violence of its caked force; at other times flattened to near extinction by the equanimity of the blue; and— at a spot where the eye would want to return again—achieving finally a lovers' merger, so that blue is deepened by violet's shadow and her imprint is left on the long night of his memory.

The painting's challenge would be how well I could capture

that state of *precariousness*, how well I could evoke, through paint, choices hanging in the balance, the way different thicknesses (like different individuals) strove to impose their color against all that would go on anyway. That their color was a reflection, a variation, an emanation of my own had come to me only in the course of this evening. Had not Ambrose's act in some way been an echo of my own darkest wishes? Weren't we all involved in the same contest between living and dying, between doing what we wanted and needed to do and not doing it? Some of us drifted fairly steadily along the elected path, like Milo; others went looking, like myself, for the easy miracle route; and those like Ambrose . . . fell prey to the charming detour? Confused the detour with the next leg of the journey?

"Boy, if I haven't gone and made a mess," he'd said. It was the night he'd left Carol, the first and only time in my New York life when he'd dropped in on me unannounced. (For decency's sake, shouldn't I call Carol and let her know? I honestly had not thought of her till this moment, the woman Ambrose had suddenly married soon after I came to New York—and just as suddenly left, a little over a year later. Would she want to know? What would it be to her now, that the man who had caused her so much pain had finally chosen to end his life?)

"But what's happened?" It was very late. His knocking had waked me up. Yet I was flattered that he'd come to me and of course I was curious, the way most human beings are, to know the gory details of the breakup.

"Oh, honey, I've gone and made a mess, that's what. You wouldn't happen to have a little bourbon in the house, would you? Or blended whiskey?"

"All I've got is some Drambuie. I could put some ice in it." It was a hot September night. I had not even known they were fighting.

"That sounds wonderful, thank you."

And there we'd sat, Ambrose sipping his Drambuie and ice, and me trying to squeeze in the pertinent question, to find out what had happened.

"Well, let's see what I can salvage from my mess," he said.

"I'll go to Mexico for the divorce. The sooner she's rid of me the better. Then she can marry a man worthy of her. I have in mind a little plan, to sort of tie in with my book. I've been checking through Connie Ryan's book on D-day. It has a list of all the men in the 101st who took part in the liberation. You know what I've been thinking of doing? Looking up these men, finding out what they're doing today, how they've adjusted to civilian life, how they feel about this war we're in now. I could use it as an episode in my novel—you know, the hero looks up some of his old buddies twenty years later—and, I was thinking, I could also publish it as a separate piece of reportage. I was speaking to a friend of mine this afternoon, he's an editor over at the *Saturday Evening Post*. He says he can get me an advance for my travel expenses. I could visit some of these fellows on the way to Juárez, rent a car and sort of make it into a working divorce."

"But how exactly did you make a mess?"

"Aw, honey, you know. Two people marry, each expects the other to fill up all those empty hollows. But Carol's a fine woman. Too fine for the likes of me."

"But . . . were you"—I hesitated to say it aloud—"unfaithful?"

He looked at me attentively, as if I'd given him an answer to a question of his own. He didn't seem annoyed at all. "Something like that," he said.

"Oh. Would you like me to fix you some eggs? An omelet? I could make us a bacon omelet."

"Great idea, sport! I'm feeling more positive already."

He stood in the doorway of the kitchen while I broke eggs into a bowl and fried strips of bacon. "It's an exciting time to be alive," he said. "So much is happening here in our country. I'm beginning to think that Italian sojourn was a little bit of a regression for me. Not that it wasn't enjoyable, I'm not saying that. I've been waylaid by the past too long. It's so nice and complete. That's its charm. Now I'm going to stick my nose out into these sixties and see what's in the air!"

8

"A. Valentine"

I really did not feel justified in telephoning Carol at six-thirty
in the morning to give her such unhappy news. So while Milo
perked our coffee (he was pale and shaky this morning despite
his insistence that he'd slept a dreamless sleep) and set out
enough cereals and fruit and wheat germ to turn me into a su-
perwoman, I looked up C. M. Gruber, still at Central Park
West, in the phone book, and made a note of the number. I decided to call her from the Port Authority Terminal just before
I boarded my bus. This was sheer cowardice on my part. I didn't
want to talk any longer than necessary. Not that I hadn't liked
her; it was just that the mere thought of her had made me feel
guilty ever since their breakup. I felt that I shared some portion
of Ambrose's swerving temperament, that she had seen it in me,
and condemned the pair of us—after there was no longer any
reason for her to be loyal to the name of Clay—as two indolent,
capricious Southerners unable to stick to any project or relationship for long. She and I had endured (at her invitation) one painful post-divorce luncheon at Schrafft's, where she had insisted
she wanted to remain my friend and given me a little lecture on
the importance of Drive. "Next time, you call me," she had said.
I kept meaning to and putting it off. One day a long time later
I was walking down a certain block of Madison and noticed that,
for some reason, I felt less oppressed. I puzzled it out. What
could it be? I liked this block better now. It was because the
Schrafft's was no longer there.

Without the rush-hour traffic, my taxi made it to the terminal with time to spare. I found the Adirondack Trailways counter, bought my ticket and asked the gate number. Then I went
to the dim lounge, where a handful of in-transit souls sat hypno-

tized by little TV units attached to the arms of their chairs.
There were four empty pay phones. "Okay, Violet, get it over
with," I said.

She answered, sounding rather cheerful.

"Hello, Carol, it's Violet here. Violet Clay."

There was a silence. Then (with a tad too much heartiness?):
"I haven't forgotten you, Violet. How nice to hear from you
again. What have you been up to?"

"Oh, nothing. Pretty much the same." Up flashed a parodic
silent-movie vision of myself falling in and out of bed with a series of dark-tempered men, weeping, slugging back vodka,
slashing a hack canvas with angry black strokes. "Listen, Carol,
why I called . . ."

"Yes?" She sounded a shade more distant. Was she afraid I
had broken the long silence in order to ask for a loan?

"Ambrose is dead. I thought you'd want to know."

No answer.

"Carol?" My bus left in ten minutes.

"What happened? Was it an accident?"

"No. He shot himself last night."

"Last night? Only last night? Where was he? Where are you
calling from?"

"From the bus station. Actually, I have to hang up in a minute. He was living in a place called Plommet Falls. I'm on my
way up there now. It's in the Adirondacks. He'd been living in
a cabin up there, ever since he came back from Mexico this past
spring."

"In a cabin?"

"Yes. He went up there to finish his novel."

"Oh," she said wearily. "The same novel?"

"I'm not sure," I hedged, defending Ambrose's spring intentions against the wintry foreclosure in that unfooled Yankee
voice. "Who knows?" I said. "Perhaps he finished it. I'll know
a lot more in a few hours. I've got to go up there now and take
care of things. Listen, I just thought it was right for you to know.
I hope I haven't spoiled your day."

"*My* day?" For the first time she sounded close to tears.

"Wait a second, Violet, let me think. I've called a meeting of the board of directors for ten, at the Newark factory, but we could go together to the Adirondacks . . . my chauffeur could drive us. We could leave around noon. Why don't you cash in your ticket and come on over here and we'll go together."

"I really can't, Carol," I said, tempted only momentarily by the prospect of being whisked classily up to the mountains in the back of a chauffeur-driven automobile; it would be a different sort of travel, hermetically sealed in Carol's world. The very nature of my journey, I felt, required a solitary openness to whatever thoughts might spring naturally from its occasion, undeflected by any other person's interpretations. "This lady's already made plans to meet my bus and take me to the funeral home."

"Oh. Was . . . was he living with someone, then?"

"No, no. This was his landlady." Poor Carol, still jealous, I thought. "Look, I could call you from up there, when I know more. Now I'm really afraid I've got to run or I'll miss the bus."

"Have you called the *Times* yet?" she asked.

"The *Times*?" I asked, mystified.

"It's probably too late for Sunday, but they should have it for Monday's obituaries. I could do that if you like. Write up a paragraph and call it in. We shouldn't mention the cause of death, I don't think."

"Well, okay. If you think they'll put it in." I felt suddenly protective toward his memory. I couldn't bear the thought of Ambrose not making the *Times* obituary page.

"Of course they'll put it in! He published a book, and he won all those medals. Let's see. The Distinguished Service Cross, the Bronze Star . . . oh, yes, the Purple Heart. His ankle never did heal correctly. It always had that funny knobbly place. . . ." I thought I heard her voice break.

"Carol, I feel like a heel, but I have to hang up. Listen, I'll call you from up there and tell you what I find out."

"Will you call today? I'll be home by midafternoon at the latest. Oh, what was the name of that club he was in, the one for Southerners? He took me to their dance at the Plaza once."

"The New York Southern Society?"

"Yes. Shall I put that in, too? He enjoyed being in that. In fact, I think I have the old program somewhere. He was on a committee."

By the time I finally managed to hang up, I had to race downstairs to my gate. Dear Carol; the *Times* was her arbiter of reality. If it wasn't in the *Times* it didn't count.

There was a line of people waiting to board the bus, many of them young, wearing heavy boots and orange backpacks. What if I didn't get on? But the driver took my ticket and I did. I was afraid I wouldn't get a seat by the window, but I did. I froze myself in an aloof position and hoped nobody would sit next to me. Nobody did. Then I wondered why they hadn't. Across the aisle, a boy and a girl took off their backpacks and settled themselves in. They were very beautiful and seemed almost replicas of each other. They both had long shining blond hair and their lanky, narrow-hipped bodies were practically interchangeable. I remembered how surprised I had been in my first life drawing class when the teacher told us that the male and female skeletons had exactly the same sets of bones, the same number of bones, and the same kinds of bones. What had I been expecting—Adam's rib in the female? Or a penis bone in the man, like the one in my uncle's old joke about the duchess? But if our teacher had shown me these two across the aisle, I would have been less surprised. There was not much of a male-female dividing line in their structures. Were the structures of male-female relationships changing as well? I couldn't, for instance, see this lanky girl waiting at home by the telephone for her boy. She'd pull her Levi's up over those long bones and lace up her boots and stalk out into the night and find him. And if she didn't find him she'd probably go on walking. Today they'd clamber up the side of a mountain in their look-alike clothes and tonight they'd settle down, after a supper from cans, in identical sleeping bags under the August moon. And then? Would one of them shift his skeletal frame through the moonlight to the other's sleeping bag? Which one would come to the other? Or didn't those things matter anymore? And once together, would they shed this deceptive look-alikeness and plunge into the old, time-honored mysteries of the flesh? Or was mystery between the sexes as old hat now as sleeping on either side of a sword?

I watched these two as the bus sped through an ugly industrial section on the other side of the tunnel. The boy had put his knees up against the back of the seat in front of him, scrunched serenely down on his spine, and was either sleeping or preparing to sleep. The girl had taken a paperback book out of her knapsack and seemed to be gazing at the print rather than reading it. It looked like science fiction, with a cover depicting a rather cartoony tropical paradise. I wondered if she'd ever read a gothic. Or would she laugh at the silly old plots on which my emotions and expectations had been weaned? What would it be like, I wondered, to have been born this girl instead of myself? Somehow, in spite of all my travails, I decided it would be less interesting. She was all light and surface; there wasn't any chiaroscuro. No signs of low simmering anguish or volatile desires. Or perhaps I was being unfair. Give her ten more years; she'd grow some shadows. But even the shadows would be a different generation from mine. I doubted, for instance, that she worried about being an old maid. Did some unrealized ambition smolder in her breast like chronic heartburn? Maybe so, maybe so. I couldn't see any signs of it threatening to ruin today for her, however.

I looked out the window and noticed, for the first time in weeks, that the world still had a sky, a very light, cloudless Prussian-blue one, give or take the bottom mile or so of industrial smog. New York from across the river resumed the manageable proportions of a maquette, a harmless little table model on which I could project my dreams. It had looked like this when I rode the Carey bus into its center nine years ago from Newark. I still felt the old twinge when I looked at it now. I still wanted to leave my mark on it, even though it had left so many marks on me.

Just learning to survive, those first months, had been exciting. I'd had several immediate small victories, mitigated, I'll admit, by what came after, but quite exhilarating in their own hour. I'd found a job doing sketches, a beautiful older-sister sponsor who took me under her wing. I'd even had the perfect apartment, the one I secretly wanted, dropped into my lap rent-free.

My uncle, as I have already mentioned, promised to put in a good word for me with the "nice lady" he knew over at *Vogue*, to help me find an art-related job to tide me over till I could establish my reputation as a painter. Well, after our evening together, his and mine, about a week went by during which nothing happened and nobody called. I almost picked up the phone to call him several times, but I didn't want him ever to feel Little Niece Violet might become a drag on his bachelor life. I restrained myself. I haunted the Museum of Modern Art by day (it was much less painful to confront the Safely Famous, many already old or dead, than it was to return to the scene of my early defeat and gaze on the works of my luckier peers) and sketched and brooded by night on my bed at the Martha Washington. When the phone *did* ring around nine o'clock one evening, I had become so used to the silence that I almost jumped out of my skin.

A very friendly-sounding woman introduced herself as Sheila Benton. "I'm health and beauty editor over at *Vogue*. Also a very close friend of your uncle's. I was wondering were you free for lunch tomorrow."

I was indeed free.

"Wonderful. I'll take you to this little French place I'm fond of. Will you, by any chance, be seeing Ambrose before tomorrow?"

"I don't plan to. Did you have a message for him?"

"No, not really. Nothing special at all. Well, then . . ." She told me how to get to her office. "Around noon? And be sure and bring your portfolio. Particularly any little pen-and-ink drawings. I really must run along now. *A tout à l'heure!*"

The next morning I went through my Anne Fogarty, good pearls and Chant d'Arômes ritual, the same as a week before, only this time, thank goodness, I didn't have the curse. I arrived at the Condé Nast building fifteen minutes too soon and lurked downstairs at a newsstand, gazing with some disbelief at the glossy perfection of the women on the magazine covers and then furtively comparing my reflection in a long glass case full of cigars. I seemed unusually square-faced and truculent-looking today. I softened the effect with a smile, and rode up on the elevator to Miss Benton's floor, imagining that I already worked here.

I couldn't help staring when she came out to the reception room to meet me. Could anybody not pressed into the deceptive two dimensions of a magazine cover actually look so perfect in the flesh? What a face. What a shape. And her whole person was clipped and colored, scented and coordinated to such a pitch of grooming that I became uncomfortable, for the first time since I'd shed Pequeña Bombal's influence, about my unpainted nails, unprofessionally coiffed hair, and last spring's hemline.

Miss Benton, however, seemed delighted with me. "What a *petite* thing you are! You've got Ambrose Clay's raven-black hair. Also, you know, you resemble him around the cheeks and nostrils a little. Won't you come this way? I'll show you my little cubbyhole." She led me down a hall, setting a jaunty, swinging pace, her beige shot-silk skirt swishing, her magenta silk blouse rustling, the little gold chains around her neck and wrists ringing like tiny sleighbells. Behind desks in the cubicles we passed, women sat framed by open doorways as if on display. Even the older ones looked as though they'd been up all night with a makeup man, getting ready to come to work.

"Here we are!" sang Miss Benton. "Why don't we sit down and see what you've brought me first." She made a good-natured attempt to clear a part of her desk, which was crammed with sample bottles of liquid makeup, packages of cold-water soap, tubes of hair conditioners and suntan lotions, false eyelashes, night creams and so on. Her nails were painted the exact shade of her blouse, and as she bent to tidy up, I got a glimpse of beige lace ornamenting a generous bosom. Her hair, a burnished red-gold, she wore in a sort of warrior's helmet haircut.

Together we looked at my drawings. Whereas the week before I had been painfully conscious of a delayed reaction on the part of my gallery critics, Miss Benton's reaction seemed to come a little too quickly. She pronounced my nudes in conté crayon "charming," my watercolor "Studies for Three Graces" "*comme il faut*," my lithographs of the Dark Angels (minus the one I had lost to biology) "deliciously spooky," and when she saw the little sketches I'd been doing from my window in the evenings at the Martha Washington, she seized on them at once. "Now, *this* is the kind of thing . . ." She held up the one of a window sill crammed with cosmetics. "And I can tell from the nudes that you'd be able to do little drawings of women doing exercises. Just line drawings, you know. Oh, what is this lovely old house with the iron gate and the piazzas?"

"That's just a pen-and-wash thing I did several summers ago. It's our old house in Charleston. It's been sold now."

"That's Ambrose's house? The house where he grew up?" The bosom heaved under the magenta silk blouse. I was beginning to put two and two together. Still, a job was a job.

We walked to the French restaurant, as it was a nice day. I saw men turn their heads as Sheila (as I had now been ordered to call her) swung briskly along in her career girl's stride, bright hair bouncing, gold chains jingling. "I'm pretty sure I can get you seventy-five a week for a start," she said. "You'd *legally* be my assistant—the editor's promised me one for ages—but I see no reason why we couldn't run some little drawings as part of my column. The art department is run separately, you see, but this way you and I can work closer together. You'd help me research my column as well. Would you mind that? Jobs are hard to find here. And of course, this would only be a *faute de mieux* for you, till you break into the art world."

Over our lunch in a tiny basement slightly larger than her office, attended by three waiters with whom she took every opportunity of exchanging French phrases, we discussed what I would do for her. "I've already had one idea," she said, daintily prying loose an artichoke leaf with her magenta nails. "I'll send you over to Michel on Fifty-seventh. He's my hair stylist. A real wizard with hair. He'd do wonders with your thick black mane. Not that it isn't nice now. But he could bring out its natural weightiness with a little shaping. And you could do sketches. Before and after, you know. I'd call the column something like 'Bringing Out Your Hair's Natural Shape.' The natural look is the thing these days. All that teasing damages your hair, you know."

I agreed there was no reason why I couldn't begin work the very next day. When we parted at the entrance of the Condé Nast building, she actually kissed my cheek. "I'm so pleased about this, Violet. Do say hello to Ambrose. Will you be seeing him later?"

"Not *today*," I hedged, not wanting to admit I'd seen him only once since I'd been in town.

"Well," she said, with a cheery little lilt, "if you see him before I do, tell him Sheila sends her best!"

I said I would, noticing, as we waved goodbye, how soft her silver-blue eyes were. They were the least voguish part about her, limpid and trusting, rather like a blue-eyed dog's eyes.

That night, I felt I had a good excuse to call Ambrose, to tell him I had got the job and thank him. He answered his phone in that same reserved way I'd noticed the first time I called him, as if he wasn't sure he wanted to talk to the person at the other end. But he warmed up when he heard my voice and said he'd been meaning to call me this very same evening—it must be telepathy. "Truth is," he said, "I've got a little proposition for you. How would you like to apartment-sit at Two hundred Waverly for the next three weeks or so?"

"Are you serious!"

"Sure I am. I'm off to Italy on an assignment for *Holiday* magazine in a couple of days. Why should you waste your good money on the Martha Washington when you could spread out at my place? Besides, I need someone to water my begonias."

"Boy, this *is* my day," I said. I told him about the job. "I owe it all to you. I have a strong feeling it was your friendship

with Sheila Benton more than my artwork that got it for me."
I put just a touch of insinuation in my voice in case he wanted
to respond to it.

He didn't. "Sheila's a real fine girl," he said, "but you are
a finer artist. But I'm glad I could put you two in touch. Now
listen, tell you what. My super's name is Finney. I'll leave the
key with him, and then when you get ready to come over, just
ring his bell. He lives on the ground floor."

"But aren't I going to see you before you go?"

" 'Fraid not, honey. I'm going to be running all over the
place these next two days. And I've got to get my smallpox
booster and do research at the library."

"For the novel?"

"No, no, for my *Holiday* piece. It's going to be called 'The
Writer's Italy.' I can't imagine why nobody's thought of it before. This editor I proposed it to got real excited. Violet, stop
and think. How many writers can you think of to whom Italy has
been important?"

"Well, Dante . . . or do you mean writers of other nationali-
ties as well?"

"Sure! Dante and Boccaccio, and also Byron and Keats and
Shelley and Forster and Lawrence and James and Mann. And
Mrs. Wharton . . . The list is endless. What I'm going to do is
talk about the writers *and* their characters in Italy. You know,
Von Aschenbach in Venice, not just Mann."

"And Isabel Archer got proposed to in Rome," I reminded him.

"Hey, that's right. You ought to be going with me. You'd be
a real asset."

"I'd love to. But starting tomorrow, I'm a working girl. By
the way, Sheila said for me to tell you hello if I saw you before
she did. So I guess this will have to do, since I won't see you
for a few weeks."

"I guess it will," he said, not too enthusiastically.

We talked a few more minutes and made arrangements for
me to take up residence at Waverly Place in three days.

Thus began my Euphoric Era in New York, short-lived as it would prove to be. My progress—or the illusion of it—rode uptown on the subway every morning to my job. It went with me over to Fifty-seventh, where Michel the Wizard Hair Stylist tilted his tight-trousered pelvis against the side of my chair and snipped and set and combed while I rapidly sketched out of existence the old un-*chic* Violet and redrew her as a svelte duplicate-in-miniature of her new boss, with the same warrior's helmet hair style. It followed me "home" after work, to my uncle's lived-in lair, where I overwatered his begonias, played his records, and snooped a little. On the nights I didn't eat with Sheila, I made entries into a new hardbound sketchbook I had bought: one day if I became famous, these notebooks (I had in mind the diaries of Paul Klee) would be of inestimable value to art scholars. The verbal entries I therefore made in ink; and whenever a pencil sketch turned out particularly well ("Self-Portrait Sketching in Bed," for instance), I must admit I sprayed it with fixative. My energies, not yet dulled by habit and routine, struck out in all directions. I had in mind dozens of projects— which would all have to wait, of course, until I had saved a bit of money and moved into a place of my own. My spirits were so high that I could even look back on the Gallery Fiasco Day as an important spiritual lesson for me, and—after I had made my name—a story both touching and encouraging to other young artists coming up. To preserve the memory before it faded, I jotted down the impressionistic details of the day and illustrated them with small drawings: the lady in the red hat, old Mr. Green standing in awe before several giant-sized burdocks and a few violets growing out of the gallery's floor. The Frank Stella imitations on the walls. I colored my burdocks and violets with inks, but left the paintings on the wall black and white. History would appreciate this ironic touch of prediction. I even managed a cartoon of distraught Violet, naked in her bath, steeping in the pink waters of her first humiliation.

Sheila and I at her initiative had become intimates immediately. She was only six years older than I. The only daughter

of a Dallas dermatologist, she'd come east to attend Miss
Finch's. During her second year there, her mother had died
suddenly. She'd gone back to school briefly, then dropped out.
After that she'd lived in Paris for a year with a rich aunt. She'd
come back to New York set on becoming a high-fashion model,
but both Powers and Ford had told her she was too well en-
dowed up top. She got a *"faute de mieux* job" at B. Altman's,
after which she went to *Vogue* as an assistant to the fashion assignments coordinator. "And then one day the magazine was doing a special section on skin care and I called Daddy on the
WATS line to ask him a few things, and ended up writing most
of the copy, which everybody liked, and . . . here I am!"

But where she was, I very soon learned, was not where she
intended to be for long. I had begun to suspect where her real
ambitions lay the first day we met; I suspected a bit more when
she insisted on buying my pen-and-wash drawing of the house
on the Battery and paying too much for it even after I had
pointed out a critical flaw in perspective between the second-
floor south piazza and Ambrose's old room to the north; but the
truth had really hit home that first evening I went to her apartment for supper. As soon as we were inside, she gave me a drink
(in those days, I still preferred a Coke) and told me to look
around if I liked while she cut up things for our salad. I browsed
about her modish living-dining area, furnished more appro-
priately for a southwestern climate, with glass tabletops and
bamboo furniture and bright floral prints. There were lots of
mirrors (well, why not, in Sheila's case?) and some hard-edged
pastel canvases that had probably been bought because they
matched the curtains. There weren't too many books, although
she had all the current fashion magazines on a display rack at
the end of her wall shelves. I did notice a sumptuous new volume on Italy on her coffee table. "Do you mind if I use your
bathroom?" I called. "It's through the bedroom!" she called
back. A thrilling tension went through the entire apartment as
I crossed the threshold of that bedroom. There, across from the
king-sized bed covered in a quilted rust satin, above an enor-

mous kidney-shaped dressing table with more perfume bottles
than I had ever seen, all around and above the three-way mirror, were at least a hundred pictures of Ambrose: Ambrose from
all angles and in various dimensions, Ambrose in sharp-focused
black-and-white, in grainy gray, in all his colors; Ambrose wearing tennis clothes, Ambrose in a raincoat looking like a cheerful
spy, Ambrose with his arm around a Sheila with a different
hairdo, Ambrose in a bathing suit with his back to the camera,
about to venture into the sea. A surfeit of Ambroses. Pequeña
Bombal's single votary photo of him on her schoolgirl dresser
was but a chaste prelude to this exhibition. I picked up a bottle
of Bellodgia and abstractedly oversprayed myself. The exhibition had been mounted as a sort of collage mural. Whoever had
done it had a good eye for balance and design. There was one
Ambrose, wearing a tux and black tie, blown up even larger than
life size—probably someone on the *Vogue* photography staff had
obliged her. I think I completely forgot to use the bathroom.
When I went into the kitchen, Sheila stood shredding a carrot.
She looked up and met my look. "Well, *ma petite soeur,* now
you know," she said, blushing happily.

As we sat at her round glass table eating our chef's salads,
she inquired with friendly interest about my life and my plans
for the future. I gave her a portfolio sampling, mostly cartoons
because I was in a good mood, of my travails as a boarding school
orphan, my summer in stifling Charleston with Granny, my
brief marriage to Lewis, my decision to start all over again and
make my name as an artist. Whenever my history touched in
any way on Ambrose's, she became raptly attentive. "Did he
come often to your school, then? What was his life like during
those years when he was in Hollywood, doing that ill-fated
screenplay? So many writers have had bad luck with Hollywood,
haven't they! It's interesting, though, that he never married.
Did you meet any of his girlfriends in those days? Of course,
that's long ago, that's the past," and she laughed. "I would have
been in grammar school. When Ambrose was my present age,
I was eleven! I'm twenty-nine now. You're fortunate to be only

twenty-three. Twenty-three and you've already been married. Nobody can ever call you an old maid." She sighed and put down her fork.

After supper, we curled up on the couch together and she brought out a scrapbook. In the scrapbook were articles, some from magazines I'd never heard of, neatly clipped and inserted between transparent sheets of plastic. They were articles on food, drink and travel, and an occasional movie review. They were all signed A. Valentine. "His *nom de plume*," she said. I pretended to know. I scanned a few articles. Some of them were only a couple of paragraphs. A. Valentine wrote a stiff, understated, condescending prose. There was no sign of Ambrose's rangy, enthusiastic, hyperbolic speaking style. A. Valentine had never been a boy from down home. He seemed to have been drinking and dining and going through customs since the beginning of the world. I noticed foreign phrases scattered wearily through his low-keyed praise of newly opened bars and restaurants. I was a little disappointed at him, who cared so much about getting his "one true sentence" a day. Why waste words on these things? Money, of course. The dear old till. I, too, was now indentured to the till. Why else would I spend my days drawing haircuts and tubes of suntan lotion? I resolved hereafter to create technical challenges for myself. Starting tomorrow, I would draw every bottle and beauty aid upside down.

"Of course, for this big *Holiday* piece," said Sheila, "he'll no doubt use his own name. That's the kind of piece that can bolster his reputation. He keeps the two separate, you know. The fluff and the real stuff, as he puts it."

"Oh, do you have any of his real stuff, then? I haven't kept up as well as I should with what he's been doing."

"Well," she mused, turning the pages of the scrapbook but not finding anything representative of this higher category, "just *now* he's putting his best efforts into the new novel. Which is as it should be, don't you agree?"

I agreed. "Have you read much of it?"

"He read some of it to me once. It was just after we started going out together. One weekend we went to Fire Island and he read this really touching scene—I'm pretty sure he said it was a chapter from his new novel. It was that scene where the lonely little boy is wandering around the big house trying to amuse himself and invents this sinister man who leads him upstairs to where his mother is making love with a stranger. You know that one?"

"I *think* I remember it," I bluffed, wanting to learn more yet keep her from knowing how little I knew. "But I can't recall . . . Who was the stranger? That part seems to have faded."

"Oh! I was hoping you could fill me in on these details, Violet. Did your grandmother have some lover, perhaps?"

"Not that I know of."

"But of course she wouldn't have told you, would she? The Clay family is so full of mysteries! All so convoluted in that typically *Southern* way. The first book was based on your mother, he told me that. All so strange! You know, I've even thought I owed a debt to her at times."

"A debt to my mother?"

"Yes. For keeping him so charmed by her memory that he didn't marry all those years. But I have to say, Violet, that there are times . . . well, when I have had reason to think that his allegiance—sacred as it has been—shows signs of fading. Do you mind that I've said that?"

"No, I don't mind."

"And you *wouldn't* mind if . . ." The faithful-dog eyes entreated me with all the fullness of their limpid blue appeal.

"Of course I wouldn't," I said.

She threw her arms around my neck and kissed me and called me her *petite soeur,* which, till the end of our relationship, became her pet name for me.

After Ambrose had been gone about two weeks, we each received a postcard. Sheila's showed a detail from Botticelli's "Birth of Venus." Her hair was the same color as Sheila's. *I greatly appreciate your kindness to Violet,* said the message, *and am sure she'll prove herself a real asset. The weather so far*

has been beautiful. Will leave for Rome tomorrow. Affection-
ately, "A.V." My card had a self-portrait of Hans Holbein the
Younger. Have just spent an enriching morning at the Uffizi.
Kept wishing you could see these great paintings. Well, when
our ships come in! Look at Holbein's searching eyes, the real artist ready at any minute to pounce on his truth. Love, Ambrose.
I was a little surprised that he hadn't signed Sheila's card "love,"
as well. But she seemed quite pleased that he'd sent her a card
at all, which I thought strange, considering how things stood between them. And then, that evening or the next, when she and
I were curled up on her sofa looking through her glossy picture
book of Italy, sort of tracing his journey, she told me she'd
bought this book "after you told me about his Holiday assignment." I took this to mean he hadn't told her and I thought that
strange, too.

The Saturday following this, I was just heading out into a
lovely morning, on my way to spend as much as I could of my
pay check at a fabulous art supply store I'd just discovered. All
the artists in the Village shopped there and I got a great com-
petitive stimulus from watching to see what papers and brushes
and colors they chose. There was mail in Ambrose's box and I
debated whether to look at it now or to wait till I came back so
I wouldn't have to carry it around in my purse. My innate curiosity won, of course. Along with what looked like a bill from Mark
Cross and a reminder that his subscription to Playboy was about
to run out was an airmail letter for me from the American Em-
bassy in Rome. It was from Ambrose. I read the first sentence
in his ceremonious, free-flowing hand beneath the imposing
seal. I stopped walking and reread it. Then I leaned against the
wall of his building and read the whole letter.

Violet honey,
    Your decrepit old uncle was married here at the consul's office
about fifteen minutes ago. This p.m. we leave Rome for Siena,
where we'll be staying probably through the most part of the summer. Things happened pretty fast but then miracles generally do.

Carol believes in the things we do. She says tell you she plans to write you a long letter soon. I am a lucky man and a thankful man. For the first time in years, I feel I'm dealing with a full deck. Hope you're finding the apartment congenial. I may be asking you to send me a few things, my lightweight suit and some more shirts. The coleus (with the fringy leaves) will need to be watered more than the Wandering Jew, and the begonias mustn't have direct sun. Don't worry about rent, I'll take care of it through my bank. Now's your chance to get on your feet. This marriage is going to be good for everybody, wait and see.

Tuo zio fortunato,
Ambrose

After I had assimilated this extraordinary news, my first urge was to put the letter back in the box and pretend it had not arrived till Monday. I was having supper at Sheila's, and one reason I had so looked forward to this day by myself was that I knew I had somewhere to go at the end of it. How could I go and eat her food now? But on the other hand, I reasoned, surely he must have sent her a letter, too. She would want to talk about it. She might even be telephoning me upstairs right now. Should I go back up? But the sun was so warm and the day so lovely. Perhaps I should get on a subway and go uptown to her immediately, get it over with. But if she *hadn't* received the news, I'd just succeed in blackening this nice spring day for her.

Yet at the same time my thoughts raced frantically back and forth on Sheila's behalf, another part of my mind had set up its own counterpoint of jubilation. I couldn't deny it. Ambrose was happy and I was happy for him, and I could stay on in his wonderful apartment and paint. *Really* get my feet on the ground. I already envisioned a roomful of new paintings by the fall . . . a second, triumphant trip up to the galleries. Or maybe this time the gallery owners would come downtown to me.

But I would need to keep my job as Sheila's assistant, in order to provide myself with food and the other daily necessities.

By this time I had reached Washington Square. Still debating whether to call Sheila, or go on through the day as planned and simply show up at her place at six and let nature take its course, I walked block after block up Fifth till I found myself at the Forty-second Street library. I felt I could more easily walk to Montreal than face Sheila. Then "Jesu, Joy of Man's Desiring" pealed through the spring air like a nudge from God toward my charitable impulses. A black man playing the xylophone had gathered a large crowd around him on the steps of the library. I put a quarter in his hat, thinking of charity versus tinkling brass, and decisively crossed the street and headed east toward Sheila's. I stopped to buy a bunch of jonquils at the outdoor market across the street from her building. Do unto others, I thought, and if I were in Sheila's shoes I would want to know where I stood immediately so I could make other plans before grass grew under my feet.

She was surprised when I announced myself on the intercom at half past eleven in the morning.

"May I come up for a minute? I was just passing," I said like an idiot. Starting off on the wrong tack already.

"Violet! I'm not even dressed yet. Sure, come on."

The door buzzed. I went up to her floor. She was waiting happily in her open door, in an orange kimono. Without her makeup, she looked like a scrubbed schoolgirl. I felt a dark flash of hatred for the stranger Carol.

"What a sweet thing you are," said Sheila. "You've brought me flowers. I'm glad you stopped by." She hustled me in. "I'll make us some tea . . . or would you rather have coffee?"

"I'm not sure you'll want to have *me*," I said, sinking down on the sofa where we had so recently sat with our feet up, looking through "A.V." 's scrapbbook. "I've just had the strangest letter from Ambrose. . . . I feel perfectly terrible."

"Why? What?" She sat down beside me. The shining look went out of her face.

"Well . . . shit. It seems he's gotten married."

"That's impossible," said Sheila. "If he ever marries, he's going to marry me. You're lying."

"No, I'm not. I wish I were." I held up my hands in a gesture of impotence.

Sheila was looking at me as though I had brought something

really filthy and laid it down in her hospitable room. Well, I had.

"What did the letter say? Do you have it? Let me see."

"Sheila, I'm not sure you ought to see it. I mean . . ."

"Oh, come off it, Violet. Let me see that letter. That is, if this isn't some joke of yours."

I handed over the letter, feeling wounded. Sheila was not responding very decently to my charitable impulse. I examined the hard-edged paintings that I didn't like while she read Ambrose's letter.

She took a long time reading it. Perhaps she read it several times. "*Je suis foutu*," she whispered savagely at last.

"I'm sorry," I said. "I was just as unprepared for this as you were."

"I wouldn't go so far as to say *that*." She was looking at me so coldly I felt shivery. The jonquils lay in their paper on the glass-topped table, where I had eaten her food. "Did you know about this woman? Did you know he'd been seeing her?"

"I never even heard her name till I opened this letter. He met her over there, from the sound of the letter."

"No, he'd been seeing her here, behind my back. He took her to Italy. This was all planned out."

"Well, then," I said, wondering how soon I could leave, "you know more about her than I do. I wasn't even sure she was American."

"Let me see that letter again," she said, snatching it back. She read through it once more, moving her lips. "*Tuo zio fortunato* . . . pretentious bastard. 'Good for everybody,' eh? I'd like somebody to tell me how it will be good for me."

"Well," I said, "isn't there some good in knowing the truth? Then you can proceed from there."

"The point is, *ma petite soeur*," and now she put an acid inflection on my pet name, "I don't want to proceed anywhere. So what are we going to do about that?" She folded her arms and stood up, looking down on me, as if this were just some nonsensical joke that I could set right anytime I chose.

I, too, stood up. "I think I ought to go. It can't be pleasant for you, having me here." I couldn't wait to get out of there.

"I've got to think," muttered Sheila, pacing up and down with her kimono trailing majestically behind her. She wrung her hands mechanically, going back and forth in front of me. "Just let me think."

"I'll call you later," I said, letting myself out. She was still pacing and did not answer me.

Made braver by the real trouble of someone else, I decided to experiment with the New York subway system and discovered the E train, which got me to the Village without a single change. I bought a hot dog from a vendor and ate it sitting on the rim of the fountain in Washington Square, trying to imagine who Carol was and what she would turn out to be like. I reread the letter, searching for clues. She "believes in the things we do" must mean art, since the whole basis of Ambrose's and my new relationship resided in this. A lucky man, a thankful man . . . hmm. How come he hadn't said a happy man? But wasn't "dealing with a full deck" one definition of happiness? I would just have to wait. Water his plants, work on my painting, and show myself worthy of a rent-free summer.

When I puffed up the five flights of stairs around four, carrying a secondhand studio easel, solvents and a number 22 sable, which I actually didn't need for the 14-by-18-inch canvas I'd bought, Ambrose's phone was ringing. It stopped when I got inside, then almost immediately started again.

It was Sheila, quite hysterical. Where had I been? She had been calling me all afternoon. "We're still having dinner. Aren't we? I can't stand to be alone. I'm afraid I'll do something awful. Do you know what I almost did, Violet?"

She had booked an afternoon flight for Rome. Then realized he would already have left Rome by the time she got there. "That's when I started calling you. . . . I couldn't remember where he said he was going. I was pretty sure he said Siena, but then I thought no, Sicily. Now that plane's left. I had to call the airport back and change to tomorrow's flight. Are you still coming? Only"—she laughed wildly—"I haven't got any food, I haven't shopped. Wait, I have a better idea. I'll just hop in a cab and come down there."

"Are you sure you want to do that? I mean . . ." Yet, I thought, much better she comes here than goes to Siena. Well, there went my quiet weekend of painting. I had planned to begin my self-portrait, something on the order of Holbein the Younger.

Now she gave a different laugh, a sort of menacing snarl. "And why not, *ma petite soeur*? Two hundred Waverly has been my Village *pied-à-terre* for three years. Just as *my* humble abode has been a certain person's cozy uptown retreat. That is, unless you'd rather I didn't come. Perhaps you want your cozy retreat all to yourself."

I assured her I did not, that I was her friend and would expect her as soon as she could get there. Then I rushed out and bought a barbecued chicken, a pound of potato salad, and blew the remainder of my week's salary on a fifth of gin, my departed grandmother's favorite antidote to psychic pain.

It was an eye-opening twenty-four hours in more ways than one. Accompanying Sheila up and down the scale of human emotions ranging from Camille-like prostration to violent vituperation, I found myself wondering if you could ever know what someone else was really like. Perhaps no one had a stable personality, but people simply vibrated different emotional frequencies, depending upon the lights or darknesses of the moment. She had arrived wearing no makeup, her bright hair completely obscured by a kerchief, clad in some nondescript gray slacks and a grizzled shapeless top that I swear to God resembled a hair shirt. The glossy health and beauty editor with her vivid-bright colors was nowhere to be seen. Also gone was any sign of the blushing friendly Big Sister. The trusting dog-blue eyes were shot with hours of weeping and rage.

We talked mostly about him. Rather, she talked. "For three years we went everywhere together. He depended on me for everything. I was the one who went to Tiffany's and bought your wedding present and had it sent. He said he could always trust in my taste. I almost got a silver calling-card tray, but who uses those anymore?"

"I loved the little vase," I said, rather disappointed that my uncle hadn't selected my wedding gift himself.

"I remember looking at the stationery that day. I chose the kind I would order when . . . It was a light-gray background with a thin border of blue. I was going to have the 'Mrs. Ambrose V. Clay' in blue italic, and our address . . . We would have had to move out of here; it's too small for two people really to function, no matter how in love they are"—and she dismissed the room with an airy flutter of her hand. "I mean, there isn't even a decent closet where I could hang my clothes." Then she seemed to falter, unsure of where she was. "Oh, God!" she shrieked. "It can't be true, it can't, it can't! Please tell me it's not true!"

I poured more gin into her ice and tonic and worried about the neighbors.

A few sips later, the wistful woman who'd shopped at Tiffany's dissolved into a vengeful harpy who narrated to me in a low, brittle voice, how, several months ago, she had hired a detective to follow Ambrose. "I'd seen him flash by in a Mercedes with a woman, only an hour after he'd left my apartment to 'go home and write.' Yes, my dear, I had your slippery uncle trailed for one whole week. That's all I could afford, and the detective was a low-bred little man. Well, would you like to hear what I found out? Don't look so worried. It does you good to know the truth—weren't you preaching that to me just this morning? My little detective came back with his greasy black notebook and enlightened me considerably. Three afternoons a week, from one to five, your illustrious uncle was a salesman at the Mercedes-Benz showroom on Park Avenue. On the other afternoons, he played squash and swam at the Sixty-third Street Y. On the evenings he couldn't see me because he 'had to work on his book' he sat downstairs in the corner bar telling dirty jokes with some gray-haired woman and playing boogie-woogie on their ratty piano. And the rest of the time—God forbid he might have to go back to his lonely room and face that novel!—he was over in Sheridan Square, loafing in the bookstore. Well, *ma pe-*

tite soeur, voilà! Your uncle, the dedicated author who robbed me of my best years. At least you get the information free. I had to shell out a hundred and fifty bucks."

"At least you found out it wasn't another woman," I replied, a little crestfallen from these revelations.

"That was three months ago. Who knows what he's been doing since then?"

"But I thought you saw him frequently."

"Not lately. He's been acting strange. Every time I call him, he pleads his book. What a joke, that book! He isn't interested in writing a book. It would be too much like work. He used that book on me the way married men use their worn-out wives on their mistresses. To get away when they're bored."

"Maybe you're better off now," I said, helping myself to more gin. "Look at it that way. That you're well rid of a slippery fake."

This triggered the appearance of yet another Sheila. "Don't say that," she moaned. "He was the gentlest, kindest man I ever met. Oh, poor, poor darling. He's going to be miserable with this woman. She trapped him some horrible way, I'm sure of it. When he understands, he'll come back to me. I know it. I feel it."

On this note she passed out. I hauled her dead weight, which could still stagger, to the big brass bed and covered her up and ate the potato salad and both legs of the chicken. I tried my new easel in various spots and drank a little more gin. Finally I got sleepy and put on my nightgown and slipped into the other side of the bed. I was waked sometime later by a persistent melancholy tune washing over my eardrums in wave after wave of amplified sound. The hi-fi was on full blast. I leaped out of bed and round the corner. There stood Sheila in a trance before the machine.

"Jesus Christ, Sheila! You want me to get evicted?" I turned down the volume.

"Do you know what this is?" Tears splashed down her cheeks. She held out a plain record jacket. "It's the music sound track they were going to use for his movie. They had already re-corded it before everything fell through. We used to lie in bed and listen to it."

"I've never heard it before."

"Come," she said, starting the record over, "let's just lie quietly and listen to it. Then I think I can sleep. Come back to bed. I'm sorry I woke you."

I decided it was best to humor her. We lay side by side and I listened for the first time to the background music to the story that had been based on my mother. It was the sort of music the trained ear is embarrassed by and the emotions secretly adore: a searching but comfortably repetitive melody of low strings against a background of muted horns that evoked the sea.

"We would lie here and he would tell me all his hopes and plans," she said. "He had this way of stroking the back of my neck." She turned sideways away from me and reached over and guided my hand to her neck. It was very feverish.

"Like this?" I asked.

"No, lighter. Just teasing, like feathers. Yes, like that. Oh, God, is it possible? If I could have looked into the future a year ago—I was probably even lying in this bed—and seen this com-ing . . . He might even have been stroking my neck." She burst into the most heartbroken sobs I ever hope to hear.

"Don't play games like that with yourself," I said, curling up against her, as years ago I had lain beside my roommate Pe-queña, who often woke up and confused the darkness with going blind. The sound track for the dead *Lora Lee* switched itself off. When my arm got too tired to tickle her neck anymore, I kept it protectively round her and we fell asleep that way.

On Sunday I fed her breakfast and at about three in the after-noon she pronounced herself over her foolishness and asked if she could borrow my lipstick, which I thought was a good sign. She took a taxi uptown and said she was going to write to her daddy and have an early night.

Monday I arrived at work at the usual time. Sheila was not there yet, but she was often tardy, so I got out my inks—I worked in a closet-sized cubicle next to hers—and started work on a series of summer shape-up exercises. At ten-thirty her phone rang. It was Sheila herself.

"Hello, Violet dear. Would you do me a favor and tell Marge I won't be in today?"

"Sure. Are you feeling okay? Maybe I could come by on my lunch hour."

"Oh, I won't be in, I'm afraid. I'm feeling fine, though, since you ask. The reason I won't be able to make it to the office is . . . Do you promise you won't tell a soul?"

I promised.

"I'm getting married. That's why I won't be able to come in today. Or tomorrow, for that matter." She gave a faraway tinkly laugh. "You'll just have to carry on without me."

"Sheila? Are you kidding?"

"No, dear, I have never been more serious in my life. It's you who've been kidding *me*."

"Sheila, I don't understand."

"Oh, yes you do, you naughty girl. Though I can't say I blame you for wanting to keep him to yourself. But luckily I saw through you. I'm on my way to him now."

"What airline? What flight?" I had the presence to ask, for an unpleasant truth was surfacing.

Again the glassy faraway laugh. "Now, Violet. *Tout va bien.* Don't try and spoil it again."

She hung up.

After I regained my calm, I used that telephone within an inch of its life. I beat her to the TWA building at Kennedy by an hour. I had encountered what might be called "madness" only once. One day in sixth grade at Pine Hollow our math teacher started throwing chalk at us and chanting, "Dirty little beasts, dirty little beasts!" Someone slipped out and got the principal. Several days later we were informed that Miss Greany had had "a nervous breakdown."

But how could anyone, watching Sheila saunter through those glass doors, as composed as if she'd just stepped off the cover of the magazine she worked for, think she'd had a nervous anything? Ever since that day, when I watched her glide up to the ticket counter, set down her little Louis Vuitton overnight bag and slap down her credit card, I feel differently about the beautifully composed people I see crossing my perimeters. I no longer dismiss them as all-of-a-piece figures, luckier and simpler than I. Of course, the overnight bag was one of the giveaways to Sheila's condition. The doctor from Payne Whitney who had met me at the airport and now waited with me explained this. The distressed Sheila was acting out going to Rome; the practical, clothes-wise Sheila had not packed to go any farther than where she knew, somehow, we'd have sense enough to get her to. She had been there before.

I had called her father, the dermatologist in Dallas. I explained who I was and he said yes, his daughter had written to him about me. He believed Sheila had been seeing a good deal of my uncle for some time, as well, he added dryly. Then I had to tell him Ambrose had gone and gotten married and the effect of this on Sheila. "She was terribly upset at first, then she got better, but now she suddenly says she's flying to Italy to marry him . . . or maybe she's just kidding me."

"She's not kidding you," he said, and became very professional. He told me he was going to call a friend at New York Hospital and asked me to sit there till he called me back.

Now I said to the doctor, a pleasant-looking balding man in his mid-thirties, wearing tennis shoes (Dr. Benton had caught him just as he'd been leaving for his game): "Shouldn't we stop her before she buys the ticket?"

"No, let her complete the transaction. It's no problem canceling a credit card charge." He laughed ruefully. "Some part of her knows that, at this moment."

He had helped treat Sheila during her last stay at the clinic. He had been an intern then. It was after her mother died. She had calmly received the news by telephone—it had been a first heart attack—and flown home to Dallas. She went to the funeral and did not break down once, kissed her father goodbye and re-

turned to Miss Finch's. Several weeks later, she began telephoning home, asking to speak to her mother. The first few calls
were taken by the maid, a Negro woman who had cared for
Sheila since childhood, and who, for some kindly superstitious
reason of her own, would simply reply, "Sheila honey, your
mamma's not here now, you know that." But then Sheila wanted
to know when she would be home, why didn't she ever stay
home anymore? By the time one of her calls reached the doctor,
Sheila was screaming. She accused him of hiding her mother to
punish her for leaving them. Dr. Benton had taken the next
plane east.

Now the nice balding doctor went up to Sheila, who blinked
flirtatiously and asked what he was doing at the airport. Was he
going to Rome on the same flight, by any chance? She either did
not see me sitting in the background, or she pretended not to.
The doctor explained that her father had called and wanted her
to have some tests before she left the country. She nodded, very
serious and amenable. She seemed to have forgotten the ticket
she had just purchased and slipped into her purse. She agreed
to ride back to town and check into the clinic and have the tests.
"Isn't it lucky that I brought my gown and toothbrush," she told
him. Then he pointed out my presence and said we could all
ride back together.

"Why are you here, Violet? Why did you come?" asked
Sheila. "Why aren't you at your desk, at the office? I told you
not to come out to see me off. It's such a waste of money. I'm
in very good hands, I can assure you." She opened her handbag
and took out a crisp twenty-dollar bill. "Take this and run along
back to work."

I started to refuse it, but I got a look from the doctor.

"Violet will make her own way back," said Sheila firmly.
"She's a big girl now." Then, before we went our separate ways,
she nudged me aside and whispered in my ear, "I have known
this doctor for years. He has always been in love with me . . .
hopelessly, of course. He somehow found out I was going to
elope with your uncle. I'm going to play along with him and go
quietly so he won't make a scene. I hate scenes, don't you?"

Then she winked at me and giggled like a schoolgirl, and off they went, the doctor springily, in his tennis shoes, and Sheila erect and beautiful with her swinging career-girl stride. He had taken the Vuitton bag and held her arm lightly, like an escort.

I returned to town on the airport bus. Then decided it was too late to go back to work and took a taxi down to the Village. I would probably lose my job anyway. With the rest of Sheila's twenty dollars I bought a cold supper and some more tonic and another fifth of gin. I thought of Ambrose, lucky and thankful with his bride in Siena, now safe from the transatlantic arrival of a certain beautiful skeleton from "A. Valentine" 's closet. And of Sheila, surrounded by anxious professionals all dedicated to cleansing her mind of this new layer of painful shadows. Having been the Strong One all weekend, I now felt let down when there was no pressing reason, nor any audience, for my further good example. I curled up in the window seat, my head tickled by the friendly swaying of the hanging coleus, watching the afternoon fade, sipping a cool gin and tonic, and reading Ambrose's old letters to my grandmother. He had divided them up, according to various periods of his adult life, in separate plastic sandwich bags. There was a bag for Basic Training, a bag for Newbury, England, where he'd been stationed before D-day, a bag for Hollywood, a bag for New York, and one bag labeled simply "On The Road." He had marked various passages of certain letters and, in some cases, written notes in the margin— "Use for scene on beach," "Have L. say this." He obviously planned to use these letters in his novel. When I had first discovered the letters in the bottom drawer of his desk, I had determined to inflict a moral handicap on my snooping intentions by making myself read them in chronological order. The Basic Training ones were a drag. He was either "on duty," or having dinner with "one of the boys who lives at home" (much description of food), or washing out his clothes (with a touch of self-pity) back at the base, or speculating (with a touch of Rupert Brooke) on his impending active duty.

I felt I'd done enough for him in the past forty-eight hours to warrant my skipping to the New York bag (by far the thickest), to see what else I could learn about the secret life of A. Valentine up until the death of my grandmother. I had not found any trace of her side of the correspondence.

"Many thanks for the small loan," I read, in one of the early letters. His writing was leisurely, with lots of flourishes, as if the hand had been in love with its own penmanship. "Am changing my tactics on *Last Hero*, using more understatement now. If I get on paper what I want, we'll throw a shindig that'll send all the old biddies on East Battery to their fainting couches, then we'll build a bonfire and roast marshmallows over the embers of our old mortgages." "Have been in a slump," began another (written the summer I'd been with Granny). "Better now, thanks to your care package and the good advice. A man of words had also better be a man of deeds, you're perfectly right." And a bit later, "You are one angel Momma. And thanks also for the nice socks. Have been reading Dostoevsky's *Diary of a Writer* tonight to put some fire into me. Women are our great hope, he writes, they will manage to save much."

Summer Activities

True to her promise, Ambrose's new wife wrote to me within the week.

My first thought upon turning over the envelope and seeing a crest on the back with *Castello Marciano, Siena,* in raised script beneath was: Of course! Ambrose has married a princess, castle and all. It seemed fitting somehow, since he had waited so long to marry anybody.

But on skimming the closely written pages, to take the edge off my curiosity before I could settle down and read calmly, I learned that her maiden name was Gruber, that she had grown up in New York City, that she was forty years old—born, coincidentally on February 14, 1926, the same day as Ambrose—and that she owned several factories in New Jersey that manufactured an imitation leather known as Dura-Pelt. And every spring she made a working-holiday trip to Italy's leather capital to garner new ideas for her own future lines.

"I first laid eyes on your uncle," she wrote, in a brisk and regular script I would come to know well, "in the Uffizi, in the room with all the blondes, as I now tease him. All those North Italian girls with their pale tresses, the Botticellis. A handsome twentieth-century man surrounded by a roomful of beautiful fifteenth-century women. It was an aesthetic sight in itself. As an artist you will understand this."

She had thought he was Italian. But a while later, he sat down at the next table from hers in an outdoor café and after writing several postcards (the ones to Sheila and me?) looked up and asked her in careful Italian if she knew where he could buy stamps. ("The funny thing was, he thought *I* was Italian, because of my black hair and Gucci shoes. And then we began talking and discovered we both lived in New York and he joined me at my table and we had lunch and some wine. Then we mailed his postcards and went to look at Dante's house, which was very near.")

He told her about his *Holiday* assignment. He'd already done Venice and the photographer was meeting him the next day in Rome. "And I offered to drive him, since I had a car and he had been planning to take the train."

She wrote, rather disarmingly, that "I fell in love with him almost at once, on the first day I think. He fell in love with me too, not at first sight or anything, but after we had been together a few days and discovered more about each other." I read much into this sentence.

But I had been correct about the castle. It was a real castle, in the Tuscan hills, built by a fourteenth-century duke. It had an Olympic-sized pool and central heating. ("Some friends of mine in the leather business bought it and fixed it up; they rent it out, mostly to Americans who have always had a yearning to live in a real castle.")

She and Ambrose would stay through the summer, she said. She had been married to her job long enough and it would be good for him to finish "The Writer's Italy" while in Italy; it would give it that bit of extra snap. ("Then also, he's full of ideas for his new novel, which sounds very exciting.")

She promised to send "some snapshots of the castle and the late-blooming lovebirds" in her next letter and told me she had half a notion to tempt me into flying over and joining them. "But I *won't* tempt you, because you're starting to make your own way and that is so important. I went overboard in making mine (after my parents were killed in a stupid car crash twenty years ago, I just had to prove that my father had been justified in leaving so much responsibility in my hands), so much so that I had practically forgotten how to live. But your uncle is lovingly reteaching me. Now I look around me and take deep breaths of air and enjoy each moment as it comes."

Then she tactfully damped down the ardor that was beginning to rise from the page by saying that Ambrose sent his love and said not to bother about sending any shirts, he would have some made in Florence, and that she already thought of me as the sister she had always wanted.

Well, I thought, each time I reread her letter, it's no crime per se to marry someone with money. And who is to say he didn't fall in love with her *before* she told him she owned factories? And she does sound interested in his work. Now he can get on with it with no distractions. He doesn't even have to bother sending for his old shirts.

Knowing she thought of me, too, that she already claimed me as a sister, made my present financial situation less threatening. Not that I would ever ask her for anything. But knowing she was out there with Ambrose, annexed to the Clay family for better or for worse, I could take a more tranquil attitude toward the future. "This marriage is going to be good for everybody," Ambrose had said, and now I felt the same.

Not surprisingly, I had been let go from *Vogue*. The new health and beauty editor would want to hire her own assistant, if she felt she needed one. I was given two weeks' pay for my services, which was generous, considering how little I had actually contributed to the magazine during my short occupancy in my adjunct mini-cubicle.

Sheila was doing nicely over at Payne Whitney. Her father invited me to have dinner with him at the Plaza. He was a slim gray-haired man who watched his diet. He thanked me for my quick thinking and for being his daughter's friend, and said he knew I'd understand that she wasn't quite ready to meet me again. He claimed to know very little about the workings of the human mind; his specialty, he said, was skin, and he had his hands full just keeping the many afflictions that could affect that surface in control—or sometimes not. He reported that his daughter was responding to medication, had stopped looking out the window, waiting for Ambrose to come and marry her, and had even admitted to the doctors that she hadn't seen Ambrose a whole lot within the past year. Dr. Benton planned to take her back to Dallas at the end of the week. She had already been on the phone to Neiman-Marcus and had a job waiting for her. Her father said that in his humble opinion, everybody had one or two crazy areas, just as there were certain areas of the epidermis that, through a combination of factors, were more liable to "breakouts" than surrounding areas. Sheila's mental makeup was on the whole very sound and practical. "It simply refuses to tolerate the loss of loved ones, that's all." He very much wanted his daughter to fall in love and marry, he said, before anything happened to him.

As for me, the high was beginning to fade from my New York experience. I, too, now ran for the subway, even when I wasn't in a hurry. I had stopped noticing my surroundings as much. Being unemployed, I took to sleeping late, and then it needed all my will power to stay inside and paint when the sun was already high. Even as I worked, my mind was distracted. I was thinking: I *should* begin looking for another job soon; or, more ignobly: If I don't go out for lunch soon, all the interesting-looking people in that restaurant will have finished their lunch and gone back to wherever they go. I ate in the same restaurant every day— joint would be a better description of it. Most of the clientele ate eggs and hash browns at noon and had paint on their clothes and under their fingernails. I gave as much thought to the book I took along with me to "read" as I did the painty *déshabillé* I affected to signal to the interested eye that I would be worth striking up a conversation with. But so far, my *Either/Or* and Fry's *Last Lectures* had seemed only to reinforce my isolation. Perhaps the eye that I would have been interested in decided it would be useless to compete with such perspicacious companions. I was left to plow undisturbed through "The Diary of a Seducer," and "Negro Art" until I all but floated back to my apartment on coffee refills, to dutifully resume work on "Self-Portrait."

I am sorry to report that the thrill had gone out of it almost as soon as I'd set up my work space and done the preliminary sketch and imprimatura. Why had I wanted to do a self-portrait anyway? The impetus was Ambrose's Holbein postcard, probably. But exactly what, at this point, did I want to record for posterity about my self-concept? The trouble seemed to lie here. What about me was interesting enough to commit in oil pigment to canvas? In retrospect, of course, should I become a legend, any aspect of my youthful self, like Dürer's silverpoint of himself at thirteen, would be cause for celebration. Meanings would be assigned to chance brush strokes, flaws in perspective, even.

The afternoons were long, especially now that there was no prospect of company in the evenings. One afternoon, out of sheer need to be recognized for myself, I made an appointment with Michel, the hairdresser of Fifty-seventh, for a wash and trim. "And how are things at *Vogue*?" he asked, shampooing me himself. I brought him up to date, saying merely that my boss had decided to move back to Texas. "Ah, so now you will be looking for something else," he murmured. He seemed to have a genuine French accent, rather heavy at that. "Oh, I may just stay home and paint during the summer," I said, "or at least till my money runs out. My uncle is honeymooning in Italy and he's left me his apartment, rent-free." "You are a fortunate girl," he replied, smiling. He had nice teeth that reminded me of a small animal's. "Relax your neck, now. Your neck is so tense." "What are you doing?" I asked. "Massaging the scalp a little. Lean back. Relax." His fingers made strong, practiced little circles around my head, working from back to front. By the time he reached my temples, I was almost in a trance. "You like that, eh?" He stood above me, a small, self-proud man, his pelvis tilted close to my cheek. A look passed between us. I quickly closed my eyes, embarrassed. "Did you learn that in your school?" I asked, trying to sound like a patron. "I learned the relaxation points . . . here and here," he said, "but the touch is my own."

A few nights later the phone rang. "Is this Violet Clay?" said a man. I thought it was a crank call, someone parodying a heavy foreign accent. It was Michel. "How did you get my number?" I asked. "Oh, that is not so difficult. I made a few false tries, that is all." He asked me how my painting was going and how I was enjoying my rent-free apartment. He then asked if I would like to go out with him sometime.

"Thank you," I said, "that's very nice of you. I'd love to, but . . . you see, I'm trying to finish this painting."

"You paint all day and all night?"

"No, but . . ." I hedged. "It takes a while for me to work up the right mood. I'm ridiculously easy to distract, so I just have to make it difficult for myself."

"I think you also like to make it difficult for me, eh?"

"No, no, it's not *that*. . . ."

"Perhaps there is something about me . . . some reason you would prefer not to go out with me," he suggested.

Which was of course the whole thing. I was lonely, but not

desperate enough to start dating my hairdresser. "No, you're very nice. I'm sure any woman would be pleased to go out with you."

"Well, what is the problem? A friendly dinner will not upset your painting. It will relax you. You are a very tense girl."

"I am?"

"Yes, I noticed it when you came to the shop. But I don't want to make you more tense. Have you a pencil? Yes, all artists have a pencil. Here is my number. I am almost always home in the evenings. Me and Beatrice. That's my toy poodle. When you feel like some company, a nice meal, pick up the phone and call Michel."

Really touched by the gallant way he'd let me off the hook, I took down his number and thanked him. I said it might be some time, I just couldn't predict how my summer would go.

"I understand. Anyway, it has been nice having this conversation with you."

Then I hung up and felt like a bourgeois snob. I saw him as a kind man, who had noticed my tenseness. My loneliness probably stuck out a mile as well. And he was attractive. Those small, healthy animal teeth . . . and foreign accents always added that little bit of mystique. If I had met him, say, at a diplomatic party, I would not have had a moment's hesitation in accepting his invitation. Besides, a man who spent most of his evenings alone with a dog named Beatrice could not be too bad. I picked up the phone and called him back.

"Hello," he said. "And how has your summer been going?"

I got into the habit of going to Michel's several times a week. We both hated eating alone, we discovered. He lived in the East Seventies in a modern high-rise building with a fountain in the downstairs lobby. I'd meet him at the corner of Fifty-seventh and Fifth when he got off work, then we'd take the bus to his street, go up and get Beatrice and take her back down again for her walk, and then Michel would cook supper (he was an excellent chef, baked his own bread and made his own tarragon dressing) and we'd eat it in front of the TV. He already had a color set. When we got better acquainted he showed me movies of his immigration to America and the friends he'd made on the ship. I noticed that his teeth in the movies were brownish and broken; he had had them all capped as soon as he prospered in the New World. He was in love with all modern devices: his apartment was crammed with complicated stereo components and lamps that bubbled up designs in colored oils. After we'd eaten, and drunk a bottle of Bordeaux and watched our programs (Ed Sullivan was Michel's favorite), he would go around switching on gadgets, and as soon as the lamps began bubbling their oils and Frank Sinatra had settled into his first album, Michel would lie down on one of the angora rugs, very still and fully dressed, even with shoes, and then it would be my duty to "awaken" the Reluctant Robot. I would have to do all the work, undress both of us, a little at a time, till our two pale bodies danced with eerie reflections from the bubbling colors. I would endeavor, in the manner he'd tacitly instructed me, to bring to life his furled sex. This was not always successful. But on the evenings it was, he would writhe and moan and finally begin chanting in rapid French; then suddenly his flesh would become steel and he would turn on me like a machine man, and I'd find myself in the grip of a monster with a mindless will. It was the nearest I've ever come to being satisfied by a machine, quite agreeable in its impersonal way. Then we'd lie meditatively on the angora, often with furry Beatrice wriggling around between us, neither of us speaking, watching the patterns the lamps made. Around midnight, he and Beatrice would escort me down on the elevator and I would be sent home, like a lady, in a taxi.

On the evenings I did not go to Michel's, I had concocted for myself a rather desperate little act to relieve the loneliness. I would dress very carefully and then "whisk down" to the little corner bar—the one with the old piano to which Sheila's detective had tracked Ambrose—and buy a pack of cigarettes, and whisk right back upstairs again. It made a break in the long summer night to follow, and it gave me something to look forward to. I understood perfectly why Ambrose had sought refuge down there. If I had been a man, I, too, would have sat at the old painted piano and played boogie-woogie and waited to see who'd come along. But the ideals of Southern womanhood were still too strongly ingrained in me: I might play robot games on the floor of my hairdresser's apartment, but I would never sit down by myself with a drink in a public bar. What I vaguely hoped for, however, was that on my nightly cigarette run (I didn't exactly smoke; I could never learn to inhale), someone would detain me, in a gentlemanlike way, and ask me to sit down. But such a person, when you thought about it, could not possibly be a gentleman to make the kind of time he'd have to make if he were to snatch me out of that split-second nightly sprint.

One evening, I was just on the verge of giving up and retreating back to my lonely pinnacle for a solitary read (I was attempting to reread my uncle's first novel, *Looking for the Lora Lee*) when a husky, amused voice called from the darkness of one of the booths, "Where's your guy? Where's old Fitzie? Haven't seen him around lately." It was the "lady pornographer" with her witchy hang-down hair. She beckoned me over to where she was sitting comfortably in the company of her drink and an ashtray full of cigarette butts.

I sauntered over, trying to keep the pleasure from spilling absurdly from every crack in my face. "Hi," I said. "Ambrose is in Italy. By the way, he's not exactly my guy. He's my uncle."

"Your uncle? Sit down. Have a drink. What's Fitz doing in Italy?"

"He's on assignment for a magazine." Having just lost one friend to Ambrose's marriage, I was being more cautious.

"And what about you? You live around here? What would you like? I'm drinking Scotch. But maybe you'd rather have beer."

"Yes, thank you. Beer would be nice. I'm staying at Ambrose's place till he comes back."

She was looking me over, smiling a sort of side smile and nodding ironically, either at something she was thinking or at something she found amusing about me. Close up she looked older than she had on the street. She smelled of years of cigarettes.

"How about letting me have a fag," she said. "I'm fresh out."

"Sure." I handed over the pack. "Help yourself. Take a couple for later, too."

She raised her eyebrows and expertly slit open the pack with a dirty nail. "Thanks. What did you say you were doing in New York?"

I remembered how Ambrose had said she had once been a successful painter, with shows and everything. Suddenly I felt very shy across from this ironic-smiling, world-weary woman. I made light of myself. "I'm just one more Southern girl who's come north to seek her fortune."

"Hmm," she said, lighting the cigarette and taking a hungry drag. "And what are you going to do to seek it?"

"Well," I said, "I'm a painter like you. My uncle told me you were a painter."

"Used to be. Now I'm more of a designer. I design other people's dirty thoughts. What do you do—abstract?" She said this last word with such a sneer that I realized there was no need for me to be defensive about my figurative leanings.

"I have done a few," I said, "but to tell the truth, they bore me. I'm just not interested in setting up some problem about hot and cool or white on white or flat on flatter. Or ruining my eyesight making tiny little straight lines that ruin everybody else's eyesight when they're hung on the walls."

"You'd better get your pretty ass back to the South, then. You're hopelessly out of fashion." But she was looking at me with more liking as she said this. What had happened to her career? Had she gone out of fashion?

"Surely," I said, "there are some people who still like to see paintings with some reference to the human element."

"Surely." Was she mocking my accent? "People wealthy enough to have their portraits painted—flatteringly, of course. Or there's always the women's mags, illustrating for them. Or there's what I do, which is all too human. Only humans could imagine such degradation."

"If you feel like that, why do you do it?"

"There are certain advantages to not starving for one's ideals. I'm saving up for my old age. I'm going to retire to Vermont. I've already bought a farmhouse there."

"And then you'll go back to painting," I said encouragingly.

"Nope. I'm going to raise dogs. I'm going to have little doggies running all over my ten acres, barking their hearts out for joy at being able to run where they like and shit where they please, when they please."

"I think I saw your dog that night I was with my uncle," I said. Then, because I didn't want to go on about painting: "It was a very attractive dog, very unusual."

"You saw Tang? My little Tang's worth ten human beings." Her voice rose a pitch and all irony went out of it as she told me about Tang. He descended from a very valuable litter of Shih Tzus brought from China to England in the 1930s by Lady Somebody. Tang's ancestors had been raised by eunuchs at the Chinese court. The best dogs had their portraits woven on tapestries and the eunuchs who had raised them were given gifts by the emperor. Tang himself was lively, arrogant and highly intelligent. She told me the tricks Tang did and how he had once almost died choking on a chicken bone. I guess I acted interested and made all the proper responses because she got quite friendly and asked me how I planned to support myself until I made my fortune.

I told her my *Vogue* story. "I still have a little cash left because I don't have to pay any rent at the moment. But I really do have to get something soon. I suddenly had an idea. Why not see if I could get on at her place of work? It would probably pay ten times what aboveboard magazines did, and I could work at home and have time for my own painting as well. "I'm very good at doing figures, bodies in all sorts of positions," I told her. "Do they happen to need anyone else where you work?"

"There's no one *place*," she said. "I'm free lance. They call me. You might say I've become known in my field."

"Oh. I see."

I must have touched her sympathies in some way, because, after stubbing out one cigarette and lighting another, she said, "Maybe Landsborough might have something for you. It's not a fancy place, but if you need to pick up a buck or two . . . I used to do stuff for him. He's a nice guy. A cripple, but with an eye for the girls. Let me have that pack again."

I thought she was going to demand another handful of cigarettes for the price of her job tip, but no, she only wanted to tear off a corner to write down a telephone number.

"I think this is still right," she said. "It's been a long time since I did stuff for him. But if it's wrong, it's Landsborough Productions—you might look it up in the directory. If it's not there, he's gone out of business or left town or something. Anyway, it's worth a try. If he's still in business, you trot on over and show him your stuff. You're a cute kid; he'll probably come up with something."

"Thank you. I really appreciate this."

"Glad to do it. How long did you say old Fitz'd be over in Italy?"

"It's sort of nebulous at the moment. He's doing this long assignment for *Holiday*. It might be all summer."

"Some assignment. Well, it's nice if you can get it. I'm happy for him. He deserves a break. He's kept us all laughing down here many a night, and I say a guy that can make others laugh deserves to have a few breaks. Don't you agree? Want another beer . . . Hey, I don't even know your name."

"Violet. Yours is Elvira, he told me. No, thanks. I ought to get back."

"He told you, eh? Isn't it a pisser? Named after a great-aunt. What else did he tell you about me?"

"Just that you all were good buddies."

"That we are," she said, looking almost young and shy for a minute. She blew out a long stream of blue smoke. "You tell him Ellie says hi when you write him, okay?"

"I will."

We shook hands. Hers was dry and weary. I suddenly saw

myself twenty years hence, sitting in a bar with long untidy gray hair, counting the days till I could retire to the wilderness and raise dogs when once I had hoped to be a great painter.

"Call old Landsborough," she said, "but watch his hands."

Carol's next letter arrived. Several color prints fell out. One of the happy couple, standing by the pool, the famous Tuscan hills in the background. Carol wore a simple one-piece suit, like a racing suit. There was nothing awful about her body. Her hair was dark and wet. As she was facing into the sun, it was hard to tell about her face. Her teeth were good and white. Her smile seemed very happy. Ambrose looked less of the man about town, possibly because his hair fell down over his forehead and was not parted in its neat F. Scott Fitzgerald way. There was a tiny roll of flesh around the waist. He, too, looked pleased with life. Then there were two pictures of the castle, one taken close up, from in front of the peeling stone walls where they parted for the iron gate, and one from the bottom of the hill, on the other side of the vineyards. The castle was a dark ocher, with faded orange shutters, and looked more like a rambling old country house with a perpendicular wing at either end. In one of the photos were two men in the distance. They were wearing what looked like pajamas made out of mattress ticking. From their demeanor, I guessed they must be servants. Had one of them taken the photo of Ambrose and Carol? In the letter, Carol described the high ceilings, the parqueted floors, and the red-black-and-white mosaic tiles in the bathrooms. And the marble stairs, the old portraits, the flowers in the garden, the stone fireplaces. An eighteenth-century harpsichord with candleholders built on. She wrote that the headboard of their bed had medieval figures carved into the pine, "Some kind of procession, with horses and flags. . . . Ambrose thinks it's the *palio*." She described what the *palio* was ("a local horse race with costumes and religion thrown in—the first one takes place in early July"). She said she and Ambrose were taking Italian lessons and had met a very nice American couple; he was a Fulbright professor whose specialty was the influence of the Italian Renaissance on Germany. ("He's taken a great interest in Ambrose's article, given him all sorts of information he didn't know. . . . Apparently Goethe believed no poet's apprenticeship was complete unless he knew his Italy . . . so Ambrose is deep into *Wilhelm Meister* and then we're all going up to Lago Maggiore because he feels he must get the atmosphere right. I'm hopeful that he'll soon be winding up this assignment and getting back to the novel. . . .")

My own "assignment" was not turning out at all. Every time I looked at my self-portrait, a sick feeling rose up in my chest. It got to the point where I didn't even have to look at it for the idea of it to sap my spirit. One morning I lay in bed, made my resolution, then before I could change my mind rushed over and took a big brush and a jar of gesso and covered it over. There: all white again. I was too divided at the moment, I told myself. How could anyone paint from the wellsprings of the soul with half her vision focused on dwindling cash reserves? For days, the scrap with Landsborough's phone number had bided its time stuck in the corner of Ambrose's mirror. Now I felt its hour had come. I called and a man's rich Scottish burr replied, "Landsborough Productions, Stewart Landsborough here."

I made my pitch (I was so nervous, I had written it out first on a piece of paper) and he said he had nothing to offer an artist at the moment. "My firm does mostly reprints these days. The market for new war books has sadly declined. How is Elvira? Does she still wear her lovely long nut-brown hair to her waist?"

War books? Was he trying to put me on? "I'm afraid it's mostly gray now," I said. No, maybe he was testing me. After all, I might be a policewoman in disguise, trying to get him to reveal his dirty enterprises over the phone. "Look, Mr. Landsborough, couldn't I just come and see you for about ten minutes and show you what I can do?"

"Gray, is it? Has it been that long? I suppose it has. We're all getting on. How do you happen to know Elvira?"

Ah, I was beginning to see. He had to make sure I wasn't a policewoman trying to break his front. "Actually, she and my uncle are good friends."

"And who is your uncle?"

"Ambrose Clay, the writer."

"What has he written?"

"Well, his most popular book so far has been *Looking for the Lora Lee*. It came out a little while ago, actually."

"It sounds familiar. In fact, I think I read it. About a girl on a yacht giving a GI a hard time?" He pronounced it "girrul."

"That's the one! Actually, the girl is based on my mother. She's dead now, of course."

"I'm sorry to hear that." He asked me a few more questions about myself. "You sound like a very enthusiastic young woman. As I say, I've nothing for you, but if you'd care to drop by my office about eleven-thirty next Tuesday, perhaps I can come up with some suggestions after we've talked."

"And you've seen my work."

"Yes, by all means bring your work along." He made it sound naughty and poetic: "*wirr*uk." I felt we understood one another perfectly, without ever having once referred to pornography. Why, social intercourse in this city was turning out to be very much like Charleston. Everything based heavily on nuance and whom you knew. I felt very pleased with the way I'd handled things, and set about to "wirruk" up my porno portfolio for Mr. Landsborough between then and Tuesday.

Sick of my easel's reproaches, I covered Ambrose's dining table with newspapers and got water and inks. Now to think of something dirty. The only pornographic art I had seen was Rowlandson's and Picasso's and Dali's. What exactly *was* pornography? That it was intended to arouse sexual desire I knew, but that depended on whose desire you were trying to arouse. When I was sixteen, I had been throbbingly aroused by a scene in a historical novel when a woman announced to a man she wanted to "give herself to him completely." Whereas it might take more than that for the jaded pervert who went to blue movies every afternoon. What level should I aim for? The thought of hard-core stuff made me sick. It made me hate the thought of my own body and its processes. Maybe something light and witty, a combination of playfulness and eroticism. I set to work, already imagining myself bringing a fresh dimension to the old art. Elvira might be the lady pornographer; I would be the lady-like pornographer.

I shuffled through my own recent erotic experiences. What could I use from them? I tried a quick "comic strip" of Michel's and my ritual—a metal-jointed robot with a single human attribute lying curled like an early spring fern, and then its progressive cultivation by the maiden till it bloomed dangerously and turned to steel and retaliated upon the maiden's tender bud. It was not very good. It was coy—banal, wooden in movement, and lacking any surprise. All it succeeded in doing was making me telephone Michel to invite myself for dinner.

I was much more successful when I left the men out altogether. I did a somber pen-and-ink sketch of a beautiful woman resembling Sheila lying on a bed and calling upon her own body in a roomful of pictures. Then I mixed an orange gold and colored her spread kimono and all her hair. The black-and-white man in the pictures wore a selection of Toulouse-Lautrec capes, Charles Dana Gibson dinner clothes and Bogart trench coats. The placement of that single color made an interesting sort of statement on her activity, I thought.

Then I did a woman with long witchy hair, kneeling arse-up beside her bed, being diddled from behind by a small dog with a chrysanthemum face and a plumy tail. I left everything in grays and inked in the caption: "My doggy's worth a dozen men."

Then, getting into the swing, I did two women in a big brass bed. I took this one more seriously. There was the charged echo of the poignant night with Sheila to guide me toward a truly sensual rendering of what it might be like to give oneself up to the caresses of your own kind. With the use of sepia highlights, I heightened the mirror effect so that they became like reflections of one another. "Narcissa's Lover," I captioned this one. Because of the tilted-forward angle of the bed, it resolved itself into a flat picture plane against which the two rounded figures seemed to hang swaying in their rapturous embrace. It was easily the most moving and lyrical figurative study I'd yet accomplished.

I was amazed to find I had worked uninterruptedly for a whole afternoon on my "porno portfolio" without once thinking self-consciously: I am now painting what will one day be seen as a breakthrough work of the young Violet Clay. For the first time since I left art school, I had painted with such keen absorption that my mouth watered, my cheeks burned and time suspended itself.

When I walked into Landsborough's office on Tuesday, I really admired the thoroughness of his "cover." On the walls hung framed enlistment posters for four American wars. In the showcase featuring Landsborough Productions were paperback books with titles like *An Anthology of Famous War Stories*, *Alexander the Great (for Young Readers)*, *A Boy's Guide to Great Battles* and *The Valorous Years*. Landsborough himself, with his neat black mustache and reconnaissance-sharp blue eyes, looked like a professional military man himself when he emerged from an inner office to greet me—except for the pronounced limp, of course. One leg was shorter than the other.

"How do you do, Miss Clay," he said, giving me a crushing handshake. "I'm afraid my girrul's out sick, so I'm my own receptionist today. Let's go into my room; this front one is just for show."

"So I figured," I said, catching his eye with what I hoped was a knowing look.

He reciprocated with an equally direct look, which then roved stealthily over the rest of me and finally came to rest, respectably, on my leather portfolio. "Come, show me your work," he said, and led me into his inner sanctum. The walls in here were covered with battle scenes. Well, you couldn't be too careful, I guessed.

He sat down beside me on an old plaid sofa. "Now then," he said, taking out a pipe and regarding me while he massaged a spicy-smelling tobacco down into the bowl. "What have you brought me?" He lit up and sat back, waiting to be entertained.

I had a moment of embarrassment and then unzipped my
portfolio, very businesslike, and took out my small sheaf of erot-
ica. "These are just samples," I said. "There are lots more
where these came from." I passed them over to him and concentrated on the family pictures on his office desk. A nice-looking
blond wife with a pained smile, a girl of about fourteen ice-skat-
ing on a pond with a smaller boy. My cheeks felt hot. I hoped
he wouldn't notice and think I was a neophyte at this line of
work. I heard him leaf through the heavy watercolor papers. I
heard him puff, then puff again. Aromatic smoke trailed past my
eyes till they burned. I couldn't bear it anymore. I had to look.

He had the papers stacked neatly on his lap. He was just sitting, puffing on his pipe, studying me with the sharp blue eyes.
"You have very fine draftsmanship, Miss Clay," he said with his
burry r's.

"Thank you."

"And a sense of humor, as well."

"Thank you."

"Remarkable drawings, really, for such a modest young girrul."

"Do you think you might . . . use some of them?" My hopes
rose.

"Use them? These particular . . . er . . . works?"

"Why, yes. I mean, I don't exactly know what level you aim
for in your books. I probably wouldn't work out too well illustrating the hard stuff, but . . . my sort of thing's more a witty,
lyrical eroticism, I think."

"It certainly is," he agreed. "But tell me, Miss Clay, where
do you think I could use your 'sort of thing' in the kind of books
I print? Not in Churchill's boyhood reminiscences, certainly.
Nor in the reissue of *All Quiet on the Western Front* I'm bringing out this fall."

"Well," I coaxed, "how about some of the *other* books on
your fall list?"

"But that *is* my list," he said. "As I told you on the phone,
my market is a sadly declining one."

I thought it was time to lay my cards on the table. "Look, Mr. Landsborough, what about the pornographic books, the ones Elvira did drawings for when she worked for you?"

He looked really abashed. "Elvira? But . . . Elvira did jacket designs for me, when I still had a hard-cover line. What on earth are you talking about? What's this about pornography?"

"Look," I said, "Elvira makes no bones about what she does. I don't see why you should, either. I can promise you I'm not a member of the vice squad or anything. Besides, I thought the Supreme Court had loosened all that up anyway. I simply need a job to bring in a little food money, and later some rent money, and I prefer to work at home so I can paint my more serious stuff at the same time."

"This isn't your serious stuff, then, what I've just seen?" He was beginning to look amused as he sat there watching me and puffing that infernal pipe.

"Of course not. I sat down one afternoon and did these just for you, after Elvira gave me your number. She said she'd once worked for you, and I naturally assumed . . ."

"So Elvira's gone over to the porns, has she?" he mused. "Wonder why? She had such big plans. That's why she left me."

It was becoming clear to me that I had made too big an inductive leap, which had led to this gross mistake. "Oh, God. I feel like such a fool," I said, beginning to shrivel.

"Oh, come, come. No harm done. I think"—he began to chuckle—"it is really very funny." He took another puff, then removed his pipe from his mouth and burst out laughing. "It is hilariously funny! Me a publisher of dirty books! It would certainly solve some of my financial woes; perhaps it's not too late for me to look into the market. Why, what's the matter? Good gracious, Miss Clay—Violet—don't cry. There's nothing to cry about. Please don't. Now please don't. I have absolutely no defenses against a woman's tears." Out came the proverbial handkerchief.

"You must think I'm terrible," I wailed. "Coming in here and showing you these . . ."

"I think they are delightful," he said. "Now wipe your eyes. I'm going to take you to lunch."

"Oh, no, please."

"Why not? A girrul has to eat, doesn't she? I know a nice pub nearby. We'll order ourselves a Guinness, or an ale, whichever you prefer. It's the only place in New York that serves genuine Cornish pasties and Scotch eggs. Come, don't spoil your eyes. You'll need them for your wirruk."

"I don't have any work to speak of."

"We'll put our heads together over lunch and see what we can come up with. I've been in this business over twenty years. I have a few connections in the trade, you know."

"You're very kind," I snuffled.

"You're very nice yourself," he said, putting his hand gently on my knee. Too late, I remembered Elvira's warning.

10

Autumn Realities

If I were doing "The Apprentice Years of Violet Clay" as a cartoon strip, I would signal the end of my Euphoric Era by drawing Stewart Landsborough and me sitting side by side on his plaid sofa, my portfolio on the floor beside us, his hand on my knee. It would prefigure the rest of that summer when Ambrose was in Italy spinning out his honeymoon—and his *Holiday* assignment. And as Ambrose's shape-shifting summer article, "The Writer's Italy," would prove sadly emblematic of his second novel's fate, the second half of my first summer in New York would contain most of the seeds of my nine-year-long Era of Compromise.

Landsborough took me to his favorite pub, where we filled up on British Isles snacks and he introduced me to my first Guinness—first four Guinnesses, to be exact. In the beery haze of our high-backed wooden booth, we exchanged life stories. I shaded mine with Orphan Annie pathos to mute down any overly garish impressions my erotic drawings might have made. He, in his turn, disarmed me by his unself-pitying tale of how he'd got what he called his "gammy leg." At eighteen, he'd come to visit his rich cousins in America—the uncle had made a fortune in chewing gum. During a camping trip in the Rockies, Stewart had contracted polio. The uncle, feeling terribly responsible (and also indebted to God for sparing his own sons), lavished his nephew with the best to be had in physical therapy and settled an immediate legacy on him. "Then the war came. As I couldn't enlist on either side of the pond, I went into journalism. I was rewrite man on the old *Trib*. Then when the regulars came home from overseas, they wanted their old jobs back, so I bought into a pulp syndicate and learned that trade. When the war stories started trickling off the presses, I saw the potential book market—this was already the end of the forties; everybody was beginning to have the blahs. Well, it was high flying while it lasted." He sighed and laid down his pipe. "Now all folks want to read about is sex and their own neuroses. They don't give a damn for high courage anymore; all they want are new ways to indulge themselves." He clamped a hand over mine. "What do you say, my poor wee fatherless sprite?"

"I suppose you're right," I agreed, moved in spite of myself by this epithet.

Arm in arm, like two Dubliners after a pub crawl, we swayed back to the inner office at Landsborough Productions. I wondered if he even had a secretary. His office phone turned out to have a wall plug and the plaid sofa to conceal a bed. Orphan Annie comes to the city and is seduced by Daddy Warbucks, I thought. But somewhere, it didn't count. I was still nobody in this town, nobody knew me, therefore it didn't really count.

"Love affairs," I would explain rather high-mindedly to Jake some years later, after our passion had worn thin and we were beginning to go in for philosophical discussions, "are sometimes a way of exorcising one's own psychic ghosts. At different stages in the psychodrama of your life, you suddenly find you need to go to bed with your father or commit incest with the brother you never had. Or sometimes you need to balance things out by cohabiting with someone who represents Community Values . . . or maybe sheer Eccentricity. Many of our lovers are just projections, externalizations."

"Violet, if they gave a Nobel Prize for whitewashing, you'd get it. I never knew anyone so adept at manipulating the language to call a spade everything but a spade. What 'psychic ghost' do I represent, then?"

"I don't know. Besides, I said *sometimes*. Perhaps you're the exception. Also, maybe some love affairs last longer because each lover keeps changing into the next necessary projection desired by the other. What would *you* call the spade, then?"

"I'd call it promiscuity," he replied ominously, folding his short, muscular arms and looking like a bully.

But whatever epithets I might coin to justify or condemn the caprices of the past nine years, nothing could bring those years back, any more than pinpointing where Ambrose chose wisely or wrongly could raise him from the dead. At some point, for each of us, our summer promises had taken on the autumnal tinge. The decay was unobtrusive at first, just like the slightly tired green on the trees along the Thruway outside the window of my bus. It was too late to see them in their spring glory, as Ambrose had when he'd driven north to the Adirondacks four months earlier. I knew from a recent nature editorial in the *Times* that leaves stopped producing chlorophyll in mid-July. But they would persist in their disguise of being active till the first frost compelled them to admit the game was up. I wondered if—unknown to myself as yet—the game was already up for me.

People talk glibly of selling out. "So-and-so was a writer,

then he went to work in an ad agency. He sold out." "So-and-so
the actress—you know what she's doing now? Hand-cream com-
mercials. She sold out." But looking back on it, I didn't feel I
was selling out when I took the job at Harrow House. Georgia
O'Keeffe had done illustrations for an embroidery company in
Chicago in her mid-twenties. Since I had to earn my living,
wasn't it better to earn it at the drawing board, where, at least,
I would face daily challenges and choices involving line and
color? And illustrating romantic fictions was a step up, I told myself, from line drawings of thigh-reducing exercises and little
bottles of beauty potions.

And, as I've said previously, Williamson, who was art director in those days, had a way of making it all right. That first day
in his office, among the cozy bric-a-brac, he made us each a cup
of Lapsang souchong and we talked first of Landsborough (who
had sent me to his old friend "in the trade") and then of the noble tradition of book illustration. ("Why, people looked forward
to the drawings by Phiz as much as they did to Dickens' next
installment," he proclaimed in his reedy voice, his nervous bony
hand, prehensile when it came to books, curling behind him to
a place on the shelf he knew by heart, plucking out a collector's
edition of *Bleak House* to illustrate his point. . . . "Or take
Doré: when most of us picture Heaven or Hell, we see *his*
Heaven, *his* Hell.") By the time I left his office with my first
assignment, his already cluttered desk was piled high with
books: an 1894 edition of Charles Dana Gibson drawings; a fascinating book-length poem called *Lucile* (Boston: 1881), with
dozens and dozens of high-quality engravings (including those
of an artist listed modestly as T. Cole) of beautiful women sitting
alone at the edge of craggy precipices, or reclining pensively on
Victorian chaise longues while earnest and well-dressed gentle-
men plied their suits, or of isolated houses swathed in overgrown brambles and eerily lit by the moon. I couldn't wait to
get out my paints and add my contribution to "the genre," as
Williamson called it. In fact, looking at my lithographs of "Dark
Angels Fly at Night," he had actually likened my style to that
of Samuel Palmer.

At the time, of course, I did not know that I was turning less green, that the Era of Compromise was subtly setting in. On the contrary, as the summer wore on I was very much under the illusion of my "progress." I was always rushing somewhere now— down to the art store to pick up more illustrator's board, uptown to meet Stewart for a tête-à-tête lunch at that dark little pub, or to Michel's for an evening of fun and games, or to deliver another maiden in distress to Williamson, who would give me tea and praise and write out a voucher for two hundred dollars (in those days) for me to take upstairs to the business office. Then I'd head home with another batch of proofs, or sometimes one of Williamson's own detailed précis, which were little pearls of gothic narrative in themselves, and, on the evenings Landsborough came down to me, I'd often be working when he arrived, my next maiden and her house already sketched in—I liked to hear him clump unevenly up the stairs and find me plying my trade as the sun went down and kiss me and call me his "plucky girrul." I was proud of how well I was surviving in this city that was supposed to be so difficult to survive in. I felt like a woman about town with my busy schedule and double life. When the phone would ring I'd say to Stewart, "I won't answer it; it's just some woman for my uncle," when I knew it was Michel; I'd explain to Michel I had to "work" tonight, when I was seeing Stewart, remembering how Ambrose had used this same old trick on Sheila. A chunk of the old fickle Clay, that was me! Also contributing to my illusion of momentum was the lovely false consolation of the deadline. "How soon can you have this ready, Violet?" Williamson would ask. "I don't want to stint your quality, but would a week from today. . . ?" And I'd get high on my own sense of importance as I blocked out my third . . . fourth . . . fifth maiden in distress. So much of one's self-image depends on feedback. I knew, as I cribbed a Norman façade or a sixteenth-century manor house from Pevsner's useful little book, or stood in front of the mirror sketching my fist against my mouth in an attitude of shocked maidenhood, that uptown Williamson waited for this painting, was perhaps even now thinking of me at work on it. Whereas with my fizzled-out "Self-Portrait," no one had anticipated its completion or imagined its stages of creation.

By August I had grown so accustomed to the unearned accouterments at 200 Waverly that I was slightly miffed when Carol's note arrived announcing their return on such and such a flight at the end of that week.

I went out to Kennedy Airport for the second time, this being admittedly a more festive occasion (I had splurged on a bottle of champagne in their honor, lugging it out on the bus in a Bonwit's shopping bag); it was still in those times when you could stand upstairs on that glass-enclosed balcony and watch people going through customs—before the dope-ring signalers spoiled it for everybody.

I was watching so intently for the first sign of Ambrose and Carol that some moments went by before I realized I had looked upon them, opening their bags for customs, and then looked away, not recognizing them. For one thing, Ambrose had on these light-colored, pointy shoes that some minor official of the Mafiosi might wear; for another, he had grown curly sideburns and put on weight. The two of them were very tanned and had obviously been leading the good life. While Carol was chatting animatedly with the customs official, who appeared to be in a good humor with her, I watched Ambrose. A funny, petulant expression crossed his face. His eyes roved round the customs hall as though contemplating escape. Then he tipped back his head and lazily scanned the upper floor. When he saw me, his expression changed instantly. Up went the hand in a jaunty wave, one cohort to another. Then he touched Carol on the arm and said something and she looked up and they both smiled and waved.

I hurried down to meet them. Ambrose kissed me. "It sure is good to see you again, sport," he said. He'd been drinking on the flight. "Violet darling, at long last," said Carol, embracing me. She smelled of some very good perfume. She wore a well-cut, open-necked black suit that emphasized her tan; even the disciplined threads of white in her neat black French twist seemed svelte accessories to her outfit. I fumbled in my Bonwit bag and presented her with the bottle of warm champagne. "How sweet," she said. "Thank you, Violet. Look, Ambrose, champagne for our homecoming."

"Very nice," he agreed abstractedly, already looking around for a porter.

Carol and I followed behind to the taxi rank.

"Well," I said, "how was Italy? Weren't you a little bit sorry to leave your castle?"

She frowned into the sun, walking crisply along with the awkward champagne bottle, the toes of her long, narrow shoes turning a little outward. "It was a beautiful three months, Violet, I won't deny that, but I'm very glad to get back. To tell you the truth, I started feeling slothful towards the last. I need my work to complete me, to make me feel I've used up the day. Are you like that, too, by any chance?"

"Oh, yes. I feel awful when I don't use my day well."

"You don't know how happy it makes me to hear you say that. I'm sure you and I are going to get along. I loved your letters, by the way, with those darling colored drawings of Ambrose's plants missing him. I think it's good for him to get back, too. New York stimulates people's drive. Italy's a bit too full of pasta and all that *dolce vita* procrastination for my stern Yankee tastes."

Did I detect the beginnings of sourness in those efficient Northern vowels, the first decibel of bridal disillusion in the astringent tone?

I had brought Ambrose's latest mail out to the airport and he sat in front with the driver reading it while Carol and I sat in the back and I built my initial impression as the hard-at-work ingénue struggling toward a place in the sun.

"And you're able to do a cover a week?" said Carol approvingly.

"I think I'll probably be able to do two, when my work catches on. I've just seen the proof of my first painting. It really looks great, even with the four-color process."

"Now, Violet, does your painting get photographed and then separated for engraving, or—"

"Why, that ninny!" Ambrose burst out. "That thickheaded, uncomprehending boob!"

"Darling, what?" cried Carol.

"Contemptible flunky!"

"Who, Ambrose, who?"

"The mercantile mentality of these people overwhelms me. . . ."

"*Whose* mercantile mentality?"

"That goddamned Rosen, over at *Holiday*. He won't grant me my extension. 'The boss says no.' Don't they ever run out of bosses when they're too lily-livered to answer themselves? It seems my article has to make the issue with all the Italian wine ads, or else forget it. As if it has a goddamned thing to do with wine!"

"Well, don't you still have at least a week on your old extension?" asked Carol.

"That's not sufficient. Hell, I could have shaped this into something really fine if I'd had that extra month."

"But wouldn't it be better to type up what you've got and hand that in?" persisted Carol.

" 'Hand it in'? Honey, this isn't some inventory report. It's an in-depth essay about the love affair of the greatest writers in the Western world with a country."

"Pardon my mercantile mentality," murmured Carol.

The color rose on the back of Ambrose's neck. Then, slowly, he turned and gave her the appealing look of a naughty boy who expects to be forgiven. "Aw, honey," he said, "let's not give this cretin the satisfaction of spoiling our homecoming. You don't want Violet to think we've started squabbling like old married folks." He winked at me. "Besides, if I break my back, I think I can probably get something to Rosen by the end of the week."

"We'll live at my place, for the present," Carol explained to me. "There's so much room. It's one of those rambling old West Side apartments that a whole family can grow up in without getting in one another's way. *I* grew up in it. Ambrose will no doubt want his studio outside. A man needs to go out to work every morning." Then, in a conciliatory gesture, she reached forward and stroked Ambrose's neck with the back of her nails. "I'm sure you can finish it beautifully by the end of the week," she said. (I was wondering how much longer I could keep the apartment.)

The taxi deposited us at a somber, well-kept building across the street from Central Park. An old doorman rushed out at once, wreathed in smiles. "Welcome home, miss! Or *Mrs.*, I should say now." Carol introduced Ambrose and me, and the old man welcomed us. He bustled us all three along to the elevator and while we were going up Carol told us, "Parks has been here ever since I was a little girl. Apparently I once asked Father if Parks was his father." She giggled, seeming suddenly to shed years in her childhood environs.

We got off at the fifth floor, already in a sort of private foyer, with a large oval mirror and fresh flowers arranged liberally in a Chinese vase on a lacquered table. Carol pressed a bell and the door was thrown open almost at once by a tiny brown woman in a black uniform with white apron, who fastened herself on Carol like an appointed fate and began to weep. Carol also burst into tears and Ambrose and I stood awkwardly by while the two women clung and sobbed and alternately patted each other's backs for several minutes at least. Then Carol straightened up and rather shyly asked Ambrose if he would carry her over the threshold. It seemed a bit ridiculous. I sensed he felt that way, too, but it was done, and once inside, we were introduced to Elena—who had also been with Carol for eons. (She had pressed her thin little lips together and looked the other way disapprovingly while her mistress was being hauled over her own threshold.)

My experience of city apartments had not prepared me for Carol's. To me an apartment was by definition transient, a place where you marked time till home came along. But this was clearly home for Carol. Its rooms spread out in all directions, like a house. Its walls and floors were covered in that layered, solid fashion that bespeaks a long, assured residence and the slow accumulation of things for themselves and not because they "go" with anything else.

Carol parried phone messages from "the factories" and sent away my champagne to be iced, and discussed with Elena which bags were to be unpacked where. "Mr. Clay's things should go in Father's old room, Elena. He'll want his own space to spread out. Also there's a desk in there." She brushed past Ambrose, who was standing at the window, looking down into the late-summer green of Central Park, and murmured playfully in his ear, "If you're good, you won't have to *sleep* in Father's room."

Ambrose laughed shortly. "Much obliged, madam."

"Is this a Gifford?" I asked about the large painting over the beige sofa, a sunset over New York Bay.

"No, it's anonymous," said Carol, coming over beside me. She had kicked off her shoes and she stood flatfootedly, digging her long, dark-stockinged toes into the thick pile of the carpet. She was completely at home in her own territory now. "But a very good anonymous, we always thought. Definitely worthy of the Hudson River School. However, the little woodsy scene over the mantel is an authenticated early Inness. And later I'll show you several rather valuable Dutch interiors in some of the other rooms."

"The Grubers are patrons of the arts," said Ambrose pleasantly, still with his back to us, gazing out the window. Something about the way he stood made me think of a sleek plump panther, testing the view from his new cage.

"*Minor* patrons," corrected Carol. "And now look at me: I've married into a family of artists."

"Who'd better not be minor, if they know what's good for them," quipped Ambrose, with a slight edge in his voice, I thought, although I could not see his face.

I dozed, on and off, until Albany, where we got a change of drivers. The look-alike blond couple got off at Lake George. As I watched them leave the bus with all their gear, clumping down the metal stairs in their thick boots, then squinting purposefully

into the sunshine and shouldering their orange packs, I recalled
that O'Keeffe and Stieglitz had once had a place at Lake George.
I was in her territory. This stimulated me fully awake and I
looked out my window with a painterly eye, trying to see the
landscape as she might have seen it. But these ranges looked too
cool for her, too mythically suggestive, not earthy enough. If I
were painting them, I would feel strongly tempted to do a bit
of anthropomorphic meddling: they looked so much like morose
blue giants lounging torpidly atop the faded noonday green.

When the driver announced, "Plommet Falls, request stop
only," over the intercom, I pulled the cord and hurried forward
and within seconds found myself in the middle of an abandoned
crossroads with a derelict old wooden hotel and a handful of unappetizing storefronts.

I couldn't imagine what had made Ambrose want to stop at
this desolate little junction. Far from being inspiriting, everything seemed dead. When had a guest last entered the Old
Coach Inn, whose porches crumbled and whose chipped Doric
columns all bore large warning notices that this edifice was no
longer safe? At least fifty years had passed since the moth-eaten
raccoon in the taxidermist's window had been a threat to any
camper's stores. Next door was a grocer's, whose window supplies didn't look much fresher. Was this the "country store"
from which Ambrose had made his last happy phone call to me?

There was a single car in sight, parked in a patch of shade
round the side of the old inn. It was a shiny green Gremlin with
a HUNTERS PAY FOR CONSERVATION bumper sticker. At first
I thought a child was playing some game with me, waving and
ducking up and down in the driver's seat. Then the glass was
rolled down and someone sang out, "Yoo hoo! Violet Clay?" I
recognized the odd, rarefied voice of last night's telephone call
and went over. "I'm Minerva Means," said the diminutive lady,
seventy if she was a day, yet somehow giving the impression of
a wizened child peering out at me. She wore a pink cotton pant
suit and a matching grosgrain hair ribbon in her surely dyed
black hair. For this time of day, for any time of day, she was ludi-

crously made up. "Get right in, to the air-conditioning," she said, "out of this terrible heat," already rolling up her glass again. I went around to the passenger's side, thinking how Carol need not have worried about any competition here. The door was locked. She sat behind the wheel, staring straight ahead, a fixed little smile on the wizened face. When I knocked on the window, she gave a nervous start, recalled herself and unlocked my side.

"So sorry," she sang out. "I'm not quite myself today, dear. This has been an awful shock. Is there any room left back there for your bag? Slip it on the floor between the seats. That's right. In addition to everything else, a prisoner has escaped from the big state prison near here—or 'correctional facility,' as they say nowadays—and I've taken to carrying my valuables with me when I leave the house."

Sure enough, on the back seat of the little car were piled several fur coats in their plastic bags, a silver tea service, also under plastic, and a stack of leather boxes stamped with fleurs-de-lis.

"These days, you have to protect yourself," she said in her child-pitched voice. "Nobody else is going to do it for you." She looked me up and down and seemed to approve of what she saw. "Fasten your seat belt, will you, dear—otherwise the buzzer will make a racket."

I did so, and she pressed a dainty foot, clad in a white vinyl ankle boot, upon the accelerator, and off we went at a snail's pace through the desolate little village with its substandard frame houses and ragged lawns sporting various-sized collections of old cars on cinder blocks.

"This is not exactly Beverly Hills," she said. "I wouldn't look, if I were you. It will make you all the more depressed. I wish you could have seen Plommet Falls in its heyday. Now it has become a village of mechanics, and mechanics on welfare, at that. Don't worry, we'll soon be into the part they can never spoil. I'm taking you to Mr. O'Halloran's first."

"I was wondering how my uncle happened to stop in Plommet Falls. Do you know how he happened to pick this particular village?"

"Well, dear, as far as I know, he went to Dean's real estate office down in Schroon Lake. Ever since I had my fiasco with the hippies who burned down my other cabin, I let Mr. Dean handle my rentals. But the moment I spoke to your uncle on the telephone, I felt I wouldn't have to worry. And then he came up to the house and I had no reservations whatsoever. Such a gentleman. It was a pleasure to rent to him—more like having a relative nearby, really. That's why, when this little Indian from the Meditation Ranch in Schroon Lake started pestering me about a fall rental, I made sure Ambrose didn't want to stay on. I drove up to the cabin to ask him. He was sitting outside smoking his pipe, that lovely *relaxed* way of his; I told him I'd just come to find out his plans and if there was any chance of him staying on I wanted to get this little Indian guru off my neck once and for all. He laughed and laughed. Then he insisted on bringing out a chair for me and we sat there enjoying the afternoon and talked about all sorts of things. That's the way he was. Always had all the time in the world for you. He always made me feel so clever and entertaining. Then I said I had to be going and he promised to let me know his plans within the week. Two afternoons later, he stopped by my house. He was walking with the little girl, Cheyenne, the daughter of the neighbor I was telling you about. . . ."

"The little girl who actually found him?"

"Yes. I'm afraid so. Such a terrible thing, her finding him like that. I'm sure he never meant that to happen. But . . . I was thinking last night, lying awake after the troopers had gone . . . who did he imagine would find him? It was pretty certain to be one of us. And Samantha was much nearer; she has to use the road that goes right past the cabin. Oh, dear, I just can't quite take this in yet."

I somehow could. Not the particulars, but the fact. "But you were saying how he came by your house with the little girl."

"Yes. He said he had thought the matter over and though he'd been tempted to stay on a while longer he'd finally decided it would be better to get on with his original plans. He said I could count on having the cabin vacated in a week. 'But I thought you intended to stay till the end of the month,' I said. Then I felt bad because I was afraid I'd rushed him off. I told him that, and he put his arm around me and patted me and said, 'Don't you think any such thing. Once a person's made up his mind to leave, it's better just to go on and do it. My time's up here.' That was a week ago today, when he came to tell me that. I don't know how many times I went over those words last night. Saturday a week ago. And then they walked down my driveway and up the road. The child hung around with him a lot. I just can't think how he could have . . . and yet Samantha was telling me—I saw her this morning—that Cheyenne was acting very stoical about it. But Cheyenne is that way. A very cool child. She keeps her own counsel."

"How old is Cheyenne?"

"Let's see. Eight. No, she was eight when they came here two years ago. She must be ten now, mustn't she?" She gave a high-pitched laugh, sounding not much more than ten herself. "It's just the mother and daughter. Both of them are very reticent about the father and I don't like to pry. My mother always told me if people want you to know something they'll find a way to tell you. People here assume the child is illegitimate. But I like Samantha. Or Sam, as she calls herself. She's an excellent neighbor. I suppose you could call her a liberated woman. She can do carpentry and plumbing, fix anything. You should see what she's done to that old ruin of a hunter's shack her father left her. Yes, in the two years she's been with us, she's made herself quite indispensable around here. She'll bring you a cord of wood in the back of that jeep of hers, she'll repair your gutters, patch your roof. No going on welfare for her. And with an illegitimate child most would. No, Samantha is a good girl. Hard-working. Handsome in her own way, too."

"She sounds worth knowing," I said, already wondering what she and Ambrose might have been to each other.

"Mmm. Now you may look out the window again with pleasure. This is the Plommet Falls that can't be ruined. See? All that on your side is national forest plantation. Isn't it something the way they put in those pines so straight? And on my side you have the old family homes. Some live here all year round, like I do, and others open their houses just for the summer months. Of course, when Mother and Daddy were alive, we lived in Albany in the winter; we'd close up the house as soon as hunting season was over. Daddy was quite a hunter. It was the death of him, I'm sorry to say. Mr. O'Halloran's father buried my father. Mr. O'Halloran himself took care of Mother. But that was much later. She's only been gone fifteen years."

The afternoon sun sailed in and out between the tall needly pines with their long, clean trunks. Minerva Means' beribboned black head barely crested the dashboard as we wound slowly up the steep curved road.

The houses, large old brown-shingled boxes, some with Victorian gable roofs, sat aloofly back from the road, protected by rough stone walls or cloaked in thick foliage, offering the occasional, imagination-provoking glimpse into the summer lives of their inhabitants: a glossy magazine turned face down on a green wicker chair; a man's bathing suit with white drawstring drying on the wooden railing of an upstairs sun deck. I was reminded of Lewis's summer cottage in Flat Rock, how as a new bride I had sat on its deck, trying to imagine the lives of the people down below who slowed their automobiles and peered up through the openings in the trees to get a glimpse of my tan shoulders and yellow sundress.

"Odd, isn't it," Minerva was saying, "how undertakers never seem to *go into* undertaking. They always take over from their fathers. I know you're going to like Mr. O'Halloran. His wife, Sadie—she's quite a bit younger—keeps trying to get me to go to Florida with her. She goes every year. Can't stand the cold weather. I'd like to go. I've never seen the ocean further down than Cape May. But I can't go. I can't leave the house. If I went, I'd just worry about the house all winter."

We turned into a circular shaled driveway. A gleaming black Cadillac was parked in front of the door. The house was square and brown-shingled, like the others I'd seen on the road, with dark-green trim on the windows and door. Only everything was neater here, more visible, the lawn clipped low and smooth, the new lamp fixtures, made to look like old lanterns, a little too shiny. A gothic-lettered sign, O'HALLORAN'S FUNERAL HOME, EST. 1884, hung over the porch.

A bleached-blond lady wearing lots of perfume and a silk print pant suit of turquoise and lavender swirls opened the door. She hugged Minerva, calling her "Minnie Mouse," and very cordially took my hand in hers and offered her condolences. "Dick's changing; he'll be right out," she said. "We had ourselves a few holes of golf, but it was much too hot to play."

"Oh, much," piped Minnie in her high voice. "Sadie, oughtn't I to drive the car round back? I've got the coats and silver and Mother's jewels in there. That escaped convict—did you hear? Everything goes wrong at once, it seems."

"Oh, Minnie, you silly. That was all the way up in Dannemora. You mean to tell me you dragged all that stuff out in this heat?"

"Desperate criminals can get a long way in a short time," said Minerva, her voice wavering a little, like a child who anticipates being balked.

"All right, darling, if it makes you feel better," capitulated the other at once. "You drive it around to the annex. You're looking very pretty today. I love you in that pink. Violet, would you like to freshen up after your long ride? Come, let me show you where to go."

Not one word pertaining to death was mentioned over luncheon, which I was given to understand had been prepared for me, after the long trip. We sat outside, on a flagstone patio under a striped awning, amid the fragrance of roses and the splash of a little fountain, and Mr. O'Halloran, a pink-faced man with curly white sideburns, asked polite questions about my life in the city. "I am fond of New York," he said, "though I haven't been down there in a while." This incited laughter from Mrs. O'Halloran, who explained that by "a while" her husband meant 1949. O'Halloran smiled with good nature and said yes, his wife was the traveler in their family; he himself preferred to stay home and potter about the place. "Though I have," he said to me, "visited Charleston, many years ago. I noticed from his papers that Mr. Clay was born in Charleston. Were you born there, as well?"

As if by prearranged signal, the women rose and began to clear the table. "Minnie, I want to show you the darling beach outfit I bought last week in Albany," said Mrs. O'Halloran, patting her husband's cheek in passing. Off they went, like two girls, leaving us grownups to serious matters.

"I especially loved the grounds of those old churches in Charleston," went on O'Halloran reflectively. "Let's see, isn't it St. Philip's that has the graveyard with the Spanish moss? And the other one, the one whose bells have crossed the Atlantic five times . . . ?"

"St. Michael's," I said. "That's one of my first memories, those bells."

"Lovely place, Charleston. Is there, perhaps, a family plot waiting in one of those historic old churchyards where you will wish to bury your uncle?"

Well, well, I thought. For a diplomatic transition, that gets full marks. "I'm afraid not," I said. "My grandmother got the last space in our family plot." I saw no reason to dispel his romantic illusions by adding it was not in either illustrious churchyard. "I really don't know what the best thing to do is. I don't recall Ambrose ever expressing any wish about such matters."

"In that case, you must be guided by what you think best, then. You are, I believe, the next of kin?"

"Next and last."

"I see. Well, you be thinking about these things. I will, of course, be glad to take care of matters for you, but I should in all fairness inform you that although I'm the coroner here, there are other funeral directors in the vicinity. There are some papers you must sign for me after you've viewed the body, but after that you are free to make your own arrangements."

"Oh, of course I'll stay with you. I wouldn't want to go anywhere else." After that nice lunch, how churlish, besides.

"I thank you for your confidence. We *are* the oldest establishment in Essex County. I'll do my very best for your uncle. Just so you know where we are, the decisions to be made are these," and he ticked them off on his fingers: "How you wish to put the body away. And then where, of course. And thirdly, what kind of burial service you think would be appropriate. What was your uncle's religious preference?"

"Episcopal." As far as I knew, the last time he'd set his foot in church was for my grandmother's funeral.

"The rector down in Schroon Lake is a congenial fellow. We might give him a ring later. You may decide on one of our local cemeteries. Now, do you feel like stepping over to the annex and viewing the body? It's quite all right, nothing to be nervous about."

The "annex" sat discreetly behind a row of Norway spruces. It was a remodeled barn, painted a pale yellow, with the dark-green trim used on the main house. It faced away from the house and had its own parking lot. In a shady area, a young man was hosing down a hearse. The one Ambrose had come in?

"Will it be too cool for you in here?" asked O'Halloran, as we walked down a dark-tiled hallway. The building was air-conditioned, but I was shivering for other reasons.

"No, no, I'm fine."

"He's in here," he said, going first into a dark room and switching on the fluorescent light. A man with a gray beard lay on a trolley, covered up to his chin by a sheet.

I was just about to explain to O'Halloran that he'd made a mistake, but no, it was Ambrose, all right, looking like some saintly ascetic. I'd never seen him with a beard. It completely changed his looks. Elongated the face. Made him look old. All the white, of course. How strange that the beard should be so much whiter than the hair. Except for a discolored area around his right temple and closed eyelid, he looked serenely untouched. There was something about the mouth that looked prim . . . as if he were congratulating himself on some achievement.

"Do . . . dead people often look so . . . pleased to be dead?" I asked O'Halloran, who stood tactfully to one side.

"There *is* a certain repose in many instances," he replied. "It often has nothing to do with the manner of death. An old person who has been ill for a long time, expecting to die, will often have a surprised look, as if he's been caught off guard. And sometimes, when the death has been a violent one, the person will look perfectly calm, as though he'd been carried off gently in his sleep. You recognize your uncle, then?"

"Yes. I didn't know he'd grown a beard."

"Well, when you're ready, I'd like you to step down to my office and sign those papers. Then perhaps we can discuss the other arrangements."

"Why is he . . . I mean, he's naked under that sheet, isn't he? Did he shoot himself naked?"

"No, that's because of the autopsy. He was fully dressed. I have his personal effects for you in the office."

"But why an autopsy?"

"That's standard procedure in a case like this. Just to make sure. Though, based on the contact wounds and other evidence, it's unlikely there'll be anything new to learn. Would you care to be alone with the body for a few minutes?"

"Yes, thank you," I said. As soon as he had closed the door, I whipped out the small sketch pad I always carry in my purse and stood shivering and sketching the remote new contours of my uncle's dead face. I knew if I did not, that my memory would falsify this last impression, would retouch it with some of his old roundness, or else exaggerate the new asceticism. If his face at the moment of death had left me any message, I wanted to have it intact—or at least as best as my combined hand and eye could catch it. My emotions were curiously in abeyance for the time being. I felt only a taut fascination for this mysterious face. It was so remote from the living man I knew that after I had made the sketch, I was able to push back the hair that O'Halloran had combed tactfully forward over the bruised forehead and look calmly at the hole. It didn't look big enough to put an end to forty-nine years of pulsing, dreaming life. His dark hair was surprisingly silky to the touch. The silky hair of the princess, I thought, whose scalp you must get inside, as he told those young writers-to-be at the Pine Hollow School, that long-ago day when he was in his robust prime. Had he any inkling, then, of the dark future he might be creating for himself when he suggested to the little girls they write about something they didn't want to happen, then hurriedly retracted himself?

I gave him one last, long look, knowing that even in his casket I would not see him this way again. Now it was O'Halloran's turn, an artist by his own lights, to prepare these remains for their final appearance as "Ambrose Clay."

11

A Cabin in the Woods

"I'll take you up to the cabin now," said Minerva. We drove up a steep, lonely road with thick pine forest on both sides. "You can look around while it's still daylight. I can leave you there, if you like. You might prefer to pick out his burial clothes on your own. Then whenever you get ready, walk on down to my house and we'll have some supper. You're welcome to stay with me as long as necessary. There's plenty of room. In the old days, when Father was alive, we often had ten or twelve people for the weekend. When we ran out of bedrooms, Mother just put up camp cots on the porches."

"That's really kind of you."

"Oh, it will be nice to have company. My sister is the only company I ever have, and she's so busy she seldom gets up from Albany anymore. She's in real estate. All she ever thinks about is buying and selling property. She's been after me for years to put up more cabins; I've got the acreage for them, she says, as if that's all it takes. But I don't have the temperament for it. I worry too much. I worry whether the tenants have left their stove on or if they're tramping around in their ski boots ruining the wood floors or if they'll come and do their skiing or hunting and then steal all the furniture and leave in the middle of the night. And everything I worry about comes to pass. That's the worst part of it. I told you they already burned one cabin to the ground. I knew it was unwise to rent to hippies, but they were rather sweet, a young couple, and so excited about living in the woods. Also, it's not the easiest thing to find year-round tenants, even when you've put in electricity and plumbing. People don't want anything to do with these steep, icy roads. That's why I guess I must consider myself lucky to have that little Indian guru, though I'd much rather have gone on with your uncle. Oh, dear. This time yesterday, he was still alive. Sam and the child saw him cleaning out his car with a whisk broom. They waved and drove on past because they'd already said goodbye earlier. They thought he was getting a late start. Later, after supper, on an impulse, Sam sent Cheyenne over to ask if he'd like to have some dessert with them. This morning she told me she wished she'd gone herself."

"I'd like to meet Sam. Do you think she'd mind if I talked to her?"

"Of course not, dear. She's sure to have seen a great deal more of him than I did. You'll have plenty of opportunity. The funeral's not till Monday, and then you may have to stay a bit longer to settle the estate. You don't have to be running back to a job, do you?"

"No, I don't have that particular pressure just now," I said. It had been a relief to forget my troubles for several hours, to be caught up in the immediacies of Schroon Lake burial plot prices, the choice of a casket, setting up an appointment with the local rector, telephoning Carol, as promised, to inform her of funeral time and place. The activities surrounding an accomplished death seemed so prescribed and solid next to the great yawning question of my own nebulous future. "I doubt if there'll be much of an estate to settle," I said. "As far as I know, Ambrose was as poor as I am."

"Ah, but there's red tape, no matter if you're penniless," said Minerva. "Forms to be filled out for the Internal Revenue. And there's the car, don't forget. You'll have to have the title transferred, even if you plan to sell it. I don't expect you'll want a car in New York. It's awkward, it being the weekend. The banks and county offices are all closed. Otherwise, you could get a start on matters between now and the funeral." She sighed. "Poor man, couldn't think of everything, I suppose. As it was, he was more considerate than most. If you could have seen the way he had those things laid out on the table: keys, papers, wallet. That businesslike note stuck in the typewriter, signed by his own hand. Now, that's my house, through those cedars, to your right. So you'll know when you walk down again. I could come back for you, I suppose, but I hate to unload all that stuff in the back and then have to load it up again."

"Oh, I don't mind the walk. It's been years since I've been near anything resembling country." I was straining to see as much as I could of the imposing old hunting lodge with its brown gables and massive stone chimneys. It seemed incongruous, this apprehensive little woman with her child's voice and pink ribbons, living all by herself in such a dour forest retreat, like some faded Red Riding Hood, nervously protecting her valuables from thieves.

Up, up we went, the little green Gremlin puttering in second gear, till the paved road ended at the bank of a stream. We turned left and began descending cautiously down a badly rutted dirt road. Blue and purple wildflowers grew in profusion. The stream descended, too, rushing alongside us down its rocky bed. We bumped over a loose-planked wooden bridge and Minerva said, "I must ask Sam if she can't do something to steady this. Every time I drive over it, I feel like I'm going to fall through. Not that I come here all that often."

"This is all yours, then? All these woods, too?"

"Yes, dear. And all the property taxes that go with them. Daphne—that's my older sister, the one in real estate—is always after me to put up cabins or sell. But it's my heritage. I don't want to see it changed. Daphne and I feel differently about these things. She says I'm a sentimentalist. I find her too much of a realist sometimes. You can't buy new memories, I tell her. I'll never understand how she could sell the old house in Albany. Each of us got a house, you see. She sold hers within a week of her possession of the deed: a lovely old stone house, built by one of the first settlers. It had been in the Means family for a hundred and fifty years. She's quite content to live in her modern apartment. She goes out dancing every night and dances into the wee hours, but when morning comes, she's on that telephone making deals. I prefer a more reflective life myself."

I could see her point. The woods, the soft summer afternoon light, were working their charms on me. In such a setting as this, prospects became both exalted and simplified.

Minerva said, "I remember when I took your uncle to show him the cabin. Rather, he took me. We rode in his car. When I first saw him I thought he might be an actor, or some public figure who wanted to get away for a while. I remember he wore an ascot, a silk ascot. There is something about men with ascots, don't you think? I admired him, the way he kept himself up, even when he was here all by himself. That afternoon I was telling you about, when I came to ask about his plans . . . he had finished his work for the day and was sitting outside, dressed so nicely—casual clothes, of course, but as though he cared. I wasn't crazy about that beard he cultivated over the summer, it made him look too old, but that was his business, I guess."

We bumped through a long patch of shade almost as dark as a tunnel and then took a sharp upward curve back into the sun. To the right was a small log cabin with a green roof, set in a clump of dark spruces. An orange lawn chair faced the bend in the road we'd just come round. Wild lilies grew up around the windows and curled against the screens. Parked in the shade of

a pair of old birches was a well-cared-for gray Pontiac, of late sixties vintage.

Minerva pulled up into the grassy clearing and switched off
the ignition. "Well, dear. This is it."

We got out. I couldn't believe the quiet. There wasn't much
breeze, but you could hear it blowing through the lilies. And
there was the rush of water from the stream. I was to look upon
this scene many times, in a variety of moods, but my first impression remains as vivid as ever. It was like suddenly coming
across a beguiling landscape illustration in an old book—the
kind of book Williamson used to keep in his office at Harrow
House—and not knowing without reading the text whether
something marvelous or awful was supposed to happen in that
setting. And somehow being beguiled by its very ambiguity: the
way the light fell at just this time of day in burnt golden patterns
against the rustic timbers—was it sinister, or was it reassuring?
Had the shadows been put there to emphasize the sunshine, or
the other way round? Of course, something bad *had* already
happened here, but the ambiguity seemed to lie in the scene itself, in both the promise and the warning such a spot would always hold out to those who came wanting something of it. It was
as if I were seeing the place in the same light that Ambrose had
first seen it, when his fate had still been forked.

"Was that the chair he sat in?" I asked.

"Yes. It's almost as though—with that chair at just that angle
and his car parked under the tree—he'd only gone in for a minute and was coming right out again."

She unlocked the door and we went in. Bare-looking, but
neat and somehow inviting. If I had come twenty-four hours
ago, what would I have found him doing? Packing the two card-
board boxes that stood beside the large brown suitcase with
peeling travel stickers? Standing with his hands in his pockets,
his back to me, staring out at the dense woods through the small
window above the kitchen sink? (A red plastic mug was turned
face down on the drainboard.) Lying on the old horsehair sofa
next to the wood-burning stove, or on the narrow pallet bed

built into the wall, watching the sun make its rounds one last time? Or perhaps he had sat at the table covered with red oil-cloth, looking out the big window, where you could glimpse the stream running past: sat there, his fingers on the keys of the portable typewriter I remembered from Waverly Place, thinking of what to say in his note. Or had it come to him yet, how he would end the evening? Beside the typewriter was a key ring and the papers for the car.

"It looks much the same as last night," said Minerva. "Only they've taken the note. And you've got the wallet back from Mr. O'Halloran. I saw the things on the table. I didn't see . . . I didn't want to see . . . I didn't come in until after they'd taken him away. But Sam saw. He was just there, on the floor beside the couch. Mr. O'Halloran said he lay down first, to keep from falling."

"I wonder if you'd know. If you fell, I mean."

"Oh, dear, let's hope neither of us will ever know such a thing," said Minerva. "His suits and jackets are in that plaid travel bag hanging on the peg by the curtain. Behind the curtain is the bathroom. It's a comfortable cabin, plain but with the amenities. Sam calls it my 'softy cabin.' Her place is a real show-piece, since she's fixed it up, but they still have an outdoor bath-room. Which is all well and good for two young people living the pioneer life, but you just try and rent a wooden box today without the proper plumbing and electric facilities. I only put that wood stove in for atmosphere, really. Those wall heating units can keep this room warm as toast. But people like the idea of a fire. That's what happened to my other cabin. The hippies tried to make themselves a stove out of an old oil drum, to save on heating bills. If it hadn't been for our excellent firefighting squad, all these woods would have gone up in smoke. Sam put in this stove all by herself, built the chimney and all. She had just the slightest bit of help from the man who delivered it."

"She sounds like quite a girl." I was more and more curious about this paragon woodswoman.

"Oh, I don't know what I ever did without her. I used to

think it was a man that was missing, when a fuse blew out or the pump stopped or there was some carpentry that needed doing. But it wasn't, of course. It was just someone who knew how to do things."

"Where exactly is her cabin?"

"Well, if you follow the stream, it's straight down through those trees, just below the waterfall. If you take the road, it's longer, about a quarter of a mile. It belonged to Sam's father. He was a sea captain. He'd come up here by himself whenever he had time off. He was an odd sort, a hermit in his way. I remember seeing him—that was years ago—going up and down the hill in an old station wagon, fishing tackle hanging out the back, frowning as though he was scared to death somebody might say hello to him. Poor thing's in a nursing home now. It was a strange marriage, from what I gather. He was already in his fifties when Sam was born. She never saw much of him as a child. But she apparently doesn't hold it against him. Families are interesting configurations, don't you think? I've often thought a family is a whole world by itself. Now, would you like me to leave you for a little? So you can look around and maybe get his clothes ready to take down to Mr. O'Halloran's first thing tomorrow? You won't need shoes; I remember that from my own father. Mother, too, but in her case I insisted. 'I can't bear to think of her without anything on her feet,' I told him. 'All her life she complained about her feet being cold.' "

"What time should I come down to your house, then?"

"Whenever you like. I'll go and see what I can find for our supper. Here's the key. Don't forget to lock, will you?"

After she'd gone, I walked around the cabin. Except for the plastic mug on the drainboard, he'd pretty much removed all traces of himself. I sat down on the narrow bed and looked through his wallet which O'Halloran had returned to me. Several dollar bills (not likely for someone starting on a real trip) and the honorable discharge and a Y membership card that expired in 1967, his driver's license and . . . what was this? A printed calling card, in Spanish, advertising that Ambrose V. Clay, an *escritor norteamericano*, was available for English *lecciones individuales o en grupos*. He would also, for a reasonable fee, compose *cartas o documentos en Inglés*. Had he had any customers? I wondered, going through his brown leather suitcase. It was not packed as one packs a suitcase to go somewhere. The underclothes had all been stuffed into a transparent plastic bag; they weren't even folded. Sundry items had been stuffed unceremoniously into the side flaps: pipes, a pair of sunglasses, a new wallet still in its box from a shop in Puerto Vallarta, his passport, some woolen socks, three packets of 9-millimeter ammunition, and a small jewel case containing cuff links and tie clasps. Was that the ammunition a Luger used? And where was the Luger now, that eccentric-looking weapon he had unwrapped from his handkerchief with a special flourish, that long-ago birthday of mine, to exhibit to those solemn little girls?

The boxes had been taped crosswise with masking tape. It was loose. Someone, probably the troopers, had lifted it and looked in, then replaced the tape. As I did now. What had I been hoping for? The manuscript of the long-promised novel, which I could now take back to town, to vindicate him posthumously? Some notes, at least, which would expand on the nature of the bankruptcy already declared in his note to me? I recognized some of the books from his old Waverly Place shelves: the novels of Fitzgerald and Hemingway, the dictionary and the thesaurus, his confirmation Bible. . . . There was also a Spanish grammar and dictionary and a history of the Normandy invasion, it looked like. And below these, a couple of copies of *Looking for the Lora Lee*, which had been out of print now for years. He had kept several dozen copies on his shelf at Waverly Place. Where were they all now? Had he given them away? Besides the books, there was a framed photograph of my grandmother wearing a soft pleated dress from the twenties, with her dark hair crimped in the style of that day—I remembered that picture also from Waverly Place; and the black box with his war medals; and the inscribed photo from Ava Gardner. I knew that, too.

At the bottom of the second box were two 100-sheet packages of Corrasable Bond, one package still unbroken. Not many sheets had been used from the broken package, as far as I could tell.

I went into the little bathroom behind the curtain. An old-fashioned toilet with the tank high up on the wall; a tub on legs, painted dark green on the outside. Everything clean, not even a hair in the sink. A can of Ajax on the floor. I had to stand on tiptoe to look at myself in the dime-store mirror that had been nailed above the sink. The dense foliage pressing through the tiny screened window gave my face a greenish tinge. I imagined myself living here, week after week, seeing no one. Would my voice turn to a croak? Would I see visions? Would I wake up one day, scrub out the sink and tub, cram all my belongings into the smallest space possible, take one last look at the sun wheeling through the green world and then, with relief, lie down and extinguish my own flickering lights?

Perhaps, replied my face, suddenly spooky in the greenish shadows. *Perhaps if you were a little older than you are now, you would. If you'd looked into the mirror a few more thousand times, and each time said: You haven't become what you wanted to be and each day now only diminishes your chances and increases the mockery of the comparison.*

I remembered the look Ambrose's face had given him from the mirror, that time when I sat on his bed, reading the passage about charm. Nine years ago. He'd just turned forty then. In seven years I would be forty.

To get away from such thoughts, I turned with something almost like enthusiasm to the task of selecting Ambrose's funeral clothes. The first thing my eyes lighted on when I unzipped the plaid clothes bag was the famous hound's-tooth jacket. I took it out and ran my fingers along the durable wool, hearing an impossibly naïve younger self say brightly in the lobby of the Martha Washington Hotel, "I've always loved that jacket. It connects me to the past." "Maybe that's why I like it, too," he'd bounced back. And all those girls watching us as if we were in a movie, when we floated out into the spring dusk.

Could you bury someone in a wool jacket in August?

I heard a car approaching. Thinking it might be the wonder woman Sam, whom I very much wanted to meet, I hurried to the door. The car stopped. I poked my face out the screen door. A prim young man with a round butterscotch face got out of a bright-yellow Volkswagen. He wore crisp khaki shorts and his legs were curiously hairless. Across the grass he tripped, in precise little steps, in his white leather tennis shoes with three blue stripes.

"Hello," I said.

"Hello. Is Mr. Clay here?"

"I'm afraid not."

"Oh! I am sorry I couldn't get here last night. Something important came up. When do you expect him back, please?" He had some kind of accent.

"Well, to tell the truth, I don't."

"He has already left? But I see his car is still here. Are you perhaps . . . er . . . ?"

"I'm Violet Clay, his niece. And you? Are you a friend of his?"

"I'm sorry, no. I have only met Mr. Clay once. I came on Thursday, to measure the cabin and learn how to operate the stove. But he said it was not convenient. He asked me to come back. We made a date for yesterday at seven, but I was detained in Schroon Lake. Is it all right to come now?"

"Well . . . yes, I guess it is. You must be the new tenant."

"That is right. Conrad Chakravorti." He held out a plump hairless hand.

"Did you say he asked you to come back last night at seven?"

I must have looked odd, or threatening or something, because he went into a long apology about some mixup down at his meditation center . . . a speaker had arrived unexpectedly, a day early. "I really do apologize. I have inconvenienced Mr. Clay?"

"Well, I'm not sure. No, probably not." A new idea had dawned on me, very much in keeping with Ambrose's style. He knew someone had to find him, and since someone did, why not a perfect stranger? Why not set up a time for the stranger to return, find what he had to find, and efficiently notify the proper authorities? This young man looked very efficient. Even at this moment, he was withdrawing a shiny metal tape measure from his pocket. On the other hand, I thought, if he had come last night when he was supposed to, maybe he would have arrived in time to avert the suicide.

"Is there something wrong?" he asked, sensitive to my scrutiny of him.

"Well, sort of," I said, "but there's no reason why you shouldn't measure whatever you need to measure. I'm afraid I can't help you with the stove. Miss Means will have to show you how that works. I understand it's pretty warm without it, though." I held the screen door for him. He edged diffidently past me, already eyeing the place possessively. It suddenly hit me that I resented his being here and I didn't want him to live in Ambrose's cabin. I wanted to live here myself. I saw him looking at Ambrose's things in the open suitcase. "Mr. Clay killed himself last night," I told him.

He flinched. "Here? In this place?" The plump brown fingers closed tightly around the tape measure.

"Yes. He shot himself, about the time you were supposed to come. I'm not saying you could have saved him, but anyway, I thought you ought to know. Since you're going to live here. You're not superstitious or anything like that, are you?"

"Oh, no. No . . ." He looked up at the rafters as though he expected something might be getting ready to jump down on him. "It's a nice place. I need a place when the Meditation Ranch closes in September. I am very sorry about your uncle, of course. It is very sad for a man to take his life. Perhaps he was ill?"

"Perhaps. I don't think so. Go ahead and measure. I'm just getting some things for his burial." I shook out a blue oxford-cloth shirt. "It's not too wrinkled, is it? I mean, he'll have the coat on over it. And a tie."

He opened his lips to say something, then closed them. "I

have come at an unseemly time. Perhaps I should come back later, after you've had a chance to remove his effects."

"Well, it might make *you* more comfortable," I said. "Why don't you come back next week sometime? Late next week. That way, the funeral will be over, and if the troopers need to come up and look around some more, you wouldn't have to talk to them. Though to keep things clear—for yourself, I mean—I really think you ought to let them know about your appointment with my uncle last night."

12

In Mother's Room

After Conrad Chakravorti drove off, I felt a little ashamed of myself. But not much. After all, I reasoned, something had come over me and I had simply obeyed its demand. And why *should* he ease right into the space of a dead man without any difficulties? I had done him a service, in a way, telling him straight out. He was bound to hear it in trickles anyway. And even if he did decide to live here, he would feel some psychic quiverings sooner or later. After all, meditation was his line of work. No, better to know what he was in for before he committed himself to the cabin. However, I doubted he'd be rushing down to report to the troopers about his unkept appointment with Ambrose. Why ask for trouble? I was pretty sure he had alien status.

I locked up the cabin. Already I had second thoughts about my "impulse." Now that Chakravorti had gone, I began to think maybe whatever had come over me hadn't been a genuine desire to live here myself so much as it might have been a desire to keep a stranger from meddling with the atmosphere until I could finish drawing from it whatever messages Ambrose's living and dying here had left behind. Frankly, I wasn't sure I had it in me to live in a place like this all by myself for very long. How would I deal with so much unstructured time? Could I make anything more of it in the woods than I had in town? And what if I couldn't? What excuses would be left me? For years, I'd had one or another escape clause to put between me and my . . . what? Sloth? Faintheartedness? Self-indulgence? Fear of failure? There'd always been either a man or a job to blame for keeping the precious energies dissipated.

Ambrose may well have found himself in this predicament.

Before I started the trek down to Minerva's, I went and sat in the Pontiac for a few minutes. It was very tidy, not even any of the dust you always see on people's dashboards. But then, according to Minerva, who'd had it from Sam, he'd cleaned it out with a whisk broom yesterday. For whom? For me? Or for the same reason that my grandmother used to keep her drawers in order? ("If I die, I don't want people going through my underwear and things and casting aspersions on my personal habits.")

He had neglected a few pine needles on the floor of the driver's side. The sight of them brought home to me, more than anything else, how recently he had been alive. So this was now my car. My license had expired almost as many years ago as this car was old. It had been Lewis who made me learn to drive. He couldn't believe that a twenty-two-year-old American woman had never bothered to learn to drive. "Somebody may not always be there to pick you up and take you where you want to go," he'd said.

The time Ambrose had come to speak at our school, Pequeña Bombal and I had followed him out into the waning afternoon to see him off. All by itself in the school parking lot crouched a sleek foreign car with a snarling animal's head on the hood and plush red bucket seats. I almost burst with pride. "Is that *yours*?" I asked.

"No, actually it belongs to a good friend of mine," he said, "but when I want it, it's usually at my disposal. It's impractical to keep a car in New York City."

"Oh! May we *seet* in it?" cried Pequeña, jumping up and down—overdoing the *jeune fille* enthusiasm even for an eight-year-old, I remember thinking at the time.

"Well, sure," said Ambrose, smiling at her. "You two go ahead and both sit in it for a minute if you like."

She made a beeline for the driver's side and I rather sourly climbed into the passenger's seat. While she was pulling and pushing various knobs, comparing the dashboard setup to her father's Mercedes, Ambrose looking in on us benevolently, I spotted a light-green angora cardigan with pearl buttons balled up carelessly in a heap on the shelf behind the seats. I couldn't have been more shocked if I had suddenly turned around and seen a soft green snake curled there. Pequeña chattered on, animated by all the attention she was getting.

That night after lights out, her accented voice speculated playfully through the darkness, "Your Uncle Ambrose, what do you bet he has a meestress?"

"What makes you think that?" Had she seen the sweater?

"Because my father has one. It is all right. He is a widower. All men who are successful have them. It is the way of the world. You know what else I bet?"

"What?" I did and didn't want to know.

"I bet he and his meestress are spending the night together in a motel right now."

"You don't know anything," I said, thinking of the soft green sweater tossed carelessly down. Where had she waited for him, then? In town? It somehow spoiled the whole day, such a thought. What exactly was a 'meestress'?

I left the car and started walking back down the road toward Minerva's. It would be nice to have somebody fix supper for me. It was lovely to be in the open air, in the woods, in the warm sunshine of late afternoon. I felt surprisingly alert, considering I hadn't gone to bed at Milo's till after two, not to mention the drunken binge before. My angle of vision had shifted within these last hours to make me see how narrowly I had been living my life, if you could call it living. Was that me, yesterday at this time, juicing up on Stolichnaya, in that shadowy apartment? How depressing!

I stood on the rickety wooden bridge and looked down at the stream hurrying over the flat, oddly shaped rocks. I saw white cutouts beneath a thin wash of viridian green: Arp-like geometry, with a touch of Ryder's romanticism to soften the hard edges. As a painter, I had never, for any period of time, submerged myself in nature. If I did do so, which way would I go? Would she overwhelm me into making slavish replicas of her creations? Or would her creations offer themselves as guides toward my own inner shapes? The latter, I hoped, but how could I know till I tried?

I was just turning into the paved road that led down to Minerva's when a large white jeep came roaring uphill. It slowed at the last minute before the road dead-ended at the stream, and the driver, a deeply tanned woman with long braids of an uncanny silver color, executed a hairpin turn to the left with the ease of one who drove this route regularly. Beside her was a young girl with an aureole of pale fuzzy hair and wide, curious eyes. She turned round in her seat to look at me as the jeep bumped off, down the rutty road up which I'd just walked. The driver herself had afforded me only the briefest of glances.

My uncle's neighbors? Undoubtedly. How many handsome women with girl children would be likely to drive down this particular road with the reckless expertise of habit? Besides, Minerva had mentioned the jeep and the handsomeness. The woman who chopped wood and brought it to her customers, patched roofs, fixed gutters: who was she? My curiosity was all the more piqued from having seen her. What had Ambrose had to do with her? If I knew him, he'd had a try at something. Had she responded? If so, how did she feel today? Her face had shown nothing, but why should it? For all she knew, I was just a weekend hiker, wandering the woodsy roads.

Fantasizing on the many possibilities that might lead a

young, attractive woman to live in a remote spot such as this, bringing up a child in a cabin in the Adirondacks, I ambled through the remainder of sun and shade, admiring the little blue daisies and goldenrod that shot up in such profusion. I remembered my old violets-and-burdocks painting and wondered if Mr. Green was still alive, still gallery-sitting for his son on odd days, or whether both the old man and the gallery had gone the way of my lost nine years. That little painting—where was it? Stashed away with my other apprentice works somewhere in the cramped studio from which so many damsels in distress had been eked—questionably—into life, fleeing over and over again on twinkletoe sandals away from their future homes into a cobalt-blue night I could mix in my sleep. I had never sent to Lewis for the larger paintings left behind in his basement. By now his new wife, the mother of his twins, had no doubt discovered them and dispatched them where? To the annual school or church bazaar? (In an aside to a close woman friend, as she set them up against a box hedge: "Lewis's first wife, you know, fancied herself a painter. She went off to New York to make her name, though nothing has been heard from her since. There was one I obviously couldn't bring: a nude of Lewis, smoking his pipe. He was so skinny in those days! I had to cut it out of the stretchers with the boning knife, so it would go in the garbage can. I saved the wood, which was still perfectly good.")

Minerva's lodge had a certain brooding aspect that, had I not been fired yesterday by Doris Kolb, might have prompted me to whip out my sketch pad and jot its lineaments for a future cover. It had the gothic gloomy grandeur, all right. The weathered brown shingles. The gabled windows. The giant stone chimneys. But more important: the air of desolation about it, the ghosts of better days hovering in the flower beds gone to weed, the stone deer with a broken antler standing proud and neglected on the patchy lawn, the rustic porch furniture that looked as if it had stayed outside for many seasons of rain and snow and had long ago given up any hopes of ever being sat upon again. There was a queer little stained-glass window to the right side of the door, with a red rose enclosed in a yellow circle, inside a pine tree which dwarfed all but the edges of a blue sky. I pushed the bell but heard no ring, so knocked lightly on the colored window. Through it I watched Minerva emerge, as if from under water, a small timid shape, now in blue, with a touch of matching blue in her black hair. Various locks and chains were undone after she had called through the door to make sure it was me.

"Come right in, dear. I've already brought in your bag. My, you were up at the cabin quite a while, weren't you?" She was wearing some kind of wispy at-home wrapper, vaguely Oriental-looking, white dogwood print against a sky-blue background. The white vinyl boots had been exchanged for black ballet slippers. In the soft brownish interior light of the lodge, she seemed eerily younger, a diminutive eternal maiden, hermetically sealed behind the four walls of her parents' old summer retreat.

"You had a telephone call," she said. "A man from the BCI called, from their headquarters up in Saranac. About your uncle. Routine, he said. I told him he could reach you later tonight. *One* good thing. He told me that runaway prisoner had been apprehended. So we won't have to worry about him tonight."

Nevertheless, she rebolted the bolt and checked the lock and replaced the chain. I handed over the key to the cabin and decided I might as well tell her about Conrad Chakravorti at once.

"Well," she piped in her ethereal voice, "I suppose he had to know. It had crossed my mind that such a thing might put a potential tenant off. And those Indians believe in reincarnation, don't they." We stood in the vast, high-raftered room, from whose dark walls a large assortment of stuffed creatures gazed down at us out of stoic, glassy eyes. She gave a resigned little sigh. "I can always resort to Mr. Dean's real estate office again," she said. "He may be able to come up with someone for the winter if Mr. Chakravorti begs off. After all, he did find me your uncle, Mr. Dean did. And looking on the bright side, all those curry dishes he'd probably cook would stay in the walls for years and put off the desirable summer people."

"I was thinking," I said, "of taking some time off and devoting myself totally to my painting. So if by any chance the cabin does become available, I might be interested."

"Would you? In spite of everything? Though . . . why shouldn't you? After all, I live in this house where my own mother died. She's still here, in a sense. Her ashes, I mean. It's a very solid little cabin. And I showed you the units, didn't I? On the really cold nights you might want the stove, just to provide that extra bit of coziness. More of a security than a necessity. I shall certainly keep you in mind, dear, if Mr. Chakravorti falls through. Though if he still wants it, I suppose I must honor my word. That's only fair."

"Of course," I agreed, deciding to leave it at that. Not commit myself yet. See what would happen. I looked round the big brownish room, furnished in the strangest mixture of fussy antique and stark rustic: a rose-petaled Tiffany lamp hanging from the rough-hewn crossbeams; a collection of old fans in a glass case guarded by a stuffed white owl with outspread wings who looked as if he might take off any minute from his wall perch. There were several hulking cupboards made entirely of varnished twigs and displaying both porcelain figures and guns. But from whatever angle you happened to look up, some large bird or animal head looked back down. There was a wall coatrack, made of one long row of upturned deer hoofs.

Minerva surveyed the animals possessively, with a certain tenderness. "Father was an avid hunter," she said. "He wasn't just a careless killer, like some are today. He liked to say he'd had an *encounter* with each of these animals. When he prepared for the hunt, he would begin thinking about the animal he was going after . . . that white-tailed buck, for instance . . . or the wolverine there. Or even"—she daintily toed a frowzy bear rug with her ballet slipper—"old Blackie here. Poor Blackie, the moths have been at you again this summer. He would concentrate, Father would, until he could feel the movements of the animal's mind. It was almost like a love affair between them, right to the end, he said."

"Fascinating place," I murmured. It was. Mother's ashes and Father's stuffed soul mates, and this childlike old woman in her glad rags and matching hair ribbons, living out her days in a sepia wash of family history.

"Thank you, dear. I wish you could have seen it in its heyday. I try to keep things as they were, but I lack my mother's touch. She was an artist when it came to her own homes. If she put the simplest meal on the table or arranged a few flowers in a vase, it became a creative act. They say these talents always skip a generation. My sister Daphne can't boil an egg properly, and it's certainly so in my case."

Which proved to be true. We presently sat down in the waning summer light and dined, in the company of the best linen, china and hefty old silver, upon a meat and squash casserole still partially frozen at the center.

"Oh, dear," said Minerva. "I think maybe I ought to have left this in a little longer."

"It's very tasty," I said, sipping some water from a cut-glass goblet.

"That's kind of you. What I do is, I make up a dozen or so at a time. Then I don't have to bother to think of what I'm going to eat every night. If I had thought of it, I would have asked Sam for one of her lettuces, from her garden. We could have had a salad."

"This is fine. I think I saw Sam. Very tanned, with silver-looking braids, driving a white jeep?"

"That's her. Still so young to have gone completely gray. You wonder she doesn't color it a little." Her small hand went instinctively to her own jet-black coiffure. "But anything of that sort would probably be against her principles."

"What are her principles?"

"Oh, she hasn't enumerated them for me, or anything like that. She's not a great talker. Takes after her father, I guess. She talks more than he ever did, of course, but that's not saying much. And she's in a different position than he was; she has to earn her living from the people here. When I said her princi- ples, I mean only what I've observed about her. We've had min- imal social contact. When she arrived, I invited them down for supper as a neighborly gesture. She never invited me back. But she was quite nice that time. She asked all sorts of questions about the area. They'd been living down in Florida, with the father . . . Sam's father, I mean; she's been close-mouthed as a clam about the child's father. I suspect they may not have been married. I didn't even know what she was doing for a living till the Newkirk sisters over on Witch Tree Road told me they'd an- swered a general handywork ad in the *Plommet Falls Penny- saver*, for someone to trim their trees, and even when they talked to her on the phone they thought she meant her *husband* was coming. When she showed up, they didn't feel they could discriminate on the basis of sex. It was a matter of principle with them. And then when she did such a good job, they asked her if she could do carpentry work and she built them the cleverest little house for their outdoor cats, with insulated walls and sepa- rate little sleeping berths and a swinging door so that they could go in and out. Since then, she's had all the work she can handle. Word gets around. Especially if the Newkirk sisters have any- thing to say."

"I wonder where she learned to do all those things."

"Out west somewhere, she told the Newkirk sisters. She and some people renovated an old farm. Probably some type of com- mune. Though she isn't your typical hippie. Nor your typical feminist, either. The only time she's ever made any sort of fuss like that was when the principal at Cheyenne's school wouldn't let her take beginner's shop. Sam went to the president of the school board—she'd just done a big shingling job on his barn —and convinced him that a little girl living in a cabin in the woods needed to know how to use a hammer and saw more than she needed to learn to cross-stitch tea towels. Now Cheyenne's made herself a little dressing table for her room, and when she was down here with your poor uncle the other day, when he

walked down to say he wouldn't be keeping the cabin, she told
me four of her friends were signing up for shop this fall. I just
hope what happened last night, and her finding him like that,
won't mark her in any way. Though Sam said she seemed to be
taking it very well. But Cheyenne has always been a cool little
thing. Would you like a cup of Sanka? It's only instant. I don't
keep coffee for myself or I'd never get to sleep."

"I'd love some Sanka."

We rose together in the thickening gloom and I helped her
clear away our few dishes. Minerva was obviously not a person
to turn on a lamp till she fell flat on her face in the dark. In the
murky, none-too-clean kitchen, she put on water to boil and got
out two exquisite cups and saucers.

"What a brave girl you must be. Do you live all alone in New
York?"

I told her I did, which was now true.

"And you're an artist?" Her face tipped up to me, and in the
semidarkness I could see how she had looked at my age.

"Mostly an illustrator, these past few years."

"That must be exciting. My sister Daphne lived in New York
for a while when she was trying to become an actress. I went
down to stay once. I was going to take voice lessons. But I got
sick and had to come home."

"Oh, too bad."

"I'm not sorry. I saved myself a lot of time and disappointment. And I've enjoyed what little gift I have. When Mother
and Father gave their entertainments, I would do a bit of Schu-
bert, or the aria from *Gianni Schicchi*. The response was always
rather gratifying, if I do say so myself. And when Mother was
ill, during her last years, I am so grateful I was able to give her
pleasure. I often sang her to sleep."

We returned to the table and sat sipping our muddy night-
caps from fine china. The last bit of greenish light was fast disap-
pearing in the sky outside.

"Wasn't it . . . about this time last evening?" I asked. "You
know, that he . . ."

"Yes, dear, about now. But it doesn't do any good for us to dwell on it." She cocked her head shyly. "Would you like me to give you a little song or two? It's all I have to offer in place of dessert."

"I can't think of anything I'd like more," I said, disarmed.

"Let me see. I don't think I'd better try any of the arias. I haven't practiced in quite some time. Shall I sing a few of Mother's favorites?"

"By all means."

She took a last gulp of Sanka and sat up very straight and stationed her hands, singer style, in her lap. Her pale face, which seemed to float in the preternatural greenish light, took on a rapt expression. With the voice of a young angel, she began to sing:

My Mother and Father are deep in the grave
And I've given to the poor what they told me to save . . .

After I got over the shock of that pure and beautiful voice welling out of this fusty old brown room, I listened to the story the song told. It was real bathos. Lovelessness, poverty and despair. Doubled and tripled, verse by verse. Yet when death rescues our poor heroine, who despite all, never loses her virtue, I felt a lump in my throat. I was on familiar emotional ground.

After that came one about a little matchgirl named Dot.

Sobbing, shivering with the cold,
All her matches yet unsold;
Visions of a cheerless garret,
Cruel blows not soon forgot . . .

and the refrain:

"Oh, I'm only little Dot."

Whether Minerva was a born performer wasted away in these woods or whether she simply happened to identify passionately with victimized young girls, I found myself extremely moved. The back of my neck tingled and there was such a fairy-tale atmosphere in the room that I half expected to see the heavy-antlered deer and the fierce white owl and the moth-eaten bear begin to weep in concert, real tears rolling from their round glass eyes.

After that came "Mary of the Wild Moor," who returned home one wild wintry night with her fatherless child:

> "Father, oh, pray let me in,
> Take pity on me, I implore . . ."

But the wind is howling so loudly her father hears nothing.

> Oh, how must he have felt
> When he came to the door in the morn;
> There he found Mary dead, and the child
> Fondly clasped in its dead mother's arms,
> While in frenzy he tore his gray hairs . . .

This one almost did me in. The father part, I think, combined with Minerva's sweetly plaintive rendering. Sobbing waifs and life's cruel blows: Minerva's mother seemed to have had a sweet tooth for all the ingredients that made up what Jake used to call my "Poor Little Me jags."

There was then one that made me think of my own mother. Sung from the point of view of a policeman:

> Many a young girl I have saved
> From a dark and watery grave
> While walking the streets
>   At night on the job . . .

If he had been patrolling the East Battery that spring night in 1943, where would I be now? Would I like it any better than where I was?

At my urging, she sang an encore, "The Pardon Came Too Late," which showed that men could have problems, too. It had an irresistible melodramatic refrain, which we ended up singing together:

> A tear, a sigh; alas, goodbye!
> The pardon came too late.

At about the ninth refrain, we both started to giggle. I felt we were the same age. Then the phone rang, and Minerva stumbled through the darkness, feeling for the light switch. It was the inspector from the BCI, making his routine inquiries about what might have caused Ambrose to take his own life. A few minutes of his "routine" questions (he sounded as though he was reading them off a prepared sheet) and the spell of the evening was broken. With my help, Ambrose was being turned into a statistic. The inspector used the phrase "pretty clear-cut" several times, and said he had hoped to get over personally, but there'd been a double shooting in Saranac, two CB-ers arguing over their radios, now both in critical condition. I could tell from his voice he thought the CB case was more interesting than Ambrose's suicide.

I asked him what had been done with my uncle's Luger. "It was kind of special—he got it on Normandy Beach. I'd like to have it back."

"Highly unlikely you'll get it," he said. "The troopers usually destroy the weapon in a case like this."

"Even if it was a family memento? You mean they won't return his property to me?"

I heard him sigh. Probably dying to get this over with. "Maybe if they took out the firing mechanism," he said. "Tell you what. Why don't you give Lieutenant Quentin a call? He was on the case. Better yet, stop by state police headquarters at Schroon Lake and see him. Big redheaded guy. Very amenable to the ladies, so I understand. Well, Miss Clay, I'm sorry about this. I've investigated a lot of suicides in my time. Fact is, it's rougher on the survivors. There was a man in Keene Valley not long ago. Shot himself because his trucker's license hadn't been renewed. His widow said to me, 'It's like someone asking you a question and then not staying around to hear the answer.' "

"We'll track Lieutenant Quentin down tomorrow," said Minerva. "And if he's not on duty Sunday then we'll get him Monday, before the funeral. It's the nice young trooper who was

here last night. I love their outfits. They remind me of Canadian
Mounties. Of course you should have the gun back if you want
it." She waved her small hand at one of the hulking cupboards
made of twigs. "I have all of Father's firearms. Not that I'd know
the first thing about loading a single one of them. Now I think
we ought to turn in. It's been quite a day. Come let me show
you where I've put your bag. You're in Mother's room."

She led me down the hall from the big room. When I'd visited the bathroom earlier, marveling over the wooden toilet tank
with the tiny gold knob you pushed down to flush, I had peeked
into a half-opened bedroom door and wondered who would
sleep among so much white organdy.

"This is my room," she said, seeing me slow down as we
passed it. "Would you like to see it?"

We went in and she switched on a ruffly lamp. It was a veri-
table virgin's bower, white flounces everywhere, on window curtains, dust ruffles, the canopy over the bed; even the princess
telephone and the portable TV were white. Framed over the old
brick fireplace (also painted white) was a reproduction of Lawrence's "Pinkie," flanked by assorted family pictures. A wistful
adolescent frozen forever in a brown vignette peered out of an
oval frame. Minerva's hair was not so dark then; she had worn
it bobbed just below the ear lobes, with bangs.

"It's a very feminine room," I said. "It must be fun to sleep
under a canopy. It must feel so secure. Hey, wait—here's one
of my covers." Stacked on the lower shelf of Minerva's cane bed-
side table were at least fifty dog-eared gothics, with *Conspiracy
at Thorncroft* right on top. I picked it up. "Not one of my best,"
I felt compelled to admit. Though there was no use admitting
the rest of the shameful truth: how the house the girl was stumbling away from in her too tight gown had been copied from the
Penguin cover of *The Woman in White*. At the time, I think I
had been in a hurry to go away with Jake for the weekend
somewhere.

Minerva was bowled over. "But . . . I've just finished this!
You mean you . . . ? What a coincidence. To think I lay in this

very bed . . . I often look back at the girl as I read. I feel closer
to the character if I have a clear impression of her looks. I particularly enjoyed this book. My goodness! I wonder if . . . would
you mind autographing it, just inside the cover? Yes, here are
your initials, at the base of that old tree! 'V.C.' Well, I declare!"
    Feeling a bit ridiculous, I signed: "To Minerva Means, with
many thanks for the hospitality of her house. Violet Clay."
Across from my signature the blurb read: "Years ago they had
robbed her of her wedding. Now they were trying to arrange her
funeral."
    "I shall treasure this," she said. "You are the first real artist
I have ever known personally."
    "Now that I think of it," I said, "you are the first reader of
these books I've ever met personally."
    "Come, you must be tired," she said, with a touch of new re-
spect. We proceeded on to the room at the end of the hall. I
existed now as an artist for her. Yet if I had told her I had a one-
woman show currently running at Knoedler's or the Tibor De
Nagy, she would have been unimpressed.
    Mother's room was as ponderous and red as daughter's had
been flouncy and white. It was more of a Victoriana museum
than a bedroom, with the heavy red draperies and velour-pat-
terned wallpaper and velvet lampshades with black fringe. My
suitcase had been laid across the arms of a bishop's chair. The
high, rather narrow bed, also covered in red, had been turned
back for me, though I began to doubt how much sleep I would
get in here. Directly opposite the bed was the largest and most
outlandish of the twig cupboards I'd seen yet, its shelves
crammed full of family photographs in frames of every size and
material—including several in a sunburst design, also made of
the ubiquitous varnished twigs. As I saw Minerva looking round
with the unrestrained satisfaction of a faithful curator, I felt
bound to say, "What a lot of interesting furniture! Especially
these enormous old cupboards made out of sticks."
    "Depend on an artist to single out the most sought-after
thing in the entire house. I've just about made up my mind to

promise this to the Adirondack Museum. All the cupboards were made by a caretaker of ours, Bob Jarvis. A real old-timer. He would make furniture for us when he stayed here during the winter months, looking after things. Each spring, he'd surprise us with several new pieces. Father used to say, 'I wonder what monstrosity old Jarvis will have waiting for us this time.' But Mother was fascinated by the craftsmanship and insisted Bob Jarvis teach her how to do it. It's a type of rustic furniture completely indigenous to the area. Mosaic twigwork veneer. This cupboard has three kinds of maple in it, two kinds of birch, and ash, beech and wild cherry. Those lower doors carry the design of the rose inside of the pine—that was my parents' marriage symbol. My father had a stained-glass window put in both houses, with the sign of the rose inside the pine, when they were married."

"What a lovely idea. I noticed the window on the porch. But this cupboard must have taken months to make."

"Oh, it did. But the winters up here are long. When you're alone, if you don't have a project, Bob Jarvis used to say, you're a sitting duck for cabin fever. We once had a caretaker who went stark raving mad. Took his shotgun and went down to the foot of the hill and started shooting at snowflakes. Of course, Daphne is furious that I won't promise her this cupboard. I don't know what makes her think she's going to live forever; she's older than I am. But she'd just sell it, if she did outlive me. If it goes to the Adirondack Museum, there will be a metal plaque on it forever that will read: 'Gift of the Means Estate.' " She ran her small hand reverently along the side of the big old cupboard, clearly in her element and loath to leave. "And there we all are. . . . There's Mother—wasn't she beautiful—and there's Father with a buck he just shot. That was taken up at the cabin, in the days when it was just a lean-to. And here we all are sitting on the front porch. Mother made that frame out of witch hobble and shadbush twigs, after Jarvis showed her. Now, Violet dear . . . when Daphne sleeps here, she always makes me remove this urn to my room . . ."

On the bottom shelf was a pompous-looking porcelain urn, set on a golden pedestal and painted with garlands of roses. The lid was fastened down with wire clasps. I guessed what was inside.

". . . which I gladly do," Minerva went on. "Daphne would get no sleep otherwise. Her guilt would haunt her in the presence of our mother's remains. Daphne knew she oughtn't to have sold the stone house in Albany. But I mustn't bore you with family problems. The question is, if you would feel more comfortable . . ."

"I don't mind," I said. "It's her room, after all." I swallowed a yawn and suddenly realized I was bushed.

"You *are* a sweet girl. And I can't get over the coincidence of that book cover! Well, dear, I'll let you go first in the bathroom. It's comforting for me to have someone in the house. I sometimes lie alone and imagine . . . Well, I told you how my father would think about the animal he was going out to hunt. I imagine someone out there in the night, like that escaped prisoner they've just caught. I've often thought a criminal could *feel* me, waiting and frightened, a perfect victim. And my own fear could lead him, like a kind of ESP, right to this house."

I met her once more as I left the bathroom. She had changed into a white lacy peignoir and had lifted her hair into a dark topknot with a white ribbon. Well, at least she'd be dressed for him if he ever got in.

"Good night, dear." She offered up her cheek to me, somewhat in the fashion of a beloved bride. "Sleep as late as you wish."

I got undressed and climbed into the high bed. The sheets were not as fresh as Milo's had been the night before. Had they been changed since Daphne's last stay? Poor Daphne, unable to sleep with the urn in the same room. My own mother was buried in Anderson, South Carolina. My father had been attending Clemson when he met her. Her father was foreman in a cotton mill. Once my other grandparents came to visit me at boarding school. They had been to Chimney Rock, they said, and thought they ought to look in. I remember my relief at its being just before Easter. Most of my friends had already left for vacation. I was to spend it with Pequeña, in Georgetown, only her father was picking us up late, on his way back from somewhere. I walked the ill-at-ease old couple up to the athletic field because I knew it would be deserted. He wore white socks with a brown suit and kept turning his hat round and round by the brim. She spoke in whispers, as though she were in church. On the way back to their shabby car, he took out his wallet and handed me a five-dollar bill. "If you ever want to come stay with us, you just call," he said, going suddenly red and angry. "Now, Dad," she admonished, "watch your pressure." "Well, I don't give a damn. She's Liza's child after all. Why shouldn't she come and see her grandparents?" "She will, when she's older. We can't give her the advantages. You'll come when you're older, won't you, Violet Isabel? She favors Liza, doesn't she, Dad?" She fumbled in her shiny black purse for a handkerchief and began to sniffle. "Now, Mother, you promised if I brought you, you wouldn't." Was I relieved when they finally climbed back into their dusty coupe and drove out the school gates! In my dutiful seasonal greeting cards and rarer letters to them, I habitually concluded, "One of these days, I'm coming to see you, wait and see!" But they died before I could honor my promise, he first, of a stroke, she some years later of a kidney infection. Whenever I thought of them, my mother's "people," as my Charleston grandmother would have said, I felt sad for them that their only grandchild had not been more of a joy to their last years; I had a hard time, however, thinking of that grandchild as myself. "I've often thought a family is a whole world by itself," Minerva had said. I was not of their world. I was not of the Charleston world, either. More than anything, I had been in the habit of thinking for years, I existed as a world unto myself: the privilege of an orphan. To be used when necessary to prove underprivileged status, as Jake had pointed out on that day of truth when we were both going for the jugular.

Well, my last vestige of family had wiped itself out last night. Up till this time I had been partly formed by the family presences in my life (as well as by their more extended absences); but as of now, I would have to consider my heritage complete. A few stray memories might still be holding out on me, but the returns that went with being a Clay were, for the most part, in. I was as alone in the world as Minerva. Only there would be no ancestral fortress for me to hide out in daintily, drawing my consolations from its hoards and shadows, dressing and undressing myself in front of comforting old mirrors that still bore my child's imprint on their old silver surfaces. If I didn't create my own fortress soon, my ravagers were going to be more pitiless than any anticipated thief or prison escapee.

On such a note I turned off the fringed lamp and lay in a darkness so thick it smelled old. I was not in the least disturbed by the "presence" of Mrs. Means. August as she had appeared in her photographs, she connected me with no memories, fears or guilts. For a time, I lapsed into a sort of attentive suspension, watching the movies on the insides of my eyes, those retinal afterimages that often follow an active day. I saw acrobats, speeding cars, lonely blue landscapes, the imprint of an emperor's, no, Ambrose's face on an old coin. At some point, my own "hand" took over and I began to control these images, to a degree. I often draw or paint on the verge of sleep; I fill empty spaces with abandon, the images appearing always a little ahead of my brush. At such times I am just conscious enough to marvel at my own facility and wonder why I can't carry over this gift of inspired recklessness, the *disinvoltura* that Vasari so admired, into the daytime world when I have real brush and tangible surface in front of me.

I feathered in a gypsy caravan with quick watery-brown brush strokes, in the calligraphic style of Daumier's Don Quixotes. It had stopped right on top of a barren hill. I painted a curtain in the side of the caravan. It was open, as if for a show. And in the center lay a woman strapped flat on a kind of pallet bed. Then a little girl appeared in front of the caravan and a crowd

gathered below her. I painted the backs of their heads, the tops
of their old-fashioned hats. I was behind them, waiting to see
what would form next. The child opened her mouth and began
to sing. I couldn't hear the words, but supplied some of the sad
verses from Minerva's songs. I was, you understand, awake,
only I could see these things forming. And to an extent, guide
their progress. Then the scene became animated. The crowd
threw coins into the child's skirt. They were much moved. The
poor little thing had to hold on to her skirt for dear life as it grew
heavier and heavier with the weight of coins. Suddenly the
mother broke her straps; they came flying away like cooked
spaghetti. She swelled up and sort of poured out of the caravan
and began to envelop the crowd. Soon they were knocking
around inside her like toys inside a cloud. The little girl struck
up another song (this time I myself created the words: "Sad as
sad can be . . . that's little me, oh! little me"). Then the whole
thing speeded up like a movie run too fast; it took on a comical
air, as well: the little girl turned into a helium-balloon figure and
floated up into the sky, where she soon joined the others, most
of whom turned out to be plump businessmen in felt hats. I lay
there bemused for a time by the effortless process in which my
serious beginning had turned into a painted soap opera and finally a child's cartoon, until I finally got bored with my "creation" and wiped it out by simply opening my eyes.

"I'm really tired of all this old stuff," I said. It was less dark
now. I could make out the outlines of two windows and the hulking great twig temple to Mother's ruins. But it wasn't that old
stuff I meant I was tired of.

Soon I was drowsing, this time doing a superrealistic painting of an old woman in bed. I worked small areas in a deliberate,
craftsmanlike way, using smooth sable strokes to keep me from
cheating on the small details. I did every piece of fringe on her
lamp, highlighted every greeny-blue vein in her old hands
folded formally upon the counterpane. The old masters worked
like this, I reminded myself. No impressionistic shortcut or
splashy impasto. Just solid, slow attention to each matter at hand

until, one day, the entire design shines forth revealed. Then this "painting" also degenerated into a scenario. Two masked figures dressed in black rubber, like deep-sea divers, entered the old woman's room. "What are you going to do?" I heard myself croak as they approached me with menacing gestures. Then one of them made ready to part my legs while the other brandished a poker. I struggled either to wake or to scream. "Relax," said one. "We've only come to clean out your fireplace so you can build a decent fire." Somewhere a phone started ringing.

"Hell," I said, turning the fringe lamp back on. "Don't tell me this room's getting the better of me, after all." It was reassuring to hear Minerva's high-pitched voice conversing with someone. She talked for some time, first in a questioning, then in a cajoling tone. Her sister Daphne, perhaps?

I got up and opened the thick red curtains. The window was closed and locked. I opened it and pressed my forehead against the screen. A half-formed moon floated above the conical tips of the cedars. Then I went back and turned off the lamp and waited to see if there would be more light. There was. A luminous patch of night graced the lower part of the bed. Try, try again. I lay down and, as a sort of litany toward sleep, went over the things I still had to do for Ambrose: the funeral clothes to O'Halloran, the visit to the rector, tombstone couldn't be ordered till Monday morning, flowers. . . . Carol was providing the wreath through the local florist; she had been adamant, and she would be coming, as well, if she could postpone some important meeting until Tuesday. And Ambrose's interesting neighbor woman with the silver braids, would she be at the graveside service?

When I did finally get to sleep, I dreamed about her. She was driving us somewhere very fast, along a bumpy road, in a high vehicle, a sort of cross between a jeep and a bus. It felt good being with her; she was the young mother I'd never known, yet we were both the same age. She scolded me good-naturedly for letting my license expire. The only thing that impeded my total enjoyment of our trip together was that I had to keep watching the back seat to make sure something wouldn't fall on the floor. This something turned out to be Ambrose, dressed in his hound's-tooth jacket and cavalry twills, who lay pale and posed like Wallis's "Death of Chatterton" on a piece of old fringed brocade. He was reciting something softly under his breath—his last words, maybe? He bounced precariously toward the edge of the seat. "Please, can't you slow down a little?" I begged her. But she laughed and explained we were late already.

Despite all this, I woke early and refreshed. As I dressed, I found myself looking forward to the day for the first time in months. Not that I had anything all that pleasant to do, but just moving my body from place to place seemed a nice prospect. Of course, I hadn't had anything to drink for over thirty hours, that may have had something to do with it. Minerva's door was still closed. I went quietly through the house and let myself out through the much-locked door. I walked round the old lodge, imagining the neglected flower beds weeded and in bloom, the flagrantly overgrown forsythia trimmed down to reveal the view of the mountains that I now saw went with the site. It was still very early, about six. The grass was wet and the morning light was whitening through the cedars. Behind the lodge, the land sloped steeply down, and there, out of sight from the lodge, was a stream (the same stream that wound up to Ambrose's and down the falls to Sam's?) and, beside it, a quaint brown-shingled gazebo with an old pointy roof that looked exactly like a bashed-in gray straw hat. The picturesque old ruin set against the particular light of the sky exactly as it was now made me very sorry I did not have my inks, Bristol board and sponge. I would first go after that light: that wouldn't wait, gleaming like some very modern, radiant metal not yet discovered. If I could catch that sky, and then dip down quickly and set the shadows in place, then spend the rest of the morning squinting obsessively over every fine line of weathering and neglect . . . I would have captured the essence of a certain mood: the mood felt when you find yourself standing directly over the seam of one of time's juxtapositions. The lower half of the composition would be Time Past, with all its complex and ornate lacings and crosshatchings of things that can't be undone, only eroded or romanticized by memory; in contrast, the whole top area would glow with that blank, almost brutal, silvery-yellow sheen of a young day which has not quite made up its mind whether to be sunny or overcast.

"Yoo hoo! There you are!"

It was Minerva, wearing buttercup yellow today, making her way warily down the slope.

"I thought surely you'd sleep till eight or nine. *Did* you get some sleep?"

"Oh, I managed fine. I feel great this morning. The air up here is so clean. I was just looking at your gazebo and wishing I had the whole day free. I'd love to paint this scene, just as it is now."

"The dear old gazebo. As a child, I spent many happy hours here. I haven't been down here in ages. The poor old roof. I'll ask Sam if it can be rethatched. As far as your having the whole day to paint . . . well, you may have more time than that, if you meant what you said yesterday about wanting to rent the little cabin. Mr. Chakravorti called last night. He was having second thoughts, he said, about whether the place would be suitable to his needs after all. He and another fellow down at the meditation center are thinking of going in together, getting something larger. He said he realized yesterday that it might be a bit *too* rustic for him. I said I'd never pretended it was anything but rustic and gave him Mr. Dean's number. Did I do right?" She looked at me shyly, as people do when they've offered you something you might not want.

I didn't want to dampen her gesture with niggling reservations, so I replied, "You sure did," at once and tried to look pleased. After all, I had told her I was interested. Within a few minutes of our sitting down on the steps of the old gazebo and going over details, I found I *was* interested, even excited. My polite precipitousness had been just what was needed to push me into a decision. It *was* what I wanted, wasn't it? A chunk of undivided time—at a price I could afford—in which to set up my things and see what I could do. Indeed, the longer I thought of it, in the light of my uncle's example, it seemed I couldn't afford not to seize this opportunity.

13
Post-Mortem

"You're actually going to *live* up there?" asked Carol.

"For a while, anyway."

"But won't you get lonely?"

"New York's lonely."

"Yes, but there's so much going on. I should think you'd miss being near the galleries, all the museums. . . ."

"I've been near them for nine years. Most of the time, I could have been living in Plommet Falls, for all the use I made of them."

Carol sighed. "Well . . ." She kicked off her shoes and tucked her dark-stockinged legs up on the roomy back seat of the limousine. "If you've made up your mind . . ."

We were driving—being driven, rather—back to the city on Monday, after the funeral. I planned to dispose of my apartment, store some things with Milo, and get right back to Plommet Falls before the old fetid air of compromise blanketed my new-found sense of urgency: perhaps the most important legacy my uncle had left me.

(*Man, that is born of a woman, hath but a short time to live, and is full of misery. He cometh up, and is cut down, like a*

*flower; he fleeth as it were a shadow, and never continueth in
one stay.* The rector had read well: a genuine Englishman, on
summer exchange with the local rector. The funeral had had the
simple formal composition of one of those old "Mourning Pictures" that used to be *de rigueur* in the art classes at female sem-
inaries. Ambrose would have been satisfied, I thought, with the
tableau we made, his faithful clique of mourners, including a uni-
formed chauffeur, gathered in a semicircle around the silver
cylinder with an extravagant spray of red carnations [compli-
ments of Carol] alive on its breast like a heart. The round green
clumps of summer foliage set on straight dark boles. The purple-
blue wash of a distant mountain range. And, over it all, the rector's solemn BBC vowels reminding us all that *in the midst of
life we are in death.* . . . The only missing mourners from our
picture had been the very two I was counting on meeting there:
the handsome woodswoman with pale braids and her little girl
with the wide, curious eyes.)

Carol hadn't changed much. She had simply become a hard-
edged version of her old self. Born on Ambrose's birthday, she
was going on fifty, but she had the fashion-adept woman's knack
of knocking off ten years by shrewd grooming. She looked chic,
well cared for and in control. Of course, contributing to this effect was the patina of plain old money, evidenced in the understated, excellently cut clothes, the dark-blue limousine in which
we rode, with its soft dove-gray leather upholstery and sliding
glass panels between us and Chris, the chauffeur. As formerly
in Carol's presence, I found myself being slightly cowed by her
values as she reigned so confidently among them. I could tell
that she thought my plan to live in the cabin was more of a lark
than an act of commitment. These Clays: always able to dream
up new flights to postpone getting down to earth. So let's get
off *that* subject, I thought.

I said I thought the funeral had gone well and complimented
her on the spray of red carnations.

"Yes, he loved red carnations and he *was* born on Saint Valentine's day. We both were. My former analyst had an inter-

esting theory. He said I was initially attracted to Ambrose because he was my dark twin, the side of me that had learned to waste time and have fun. I'm not sure I buy that. When I married him, I was convinced he could be an important man. Whereas the analyst I see now thinks I was a sort of super ego for Ambrose. She says he was probably drawn to me because he thought I was capable of locking him in a room until he came out a great writer."

"Hmm. Not very flattering," I said.

"You don't go to an analyst to be flattered."

"No, I guess not. I've never gone. You didn't, when I knew you before, did you?"

"No. All this has been post-Ambrose. It was not an easy time for me, Violet." There was the slightest reproach in her voice. "It's taken me the better part of the last eight years to get over the one year and four months I spent with him. Marrying your uncle was the only romantic act I ever committed in my life. Now I'm content to make what I can of reality. It was strange, seeing him in the casket. He didn't look like his old self. He looked more as I used to imagine he'd look when he became distinguished. For just a second I had a glimpse of an alternate way things might have turned out. Within nine years, if he'd been serious, he could have finished that book. It could have made him famous. And then he might have died of something sudden . . . like a heart attack. I thought that, looking at him today, with that beard, and that dignified expression on his face, as if he'd completed his work. And I was the widow, the widow of a distinguished man, with whom I'd been happy for nine busy years. . . ."

So that's what had gone through her head when, gazing down at Ambrose at O'Halloran's, before the casket was closed, she had disintegrated suddenly into a few hoarse sobs and then just as suddenly pulled herself together. Yet I liked her better for her "alternate glimpse." It showed fanciful things were not yet completely denied entrance inside that businesslike head. It made her more like she'd been when I first knew her, through her brisk but warmly confiding letters and—briefly—after they'd come back. It occurred to me that Ambrose had harmed her most not by his failure to produce or by whatever other inconstancies he'd been guilty of, but by the mere act of taking himself away from her after having shown her what her full self could be like. For I tended to agree with her former analyst as well as her current one. I remembered what she'd told me in her very first letter: how, from ages twenty to forty, she had been so busy living up to her inherited responsibilities that she had neglected to take deep breaths of air and enjoy each moment as it comes.

"What a shame it couldn't have worked out with you two," I said. "In a way each of you *was* the other's neglected half. I remember what Ambrose said when he wrote he had married you. He said he was at last dealing with a full deck."

"Did he put it like that?" She laughed. "He had more colorful figures of speech than anybody I ever knew. 'He lies so much you couldn't trust him to call his dog,' he'd say. Ah, if only he'd put it all into a book!"

"Carol, do you mind if I ask something? What did happen to that book? I mean, while you were together. I've been through the few things he left, and there's not a sign of anything. And yet I know he had written some of it. I remember holding a chunk of it in my own hands, once in his apartment on Waverly. He even read me a passage. It was about charm."

"I can't tell you where it is now, but in my day, I had the honor of hearing two chapters. The second I hated. The first was a large factor in my marrying him. He read that to me just after we'd met in Florence and I offered my car when he had to meet that *Holiday* photographer in Rome. On the way, we decided to stop overnight in Orvieto. It seemed so romantic, a twelfth-century walled city, perched up there on its mountain. We arrived late and everything was full, except for this rather grand old dilapidated pension. Ambrose was given a sort of passageway with a curtain for his bedroom, because they had one official bedroom left and, as our passports showed we weren't married, we couldn't share it. Officially, that is." She laughed. "The passageway, however, was right off my room with only the curtain between us, but that didn't seem to count. Oh, the Italians! Anyway, we were in such good spirits, we decided to play along with the decorum. Ambrose retired modestly and dressed for dinner in his passageway and I in my baronial bedroom that could have accommodated a large family, and then we went out to dinner and afterwards walked around the narrow streets and looked at the cathedral and Ambrose was really inspiring about this book he was trying to finish in his spare time. He had a way of talking that could get anyone excited and I asked him if he would consider reading some of it to me. 'If you wouldn't be bored . . .' he said, and when we got back, he came into my big room and we turned on all the old-fashioned lamps and he went into his passageway and changed into a black turtleneck sweater and then he read me a fascinating chapter. It was about a small boy who's left to himself a lot in a large house—all the antiques were described so well, I remember—and to amuse himself he imagines he is giving tours of the house. One day he has this customer, an imaginary person, of course, a sinister man who turns things round and takes the boy on a tour—"

"Oh, yes, and they go upstairs and the boy finds his mother in bed with somebody?"

"That's right. You've read it, then? I thought you said he only read you a passage about charm."

"Er . . . that's true. I must have read this some other time. When I first came to New York, maybe." Too late, I had remembered why the story had sounded so familiar. I'd heard it from Sheila. It was the same chapter Ambrose had read to her at Fire Island, years before he met Carol.

"And yet he did have talent," Carol went on, apparently buying my extemporaneous cover-up. "I may be in the luggage industry, but I can recognize a good piece of writing. A child *would* make up something like that, so it wouldn't be his fault when he found out . . . what he must have known all along. It would be a way to deflect some of the guilt at discovering his mother. No, that chapter was psychologically brilliant. And the suspense! I remember sitting in that baronial bedroom: it couldn't have been better chosen to match the mood of his story —all those antimacassars, the heavy furniture, the baroque lamps. I remember thinking: What a shame that this man has to write something this good in his spare time only. He read beautifully, too." She gazed raptly out the window and, after a moment, shrugged. We had left the mountains behind some time ago.

I could just imagine the night in Orvieto: Ambrose, changing into his reading sweater; the baronial room in a walled city eight centuries old; the soft light from the Baroque lamps; the lonely, deserving boy peeping now and then from the eyes of the Man of Charm to see how he was doing; the rich, melodic voice reciting passages that had had their effect before . . . some of which by this time he may even have known by heart.

"I realized *after* our marriage that, for him, the performance was more gratifying than the act," she went on. "His enthusiasm for his project stopped exactly short of the drudgery. That famous *Holiday* article, for example. I could almost have written it myself after listening to him talk about it for six weeks. He talked eloquently, mind you. If only I'd had a tape recorder at all those candlelit suppers, and at Lake Maggiore when we were driving around with that Fulbright couple, and by the pool, and . . . a couple of times in bed I would have had enough to feed into a Dictaphone machine and come out with not only the article that never got turned in, but many scenes from the great unwritten novel as well. But I didn't have a tape recorder. More's the pity, I guess. My fault. I was still under the spell of being a happy, useless bride in the castle."

"Well, it was your honeymoon, after all."

"That it was. As I told my analyst, however disappointingly my marriage turned out, I certainly did have a honeymoon. As long as we stayed in that castle in Siena, the setting was on our side. It made me unlike myself and gave Ambrose the chance to be more nearly his true self than ever before. It was an illu-

sion we lived in, but as long as we were *in* it, we got along
excellently."

"But how were you then?" I awaited her answer with interest. The people I'd met in the city who went regularly to ana-
lysts all had this marvelous facility of packaging their past mistakes into shapely revisions that shimmered with insights or at
least bristled with epigrammatic hindsight.

"I languished," she said, "and he lorded. I drifted about
wearing long feminine things; I played the one Polonaise I knew
on the antique harpsichord with built-in candleholders; I wafted
down to the kitchen after 'siesta hour' and consulted with the
cook about dinner. I would see her stealing these sly looks at my
body. I knew she was thinking: This one just made it under the
wire, but now she's got herself a *bello sposo*, and the rest will
surely follow. As for Ambrose, he walked about the place as if
he owned it, or sat by the pool with a pitcher of ice and a bottle
of Punt e Mes, making occasional notes, as the spirit moved
him, in a tooled leather notebook with marbled endpapers he'd
bought for himself in Florence. We might still be there now, if
old breadwinner Gruber hadn't had to go back to work. . . . No;
the truth was, I was aching to get back to work. I looked forward
to the getting down to it, for both of us. You can just languish
for so long. My languishing span is probably shorter than most."
She laughed mirthlessly. "Certainly shorter than Ambrose's."

"And so you came back," I said, wanting to hear her side of
it now.

"And so we came back. And you met us at the airport with
your bottle of champagne. And then there was that awful to-do
about that *Holiday* piece. And then he started going down to
Waverly Place to work every day, and coming home full of enthusiasm in the evening, and for a while it was okay. Even
though the *Holiday* thing fell through I still believed in his
book. And after a while I asked him when I could hear some
more of it. He said he was battling his way to the end of a new
chapter. I said why not make a ceremony out of it, set a date
for the reading and have a champagne dinner afterwards. I

thought this would be a sort of stimulus. Many people work best under pressure; I know I do. Well, first the champagne dinner was to be Thanksgiving, then it got delayed till just before Christmas. Then, let's see, I think it was about then he decided to chuck that chapter—it had no place in the book, he said—but he was already into another one that he was very excited about. As *that* deadline approached—we were then up to our joint birthday for the champagne celebration—he warned me that I might not like some of the material in this chapter, he said he had doubts about reading it to me if I was going to take it literally. I promised I wouldn't, and at last, on the snowy evening of Saint Valentine's Day, we opened the first bottle of Piper-Heidsieck and my husband read me a very strange chapter entitled 'For Pilar—with Requited Love.' "

"What was it about?"

"It was about this little girl who had been in love with him for years. Excuse me, I mean with the protagonist for years. We ended up having quite a scene over the word 'protagonist' that night."

"But how was it strange?"

"Well, it was not at all like the chapter he read in Orvieto; that was so straightforward, like a real story. In this new thing, it was difficult to tell what time people were in and who was doing the thinking. But the gist of it was that he—the *protagonist*, I mean—had once been a sought-after writer who went to give a lecture at a girls' boarding school. This beautiful child, a little girl from South America, falls madly in love with him. She writes to him for years after, sends him expensive gifts, dedicates her schoolgirlish poetry to him. There is one poem with a line that says, 'Why must our love go unrequited?' During all these years, the man—the *protagonist*—sinks deeper into a meaningless, dissipated life. But in his letters to the little girl he still puts up the front of the popular, hopeful man who came to her school. Then—now comes the part that was hard to take —they meet again. On Madison Avenue of all places. He has become a copywriter for an ad agency and married a 'wealthy society woman' . . . all the old clichés for selling out, you see. *She*, the beautiful Pilar, is locked in one of those forever Catholic marriages to a tyrannical young husband, a diplomat at the U.N. who's a little on the nutty side. He sometimes keeps her in their hotel suite for days, until she agrees to see things his way."

"What things?"

"I don't know. It wasn't made clear in the story. Anyway, I had questions of my own that night. They have a passionate affair at his place in the Village, you see. He called me literal-minded and I ended up crying."

When, I was trying to think, had I last heard from Pequeña? The last letter, in which she professed to be a happy wife, soon to be mother, had come while I was still in college. But Enrique (what was his last name?) had been something in the diplomatic service, I recalled. Was it possible that one day eight years ago, my old roommate had rediscovered the "Primer Caballero" of her childhood on Madison Avenue and become his "meestress" on Waverly Place? And all this about my grandmother. How literal-minded were *writers*? That's what I wanted to know.

"And what happened afterwards?" I asked.

"Oh, he smoothed it over in that way he had. We had our feeble champagne supper."

"I mean, what happened in the chapter?"

"Oh, not much. That is, they had the affair. It went on and on during the whole chapter. And then one or the other of them, it was not always clear which, would have a flashback. But things kept coming back to the bed. That was what's called a 'leit motif,' he informed me that night." She narrowed her eyes and frowned at the industrial outskirts of New Jersey we were now passing through. If Chris could hear anything on the other side of the glass panel, he gave no sign of it in the erect set of his neatly barbered neck beneath the light-gray cap.

"There was one sentence that I still remember," she said. " 'She was the only woman in the world who had toes he wanted to kiss.' " Carol unfolded a stockinged leg from beneath her and wriggled a set of knobbly toes against the plush upholstery. "I hardly think he had these in mind."

"Oh, the toes," I reassured her, "probably came out of his imagination, or, you know, out of that storehouse we all carry around of how we like things to look. The Greek ideal of beauty, certain proportions . . . hands . . . feet . . ." I trailed off lamely, as she didn't look in the mood for an aesthetics lecture.

"He told me afterwards, he said, 'I am honored to grant you fidelity in real life, but you can hardly chain my imagination to the wedding vows and still expect me to plumb the passions of the human heart.' I could accept that he made up the girl who had adored him from childhood—that was a bit farfetched—but . . . there was something that smacked of recent experience, the way he described those toes."

What was the point in bringing up Pequeña's existence now? We'd never know whose toes they were in the chapter anyway. "I'm really sorry," I said. "I had no idea you two were having trouble till he came by my place one night in September and said he was off to Mexico."

"Oh, we had a few more good times. Things went up and down. Marriages don't just die from one blow. It's a cumulative thing, like snow piling up on a branch till the branch breaks. Oh, no, the sun came out again, and then I had that tubular pregnancy. We didn't tell you, you had your own problems at the time—you hated that West Side apartment you'd moved to and yet I felt it was important for you to make your own way. And you'd started going to the Art Students League, I remember. You were never free for dinner on the week nights."

"Perhaps everything would have worked out differently if you'd had a child."

"I honestly doubt it, Violet. Ambrose liked his dreams. The problem with me was I kept waking him up and telling him the day had started. Well, anyway . . . we're almost to the tunnel. Come home and have dinner with me, won't you? Elena said she'd leave a lobster salad or something. We'll open a bottle of nice wine."

"Thank you, I'd like to. But I don't think I'd better. I want to go back to the apartment and start packing immediately. First thing tomorrow I'll call the landlord and see if I can get out of

the lease. It shouldn't be a problem. People are always trying
to move into that building. I told Miss Means, the lady you met
at the funeral today, I'd try to be back in Plommet Falls by the
end of the week."

"Suit yourself, then." I could tell she was disappointed. "So
you're really set on banishing yourself to that cabin. What happens when the cold weather comes?"

"I'll turn on the electric heating units. It's not the kind of log
cabin Abe Lincoln lived in or anything."

"And he did pretty well without electric heat. But he had so
much . . ." She checked herself.

"Drive?"

"A sense of purpose, yes."

"So do I. Now. I feel if I don't start painting all day every
day within the week, I'll be doomed."

"But why not stay in your old apartment and start first thing
tomorrow morning?"

"Because that place is the scene of so much failure. It would
be like trying to start a smooth new painting on a scumbly old
canvas. Also I have to get out of there soon, anyway. The rent's
too much for just one person. I took it with someone else and
now we've split. And also," I hurried on, afraid she might think
I was angling for a loan, "and this is really the most important
reason of all, I need the *gesture* that moving up to Plommet
Falls implies."

"You Southerners and your gestures. But didn't Ambrose go
up there for the same reason, to make the same sort of 'gesture'
after wasting all those years in Mexico? I've always liked you,
Violet; better than you've liked me, I think. I mean it when I
say this: I'd sincerely hate to see you throw away your talent like
he did. Are you very sure that this move to the Adirondacks isn't
just another postponement?"

"Carol, when I first came to New York, Ambrose took me to
the Top of the Sixes and bought me my first Manhattan and
showed me his 'eagle's-eye view,' as he called it, of the city. He
was in top form that night and so was I. I thought it was all going
to be so easy. When that English priest threw the handful of sod

on the casket today, I buried my last hope for any easy victory. Also Ambrose said something else to me that night. We were talking about how the channel that lets ships into New York was called Ambrose Channel and he laughed and said, 'You got to go through me, kid.' I remembered him saying that, today at the cemetery. And I thought to myself, how nice if I could live in his place and make good a few Clay promises, after all. I feel almost religious about going back up there and seeing what I can make of it."

"Ah, in that case," said Carol, sighing. "Far be it from me to tamper with any more creative spirits, much less a religious impulse. No, Violet, I'm not making fun of you. I really hope you make it. For several years after Ambrose left, and you and I had that polite luncheon at Schrafft's, I would check the gallery ads every Sunday in the *Times*. Every week I'd steel myself for the sight of your name in one of those little squares. I had mixed feelings. I wanted you to make it, but I was bitter because I would no longer have a share in your happiness. I had hoped the three of us would be a sort of family. Well, let me tell you something. If and when the day comes that I do see your name, my feelings won't be mixed anymore. Both of us buried something up there today. I buried my resentment. There was a lot of it, but"—she put her hand on mine—"I really think I've done with all that."

I thanked her, touched by her candor. I was half tempted to say I had changed my mind about the lobster salad and wine. But just then we entered the Lincoln Tunnel and as the tiled walls, yellowish in the underground light, sped monotonously past, I felt the old inertia lurking even now in the edges of my resolve. I didn't trust myself in Carol's territory with a full stomach unquickening my blood and a good wine displacing gravity with effervescence in my head. I would sit there in her well-appointed space, the relics of her family's solidity and what her own industry had added grouped round us like testimonials, and I might begin to doubt the solidity of that little cabin, shimmering, as I had first seen it, in its equal mixture of sun and shadow. It represented my vision of what might still be done. But it was a frail and fledgling vision balanced precariously between the practical and the ideal. The least tipping of my attitude toward skepticism or sloth *could* render it into just another "gesture."

Carol rummaged purposefully in her Gucci bag. "Here's my card, so you won't have the excuse of not knowing where to reach me. I'd like it so much if you'd just call every now and then. . . ."

"I'll write. I won't have a phone up there."

"You really *are* going, aren't you. Well, I wish you luck. Will you keep in touch? I have a genuine curiosity about what will happen to you."

"I'll write, then."

"Promise?"

"I promise."

She leaned over and laid her cool cheek against mine. She still wore such nice perfume. "Oh! And don't forget your *Times.*" Arriving in Plommet Falls this morning, she had presented it to me folded open to Ambrose's obituary as modestly as if it had been her own gift.

"It's placed well, people can see it," she said now, studying it possessively. "Of course, it always depends on who else they have that day. Even when compressed into two paragraphs, he manages to come out looking glamorous, doesn't he?"

14

Between Friends

It was late Friday afternoon, exactly one week since Ambrose's suicide had put the finishing touch on my Day of Lost Options, as I'd come to think of it. I was sitting in Milo's garden, sketch-

ing his brilliant array of late-summer flowers with my new set
of Marvy Markers, their forty-eight colors listed on the inside
of the box in four languages. I had gone a bit wild at the art supply shop the day before, following my success at having sublet
my apartment to three members of a mime troupe. ("I don't
much like the idea of three," grumbled the landlord. "Oh, but
they'll be as quiet as one," I'd assured him. "That's their profession.") Three young hopefuls, full of enthusiasm for everything
to do with New York, they had padded on tensed dancers' legs
from room to room, visualizing possibilities everywhere I remembered staleness. A girl with thick flowing hair to her waist,
and two boys: a couple and their friend. The couple bought the
double bed Jake and I had occupied; I hoped our old animosities
would not haunt them. The boy would make his bedroom in my
old studio. To him I sold a table, a chair and the studio couch
from the living room. They bought the dishes and rugs as well.
They wrote me out checks still drawn on a bank in Urbana, Illi-
nois. "We'll take any work we can get, till we get established,"
they explained. The girl was excited because she was pretty sure
she had got a job doing a shampoo commercial. I had mailed myself three boxes of art supplies care of Minerva Means, and managed to compress nine years' worth of accumulations into two
portable bulks. My stereo and record collection, as well as a
dozen or so paintings not bad enough to throw away but not
good enough to live in a one-room cabin with, would stay with
Milo. The rest would go with me on the morning bus to Plommet Falls.

Milo was watering his flowers. His form hovered so grace-
fully over a cluster of brilliant dahlias that I had half a mind to
include him in the composition. In the late-afternoon light he
looked like some serene gold-dappled ascetic in a Pisanello. But
if I remained true to the hard, hot-hued flowers, I would render
him pale and insubstantial; on the other hand, if I set my mind
to capturing his ethereal grace, the flowers would appear gaudy
in contrast. No, Milo was more of a watercolor than a Marvy
Marker composition, and having decided, I put a rich splotch

of magenta right where the loose-flowing line of his creamy-shirted rib cage would otherwise have gone.

"Ha," I said, consulting the multilingual color chart. "You'll never guess what the German is for magenta. *Rotviolett.* I hope that's not symbolic or anything."

"No, your color is New Violet now."

"Hmm. It doesn't seem to be in this box. I wonder what color New Violet would be."

"Let's see," he said, turning to consider me. "I see it as a color with lots of light in it . . . an airy, spacy color . . . but also with muscle to it."

"Oh, really? But what makes you say that?" I sensed a compliment glimmering behind his description and, frankly, wanted to include it in the crucial baggage I would take with me to the Adirondacks.

"It's already begun to show in your work. Of course, I don't mean 'color' in the sense of the spectrum. I mean it as a recognizable quality in your painting. It's the way you leave light in and around things so they have room to breathe. Perhaps even to change, or move."

"But what about the muscle?" I coaxed shamelessly.

"That comes across in the way you do your lines. They have firmness, yet there's the suggestion of stretch, of going somewhere."

"But can you see this in my less good things, like the ones I brought over today for you to store?" I pursued it hungrily to the dregs.

"Well, perhaps not as much." He scrupulously drew the line between constructive praise and detrimental flattery. "But what's important, Violet, is what you will do now. It's exciting, both of us embarking on new projects, don't you find it so?"

"I was awfully glad to hear you'd started something again. I was a little worried about you last week, to tell the truth."

"I was beginning to get worried myself, if you want to know." He eased onto the redwood chaise longue next to mine, crossed his long legs at the ankles, and pressed his fingers together above his chest, cathedral style. "Seven months, in all, of lying fallow. First the fruitless trip to Greece. Then coming back and making at least a dozen false starts. Then the sleeplessness coupled with that recurrent nightmare. I don't know how many times I went through it, trying to pull that infant out of the sea, while his frightful mother did her best to do me in. Actually, it's you I have to thank for rescuing me."

"Me?"

"You remember you told me how you confronted your math teacher in your dream, and she agreed to let you make up the exam? You told me to ask my woman what she wanted, why she was trying to kill us."

"And it worked?"

"Not quite in the way you advised. I couldn't manage to carry my question all the way into the dream. What I did do, one night, was sit down and write her a letter on my typewriter. I invited her to respond and offered my services at the keyboard." A weird little smile, half embarrassed, half astute, flickered over his cool profile.

"And did she?" I loved it when Milo entered this dimension.

"She certainly did. Once she started, it was difficult to shut her up. I ended up promising to give her a full hearing in my new book . . . if she'd let me write a new book."

"If she'd let you? Was it she who was stopping you?"

"I think so, yes."

"But . . . who was she? Who *is* she?"

"She's lonely and neglected. And the loneliness and the neglect has made her angry. And when she gets angry, she is powerful. She is capable in her way of creating quite a havoc."

I squirmed in a sort of mental *frisson* and recapped the magenta marker. "And what did she say in her reply to you? Was her style different from yours?"

"At the beginning it was an outburst of all kinds of things— grievances, lamentations, potluck philosophies, ominous warnings which tended to be couched in Old Testament rhetoric. You ask was the style different from mine. I certainly hope so.

Hers was bombastic, maudlin and hysterical." In a semisupersti-
tious manner, he looked up over his shoulder, toward his workroom window upstairs. "I feel a bit nervous even now, criticizing
her. But the essence of her message was: 'I wasn't always an object to be feared and shunned. I had my dreams, just like you.
Any you'd better make it your business to find out what they
were.' "

"And so you've already started. It's going to be her story,
then, your new book? You've abandoned the idea of the male
Jane Eyre, the thing you were talking about last week?"

"No. She's made him all the clearer. I've already felt the ter-
rors he's going to feel in relation to her. What she's done, Violet
—she has a name now, by the way—is provide the psychic force
which has brought it all together for me and may make it possible for me to aim for a new level of writing. She first came into
my life through that peasant woman who had the child on my
kitchen floor in Greece. I tried to suppress her then; I found the
whole thing oppressive as well as unappetizing. I wrote off my
trip to Greece as a waste and determined not to set my next
book there. But *she* followed me home and settled her ominous
bulk right into the middle of my nightmare. I dreamed about
her for four months, Violet. When you dream the same dream
over and over for four straight months . . . well, it's a step towards the edge. I might have gone over if it hadn't been for a
favorable combination of things. Your wonderful suggestion
about getting into conversation with the figures inside one's unconscious was the catalyst. You put me in touch with Kaatje—
that's to be her name. Now I've got her, she's mine, and she's
going to work for me."

"Oh, Milo, this is fascinating. I envy you. I wonder whether
I have any figures like that who'd be willing to work for me.
Kaatje? What kind of name is that?"

"It's Dutch. No, it may be fascinating, but it could have been
the other way round. She could have got *me*, and I might not
have fared too well in her employment. Take my advice and
don't go raising sleeping demons. If and when they stir, you'll
know it. Quite honestly, I wouldn't wish them on you."

"Well, then, you must compensate me by sharing yours. Why is she Dutch? I want to hear all the details." I made a choice between Bottle Green and Oriental Blue for a patch of shadow behind the dahlias.

"It all started when I returned from Greece. At first I didn't suspect I was in for any trouble. I went to my workroom my first morning back, as I go to my workroom most mornings of my life, and I sat down to begin Arabella's next novel. I had opted, after all, for an English setting. I'd decided an island of manners and mists was more compatible with my talents than an island of unrelenting blue sky and cooks having babies in the kitchen. The first morning I couldn't write a line. I couldn't imagine any-thing—not a glimpse of a landscape, not one overheard phrase of thought or conversation, nor a single expression on a face. In the past, I could take off from any of these and go on from there. But that morning there was . . . just nothing." He hugged his arms to his chest as though he were suddenly chilled. "I con-cluded I was suffering from jet lag and went to bed and slept all that day and through the night and into the next afternoon. I woke feeling a bit fuzzy, but I went to my workroom. Nothing again. Every time I'd range round in my mind looking for an impetus, all I saw was that woman writhing on the floor, blood and water pouring out. It was then I decided to force something. If I couldn't see any beginning images, I'd just roll a sheet into the typewriter and begin to write *as if* I were transcribing them. I'd *imitate* my old methods. I selected one of Arabella's early works from the shelf, opened to the first page and simply made a variation on the first sentence. It went something like: 'When Louisa opened the solicitor's letter and learned that her great-uncle Marcus had bequeathed her his cottage in Lyme Re-gis, her first reaction was one of mild inconvenience.' " Milo laughed dryly. "I struggled through sixty-odd pages with the in-convenienced Louisa, who at last gave me to understand that she didn't want to be in my story any more than she wished to be forced to poke around her great-uncle's moldy old cottage. After Louisa came Margaret, also a recalcitrant heiress, and after her came Clare, who started out as a promising restorer of old paintings. . . . I remember I almost phoned you at the time to ask you some technical questions. By the time Clare got trapped under a top-heavy load of research, where she promptly expired, my daily stint in the workroom had become a penance I imposed on myself merely for the sake of honoring my old friends discipline and habit. After a dozen or so more false starts, I began to resign myself to the idea that Arabella Stone had written her last and Milo Hamilton would have to find other work for himself. But I continued to go every morning to my workroom. To be honest, I found I couldn't *not* go. It was ingrained into my life. But now I ceased altogether attempting fresh starts and just sat at the desk, looking out at cloud formations or letting my mind drift where it would. Suddenly one day I had a perfectly clear vision of a house."

"A house you made up or one you know?"

"It was a ruin of an old stone house on the Hudson River. I saw it just once when I was small. Then I forgot it and the circumstances completely. Which is odd, because that day was the last happy memory I have of my mother and father together. Shortly after that he went mad for the final time and never came out of it again. But this day we saw the house was a beautiful midsummer's day. We'd been on vacation and were driving slowly home to Rochester, taking the scenic route along the Hudson. When all at once this ruin of a house swam up in front of us like a hallucination. It was four stories high, with a steep single-pitched roof and nothing to soften its harsh lines. It looked as if it had been empty for years. At the very top were two small oblong windows that seemed to squint at us like close-set eyes. My father laughed and said, 'Whoever could have wanted to build such a rawboned, unlovable house?' And my mother said, 'Whoever built it probably thought it was very beautiful and loved it very much.' And my father answered, 'Ellen, you'd have something good to say about Hell itself.' Then he pulled her over to the driver's side and kissed her and when I looked out the window again the house had disappeared." He narrowed his eyes dreamily at his flowers and was silent.

"And the house, is it going to be in the book, too?"

"Yes. The house that Kaatje built. When she came into her patrimony and determined to make up to herself all she'd missed. Only it's late, you see. She's almost forty. She's never known any company except her father's and he was . . . well, he was mad. Now she's deaf in one ear from a bout of her late father's violence, and whatever attractiveness she possessed is pretty well obscured by fat. But she's determined to have the good things of life, as far as she's been able to learn what they are in that isolated region of New York in the early eighteenth century."

"Oh, it's historical, then." I wouldn't have let him know for the world, but my heart sank at the mention of the date. Up to then it had sounded so . . . promising. Something that I could use myself: a story about a woman who got started late and still managed to recoup her losses.

"Only that it starts then. I plan to carry it into the present. Though Kaatje's spirit will dominate the entire thing, it will be about her descendants, as well."

"Ah, so she finds a husband and has children."

"Not a husband," said Milo. "And only one infant. And after his birth she never looks on him again. But I'll spoil the suspense for you. I'd rather you read it. It's to be a working out of a curse, you see, Kaatje's curse, over two hundred years. But I had started by telling you how Kaatje's letter to me consolidated all this. Because the house wasn't the breakthrough, not by any means. I filed it away as an image whose time had not come, whose time might never come. Just as, on another fallow morning a week ago, I heard a voice, the voice of a young man, say, 'I'm afraid to go in there!' Just that, as clearly as though he'd been in the same room. Nothing more. When I was weeding the garden that evening, I thought: Why not a gothic novel in which the man is the figure who is acted upon, for a change? And I heard myself telling the idea to you, as I used to use you as a sounding board in those days when we saw more of each other. Well, she'll call again one of these days, when she wants to see me again, I thought, and then, for the first time in weeks, I felt hungry, I felt like cooking something. And I made a salmon mousse and went out and bought black bread and cheese and some wine, and as I was walking home I had a vision of a young man, rather like a younger version of myself, walking up to that forbidding house on the river, mounting the stone steps and then . . . just standing very still, listening. And then that very same night you called. And the nature of the evening being what it was, we spoke of things that people don't often speak about. And then you dropped your good hint about conversing with the people in your dreams. And . . . well, after a few more bad days and nights, I wrote my letter. And my fat woman let it be known that it was her house. After I had that much to go on, the rest followed with an uncanny ease. I went to the library and looked at books about old Dutch houses in the Hudson Valley. In one book I found a photograph of a house very similar to the one I'd seen with my parents that long ago summer day. And in the same book I found the seed of my story. Just the barest hint of a story, but I could tell it was right. It was as if my woman, my Kaatje, pounced on that story and said, 'Yes, I could fit very well there' "

"An actual story about something that happened?"

"Yes. In the seventeenth century in a place called Coeymans, New York, there was a Dutch immigrant who'd made his fortune in the New World. Little is known about him, except that he left a large estate to his daughter, a spinster in middle life. As soon as she inherited she began to build an enormous house, incorporating all her ideas of elegance; she also had a life-size portrait painted of herself, though she 'had no claim to beauty,' as the book puts it. The only other thing we know about her—the real woman's name was Ariaatje—was that she took seven years to build this formidable house and then, at fifty-one, she married a man of twenty-eight and the marriage was unhappy. But I've altered a good bit of the facts for my purposes. Kaatje doesn't marry. Except for . . . well, except for the brief time when the French portrait painter comes to do her, she lives quite alone. And I'm not telling you one sentence more. It's bad luck. Perhaps I'll send you some later, for bedtime reading in your cabin."

"But now you've got me fascinated. It sounds ultra-gothic already. There's something about a person alone in a certain kind of house. I told you about poor Minerva Means. Only she's just preserved like some butterfly in all her family history. No, on second thought, there's nothing very gothic about Minerva."

"On the contrary, Violet, I think the very essence of what we have come to call 'gothic,' all those winding passageways and trap doors and dark stairways, may have a great deal to do with the family. With things we haven't been able to deal with. So we put them underground or in the attic, whichever you choose. We forget they're there except when they manifest themselves in some form of brooding terror, or a growing uneasiness of something lurking, waiting to do us in."

"What? The parents, or the things we haven't dealt with?"

"I'm . . . not sure it makes a great deal of difference. I've thought a lot about this. It's been on my mind, you see. Whether or not Demuth knew he was painting his mother when he painted James's governess. Whether that armored hand on Horace Walpole's banister in Otranto wasn't his heavy-handed father's hand. I read everything I could find on the subject when I was unable to write. I know a lot more than I did about it. And a good deal more about myself." He flushed slightly.

"And do you know now why the young man says, 'I'm afraid to go in there'?" It had just occurred to me that I had been privy to the rarest of treats: a guided tour through the creative channels of another person's psyche. In some ways to offer such a tour to another was more intimate than offering your body.

Milo laughed. "Yes, I know that, too. I've been there myself. Now no more, Violet. If you like, I'll sent you some of it when it's done. Which may not be awfully long. I've been going like the wind since the evil spell broke. And you've been the midwife. You'll understand I don't use the word haphazardly when you read the first part of *Kaatje's Curse*."

"Oh, please do send it. I'm so happy for you, Milo. Let's hope your good influence rubs off a little on me. If only I can go like the wind when I set out my paints in Plommet Falls."

"But don't forget I had seven fallow months. Arabella's last book was turned in last January. It's the middle of August."

"I've had nine fallow *years*. No, it's even worse than that. I've never developed the momentum that you've had. And those 'friends' you speak of, discipline and habit—I hate to say what strangers they are to me. When I was studying at the League, I had this venerable old instructor for a while. His favorite advice was, 'Get into the habit of Art.' He'd tell how he'd often have dry spells, but—like you—he'd go into his studio and he'd say, 'Well, I've got all these paints. I'll mix a color. Now I have a color. I'll lay a little of it on the canvas and see if it tells me anything.' The other thing he used to say was: 'You must be in your studio every day, in case the angel comes. He doesn't come most days, but woe to you if he decides to look in on you and you're out!' God, Milo, what if the angel's already come for me and gone away again in disgust?"

"There's no glib answer for that one. First of all, it was your teacher's formulation. I mean, who is to say the angel only comes once? Maybe he rings twice, like the postman, or maybe he gives three chances, like most of the genies in the fairy tales. Or who is to say he doesn't give a dozen, or a hundred? Perhaps everybody's angel has a different personality. The point is, whether he comes or not, how does one behave in the meantime? One puts in one's time; or one doesn't. If you've put it in, whatever happens, or doesn't happen, you know you've done your best. If you haven't put it in, you'll be haunted by a thousand might-have-beens."

"And rather than go on living with your might-have-beens swarming around you like little stinging bugs, you pack up your gear and take out a pistol and go blam, like Ambrose. Only I don't think I'd have the courage to do that. I wonder what I would do."

"There are alternatives," said Milo. "Before my troubles resolved themselves, I had considered everything from law school to some unrewarding social work that no one else wants to do. There *are* things to do in this world besides writing books and painting pictures, though people like ourselves may tend to forget it sometimes."

"Well, I'm not going to think about alternatives yet. I can afford six months up there. I'm giving myself a grant of six months of perfect freedom. No job to sidetrack me, no difficult personal relationship, not even the traffic on the street. There'll be no excuses this time. I'm going to paint and draw every day and see what evolves. If nothing evolves . . . well, I'll just have to think of some way to be a dignified, useful citizen. But first I'm going to have my grant."

"Operation Fresh Start," said Milo.

"You're so tactful. Operation Late Start is more like it. Oh, hell, I was saving those marigolds in the upper corner for last and now all the sun's gone off them."

"It looks charming as it is."

"I *could* leave that area blank. Then the picture will be charming but unfinished. Or I could risk this blue, which will either deaden the other colors or else deepen them. I can't be sure till I try. What do you think? Shall I be cautious or reckless?"

"Reckless, by all means." He laughed, coming to stand beside me.

I filled in with the blue while he watched.

"It's right," he said at last.

"Hmm. Not bad," I agreed modestly.

"What a lovely mystical effect. You've made it a sort of garden of the spirit."

"It's yours," I said.

15
Lights and Shadows

When I look back on those first weeks I lived in Plommet Falls I think of myself as one who walked on tiptoe, so conscious was I of being balanced on the high wire of my own ultimatum. My life as I saw it then took on the aura of myth. I was not Violet Clay so much as I was the Penitent Who Still Dared to Aspire. In my solitary cabin I seemed to be always under the probationary gaze of someone who would not let me get away with a thing. Even my purchases at the village store with its creaking wood floors and fly blown noticeboard—and the pay phone from which Ambrose had called me last spring —took on Significant Form. Waiting my turn at the cash register manned by a chatty old-timer who refused to be rushed, I gloated benevolently upon my virtuous still life of staples: coffee, soap, oranges, yogurt and thumbtacks. On Ambrose's old portable I had immediately typed up the inspirational words of Albert Pinkham Ryder (Milo's parting gift to me had been *Artists on Art from the XIV to the XX Century*) and tacked it to the right of the south window overlooking the stream, above the table where I ate my meals, stretched my canvases and drew.

> A rain-tight roof, frugal living, a box of colors, and God's sunlight through clear windows keep the soul attuned and the body vigorous for one's daily work. The artist should once and forever emancipate himself from the bondage of appearance and the unpardonable sin of expending on ignoble aims the precious ointment that should serve only to nourish the lamp burning before the tabernacle of his muse.

I soon tied up Ambrose's affairs. A poor man's estate is settled quickly, but, as Minerva had pointed out, there is always a certain amount of red tape. I went down to the court house and signed tax returns; I closed his account at the local bank and opened one of my own. He had left enough to cover his own funeral and burial. His balance and those expenses coincided so eloquently that I wished the police would hurry up and finish *their* red tape and give me back his note to me. Had he written: "I'm sorry, there's nothing left" or: "I'm sorry there's nothing left"? He was a writer, after all, and that comma or the lack of it might spell the difference between running out of inspiration and running out of cash. Somehow I felt that if I could look upon the actual note I'd know whether he meant: "Violet, I know I promised I'd go off to the woods and finish my book but when I got there I found there was nothing left to say, or nothing in me left to say it with" or: "Hey, sport, sorry there's no nest egg to lighten your load, but if I get out quick this should just about cover the inconvenience my exit causes."

Well, that would come. I'd get back the note and I'd get back the Luger as well—minus its firing pin. I'd gone in person to see Lieutenant Quentin, who turned out to be a strapping phallic symbol with his red hair that stood up in front like a jay's and his own loaded pistol nuzzling suggestively against his right thigh as he leaned back in his swivel chair and hooked his thumbs under his belt and narrowed his blue eyes at me as I explained my sentimental reasons for wanting to keep Ambrose's death weapon. What kind of chick is this, anyway, I could practically hear him thinking, wanting to live in a cabin where a man killed himself, her own blood relative, and wanting to have his pistol returned in the bargain?

"You'd need a pistol permit," he said.

"But I don't want to shoot it. I just want to keep it like you'd keep . . . oh, a gold watch or something."

"A pistol isn't a gold watch," he drawled, fixing me with the sharp, light eyes.

I wonder if he finds my type attractive, I thought. "The man from the BCI said something about the firing mechanism, that if you took that out . . ." The man at the BCI had also said Lieutenant Quentin was "very amenable to the ladies."

"Declare it as a souvenir. Yes, that's possible, I suppose."

"It wouldn't make it look any different, would it?"

"It'd look exactly the same," he said, making no attempt to conceal his amusement. "If you want us to take out the pin, I guess we could do that." He stood up. His sunburned hand drifted unconsciously toward his bulky holster. "Call back in . . . better give us two weeks. The reports will have come back from Albany by then and we can wind things up."

The barest minimum of a look flickered between us. There he stood, this modern knight of the road, armed and ready, perhaps one of the purest forms our culture still had to offer in the way of elemental male power. I had the distinct feeling I could start something if I wanted. Those lonely nights in the cabin. The approach of a motor. The efficient slam of a car door with no one but the night animals to hear. Would he arrive in uniform? Even better. The neat pants with the stripe down the leg. Unbuckling the weapon. The weapon beneath.

Ignoble aim! "I appreciate you taking the time," I said, lowering my eyes like a nun.

"Glad to help anytime," he replied, shuttering his but keeping them right where they'd been.

A few days later I went to the local Bureau of Motor Vehicles to get my license renewed. "You've let it expire ages ago," said the woman. "You'll have to take the road test again." When I went out into the blazing sun to meet my examiner, there he stood, his wide-brimmed hat tipped rakishly forward, shading the sharp eyes. God is testing me, I thought. "How nice to see you again. They certainly do keep you busy," I said sociably. He merely nodded, declining to participate in such chitchat. He gave me a demerit for forgetting a left turn signal and on my third attempt to parallel park between two thin poles with flags on top he chuckled coldly and said, "Pretty sloppy, but I guess I'll let it go."

"Oh . . . that's nice of you." We sat together in Ambrose's Pontiac and he filled out the rest of the form. He had a tight, neat handwriting, every *i* dotted and all loops closed.

"Indulgent is more like it," he said, signing his name as if he had a healthy respect for it (I couldn't read from my angle whether it was Gerald or Gerard), and then we looked at each other again.

"Well . . ." I said nervously.

"How'd you get down here from Plommet Falls?" he asked in a slow, quiet voice, watching me all the while.

"Why, I dr . . . that is, I . . . this friend Miss Means . . . she had some shopping to do and so she agreed to drive me." It sounded like the lie it was, even to me.

Was it possible he was sadistic enough to turn me in for driving without a license to get to the license bureau?

He held me in his tension for a moment longer, then laughed out loud. "Give this to the lady in the office and she'll finish you up."

"Thank you very much," I murmured humbly. Okay, you've had your bit of old-fashioned flirt, I told myself. He glowered menacingly and you trembled deliciously. That's enough.

But if he suggested a harmless dinner, the old Eve in me protested, wouldn't it be not playing the game to turn him down?

"And watch those turn signals," he said, making no sign of leaving the car.

If you look now, you defile the tabernacle to your muse, thought I, and I didn't look and after a moment's tense silence he touched his hat to me cordially and left me sitting in the Pontiac alone, feeling virtuous if slightly let down.

I woke extremely early in the country. Wailing sirens, angry horns and groaning garbage trucks had become for me over the years mere white noise for sleeping it off, but now the first bird call caused me to start awake as if someone had addressed a question to me. After that I would lie in the built-in bunk bed and watch the light steadily intensify through the over-flouncy curtains Minerva had hung to surprise me and I didn't have the heart to take down in case she dropped by. The bird chorus would increase to such a din that I'd find myself really interested. Which one was which? What were they all saying? Were they simply "singing with the voices God gave them," or were they having conversations? I realized I knew so little about so many things I wanted to know more about.

As the sun mounted outside, the tension mounted inside me. All this day was to be mine, to use as I pleased. At the end of its light would I bring home anything good? I held my hands up to the window. Small square hands which still looked slightly childlike in spite of their almost thirty-three years. When I arched them back, the knuckles disappeared, leaving dimples. The daylight glowed pink between the membranes. My grandmother's story came back to me, of how her hands had "gone stiff" from lack of practice, had relinquished their right to the hard-earned Rondo and Ballade.

Did talent also go stiff from lack of use? But I *had* been painting during my extended indentureship with Harrow House. Even though my subject was set for me and I did get bogged down in piecework production, I had gone to my studio most days of the week, mixed paint, made decisions about composition, perfected techniques of facial expression, even if the faces and the expressions were, by nature of the product, in a limited range. I had at least kept limber.

Talent. Something given rather than something earned, it's generally agreed. But then you get that chilling parable in Matthew: if, say, the poor guy who had his one talent taken away again happened to have been a painter, *how* exactly did God take it away again?

"Violet can make her hand do what her eye sees," was the first description I ever heard of my own talent. Miss Frieda Lunsford, fifth-grade art, Pine Hollow School. We had been assigned Edward Hopper's lighthouse painting, to copy in watercolors. She showed us how to block in our paper first, in little squares, and she'd marked up the magazine reproduction in the same number of squares. But I wanted to get started with the paints, so I rapidly sketched in the whole thing without bother-

ing with the squares. My impatience led to the discovery of the
happy partnership between my hand and eye. Miss Lunsford
just happened to be one of those teachers who are impressed by
independence in children, especially when it is coupled with
ability, and having once pronounced me talented, she was quick
to pounce on further proof of her own sound judgment. Thus I
became known as the "class artist," the way Pequeña was the
"class beauty" and another girl was the athlete and another was
the brain. Had Miss Lunsford happened to be a more rigid sort
of pedagogue, to whom squares were more important than flair,
my story might have been different. As it was, having been assigned my attention-getting specialty, I set out zealously to
make the most of it. And eventually a glowing account went
forth from Miss Lunsford to my grandmother in Charleston, the
result being that—compliments of the generous coffers of my
godmother—I became one of the chosen few students in the
school to "study privately" with C. R. Summers, the portrait
and landscape artist of local renown.

Once a week this courtly bald gentleman and his tiny white-
haired wife bore me off between them in their stately green
Packard. "Miss Lottie," as she was called, always accompanied
her husband both ways when any female apprentice was col-
lected or returned to the school. We painted together till I was
fifteen, Mr. C. R. and I—rather, I should say, Mr. C. R., Miss
Lottie and I. In our outdoor sessions, in which he taught me to
do clouds and skies and how to give the impression of wind ruf-
fling water ever so slightly, Miss Lottie brought her own camp
stool and sat behind us under her enormous white leghorn hat,
reading or sewing, or sometimes just gazing approvingly at the
back of Mr. C. R.'s head; at intervals she would rise solemnly,
unscrew the lemonade Thermos, and say, "Don't you think you
all have earned yourselves a little refreshment?" In the cold
months she brought cocoa in a silver teapot to the skylit studio
with its man-sized easels and economy-sized cans of linseed oil
and turpentine and the imposing maroon velvet chair on the
platform where his society women sat to have their portraits

done. Every room and hallway in the Summers house was hung with his Grand Style panoramas of the Blue Ridge in all its weathers, his lonely, romantic seascapes from their annual vacation at Hatteras. Once I asked him why there were no portraits of Miss Lottie; he'd painted just about every other woman in town. "Oh, it would take a master to capture the nuances of Miss Lottie," he said reverently, "a Renoir at least. Yes, Renoir could maybe have done justice to Miss Lottie." "But . . . don't you consider yourself a master?" Up until that time I had. "Gracious no, child. Masters are few and far between. I am only a proficient craftsman fortunate enough to earn his living doing what he enjoys best."

He was more than that. He had a distinctive personal vision, masterly or not, that people were willing to pay for and were pleased to hang in their living rooms.

At any rate, thanks to him I could call myself a proficient craftswoman. When I got to college I was years ahead of most of the other art majors. I could mix any color I saw or imagined. I knew how to make my materials work for me. As for drawing, for making things "like," I had started off with that.

But in terms of developing a distinctive personal vision, I was at this point years behind my serious contemporaries: the head-starter making her late start. A good picture, as Picasso said, is a sum of destructions, and I had heaps of work still to do before there'd be enough to start destroying.

Every morning I was up before seven, sometimes earlier. I made two sandwiches, filled a Thermos with ice and the cold coffee left from breakfast and a little milk, and gathered up my paintbox and portable easel and folding stool and went out to see what I could do about transcending my old proficiency plateau and discovering in what shapes and hues my inner necessities might choose—if given a real chance—to reveal themselves.

At first Nature dictated the shapes and hues. It was bound to happen to a painter who had lived in city apartments or dormitories most of her life, this love affair between me and Nature. And she was an irresistible and maddening mistress. I followed slavishly after her with my brush. What would she do next? The only certainty about her was that she refused to stay in one pose for long. I raced her through her shape-shifting contours and shadows. Take it or leave it, she'd say, already preparing to turn into something else. I often painted while I ate my lunch and once I almost drank from the glass jar of turpentine. On through the afternoon I dipped and wiped and squinted and stroked, indulging her constant mood changes, willing her in vain to hold that elusive position for one more minute, the way we used to plead with those sadistic Life Drawing models who'd suddenly announce, just as we were getting it right, "Ten more seconds."

I became compulsive and possessive, as lovers tend to do. I wanted to capture all her poses, have them safe in permanent pigments. There were certain forest moods . . . I remember a particular one that occurred about two p.m. when the saplings were shot with a delicate greeny-white translucence, and the dark boles of their elders held on somberly to their close-valued purples and grays, thus ordering the design and giving added depth to the quality of the light. But that lasted only about fifteen minutes and memory had to improvise the rest.

And then there were the sunsets. The torment of those sunsets. Each one better than the next and no two alike. I wanted them all. The carmine-and-steel-blue one; the phosphorescent green one, the violet-and-lemon, the salmon-and-gray. I filled an entire watercolor block with sunsets. One evening I dragged myself back to the cabin with a terrible headache from trying to document an apocalyptic vermilion one from its splendor to its dregs. I drank a glass of milk, too scared to eat, and lay down on the bed, eyes closed, sure I had risked blindness. I remembered hearing about some painter who had stared at the sun too long. . . . Artistic hubris? I was afraid to turn on the lights all evening. Give my eyes a darkness bath: yes, that would be the best thing.

Even with my eyes closed, I could make out the stages in which the cabin lost its light. I was in an unusually sharpened state from painting all day so intensely I forgot to eat my second sandwich, from being dead sober (as I had been every single evening since coming here) and from having been alone so much. Sam and her daughter had not been seen around, either in their jeep or out of it, since the day after Ambrose's death, and Minerva was diligently playing the *laissez-faire* landlady downhill, secure in the knowledge I would have dinner with her on Saturday.

I was really worried about my eyes. I could do without all the things I had complained so long about not having: money, security, fame, etc. I might even get by without Ryder's roof and sunlight, in a pinch. But if I could not see, I could not do the thing that gave me most pleasure, the thing that had lived with me longer than anyone in my life. I loved my painting, I knew that now, I had loved it all along. It made me happy when I was doing it. Often in the city, even when painting my fleeing maidens, I'd wander into the bathroom the way some people go out for a stroll and look at myself in the mirror and be amazed at how the blood was up in my face. I was often amazed to see any reflection at all, I had so forgotten myself in the stimulation of painting.

All those hours and days and years of brooding over my anonymity as an artist seemed unimportant, the faraway preoccupation of another world. I knew—if only, please God, I would be allowed to keep my eyes—I would go on painting till the day I died. As long as I could paint, even if I couldn't earn my living by proficiency as Mr. Summers had done, even if it was just for myself, I wanted to go on living. Even if I were granted a glimpse of my future in which every art gallery in the world hung a sign on its front door saying: NO NEED TO APPLY INSIDE, VIOLET CLAY THIS MEANS YOU! I would still go on painting because it was something I had to do and something I thought about all the time and something that made me mean and miserable when I wasn't doing it.

Now, I don't want to make a big thing of it, but as I lay there in the crepuscular moment of dusk when the birds are emitting those last little plaintive chirps, I testily opened my eyes and I saw—

Well, actually I *saw* nothing. But the shadows were such that they lent themselves to the potential shape of a person in remorse, sitting slump-shouldered at the foot of my bed. I knew even as I "saw" it that I had sketched it with my own imagination. That was the way I would imagine Ambrose to have sat in his last hours.

If only, I thought, time travel were possible and I could reach back to those hours when this shape still housed a living soul: what message might I have given him that could have made him reconsider?

Reconsider what? the bowed figure might have asked, still declining to look up.

I don't know . . . all the possibilities.

Which ones?

Well, for example, that as long as there's one thing you still enjoy doing in the world, then life is worth going on with.

The figure darkened against my optimism like those somber older trees in the forest refusing to glow like saplings exulting in a few mere patches of sun.

You won't let me help you?

Soon I could no longer go on abetting these fancies because the shape was already merging with the darkness filling the room.

No answer.

If you won't let me help you, won't you at least say something to help me understand?

You can't understand. May you never understand. May my shadow stand in the way of your ever having to understand.

But no one said that. The words formed themselves in my head. It didn't "count," therefore, in a strictly supernatural sense. Or did it?

The next day I opened my eyes on the cabin filling with its usual morning light. I gazed fondly at my paintbox lying on the table where I'd left it the evening before. Usually when I came home from a day's work, I propped my new things up so I could see them first thing in the morning. Why had I forgotten? Oh, yes. Well, I'd do it now. Soon yesterday's greens and golds and darks right up to the vermilion sunset joined the previous days' varieties and abundances.

Whose impressive artistry was it, though? Nature's or mine? That was the next question. All headache gone, my eyes still apparently okay, I was looking for problems again.

16

The Habit of Art

Where were my elusive neighbors? Where was the handsome woodswoman who repaired barns and made complicated homes for outdoor cats, and her fatherless little girl, who had kept Ambrose company and had unfortunately been the one to find him dead? I kept waiting for the jeep to pass my door. I had rehearsed at least a dozen variations of the scene in which we'd meet and certain things would be made clear. What Ambrose's last days had been like, for instance. If he had taken all those walks with the child, surely something must have gone on between him and the mother. They were near enough and interesting enough to hover at the edges of any solitary neighbor's imagination: a woman young and striking who had exiled herself to her father's old hunting shack, where she lived the year round, apparently complete unto herself with her daughter. It was a picturesque situation, to say the least. It lent itself to imaginings. Ambrose, too, had probably been stimulated imaginatively by it.

The first few days I felt sure we'd meet. She'd come bumping along our shared road on her way to or from a job, she'd slow down, lean out the window, brake the jeep and say, "Hi, I'm . . ." Sam? Samantha? I realized Minerva hadn't even told me her last name. "You must be Violet, Ambrose's niece. He often spoke of you." *Did* he ever speak of me?

But no vehicle except my own came down the road. They must be away. Why had they not attended the burial service? About these two I had many questions. Several times I started tentatively toward their place. A quarter of a mile down the road, Minerva had said, or straight below the falls, through the woods. I had already explored the immediate woods at the back of my cabin, following the stream to the point where it became —at this time of year—a trickling waterfall. But the woods beyond were dense and I saw a path but no sign of any dwelling. Several times in the early evening I had "strolled" down the road, not having made up my mind what I would do when I came in sight of their cabin. What if one or both of them were outside? What would they say? More important, what could I say? Should I simply introduce myself as their new neighbor? What should I do about mentioning Ambrose? If I didn't mention him it might seem strange to them. Whereas if I did, there was the risk of saying something that would hit the wrong nerve, in either the mother or the child, or both.

Once I got as far as the bend in the road where a piece of their cabin and a vegetable garden were visible through the trees. It was much more modern than I'd expected: siding instead of whole logs—really more like a Swiss chalet. Even from what I saw of it I got the impression of a trim, shipshape existence: everything neat and squared off into a snugness that almost bordered on smugness. Even the hollyhocks growing around the wire fence of the garden looked as meticulously spaced as one of Agnes Martin's grids. I turned around and hurried back to my own cabin, my heart thudding guiltily as though my spying had been observed. I both envied and resented the sequestered coziness this mother and daughter had created for themselves.

"I haven't seen Sam around," I told Minerva when I went

down for the Saturday dinner. (Another frozen casserole, this time more thawed, however.)

"My dear, no one has seen Sam around. Mr. Perry phoned me, wanting to know where she was. She had promised to pollard some trees for him when she had some spare time at the end of August. I don't know why people call me; I'm not her keeper. She's reliable and she's thorough when she does a job for you, but she goes her own way. She takes off when she likes. They may have gone down to Florida to see her father again. I know they went last spring."

"What is her last name?"

"De Vere. The daughter of that peculiar Captain De Vere. Always so afraid somebody might start a conversation with him. He was a real modern-day hermit, all right. Sam takes after him a little, in my opinion."

"And the little girl goes by the same last name?"

"Oh, yes. Cheyenne De Vere. As I said, I don't ask for information if it's not volunteered. My mother didn't bring me up that way. It's a strange first name for a little girl, isn't it? The first time I heard it I mistook it for 'Shy Anne,' and I thought *that* was odd, though in a sweet way."

Minerva's wrinkled-child's face looked rather sweet itself, glowing like a startled flower which had bloomed and would die in this brownish gloom dominated by stuffed animals. For some reason I was reminded of those dinners *à deux* with my grandmother in the house on the Battery, that other summer when I had set myself to paint in earnest. There had been that same sense of destiny waiting in the wings, before my "Wasteful Sea" went sour on me and Lewis Lanier came to visit with his aunt.

I continued to think about my absent neighbors. They had hooked themselves on some sharp edge of my imagination and seemed to flap along with me, wherever I went. When I painted outdoors I was intensely aware that we shared the woods and at any moment they might conceivably come upon me. The fact that I had dreamed about Sam driving me somewhere in her jeep, the two of us in league somehow, with poor Ambrose bumping up and down in the back seat, had put me in her power in a way I could not fully comprehend. Now I actively waited for her to come back and reveal . . . what? The missing piece of something. Though whether it would be about Ambrose or about herself—or about me—I couldn't have told you then.

Only about ten days had passed since my arrival. In terms of painting time, it seemed a great deal longer. I had dozens of small canvases and watercolors and sketches pinned up all around the cabin. I had assured myself that God had not taken away my natural gift to "make my hand do what my eye saw." But I had just about reached the end of the big affair with Nature and was coming round to Klee's view that she can be garrulous to the point of confusion and that when confronting her the artist must employ taciturnity.

I knew I could fill the walls of thirty cabins with graphic homage to what I saw around me. That was something. But it wasn't enough. It wasn't going to get me anywhere.

But where did I want to go?

I wanted to go to the secret element in things, to penetrate the mysteries with my brush.

What painter didn't?

But how was I going to get there?

Some dutiful voice told me I was letting boredom make me fainthearted, "just when you were getting into the habit of art, too. Shame!"

So I dutifully went back to my graphic documentations for a few days. I did the chunky blue mountains through a clearing. More lights and shadows in the afternoon forest. Some last year's leaves rotting at the base of this year's wildflowers. I found myself quitting earlier and looking for excuses to go into town. I drove down to the cemetery in Schroon Lake to visit Ambrose's grave. Carol's opulent carnation spray had taken on the monochrome drabness of a Braque. The simple square of granite, with his name and dates, had been set in, but the grass had not grown round it yet. Then I drove slowly back to my lonely cabin and parked the Pontiac resignedly in the shade of the birches. I thought I knew exactly how Ambrose had felt, after the euphoria had worn off his noble gesture and he was faced with a solitary evening ahead and nothing to look forward to.

I went inside and looked at my things propped or tacked around the room. The naturescapes from the euphoric period did have a certain dash. One felt the energy in the quick bold strokes which let the light in loosely; it was as if the painter's enthusiasm traveled faster than her hand and she had been obliged to take reckless shortcuts—some inspired—to keep pace. But alas, the competent productions of the past few days almost groaned aloud under their sagging weight of Duty.

When your "dutiful voice" turns out to be not enough, what then? There was nobody around to ask. If I'd been in the city I would have called Milo. He would have reassured me, invited me to hop in a cab and come over for something delicious to eat, and inspired me with stories of his own creative life. Or if he wasn't available, I would have set off for the nearest bookstore to leaf through expensive art books and get a new angle on things—or maybe have gone to a movie to give my stagnating vision a chance to renew itself in distracting darkness. Or perhaps by now a new lover would have been found to sweeten the bitterness of uninspired work.

I poked through Ambrose's box of books for something to read. His collection had been greatly reduced since Waverly Place. Just his old standbys Fitzgerald and Hemingway, neither of whom I was wild about, two copies (one now jacketless) of *Looking for the Lora Lee*, his confirmation Bible, and Cornelius Ryan's *The Longest Day*. Other than his Webster's and Roget's and a Spanish grammar and dictionary, that was it. He'd probably sold the bulk of his books when he and Carol split up and he'd hit the road for Mexico. In the Cornelius Ryan book on the Normandy invasion I found pencil checks beside a number of names in the index of "D-Day Veterans and What They Do Today." There were also several phone numbers, some of which had been crossed out and replaced by other numbers, or else had "No new listing" written after them. This must have been when Ambrose had the assignment from the *Saturday Evening Post*, his follow-up piece on his fellow heroes in the 101st that would whitewash his flight from Carol into a "working divorce" and could also be used as background material for the shape-shifting second novel. Poor Ambrose. His editor friend at the *Post* had been fired soon after. How many of these men had he actually looked up? It was an interesting list. From the looks of it, the "longest day" had been their brightest hour. Now—or rather as of 1959, when the book was published—they sold insurance, clerked in steamship companies, grew mushrooms, worked in the post office or ran linotype machines. The majority had remained in the U.S. Army. Ambrose V. Clay (P.F.C.) was the only free-lance writer.

I set aside Hemingway's *Islands in the Stream*. The jacket copy said it was about an artist. What I really wanted was a book about an artist and how that artist went to his work every day and wrestled with his demons. I longed for a blow-by-blow account of what really happened when he was in there by himself, without any romanticizing, or skimming over or faking. I also took out one of the *Lora Lees*. Perhaps I would try Ambrose's novel again. Every time I tried to read it, it misted away before my eyes like the elusive Lora herself and when I finished it I could never quite remember what was really in it and what I had only wanted to be in it. Was this just my particular problem because I had been told that Ambrose's love for my late mother had served as inspiration for this personage? Or was there some fault in the novel itself?

I browsed through it, trying to see it objectively: a book in its own right rather than a first novel written by my uncle, an ex-GI of twenty-one alone in the boyhood room he'd shared with his dead brother, in full view of the sea where that brother's widow had drowned herself—even after he had offered to make her a bride again.

In the book, Lora Lee didn't appear until almost the second half. The first half was about the two airmen stationed in England, waiting for the famous June night, from which one of them would not return. Lots of barracks details. The touching, unheroic things men did while waiting to become heroes. This probably accounted for a lot of the book's popularity, coming out as it did in the last years of the forties, when, as Landsborough had put it, everybody began to have the blahs. The airman Bruce, who was fated to die, untiringly sang the praises of his beautiful fiancée, Lora, to his buddy Max. Max was, as Carol would say caustically, "the protagonist." And on the long tension-filled evenings when the men sat around strumming on guitars or writing letters home or losing their week's pay on cards, Max found himself falling in love with a girl he had never met. There she was, always gazing down on him, too, from the wall behind Bruce's bed. She wore a tennis dress and held a racket. Her limbs were silky and firm; she smiled "as people did who have never been given cause to doubt themselves." If she looked this radiant in black-and-white, imagine what she must be in full color. It seemed from the angle of his bed, she was smiling a special smile that could be seen only from his side, a smile meant for him alone.

After the war, Max visits her in her home by the sea. Lora's house had many things in common with our old house on the Battery, whereas Ambrose had made Max come from a deprived background similar to my mother's. For the first hour they talk loyally of the dead airman. What is left unsaid vibrates in the air between them. Max asks if he may come again tomorrow and she says yes, but not till dusk. She even offers him her cheek before sending him back to his hotel in town. He notes a fleeting, fugitive look in her eyes but thinks no more of it till he comes back the next evening and learns that she and her Chris-Craft have fled down the Intracoastal Waterway. Ambrose—I mean Max—hires a boat and after receiving a short lecture on navigation from a salty old type (who also tells him that "yacht" comes from the Dutch and means hunt or chase), is off in a gasoline-scented spray after his Lora. I leafed quickly as always through the respectably seaworthy chase chapters, pausing whenever there was anything personal—flashbacks of childhood, war experience, dreams for the future (he wants to be a really good journalist who will help the new world interpret itself)—and skimmed over, shamelessly as always, the dangerous storm with its high point of action and impressive nautical terms, until the final reconciliation in a cove overhung with Spanish moss in which his Lorelei explains at last the mystery of her behavior.

Which was: she had loved him, Max, all along. She learned to love him through her fiancé's letters. She'd never really loved Bruce, you see, not in that way. They'd grown up together, believed love meant taking the same things for granted. And then when he was shot down over France she believed she had caused it. By being untrue in her heart. By not keeping him aloft with her love and her need for him to come back. And then after his death, she had thought for a while she had loved him. The guilt, the self-recrimination. "I resolved never to marry. And then you walked into the house and I knew I'd been waiting for you. But I've wanted too many things in my life and got them for the asking. You were too special for that. I wanted to earn you. I wanted to make it difficult for myself for your sake."

The hero then quips that, in his opinion, they've earned each other. His arm, which was broken during the storm when his hired boat cracked up and he had to leap aboard hers and help her get the steering mechanism back under control, is in a makeshift sling, but the closing paragraph lets it be understood in the tacit language available to writers in the forties that this temporary handicap in no way impedes his prowess.

I closed Ambrose's book with a sigh and opened Hemingway's, searching around in it for the places where the hero went off to his studio. But whenever he did, he was most careful to shut the door firmly behind him. Then he came out again, having "worked well," and went into town for a whiskey or out in a boat or into memories of women. There was a nice passage about his cats in the middle, about how this one cat he loved best always refused to sleep with him when he was drunk.

It still lacked an hour or more of being dark. In the old Stolichnaya days, I had not had this trouble bridging the dusk.

I wrote Milo a short note. ". . . looking forward to Kaatje
and her grim secrets. I've been working well, trying to maintain
'the habit.' There is lots to paint here, especially if you're Fred-
erick Church or Thomas Cole. . . ."

Why did that last line send a shiver of *déjà vu* through me?
Oh, God, of course. Ambrose's postcard, mailed to me last June
from Plommet Falls. He must have written it sitting at this very
table. *On the whole very peaceful here. Lots of beautiful scenery
to paint, or to write about, for that matter, if you're Thoreau.
Hope you are taking good care of yourself. Meanwhile, as the
British say, we must press on.*

We sure must. "I am starting on a new tack tomorrow," I
wrote on, as much to myself as to Milo. "There comes a point
where one becomes a mere copyist of externals. I don't want
that. I want to take off from those externals, as you took off from
your Greek woman in the kitchen, and find my way toward my
most urgent mental forms. If it means invoking demons, let
them come."

Then I wrote a note to Carol. "It is quite comfortable here,
though I wasn't prepared for how noisy nature can be. This afternoon I went to the cemetery. They've put the stone down;
it looks good. Your flowers are still there, a little faded now. I
work every day from sunrise to sunset. So far I have done . . ."

I got up from the table and walked around the room and
counted.

". . . twelve watercolors, some with gouache; twenty-two
inks and washes, fifteen pastels and ten small oils." The quantity
looked rather impressive on paper. Carol approved of quantity
and I still had time to fuss over the quality before any outside
eye would be invited to judge.

I addressed the two letters and sealed them and propped
them side by side against the two novels. So much overlapping
here. Almost a new category of still life: a *vanitas* of associative
hieroglyphics. A man's wishful projection of a woman who could

fulfill his dreams, and next to her the real woman who tried and failed to wake him up. Books filled with romance and the sea and the mirage of effortless successes. Milo in Brooklyn Heights painstakingly erecting his scaffolding from a precarious blend of nightmare, memory and a quest for a whole self. Me in Plommet Falls still poking round for the proper soil on which to build. Mothers who died and left their imprints, some of which got changed past recognition through art. People being so many things to other people that it was easy to lose track. I wrote one sort of letter to Milo, another sort to Carol, showing each the side I wished each to see. My mother, the poor girl from South Carolina who cried and cried and ate the wrong end of her broccoli, had inspired the rich Lora, who smiled "as people did who have never been given cause to doubt themselves," and, in turn, Ava Gardner, the poor girl from North Carolina who had probably never been in a yacht till she filmed *Pandora and the Flying Dutchman* with James Mason, had insisted the part of Lora was made for her. Angels, prods, warnings, models, demons. With what variations we occupied one another's thoughts!

I went to stand in the doorway. Night was coming on. There wasn't going to be a sunset, as the sky had gone overcast. The air was muggy. Everything was very quiet and ponderous and a sort of gray-green color. I heard a rumbling sound like thunder. The pregnant gray-green monotony before a storm. Just the way I felt tonight. Well, let it pour. I would have to stay indoors tomorrow and maybe something would break and a new kind of light would come in. The sound rumbled louder and louder and I whimsically thought: This may signal my confrontation with my angel or demon at last, who knows?

Like a chimera, the big white jeep barreled into sight. It slowed down at the sight of Ambrose's car parked in its usual spot beneath the birches, then roared away in a sudden burst of acceleration when the two startled faces inside saw what must have looked like a ghost to them in the eerie half light: a pale figure wearing pants and one of Ambrose's shirts, peering at them steadily from behind the screen door.

17
Demons

The next day it did rain. I woke later than usual to the soft drumming on the roof, secretly glad I had been excused from trekking off into the woods in search of significant forms. I was tempted to give myself a day off, except for the fact that I had told Milo I was starting something new today. I was superstitious about sending one version of my day off in a letter and never realizing that day in my own life. It was like letting a piece of one's ideal self get away. So I decided to set up my things at the table by the window, invoke my subconscious to come up and express itself, and see what would result on paper. I would give myself till noon at least. Then perhaps I would allow myself a little jaunt into the exciting metropolis of Plommet Falls to mail the letters to Milo and Carol, pick up some food and drive home again. Little did I imagine, as I sat down, tacked a sheet of paper to my board and swirled my sable confidently in a jar of clean water, that my demons already sat watching. They had settled in some time ago and waited patiently for my first enthusiasms to exhaust themselves. The thing about demons is, we imagine them to be fascinating little creatures like the ones in Bosch's landscapes, or great hulking Henry Moore shapes, or Milo's Fat Woman rising out of the sea to devour babies. But those are somebody else's demons. They've already been given a shape. By the time a demon has been given a shape, even in the mind, he's lost part of his power. And when he's been thoroughly apprehended, all of his tentacles pried loose from the mind and transferred intact to the cage of art, he's as safe as a tiger in the zoo. People can come and shudder aesthetically at the sight of him and go away feeling enlightened. But for every captured demon, for every successfully realized "Temptation of St. Anthony" that hangs in a museum, there lie countless carcasses of those artists who expired in the grips of their monsters.

If anyone had whispered to me, "Hey, Violet, your monsters are in the room with you!" I would have at once imagined a manageable crew of colorful creatures who could, with a bit of skillful coaxing, be charmed into working for me. Whereas, it is the nature of personal demons to be the last thing you imagine. They don't even cast a shadow, they're so close to what you are.

I thought loudly to myself: "I'll just swirl around some of this blue and light purple and see what happens." But already I was cheating. I had known when I sat down what I was going to try to make happen: that "Violet in Blue" painting I had conceived in Milo's guest room the night Ambrose had died, the color violet trying to hold its own, to find its place upon the equanimity of the blue. So I was not opening myself to the unconscious. I was pretending to some invisible audience in the room that I was opening myself, so that it would be impressed at how quickly I came up with something. That the "audience" was made up of some of my worst demons I didn't even suspect. I'm speaking about the ones who are in love with the appearance of work and are perfectly willing to confuse it with the genuine endeavor that struggles up from deeper sources.

I splashed on through the morning, wasting sheet after sheet of good Capri paper. I worked fast and wet, aiming for the kind of fluidity that was going on outside my window as the watery morning dissolved and re-formed itself through successive washes.

At least I didn't kid myself about the relief I felt when the morning was over and I had put in my time. Punctually at noon, as if a factory whistle had blown, I stuck my brushes in water. I had "painted" for three hours, hadn't I? The question echoed hollowly in the pit of my stomach. The specter of Ambrose paced about restlessly in the soft rainy gloom. He had known such mornings: I was as certain of it as though his memories were now part of my mind. He, too, had willed himself to sit at this table and "Write" for the allotted hours before fleeing these four walls.

I went into the bathroom and splashed water on my face and combed my hair. I then ambled casually back to the table, not looking down till the last minute. I hoped to surprise my morning's work into looking more promising. No such luck. I saw three hours' worth of purple or lavender transparencies bleeding overbearingly or wishy-washily into an unmagical blue.

I walked out through the rain to the car and sat bowed over the wheel, just gripping the wheel with both hands and staring out at the rain. Whatever had given me the inflated notion of myself as a person who might send light into the darkness of other people's hearts by making marks on paper?

I drove into the village, wishing with all my heart I could be someone else. Or even nobody. Today it really hit me how someone could get so sick of his same old act—the false starts, the fresh failures, the noble resolutions leading in turn to new false hopes and starts—that he'd prefer to have done with it altogether.

I mailed the letters to Milo and Carol and picked up my mail. A forwarded card from Jake, mailed almost a month ago in Norway, and the September *American Artist*. I still subscribed to three art magazines, although I now turned their glossy pages more as a monthly exercise in masochism than with any mounting excitement over new trends, or flushes of healthy competitiveness when I read about a talented contemporary.

Jake's postcard showed a modern hotel sandwiched between a mountain and a fiord.

> Bracing air—fantastic scenery. I now realize I said some pretty cruel things. I didn't mean them. Hope the air has cleared for you, too. Sophie Wilder, the mezzo, is with our tour. She also busted up with her long-time lover recently. I hope you get the same good things I want for myself. Try and remember it wasn't all bad between us.

How like him. I was sure he'd started out that postcard with the noblest intentions, only to be overcome halfway through with a need to assert his romantic one-upmanship. Sophie Wilder was a very striking woman and he knew I knew it. I dropped the postcard in the post office wastebasket, tucked the magazine under my raincoat and ran back to the car. It was raining hard now. There was a parking place right in front of the store. I sat for a few minutes leafing through my magazine, in hopes of waiting out the downpour. Two women artists were interviewed in this issue. Page 44 and page 50. I turned quickly from one to the other. The first was good. At least she was old. Her first show had been held the year I was born. There was a photo of the second. She was young and pretty, posed in profile rather self-consciously over her drawing board, with a picturesque city in the background. Her photograph was more interesting than her work. She had backpacked through North Africa and hitchhiked from Mexico to Lima, Peru, according to the interview. And had graduated from college the year after I had and started off as a commercial artist and writer. "My two children's books have sold over 700,000 copies but my love is still fine art. . . ."

The downpour was preferable to this. Preparing to make a run for it, I saw through the blur of my windshield that I was parked behind a white jeep.

My heart was beating fast as I went into the store, already "onstage" for her, in case she was watching. Perhaps it wasn't even she. Maybe there were several white jeeps in Plommet Falls. How silly. Why was I acting like this? In a daze of self-consciousness, I found myself piling my shopping cart with more groceries than I could use in a week. There wouldn't be anything to shop for tomorrow if I bought all these. Meanwhile, as my hands pulled down boxes and cans, my eyes covertly scanned the close aisles. She wasn't at the checkout counter when I came in. If she was anywhere in the store, it would have to be one of these aisles.

I came upon her standing pensively in front of the drugs and sundries shelves. She was wearing one of those black oil slickers that sailors wear in shipwreck paintings. Her hair was all tucked up in her rain hat and one might have taken her for a fine-featured man had it not been that she was quite clearly comparing the qualities of sanitary napkins. She had a rival box in each hand and appeared to be reading the small print. I tactfully moved in, pretending to be interested in the toothpastes. "Oh, hi," I said, simultaneously dropping an economy-size Crest into my basket, even though I still had practically a full tube at home.

She looked around at me. Rather, I should say down at me, because she was almost a foot taller. She made no secret of not being able to place me.

"I'm Violet Clay, Ambrose Clay's niece," I said, hoping she'd take it from there. Her greenish-gray eyes widened slightly, but other than that, her face remained unmoved. "I just wanted to say hello," I went on, feeling more self-conscious by the second, "since we are going to be neighbors."

"Are we?" she asked, as if it would take more than that to convince her. She stood coolly in her space, the boxes balanced levelly in her hands. I couldn't help noticing that both boxes were the junior size. For such a statuesque woman?

"Well, I hope so," I said, beginning to find her taciturnity a bit rude. I decided to turn on my Southern charm and go more than halfway. Who knew what kind of background she had had to fight her way out of? "I came up to take care of my uncle's arrangements," I said, "and decided to stay on in the cabin for a few months myself. I'm a painter. There's lots round here to paint."

"Yes, but it will be getting cold soon." She had a muted voice with a touch of hoarseness; if it had had more inflection, I might have been able to tell if she was trying to put me off.

"Oh, I don't mind a little cold," I said gaily, feeling more and more like a fool. Why was she making it so difficult? Surely she ought to have a little sympathy for me, being Ambrose's niece and all. "Minerva Means tells me the cabin is quite warm, what with the heating units and the stove. I believe you helped put in the wood-burning stove. Minerva says you do carpentry and fix just about anything. I can't even hammer a nail in straight."

"I guess different people do different things," she said. She was surreptitiously trying to read the labels on the sanitary napkin boxes again.

"Well, I can see you're busy," I said, allowing myself a little sarcasm. But some stubbornness or maybe it was loneliness just wouldn't let me stop there. "Perhaps sometime you could come over to my cabin and have supper," I rushed on. "Oh, and bring your little girl, of course."

Her eyebrows shot up. "I hardly think that would be a good idea," she said with some feeling. "Under the circumstances."

"Oh, God," I said, wishing to disappear through the creaky old floorboards. "Of course, I'm very sorry about that . . . I mean about it being her who found him. I'm sure he didn't plan it that way. In fact, Minerva and I have discussed it; we're almost positive he asked this Indian man to come back on the night . . . well, you know, the night he did it. So that it would be a perfect stranger, and not, well, anyone he . . . cared about."

She regarded me gravely, as though I were some eccentric stranger who had suddenly chosen to regale her with family secrets in the grocery store. Standing there so tall, her tanned, slightly damp face retreating further into the rain hat, she made me conscious of my own exposed position.

"Well," I concluded, "all I meant to do was say hello. As we are going to be living in walking distance of one another, it seemed the neighborly thing to do. But I'm sorry if I seemed to pounce on you."

"That's okay," she said (ungraciously, I thought). "It's just that Cheyenne and I were doing fine without neighbors till last spring. Now it would be best if we kept to ourselves again."

"I understand," I said, my cheeks stinging. At least I could make a dignified exit. "Well, I've got to get back. Nice to have met you, anyway." I wheeled my cartload of superfluous purchases toward the checkout counter.

"Yes, same here." Her voice trailed after me unconvincingly.

The chatty old clerk took his time, as usual, in ringing things up. He informed me cheerfully that it wouldn't be long now till the first frost came.

It was still pouring when I left the store, but I couldn't face going home just yet. I drove slowly through Plommet Falls. It was raining so hard it was difficult to see. To the left winked the sign of a black bear standing on his hind legs drinking a cocktail. The Bear was the only bar in town. There were always several large rigs parked outside, as the center of Plommet Falls was only about three New York City blocks from the Northway. For one low moment I fantasized going inside, ordering a vodka tonic (they probably wouldn't have Stolichnaya up here) and chatting up a burly truckdriver.

But wait, I did have someplace to go! To state trooper head-quarters in Schroon Lake to pick up Ambrose's Luger and sui-cide note. It had been more than ten days.

If Lieutenant Quentin happened to be in the mood for a chat, well, he was certainly better known to me than a truck-driver. There would be nothing cheap about it. He'd knock off at five and maybe go home and change first and come and get me at the cabin in his own car. We'd go out, perhaps to Myra's Steak House (another attraction I'd glimpsed along the local roads), and he would tell me the rigorous training he'd had to go through to be a modern Knight of the Road: driving through prepared oil slicks at 100 miles per hour; strapping himself into a steel-topped car, then overturning himself. I'd read all about it somewhere. And then I'd say (we'd be sitting in a booth, with a checkered table cloth and a candle burning in an old Chianti bottle, our steaks tucked away in our stomachs, well into our sec-ond bottle of heavy burgundy—would he know to have ordered burgundy?), I would say, "Tell me a little about your home life." "Oh, there's not much to tell," he'd say (how did troopers dress when they were off duty?). "I live with my widowed mother. . . ." No, I didn't want him to live with a widowed mother. "I live with my sister; she's divorced and I'm helping her raise her boy. . . ." No, that sounded like something out of

Dickens. Most probably he would tilt his head roguishly (would he look as roguish without the gun, and the stripe down the side of his trousers, and his Canadian Mountie hat?) and say, "Why talk about that?" For of course he was married, to some woman who was relieved to be going to bed alone early, her pale hair in rollers—the kids, thank God, asleep—her favorite magazines stacked by her bed. . . . Poor Quentin, he had to work overtime again. . . . But wait, wouldn't she suspect something if he'd already been home to change his clothes? That was the trouble with fantasies—all those realistic loose ends.

Oh, for Christ's sake, I thought, pulling into the troopers' headquarters. You're just going to pick up your uncle's last relics. He probably won't even be in.

He wasn't. The dispatcher at the desk said all available men had been called out. There'd been a four-car accident at the Pottersville exit. But yes, he knew of the Luger. He went away and came back with a large Manila envelope with "Clay" written in pencil on the front. He made me look inside to check that everything I wanted was there.

"Are you sure they've fixed the pistol?" I asked. "Lieutenant Quentin said they'd have to take out the firing mechanism."

"We sure did," he said. Not bad-looking himself. He fished his hand into the Manila envelope and pulled out the Luger. He cocked it and aimed it toward a framed portrait of the current governor. The Luger clicked feebly, like a toy gun. "If you'll just sign this paper," he said.

"I'm sorry to have missed Lieutenant Quentin. Would you please tell him I said thanks?" *Violet Clay,* I scribbled, thinking: Well, I still have my supper and the September *American Artist* to look forward to. Thinking: If only I had waited till a sunny day, when there were no accidents. But would that really have solved anything?

"Yes, I'll tell him," he said, excusing himself to answer one of the telephones.

As soon as I got to the car, I unfolded the piece of paper. It was on Corrasable Bond and the type was smeared a little.

I wondered how many official fingers had handled it.

Violet honey,
    I'm sorry, there's nothing left.
                Love,
                    Ambrose

Of course there would be a comma. How could I ever have doubted it? In the place where he had been when he wrote that note, finances would seem a toy problem.

I was beginning to know that place a little myself.

The rain had made the cabin damp and, I fancied, colder. ". . . it will be getting cold soon," she had said. What would the fall and winter be like, when the bad weather came, if this was any indication of what I did on the first day I couldn't go outside? Had outside been a diversion, too? How long could I exist sanely within these four walls without diversions? I now realized how much I had counted on making friends with someone my own age with her own stories to tell. I turned on one of the heating units for the first time. A dusty smell came out with the warm air. I took Ambrose's emasculated Luger out of the damp Manila envelope and, after some thought, decided to keep it under my pillow. Then I sprayed his suicide note with fixative and thumbtacked it below Ryder's paean to the rain-tight roof and box of colors. At this moment, my uncle's succinct admission of his emptiness seemed more honest and somehow nobler than Mr. Ryder's gush of creative self-righteousness. Ryder had already painted "Moonlit Cove" and "Toilers of the Sea." He could afford to give forth with a bit of inspirational patronage for those still struggling—perhaps in vain. Ambrose had been one of the latter, and in his cavalier farewell had blamed no one but himself.

All this time I had been doing my best not to look at the blue-and-purple sketch paintings for "Violet in Blue." There was nothing wrong with them, but there was nothing wonderful about them either. The best ones looked like designs for a head scarf. I wanted to ball them up and throw them into the trash basket, but it seemed wasteful to crumple up all those costly sheets of 140-pound paper. If I continued to waste paper, I should make myself use the backs of the sheets. I also repressed the urge to turn them face down. Better, if I were an artist manqué, that I should look the fact in the eye as soon as possible and make other plans.

Like what?

I lay on the bed for a few hours. The rain slowed, then stopped. Somehow I would have preferred it to go on.

I went through the motions of making an early supper. There was a soup I had become attached to, Campbell's Tomato Bisque; it went well with peanut butter and saltine crackers. I had been having it almost every night, congratulating myself that it was artistic not to worry about varied menus. I had once read an interview with Agnes Martin about how she ate the same lunch every day so as not to deplete her energies over such mundane details.

The cover of the new *American Artist* was from Courbet's "The Painter's Atelier, a True Allegory Summarizing a Period of Seven Years of My Life." This seemed a personal message to me, just as the contents of this issue seemed to have been put together solely to goad me. In addition to the interviews with the two women, there was an article about the Art Students League, which was celebrating its one hundredth anniversary.

> It is a well-worn cliché that "everyone" studied at the Art Students League. This particular cliché is not simply a game of words: most of the important American artists from 1875 to the present *did*, in fact, study at the League, and many returned to teach. . . .

A list of illustrious students followed. Good Lord, even Jane Fonda and Jackie Kennedy had put in their time there. Among the illustrious faculty, I quickly spotted my first teacher, the venerable old man who had espoused the habit of art and warned us to be at home when our angels came. Out of curiosity I scanned the article for Ivor's name, though I doubted it would be there. It wasn't. I wondered if he was still teaching at that little south Florida college, to which, in another life, I would have accompanied him, to live by the sea and raise babies. Ah, Ivor, thanks to you I wasted almost two years of painting time. But no, damn it, I wasn't going to start blaming other people again. If Ambrose could bow out in a sportsmanlike way, I, too, could be sporting. I might not choose to blow my brains out, but I could at least not whine if it was in the cards for me to become one of the world's losers. There was still time to get a dignified loser's act together, if it came to that. Didn't I come from a part of the country that had made its biggest loss into a sort of debonair victory? No, I would not blame Ivor. He was just there and I had been ready for him. In some ways, he had been as inevitable as one of my demons.

It was just before the Christmas break, 1967, and there was a wine and cheese party going on in the downstairs front room at the Art Students League, where a faculty show had just been hung. I was, at this point, in a rut. Ambrose had broken with Carol in September, driven slowly cross-country, sending me an occasional card; the last card had been postmarked Oaxaca, Mexico, where he said he was "composing my soul and assembling my materials." I naturally took this to mean his novel, because in a postcard some weeks before from Texas he had informed me his article on the D-day Heroes in Peacetime was off because his editor had been fired. Oaxaca looked like a lovely place to be composing one's soul while assembling materials, and I was a little jealous of his easy mobility and exotic fresh start. I was into my second cold winter in New York, my eighteenth month doing covers for Harrow House, and entering my sixteenth month at the League, and although I had filled many Strathmore pads with nudes and completed several professional-looking still lifes and had my fling with Abstract Expressionism, I had received no sign from the city I had come to conquer that my name meant anything more to it than that of a student at one of its institutions. The snippets of teacher praise I had managed to accrue for myself did not prove, when pieced together, to make a collage of more than transitory gratification. I had been told I had "the painterly touch"; that I had a certain chromatic sensibility. The venerable old angel-watcher himself had once singled out the neck and shoulder of a conté crayon nude of mine and told the class, "Note the degree of plasticity Miss Clay has achieved in this area." But how to cover a larger area, how to impose my painterly effects on the larger world? That was the next question. I finally got up the nerve to ask the venerable man in a private critique. "When," I said, "do you think my apprenticeship is likely to end?" I meant, of course, when did he think I'd make it, but he was much too unworldly for such Madison Avenue dialect. He looked rather surprised and answered he really couldn't say, that his own had not yet ended, in his opinion.

The night of the Christmas party, all the students and some of the faculty were milling around, plastic wineglasses in hand, examining the works on the wall, passing various comments ranging from worshipful to spiteful. Depending on the reputation of the instructor and what one's taste happened to be. Nobody dared find fault with the venerable man's work because he had studied with Kandinsky at the Bauhaus, survived a concentration camp and been purchased by the Museum of Modern Art. With the younger, more obscure instructors we were not so forbearing. I was walking around with a classmate named Katharine, whom I admired because she seemed so unrushed and serene about her talent. She had stopped her painting, sent her husband through law school, had two children, and now—after making complex supper and baby-sitting arrangements—drove in from Queens two evenings a week and set up her easel as if she were still a young girl and there was all the time in the world. She admired me because, to her mind, I was already a "professional" who earned my living and paid my tuition by painting.

We had just finished inspecting the paintings of one instructor who we had decided had taken to painting his children too often in various stances on a green acrylic lawn, and now we passed on to the corner of that wall, where three small black

Woolworth frames seemed to be making some kind of protest against all the big splashy canvases.

Inside each frame was what seemed to be a little story, written in an elaborate calligraphic hand. Katharine and I stood sipping our red wine and reading.

I

An artist makes a painting.
It is hung in a museum
and many people come and look
at it. It acquires the
reputation of being a great
painting. A revolution
occurs in the country. The
museum and the painting are
destroyed. The great painting
now exists only in the minds
of the people who remember it.

II

The world's greatest artist is
sent to prison for the remainder
of his lifetime. With infinite
patience he creates a tool from
a stolen spoon. In the dark
nights of the next thirty years
he slowly etches a mural of his
civilization around the walls of
his cell. It is his greatest
work. After his death a guard
whitewashes the walls for the
next occupant. He notices the
network of scratches, shrugs,
then covers everything with
an even white.

III

A man sits in a room. He is
staring at the wall. In the
space of one second, he sees

the greatest visual theme ever
realized by a human being.
He goes out of the room, has
a meal in a café, drinks some
wine, takes a woman back to
the room.

"Brr," I said. I was afraid to commit myself further. I knew
Katharine thought of me as "up on things," living in the center
of the art capital, being a "professional." "But whose are they?"
I felt I could safely add.

"Ivor Sedge's," said Katharine. "Or Istvan Something-or-
other. He Anglicized his name some years back. One day he just
walked into class and wrote his new name on the board. He said
he was sick of having his old name mispronounced. See the little
'I.S.' at the bottom? Oh, he pretends art is dead, but he wants
you to know these miserable jokes are his, all right."

"You mean the little Hungarian who glowers all the time and
wears the military coat too big for him?"

"That's the one. I heard that one of the League's board members sponsored his passage to the U.S. after the uprising in
1956. For a while there was talk that he'd be asked to resign.
He could be really sarcastic. I had a friend who took his class
several years ago. She brought in some still lifes of flowers and
he suggested she paint the next ones with luminous paint so
they'd glow in the dark. She dropped the course."

"Hmm. Maybe I'll sign up with him," I said, half joking. But
some perverse sense of challenge woke in me. Perhaps like Ambrose I believed secretly in the magic of my personal charm and
was looking for someone difficult to test it on.

"Why go looking for trouble?" said Katharine. "From the
looks of these . . . these manifestoes, or whatever they are, he's
obviously out to destroy art. All his own paintings were destroyed in their revolution, you know. That must have been
hard on him. I was talking to the director once and he said that
Sedge was a very well known young painter in Hungary before
the Communists took over. The word is, he's gone through a

pretty rough time. Of course it's rough, having to start all over again in a new country, learn a new language. But he's learned the language now and he's been here over ten years. It's time he stopped fooling around with these jokes. The last faculty show, his entry was a "sculpture": a wooden coffin painted black with a cutout of the Mona Lisa's head inside."

"But how can you be sure they're a joke? Maybe he means them." The little framed stories had set reverberations working in me. If, by some infinitesimal chance, they were philosophically true, then that took the pressure off me somehow.

"If he means them," said Katharine, "he ought to stop teaching at the League and go sit in a room and stare at the wall."

"But he has to eat," I reminded her.

"Then let him wash dishes in a restaurant," she said. Embracing the strictly classical herself, she hated the Op and Pop inroads of the sixties. They held no philosophical seduction for her. These "works" of Sedge weren't yet even acknowledged inroads. Soon after, Katharine tossed her plastic glass into the trash basket and headed back to her husband and children in Queens, and I went home to my dingy West Side efficiency feeling at loose ends emotionally. My evenings with Michel the hairdresser had ended abruptly when he was able to arrange his mother's passage to this country. Now she sat in my place, eating his home-baked bread and watching Ed Sullivan in color. I wondered what he had found with her to substitute for our robot games. Or if they had just been makeshift antics to assuage the boredom till he could be reunited with his real love. My comradely hours with Landsborough had also dwindled when I no longer had Ambrose's nice apartment in the Village. I could see my ugly new place depressed Stewart—it depressed me. Once or twice we tried hotels. But he always had to go home in the middle of the night and I felt cheap walking out alone in the morning. Then, the crowning blow of embarrassment, I had received a note from his wife. Stewart had suffered a coronary while raking leaves at their weekend home. He had asked her to write to me so I wouldn't worry. There was no return address on her letter, so I sent a self-illustrated get-well-soon card to the office. This was returned to me in an envelope with another note from the wife, whose name was Judith. Stewart had made his peace with things, she said, and it would be better if there was no further communication. . . . She was sure I would understand. I had burned for days with indignation. What had he done—told her all, and then used her to "make peace" with his guilty past? I resolved never again to get involved with a married man.

That night I lay in the paint-smelling darkness (I then slept in the same room where I did my covers for Harrow House) and had dialogues with Mr. Sedge. First I told him his framed stories were bullshit. He said they were not. I then demanded he describe to me what that destroyed painting, that whitewashed mural and that greatest visual theme ever imagined by a human being looked like. I tried to remember what he looked like. I had ridden up on the League elevator with him once, an aloof little foreigner with the ridiculously large military coat, probably from an army-navy store. Now I did seem to recall that he had glanced at me speculatively from under his beetle brows before looking away again in weariness, as if he'd seen hundreds like me before.

I decided to sign up with Ivor Sedge. He taught Painting and Composition on Monday and Wednesday evenings from 6:45 to 10. This conflicted with the venerable man's sessions, but I felt in need of new stimulation. In the days before Sedge's next class, I fantasized various confrontations. My favorite was one in which he went around the class taking everyone's pencils and crayons and brushes away. "Now what are you going to do?" he would ask diabolically. One enterprising young man began tearing his paper in the shape of the model who was posing for us. The only other woman in the class threw up her hands in despair and ran weeping out of the class. With me, Sedge was especially sadistic. He would wait till I got going good with a crayon, then snatch it away; then I'd accommodate myself to a Magic Marker and he'd snatch that away. When he had taken away all my brushes and pens and crayons, I simply dipped my tongue into my water jar and was soon making deft strokes on newsprint paper with my wet, pointy tongue.

I was frankly disappointed when I showed up for the first class and found everyone calmly setting up their easels to go on with a perfectly conventional still life: some oranges in a bowl of Indian brass on a turquoise cloth. Most of the students had completed the monochrome underpainting and were beginning to lay on color. Nobody looked persecuted and there were six other women in the group. I went out to my locker and got a 14-by-18-inch panel and my paintbox and hurried back to set up. All the good positions had been taken, so I was forced to go almost behind the table with my easel. The tablecloth did not drape over the back side of the table, and from where I stood I could see a circle of green mold beginning to form on one of the oranges.

When the class had been in progress about an hour, he came in. Without his military coat he looked even smaller. He wore a dark turtleneck and dark trousers and hugged himself as though he were cold, although the League classrooms were notoriously overheated. Under the fluorescent lights his face already showed the next day's stubble of beard. It looked as if somebody had painted his jaw with a thin blue wash. He began making his way slowly from easel to easel, his birdlike shoulders hunched forward. His fluty, rather high voice came across the room to me in isolated swatches. His accent was heavy, but his speech was precise and piquant. "A little less blue maybe in that shadow, no?" "If you were to heighten your yellow . . . no, leave the pencil line, it makes a nice effect . . . yes, a little more white in the yellow. Now the relief of the bowl against the cloth is sharper." Far from being any avant-garde sadistic devil, he was behaving like the very model of a Middle European pedagogue.

I had my imprimatura done and was starting to build up my tonal masses by the time my turn came. He stood watching me for several minutes.

"Your composition is not bad," he said at last, "considering you have a not too fortunate angle. You come to us a little bit late. The others have worked already for one class on this."

"Yes," I said. "I'll try to catch up."

"Good. Let us hope the oranges will last till you get your color in."

"Well," I said, "if they don't, I'll just have to imagine them."

He nodded thoughtfully. His pale, elfin-shaped face with the black beetle brows seemed to float upon the dark-blue turtle-neck sweater. I noticed that he had fine black hair that curled close to his scalp like a newborn baby's hair. I also noticed that we were exactly the same height.

"Or then I could also just imagine the whole painting," I said with a touch of devilment. I wanted to force the maker of those saucy little "artworks" out of hiding.

He blinked as though he didn't comprehend. He then took out a handkerchief and coughed in it. He had a deep chest cold. "So, continue on," he said politely, nodding and passing on to the next student. He hunched behind her for a little while, like a black bird shivering inside its wings, and then he reached forward, asking her permission first, and corrected an awkward shadow with her brush. On he went around the room until he worked himself out the door, coughing some more.

The next session he did not come to class. The monitor announced that Mr. Sedge was ill and said if there were any problems he'd try to be of help. The following session Sedge did not come either.

I had a dream. The little Hungarian was lying deathly ill in a narrow bed in a room whose roof had been bombed away. "Make me warm," he kept chanting in the high, fluty voice. His teeth were chattering. I climbed into the narrow bed and put my body up against his. It was burning hot. "Make me warm, make me warm!" he cried again. Then I realized I was the one crying out, I was the one who was deathly cold. "Come, I make you warm," he said, suddenly recovered, enfolding me in his arms and wrapping his legs viselike around me.

In the next session, the monitor gave us some problems in composition and said to use whatever medium we chose. Mr. Sedge was much better. He would see each of us privately when he returned and criticize our work.

When I brought my work into his office, he was leafing through a large art book. He looked pale but held himself with less weariness. He had on a sweater that didn't suit him, an olive-green orlon with white piping. It looked like a child's sweater and perhaps it was. He had probably picked it up at some Goodwill store. "So you did not have to imagine your painting after all," he said. Was that a twinkle in the coal-bright eyes? "Prop it there on the shelf. Let us see."

He closed the art book and got up from his desk and walked first one way and then the other, squinting at my painting of the oranges on the blue cloth and the green circle of mold and the unsightly table legs where the cloth hadn't covered. The book he had been looking at was called *Emil Nolde: Unpainted Pictures*. He gave a weird little eruption that turned out to be his laugh. "I see you are not afraid of realism. You catch the powdery quality of the mold quite exactly. You are not a newcomer to painting. You are still a student, perhaps at one of the city universities?"

"Oh, I've finished with school," I said. "I earn my living by my brush. I mean, I do commercial work." I didn't want him to think I was some spoiled ingénue with Daddy paying the tuition.

"So do I do commercial work. What sort do you do?"

"I illustrate for a publishing house."

"Yes?" He seemed pleased. "I do also. For a publisher of medical textbooks. I do the nervous system and little cross sections of valves and the arteries. Right now I work on the muscles of the eye. And you?"

"I do girls running away from houses."

"Oh? Why do they run away?" He was almost smiling. He seemed in the mood to be friendly.

"Because," I said, "these are romantic suspense novels and

the girl is afraid the dark mysterious man who lives in the house is going to do her in. . . ."

"I beg your pardon, what does that mean?"

"Oh"—I blushed, imagining what he might have thought it meant—"kill her, steal her inheritance, trap her in some villainous plot. But it always turns out that all he wants to do is love her. She finally understands this and then they marry and the book ends and I get two hundred dollars for painting another cover."

"Lucky girl. I am not paid so well. But why do you want to come and paint still lifes with me at the League?"

"I want to learn everything I can about good painting. In fact"—I took a breath, preparing for the challenge at last—"I happen to think I might realize a great visual theme, like that man of yours in his room. Only I plan to try and paint it. It won't be enough for me just to have the vision, like your man."

"How do you think I can help you, then?" His eyes were very bright and snapping.

"Well, if you have seen such things, I guess I want you to show me what they look like. On the other hand, maybe you haven't seen anything. Maybe you're just a phony." I looked down at the floor; I was numb with my own rudeness.

"And if I'm a phony . . . ?"

"Well, come to think of it, it may not matter if you are. The fact that you set up those possibilities—even if you meant it as some kind of *outré* prank, even if you don't know what they saw, those artists—it has stimulated my imagination. I find myself going around saying, 'What did Sedge's hypothetical paintings look like?' And I want them for myself."

He glowered at me and stepped forward, his hand outraised. I thought perhaps he might slap me. Then he picked up my hand, his eyes riveted on mine, and started manipulating my fingers. "Take them," he said. "Here I give them to you. Hold on to them tightly, please." And he closed the fingers of my right hand around the imaginary paintings.

"What about the mural?" I said. "The mural on the prison

wall. You forgot about that." I looked at him to see if he had felt anything and if he had meant me to. Yes on both counts.

"Ah, that cannot be detached," he said in the precise, fluty voice. "That is in a secret room that only I know of and you will have to go there with me to see it. You like to go there with me tonight?" His voice took on a wheedling quality, a little ridiculous, like someone playing at being an evil magician.

"If you promise not to do me in," I said, trying for the casual note although I knew I was already compromised.

"I do nothing you don't want," he promised solemnly, and I had my last objective look at him for almost two years: a peculiar little refugee in badly fitting clothes, just as lonely as I was and a thousand times more disillusioned. After class we met discreetly several blocks away from the League and walked to his place. It had begun to snow. He linked his arm through mine as finally as though we'd just been married. For once it didn't tug when we walked because we were exactly the same height. We walked like twins linked together, block after block down Seventh, and then when it got sleazy we cut over to Fifth. He lived on Twenty-third. By this time I had convinced myself that the whole thing was very mystical and he was leading me into a conjunction with Art. I looked up at the sky. It was black and then at a certain exact place the flakes appeared, falling fast, as if they'd only just materialized at the point where I could start seeing them.

Having a private retrospective of an old affair can be dangerous. A few stray filaments of passion may still cling live to the memory, especially if one is sitting alone in a cabin in the middle of rainy woods, with a magazine and an empty soup bowl for company, having had all human overtures rejected. One tends to fondle the moments of delight and discovery until shocked afresh with, say, the novelty of the first embrace; one skips quickly over the dreary interims. The really bad times, which seemed unbearable when you were living through them, are reduced to pungent anecdotes.

How delighted I was that snowy night. Everything was magically strange. That the whitewashed walls really did exist made me quite willing to believe the great mural shimmered behind. His room (an efficiency like mine) was as chaste of any memories as a prison cell and therefore invited me to fill in its past furniture. There was a bed big enough for two, if they lay close, and a drafting table with an India ink drawing of the eye's musculature thumbtacked to its surface. The color of Ivor's body was a surprise, too; it was a warm russet color, like a winter apple. I had expected it to be white and withdrawn, like his face. And my dream had been prescient: he was warm. He was magnanimously warm, and as firm and as sure of my response as if he'd been my appointed fate.

The nice thing about retrospect is you are free to select the things you feel like remembering and play down the rest. So, spinning out the long dusk in my cabin six years after we'd said our goodbyes, I convinced myself I longed to have him here with me now. Well, partly. I wanted to have back his warmth, the nice spell he cast over me with his strangeness—before it got too strange to be compatible with the daytime world.

"You will be sorry if you do not go with me," he'd said at the end. No telling how much longer we'd have gone on if he hadn't been offered $15,000 a year, more money than he'd ever been offered in his life, to teach at a small south Florida college. He'd been recommended by his sponsor at the League.

"Look at it this way," he said—his English idioms had flowered in the space of our liaison. "You will soon be twenty-seven years old. You have no children. Your Ivor makes you happier than anyone ever—you have said so. You come with me and we get a house by the sea. We make a real life together."

"But what will I do?"

"Be happy, raise our children. I will make enough money for everyone."

"I have to have time," I said. "I have to think about this."

He had to leave at once. The college in Florida began its term early. "You have to think about whether you want to be happy?"

"But, Ivor, how can we live together when you won't even

let me see you asleep? For the whole time we've been together you sat up all night either reading or doing those medical drawings if I stayed at your place, and when you came to me you always got up and left afterwards." I realized that not only was I stalling, but I was already using the past tense. At this point I had just read Milo's book, which was all about a daylight kind of love, and it seemed to me that for twenty months I had been under a spell compounded of pure physicality, abetted by my not inconsiderate powers of symbol-making. Yes, Ivor had been my "dark stranger," my "foreign magician," my demon lover who went flapping through the daylight world disguised in his funny-fitting clothes (I had long since quit the League; the vision of his public self was too incompatible with the russet-skinned lover who covered me in the dark with his kisses, leaving no wanting edge of me exposed). But this practical offer of a "real life" had shocked me into seeing how unreal we were. He *had* made me happier than anyone ever—in the dark—but . . .

"That will be different when we are married. I will be able to sleep beside you. I will trust you completely once you have given yourself to me."

These words sent an archaic thrill through my female system, but they also reminded me of something else. After we had been going together a few weeks, Ivor would surprise me by telling me things about my day that nobody could have known unless they'd been there. He had been. At first my curiosity was piqued when he admitted he "sometimes" followed me. I was touched and flattered when he explained he liked to watch me when I was completely unselfconscious of being watched. But as time went on, it began to make me nervous. Even when I knew he couldn't be watching, such as when I was in my efficiency working on a cover for Harrow House, or shut up by myself in my bathroom, I would feel the uncanny presence of those coal-bright eyes. I made him promise to stop and as far as I knew he had kept his promise. As far as I knew. But now I had a sudden hilarious image of me as a wife, innocently shopping in a Florida supermarket, followed by a surreptitious dark figure

bouncing up and down between the cans. This image was possibly the straw that broke the camel's back of our obsessive
liaison. What Ivor and I had had together lent itself better to
the gothic mode than to the comic.

And so Ivor went to Florida alone and I stayed on in New
York and illustrated *The Secret of Seven Towers* by "Arabella
Stone." As soon as I knew Ivor really was outside the city limits,
the whole thing was shown up for the dark, obsessive thing it
was. I returned to my bright ideals and incorporated some of
their light into my illustration. From then on I received $250
per cover.

The last thing Ivor said to me—no, not quite the last—was:
"But what about the mural on the secret wall? You don't want
to see it?" He even imitated his old wheedling evil-magician
tone. But I knew he was only trying to blackmail me by reacti-
vating the charge of our first night. I had known soon after the
first night that our conjunction had nothing to do with Art.

"Tell me something," I asked him. "The first time you ever
saw my painting, what did you think of it? Be honest. What was
your first impression of my work?"

He squinted, as if trying to look again at my painting of the
rotting oranges. He was silent.

"You said something about my not being afraid of realism,"
I coaxed him.

"I don't remember," he said. "My first impression of you was
as a woman. My last one will be also, if you insist on not being
happy."

A year after he'd gone, a man named Lawrence Weiner
"typed up" his hypothetical work of art and published it in *Arts
Magazine*, to which I also subscribed. The Conceptualists ex-
ploded upon the *Zeitgeist*, propounding such chic questions as:
Suppose the greatest artist in the world was sitting in the Auto-
mat at Union Square and suddenly had the greatest inspiration
in the world. Being completely impoverished, he of course has
no pencil, no tool. So he dips his finger in a glass of water and
records his great vision on a paper napkin. The water dries and

the vision is gone. The greatest artist slumps over and dies. Did the water work on that napkin count as a great vision? Yes! said the Conceptualists. I wondered if Ivor kept up with current art trends at his school in south Florida. If so, did he see himself as a forerunner of their trend, even if he had hit upon his "Woolworth frames" as a way to keep the League from knowing he no longer painted, never intended to paint again? The first "story," about the artist who had a painting in a museum which was destroyed in a revolution: that was true. That was Ivor's painting. The museum and the painting were both destroyed in the uprising of 1956. The painting was the one that had brought him to the attention of his peers and critics and he himself considered it to be his breakthrough. It was called "Young Girl in a Blue Hat," and the model was his fifteen-year-old sister, who was destroyed in the same year as the painting. She had been one of the child demonstrators in the famous massacre at Magyaróvár.

As for the "whitewashed mural" and the "greatest visual theme," I would have to look to myself for any glimpses. "If I walk out now and you haven't said yes, you never hear from me again": those were Ivor's last words to me. As time went on, I couldn't help admiring the shapeliness of that exit. Some artists are incredibly unshapely in their personal lives. But then, Ivor had given up art. But "I am a good teacher," he once told me. "After I learned not to be so cruel."

Seven o'clock on a Plommet Falls evening. Not quite light, because of the overcast sky. Not yet dark. Options: to switch off this table lamp and go to bed and fantasize about demon lovers like Ivor, perhaps calling on my own body as a last resort; to go for a walk (too damp, too embarrassed I might intrude upon my reluctant neighbors); to go back to the table and make some more splotches and blotches on paper (please God, not tonight!).

I made up my mind to splurge on a radio the next day. At least I could make myself the present of some music.

Oh, Lord, Lord, what does a body do when all options are gone? As good a time as any to start rehearsing.

Let's see: take 'em away.

Poor old Violet, she ain't got no lover—except her own little hand.

She ain't got no neighbors, except for a poor old spinster at the bottom of the hill, a mirror image, when you think of it, of what poor old Violet's gonna be one of these days.

If she lives. Oh, boo hoo.

The last thing she wants is "good healthy exercise," tramp, tramp, tramp, through the wet pine needles, fighting off the mosquitoes.

The thing she wants most—"the great visual theme," and not on a bare wall or napkin, either . . . well, tomorrow maybe the sun will shine again.

Meanwhile, let us be practical, since we have decided not to kill ourselves. We are not yet finished and tomorrow might well be another day.

Oh, poor Ambrose. How well I was beginning to understand him.

I reread his suicide note a couple of times. What kind would I write? I had a horrible feeling it would be much wordier, that I'd get carried away in an aside and the aside would lead to a memory and the memory would lead sideways into another aside and I would end up saying, "What was it I was going to do, anyway?"

Then I walked around a little—I was beginning also to understand the motivations of the pacer: it is, after all, a poor excuse for going somewhere—and then I remembered the dismembered Luger and went over and got it from under my pillow and fondled it a bit. Such a quaint, eccentric-looking pistol. The first "gun" I had ever seen. Ambrose unwrapping his big man's handkerchief and offering it in his outspread palm to a circle of little girls.

This is my rifle and this is my gun, he once told me the sergeant had made them recite in basic training. *This is for killing and this is for fun.* Men's lore. Give it the gun. He's a big gun. He's gunning for you. Gun the engine a little bit more. "Don't go shotgunning," he had said that night in the rooftop cocktail lounge, "for the first gallery that makes you an offer."

I walked around some more till I found a spot that felt right. Wasn't it just about here? You would want to face away from the last light; it would be easier that way. I lay down, feeling the hard floor against my shoulder blades (had I lost weight?), and tried to remember my art school studies of the cranial structure: the zygomatic arch, the parietal eminences—just about here? No, here.

Above me, the lamp made a circle of light on my stack of watercolor papers. Well, won't have to look at those anymore.

I was really into the act now. The heavy, solid, oddly shaped grip, the long aristocratic barrel. Once a German carried this gun. Would have used it on Ambrose if Ambrose hadn't used his American weapon first. And both of them barely out of their childhood. Such a solid grip. Good to hold, even if it's just a toy. So masculine. Fills the spaces of a lonely hand which might otherwise be summoning up past or nonexistent lovers. The perfect fit for an empty hand.

You'd have to know what you were doing, though. Otherwise you'd make a mess, end up with half a head or blind, new problems a hell of a lot worse than the old. No wonder women preferred pills or the oven.

If I ever did it I would probably decide on pills. And their last-minute option.

And now: you think your final thoughts. What would they be? Goodbye and good riddance! Goodbye; parts of it have been pleasant but, as of late, the unpleasant has outweighed . . .

Everyone said for so long I had promise, but the promises have not been kept and . . . won't it be nice to get some shut-eye!

> A tear, a sigh; alas, goodbye!
> The pardon came too late.

Experimentally, I decided to pull the trigger. Then decided I couldn't—what if the troopers hadn't done their job right?

And then, as if some cosmic joke had been played on me, there was a loud *blam!*

It was a minute before I understood that my cabin door had been flung open, that the Luger had been wrenched from my hand and sent flying across the room and that a woman with wet silver hair streaming down her face sat astride me, shrieking like a demented witch: "Damn you, goddamn you, take your fucking sickness somewhere else, you goddamned stupid Clays! If you don't want to live, go bury yourself in your own sick shit and let us get on with it. Goddamn you to hell, get out! Get out! Get out!"

18

"Capriccio"

If life imitates art, then you could say that the breakthrough I had been looking for sat astride me (though I didn't know it yet), screaming obscenities. She had materialized unexpectedly—as breakthroughs often do—at a moment when I had stopped pursuing her and was looking at something else.

But even if art works only from what life provides, then I was to be grateful to life for sending Sam my way. What had been lacking up until now in my Plommet Falls venture was not method or even (for a change) sustained resolve, but a subject that could be a match for my inner necessities. One reason I had been able to stick with the gothic romances for so long was that each time I set out to paint that prefabricated composition—a girl running away from a house—I still had questions concerning that picture. Maybe if I painted it one more time I'd understand the connection between the prefabricated setting and my emotions. There was something about the picture that intrigued me, attracted me even.

Actually, the picture presented a fake situation. She was running away from the house that would eventually contain her. Why then was it necessary to "the plot" for her to go through the motions of running away? Because someone had to "catch" her, and coax her to come back with him into his house—just as Ambrose's hero had had to pursue Lora Lee down the Intracoastal. She had to flee as traditionally as he had to pursue; and when they both were near dead from the chase, she could allow herself to turn around prettily and admit she'd wanted this all along. I had figured out some of the answers, but not all of them. Now here came Sam, bringing with her another sort of picture and lots of questions. There was something about her picture that intrigued me also. Sam had built her own house and was running in a different direction. Was there a choice to be made between these pictures or was it a matter of finding a new composition that could sustain a balance between them?

Of course, as she sat on top of me, pinning my shoulders down with her strong hands and screaming for me to "get out," I wasn't thinking about pictures. That came later. I was wondering, first, how to get her off—she was quite a solid woman—and second, how to calm her down. Our roles were reversed from this afternoon in the store. I was the cool one now. It had taken me only seconds to realize that, for all her rough handling of me and her language, she thought she was saving me from destroying myself. To somebody outside looking in, it must have looked exactly like a nightmare repeat of Ambrose's suicide. But why had she been outside looking in?

"I can't 'get out,' " I managed to say, spitting out a strand of her hair, "or go anywhere when you're squashing me." I thought under the circumstances I sounded quite sane.

"It's better than having your brains all over the goddamned place!" But she had let go of my shoulders. Breathing hard, she sat back on her haunches, which still pinned down my hips, her

arms dangling at her sides. They were the first woman's arms
I'd ever seen that had no spare flesh on them at all.

"You people!" It was more like a cry. "What are you, anyway? Why do you want to come here and fuck up our life?"

Strong cords defined her neck from the base of the jaw to the
collarbone. Her hair at close range was a dull blond laced richly
with early white—thus the uncanny silver effect. Her breasts
were loose, and rather large, under her T-shirt. She was one
powerful female; the Valkyries must have looked something like
her.

"I didn't come here to fuck up your life," I said, in my most
reasonable tone. "I came here because I had things to do."

She snorted. "Yeah. It looks like it."

"It wasn't loaded. It doesn't even have a firing pin in it. The
state troopers took it out. I was just trying an experiment, sort
of. Would you mind getting off now? You're hurting me."

"An experiment!" She looked down at me with incompre-
hension, as though she had found herself sitting on some kind
of alien, slimy creature. "Shit," she said. She sloped herself off
me and got quickly to her feet. "Pardon me for interrupting your
'experiment.' I walked over here to tell you it was nothing personal, what I said to you in the store. I just meant that I couldn't
see us all having a meal together on top of where he . . . where
he did *his* 'experiment.' Christ, I look in the window—it's only
natural, with the curtains wide open—and there you are on the
floor, in the same position . . . about to do the same thing. It
was horrible. . . ."

She stood very straight and tall in her frayed shorts and full-
bosomed T-shirt and sockless tennis shoes. Her legs were like
her arms: extra long, brown, and without an ounce of superfluous flesh.

I struggled up from the floor. My back was stiff.

"I'm sorry for all this," I said. "I'm not exactly sure what I'm
apologizing for, but I apologize anyway. I'm the last of the family, so I apologize for him as well. I think he would want that.
I really am sorry for the distress we've caused you."

She listened to me quietly. It seemed to penetrate. Now it

was her turn to look embarrassed. "We're all right, I guess. He's the one who's dead. You're alive, so that's okay. I owe you an apology for barging into your privacy after making such a big thing about mine. It wasn't myself I was worried about." Here her lip quivered the slightest bit. "I didn't want Cheyenne to be upset any more. I took her away after what happened. We camped for a while in Maine. She seems okay now, but I want to keep it that way."

"Is she at home now?"

"No, she's spending the night with a friend. Her school started today and her period started right in the middle of school. Her first period. I went to pick her up at school and she told me. I guess I expected her to be upset or something. But she was proud of it. She wanted me to go buy her what was necessary and then for me to take her to her friend Doreen's. When you came up to me in the store today, I was just standing there trying to take it all in. My little girl had become a woman. At ten—that's so early. I didn't start till I was almost thirteen. When you came up and started talking about him, I realized I resented it that he had spoiled our last months together, hers and mine, her last months of being a child. You caught me at a really bad moment and I took it out on you."

"But you came over tonight to explain. I appreciate that. Look, please sit down for a minute. For several minutes, if you don't have to get back. I've been about to go cabin crazy, or whatever they call it here."

"Yeah. These woods can get lonely. They do even for me sometimes, even though I've got Cheyenne." She started to sit on the bed, then changed her mind and went over to the chair. I sat down on the bed. It crossed my mind that she might have her own reasons for not wanting to sit on his bed. "You really plan to stay up here during the cold months, too?"

"Well, some of them. Till my money runs out. I'm sort of buying time. I guess," I risked, going easy, "Ambrose felt he ran out of time."

She gave me a funny look. She got up and retrieved the

Luger from where she'd flung it and came back and sat down, examining the weapon cautiously. Her hands were well-shaped but they looked tough and capable. The nails were not quite clean. "Why would you want to keep a thing like this? Why would you want it around to remind you?"

"I wanted to stay reminded. It's not easy to explain. I guess I felt I could go the same way if I wasn't careful. But now I don't think I could. I don't think I could kill myself, no matter how bad things got. That was what I was trying to decide down there on the floor. I had already decided I couldn't pull the trigger, even if the thing wasn't functioning. I didn't even want to take that chance."

"That was your experiment?"

"Yes."

She put the Luger on the table. Then she noticed my "Violet in Blue" paintings, stacked to one side. "What do you do— abstract?"

"Those were sketches for something that didn't work out." I suddenly saw them through someone else's eyes and realized they were never going to work out. They didn't communicate anything. "I was doing these landscapes till today." I indicated the other things pinned liberally around the walls.

She looked around at the other sketches and paintings. Her eye didn't pause at any single one, just grazed over the collection. "Nice," she said at last, not too convincingly.

"I wish I had something to offer you. Some wine or something. Would you like a Pepsi? I think I have one left. We could split it."

"No, thanks, I could use some wine. This has been some day." She looked down at her tennis shoes. Then she looked at me as if trying to make up her mind about something.

I smiled encouragingly.

"I've got something we could smoke," she said, "over at my place. Would you like to go there for a while?"

"Well, yes."

"Come on, then," she said gruffly, and rose to her feet.

I followed her out into the rain-fresh evening, worrying about whether I ought to go back and lock the cabin. But I was afraid to say anything for fear she might suddenly change her mind and say, "Look, let's leave it for another time." Besides, I wasn't really that worried about who might get in or what they would take. Being alone with myself inside had been more hazardous in some ways.

We walked down the dirt road that I'd ventured a few times, only once getting as far as a partial view of their trim and cozy cabin. At last I would get to see what was inside.

She walked fast, taking long, stealthy strides. I kept having the impulse to grab onto her hand because it was hard for me to see where we were stepping in this nether light. I felt very much that she was the adult and I was the child in this landscape, although later, when she trusted me, she told me how uncertain she had been on that walk, for other reasons.

Her cabin, as I noticed from my one previous glimpse, had a finished quality about it that made it hard to think of as "a cabin." It had that smoothed-down, fussed-over look of the kind of small house where a retired man lives who is good with his hands and goes around looking for things to do all day. There just wasn't much left to do inside or outside Sam's cabin. "You've really made things nice in here," I said, though I felt vaguely disappointed. Things were almost too finished, too shipshape. It had been carpentered into the full living potentiality of its limited dimensions. She'd even managed to build a sleeping loft within the gable of the roof.

"It's better than we found it. It was my father's getaway shack. He used to come here by himself when he had shore leave. He was a captain in the merchant marine. He wouldn't let my mother or me come; said it wasn't habitable for women."

"He should see it now." There were feminine touches everywhere: curtains, woven things, ceramic jars filled with dried flowers, colorful cooking utensils hanging from a pegboard over the sink. Minerva's description of it as a "showpiece" was quite accurate.

"I've shown him some snapshots. But he doesn't believe it's his place. He insists his old shack was destroyed. He's had two strokes and he sometimes gets things mixed up. The last time we went to see him, Cheyenne and I, he kept mixing us up. I mean, he thought she was me as a child and he kept calling me by my mother's name. He's in a nursing home in Key West for retired seamen."

"Is your mother still alive?" I'd made up my mind to go easy, but I felt I could ask that.

"Yes. But we don't communicate. This is Cheyenne's room." She indicated a door painted a bright lacquer red, with a hand-lettered sign in green crayon—YOU MAY BE NORMAL WHEN YOU COME IN HERE BUT YOU WON'T BE WHEN YOU LEAVE—Scotch-taped on it. "Would you like to see it? I'm kind of proud of it. It wasn't even a room when we came here, just a lean-to, for storing wood, attached to the outside structure."

She opened the door and we went in. It was a small sanctuary with a low slanted ceiling into which were fitted two built-in bunk beds, one above the other, covered in brightly striped mattress ticking. There was a small desk and a dressing table and a built-in storage cabinet, also painted in the red lacquer, which Sam opened to reveal a marvelously planned interior. A space for clothes and shoes, another for games and stuffed animals, a shelf for books, a narrower one for papers and crayons.

"Did you build all this?"

"Except for the dressing table. Cheyenne made that all by herself."

"Gosh, she's a real little handywoman." I remembered Minerva's story about Cheyenne breaking the sex barrier for shop classes at the local school, but thought it wiser not to allude to it. "What a treat, to have a room like this when you're a little girl. It's so compact and safe and yet there's something secret about it, too."

"She's enjoyed it. She likes to have her friends over to spend the night. There's always a fight to see who'll get the top bunk. I suppose she'll outgrow it soon." She sounded wistful.

"Well, then she can build her own cabin," I said, curious to know what Cheyenne told her friends when the subject of fathers came up.

"That's not a bad idea," Sam said, looking at me with new appreciation. "Maybe I'll tell her that. She can start planning it. If she has something like that, maybe she won't waste so much time chasing boys. Hey, that would be something, wouldn't it? I would have given anything if my father told me I could do that. There's enough land. We've got almost three acres. She wouldn't have to build in sight of me, even. I mean, I'd be near, but there'd be trees between so she'd feel she had her own space. Come on up to the loft and I'll show you my space. We can smoke something and relax."

"Great," I said, following her out of Cheyenne's tidy little sanctuary. Did Sam really mean her daughter could start building a cabin? I meant when she grew up; actually, I had meant it more as a figure of speech. But now I could see it, a tiny cabin built by a ten-year-old, hidden from Mother's eyes, but on the sanction of Mother's land. The perfect adolescent dream: freedom within safety, if such a thing existed.

Sam took a ladder out of a closet, hooked it to the floor of the loft above and climbed up. "Watch your head," she called back. "Don't try to stand when you get up here. It's too low."

"Okay." I climbed slowly. I didn't really want to smoke anything. Smoking made me soft and hazy and right now I wanted to be alert and focused. I was feeling a little like Minerva's late father, who tracked his animal gently, with his intelligence, until he could feel the movements of its mind.

Her loft impressed me as the downstairs of the place had: finished, complete, all rough ends smoothed, all mysterious corners opened up, nothing left to be done except bask in one's own competence. No wonder her father hadn't recognized his old shack in her snapshots. To his mind it probably had been destroyed. In his time it was probably all rough ends and spooky corners, spiders peacefully laying their eggs in the high pre-loft rafters while down below the captain sucked his pipe in woman-less contentment, knocking his ashes into the open fireplace (which had now been rendered useless by the big modern wood-burning stove in the middle of the room).

"I've never seen a carpeted loft with built-in bookcases," I said. "This is some hideaway." I scanned the book titles, mostly how-to books, at least a dozen on carpentry and building, and a dog-eared Dr. Spock. "You are completely self-contained."

"Not completely," she said, opening a drawer beneath the bunk bed. Out came the proverbial plastic-wrapped stash and a charming little ceramic pipe. "We have an outdoor john. My father didn't check out the ground adequately, and he built this place on bedrock. There isn't proper drainage for a septic tank."

So the old man had bequeathed some unalterable rough edges after all. I could see him get up from the fireplace and unzip his fly as he ambled over to the door to piss leisurely into the night outside.

"Sit down," she said, patting a place on the bunk bed. She was already settled into a lamplit and pillowed corner, lighting up. She took a deep drag on the little pipe, closed her eyes, and held her breath. After a minute or so she said in her slightly hoarse voice, "This crop is kind of rough. I think it's because the growing season's so short here. But it'll relax us." She took an-other quick drag and then passed it to me.

"You even grow your own pot?" I arranged a pillow between my back and the wall and took a modest drag.

She nodded. "It's not the greatest. But it beats having to de-pend on contacts. I don't want to go to prison for relaxing a little in the evenings after I've been knocking myself out shingling some local magistrate's garage. I got really edgy when that trooper came over here the night of . . . you know, that night. Questions, questions, questions." She took the pipe back and drew on it fiercely.

"That must have been a terrible night for you." Careful, Vio-let. Don't rustle the underbrush. I took back the proffered pipe.

How many more drags could I manage without losing track of what was being said?

"Yeah. He'd keep looking at my loft and saying how nice I'd made everything. I kept expecting him to say, 'Now if you don't mind I'll just take a look around up there.' Hell, if it had been light, all he would have to do would be walk out back and there it would be, right behind the tomatoes."

"But he didn't? Want to look around?" Keep gently to the subject.

"No. He was mainly interested in whether I could tell him anything about Ambrose. Whether he'd been depressed or anything. I told him all I could, but he was mainly Cheyenne's friend. I was away most of the time, on jobs. Summer is my busy time. Cheyenne, when she wasn't with her own friends, had to amuse herself. She got in the habit of going over to his place. I told him to send her home when she got to be a nuisance, but he said he wasn't all that busy."

Wasn't all that busy.

"I wonder if he was depressed," I said, looking intently at the little ceramic pipe. "Maybe his novel wasn't going well."

"You'll let it go out if you don't take a drag. I couldn't tell you about that. No, he didn't seem depressed. He was always very friendly. He had a smooth way; he put things well. Cheyenne said he could be really funny, but he was more formal with me. Poor guy, he was probably very lonely." She took the pipe, sucked in deeply, closed her eyes and sank back on her pillows. She passed the pipe to me. "Christ, when I first saw him sitting in front of the cabin like some dude in his deck chair, with that white beard stubble all over his face, staring at us as we drove by, I told Cheyenne, 'You stay away from that old guy. He looks crazier than Minerva's last hippies.' But he turned out to be harmless. Except to himself, I guess."

Old guy! Harmless! Could we be talking about the same person? But we were. So strong in me were my lifelong impressions that I'd already repressed the white beard, even though I had sketched the dead face so I wouldn't forget it.

"Minerva said he told her he was moving on. Did he ever say anything to either of you about where he was going?"

"No, he didn't say. Didn't he write to you, or weren't you two close?" She opened her greenish-gray eyes and looked at me obliquely from beneath lowered lids.

"We were and we weren't. He was the kind of person—well, the kind of uncle anyway—who, when you were with him, made you feel you were the most important element in his life. But sometimes I didn't hear from him for half a year, maybe more. I only had one card from him the whole time he was up here. And it gave practically no impression of the place. He didn't even mention he had you two as neighbors."

"Huh. Maybe it was early, before we came back."

"It was June fifteenth. I remember the postmark. I looked it up the night he died."

"Huh. We came back in late April. We went to see my father during Cheyenne's spring vacation. Ambrose and Cheyenne had become friends by June. I even had him for dinner." She laughed ruefully in her rather hoarse voice. "He wore a white suit and a tie. And he brought a box of candy for Cheyenne. Funny he didn't mention us." It seemed to surprise her.

"Oh, people often leave out the most important things on a postcard," I threw out.

"I wouldn't say we were the most important thing," she hastened to correct me. "He may have idealized us a little bit."

"What makes you say that?"

But I had rustled the underbrush. She withdrew. "I don't know. Just an impression. Just his good manners, maybe. Like you said. Making you feel you were important. Poor guy. I just wish he hadn't done it here. To have been friends with Cheyenne like that and then done it where she could find him."

"But . . . I was trying to tell you today in the store: I don't believe he meant that to happen. I think he had the whole thing planned so it *wouldn't* happen. He'd made an appointment with this Indian, from the Meditation Ranch in Schroon Lake, who was interested in renting the cabin. The Indian showed up the evening before, to take measurements, and Ambrose told him it wasn't convenient and to come back the next evening at seven. As it turned out, the Indian got tangled up in some mistaken early arrival of a speaker at his center and couldn't make it back. But if he had, he would have found . . . what Cheyenne unfortunately found. And the Indian would have gone to tell Minerva and Minerva would have called the troopers. The whole thing might have happened without you two ever knowing a thing until they'd taken the body away."

"Jesus. I wonder . . . but we'll never know. How can we know what he planned or didn't plan? But one thing I'd forgotten till just tonight. We heard the shot. We didn't know that's what it was but . . . I was over here washing my hair tonight, thinking about that scene between us in the store today—you talking so fast, telling me all this—and then I remembered. You see, what made me send Cheyenne over to his place that night was, I heard the shot. I didn't know it was the shot at the time. I mean, who was expecting a shot? I didn't even know he had a gun. What happened was, Cheyenne and I had just finished dinner and we were sitting at the table talking. Cheyenne was telling me some gory story about a schoolmate who'd been hospitalized because her father beat her up. Then she said, 'If I had to have a father, I'd want him to be somebody like Ambrose Clay, who would stay home and entertain me while you were off at work.' He told her a lot of stories, about his travels, being in the army. He even told some—based on you, I think—about this girls' boarding school. Cheyenne liked those especially. And then she and I started having this pretty heavy conversation about the subject of fathers. I said there wasn't much difference in me having a father who was away at sea most of the time and who couldn't wait to get away from me and come here when he was on land and her own situation. And then from up there came this loud crack. You know what I thought it was at first? I thought it was Ambrose slamming his screen door as hard as he could because maybe he wanted us to know he was getting ready

to leave and he thought we should come and say goodbye. I
mean, we'd already said goodbye the night before. He was waiting outside his cabin, sitting in his chair, and when we drove by,
he waved us down and came out to the jeep and told us goodbye.
He even came around to my side and kissed my hand. He said
we had made his summer extra special, but now he had to be
getting back to . . . I think he said . . . business. He said he
planned to leave first thing in the morning. When we left early
next morning, his car was still there. 'He'll be gone when we get
back,' I said. I took Cheyenne to the dentist's in Schroon Lake
and then we went shopping for some new sneakers and then I
dropped her off at her friend Doreen's and went on by myself
to finish off some shelves I was doing for these old ladies in the
village. Then I picked up Cheyenne about five and we drove
home and when we passed the cabin, his car was *still* there,
parked under the trees. And he was inside, sweeping the floor
with a whisk broom. I still thought he was just getting a late start
and it would be embarrassing to everybody to go through the
whole goodbye scene again. So I blew the horn and he looked
up and waved and we waved back. That was about it. Now,
when I heard the crack, I said, 'Cheyenne, why don't you run
up the hill while I get out the dessert and ask him if he wants
to have some Sara Lee cake and a cup of coffee before he hits
the road.' So off she went. And I set out three plates and three
forks and I remember thinking I maybe should have invited him
for dinner, that maybe he'd been expecting it and that's why he
was sort of hanging around, sweeping his car, so he'd be outside
when we passed. Then Cheyenne came back alone. 'Wouldn't
he come?' I said. She just stood there in the door, looking at me
and scraping her new sneaker up and down her leg. 'What's
wrong?' I said, because I knew something was, but still I had
no idea. She said, 'Now, Mother, don't get upset. Do you promise?' I said I promised, what was there to get upset about? She
said because Ambrose had shot himself in the head with his pistol from the war. My first reaction was, 'You mean he kept a pistol up there, with you around all the time?' I was really furious.

'Mother, he's hurt himself bad, he may be even dead,' she said, and started to shake. I put her in the jeep and we drove up there. I made her wait outside. I went in and it was clear he was dead. And I saw the note in the typewriter and an envelope addressed to you and I knew he had meant it to be that way."

"And then you went and told Minerva and you all called the troopers?"

"Of course," she said shortly. "What else?"

"Right. What else." I sighed. "I guess I'll never know exactly what made him do it. I mean, I know generally. He left New York eight years ago this fall and drove west and ended up staying in Mexico until last spring. The realistic part of me knew then that he was running away. I think I was surprised when he did come back and announce his intention to make up for lost time. I think I've known for years that he wasn't going to write that novel. I just didn't want to face it because it might mean I had to face . . . similar things about myself. That I might never get serious about my painting, I mean."

"And that's really why you're here?" She looked at me carefully. "Like you said over at your place, you came here to paint? You're buying time?"

"Why else would I be here?" I asked her.

If I'd been more alert, I might have heard a sort of *click* when the tension was broken between us. Thinking about it afterward, it must have come at about that point. Then she poked at the ceramic pipe. "Do you want to have another one or should we save it for the next time you come? I expect I'll be alone lots of evenings. Cheyenne seems to be popular. She's a kind of ringleader, Doreen's mother told me."

"Maybe I ought to get on back," I said. "I want to get up pretty early and see if I can paint." There were still so many questions I wanted to ask. How had she come to be where she was? Who was Cheyenne's father and where had people like Doreen's mother been told he was? What would it be like to be self-sufficient in this beholden-to-nobody way, able to build your own cozy quarters and live in them and go your own way and raise your own child, no help wanted? Why didn't she communicate with her mother? How long was it possible to live without a man?

She unfolded herself from the bunk bed. "I'll walk you back."

"No need to. Nothing will get me."

"You can't see in the dark. I noticed it as we walked here."

"I'll go carefully. My eyes will adjust."

"I'll walk you. I wouldn't want you falling off the side of the mountain," she added gruffly, going first down the ladder.

We went outside into a cool mountain night.

"Oh, look, stars," I said. "It cleared up after all. God, I don't believe I've ever seen such a skyful of stars."

"It will be nice tomorrow," she said. "I guess I'll go over to Mr. Perry's and see if he still wants his trees trimmed."

"It must be great, to be able to do so many things."

We climbed the road under the stars. Sam was right; I couldn't see much in the dark. There was no moon. I kept my eye on her pale shorts as a sort of guide.

"It's a good thing I can do something. I've got no education. I didn't even finish high school."

"Well, I would never have known it," I assured her. Maybe that accounted for her lack of interest in my paintings.

"Thank you. I'm not proud of it. Maybe when Cheyenne's older and I've got some more money saved, I might try and finish. This landscaper I know in the village did that. He took an aptitude test and they passed him on through high school and then he went to the community college up near Lake Placid. I was thinking I might try and get a degree in architecture. Do you think I'd have a chance? I'll be thirty next year. I probably look older with this hair. It runs in my mother's family. She went gray at twenty."

"Have a chance! You'll probably have more practical knowledge than your entire class put together. And the hair is very attractive. It makes you look like some sort of Nordic goddess. Anyone can see from your face and body that you're not very old."

"I'm not a goddess, either," she said, sounding affronted.

There was a silence. Then she asked, "Are you sure it was eight years ago that your uncle took that trip west?"

"Yes, it was September of 1967. I remember that time very well. Why?" I was surprised that she would bring up Ambrose again.

"You're sure? Not before that?"

"Oh, years before, when I was a little girl in boarding school. They were going to make a movie of his first novel and he drove to California once, I think."

"Oh, no; I meant like about, say, the summer of sixty-four?" Her voice suddenly sounded anxious.

"Oh, no. He was in New York that summer. I happen to remember, because I was staying with my grandmother that summer and she got letters from him. Sam, there's some reason this is important. Please tell me what it is." It was the first time I'd used her name. It occurred to me that no one had ever even introduced us and that she had not introduced herself.

"It's not important," she said. "Only, once we were talking, your uncle and myself, and I told him how I had hitchhiked west once, when I was younger, and he said if he'd been driving by he might have been the one to pick me up and we might have known each other sooner. You know how people talk about these things. But it isn't important now, really. It really isn't."

"Okay." I have more time, I thought, to find out whether it is or it isn't.

The pot must have crept up on me, because I barely got undressed and fell on the bed before passing out. I slept deeply and woke with a bright September sun streaming through the cabin windows. I had no idea what to paint that day, and lay for longer than necessary, procrastinating. I went over the previous twenty-four hours. The fact that they had taken place in the rain and then the dark made them like a dream interim, cordoned off between two sunny days. I thought a lot about Sam; I knew more about her than I had known this time the day before. But I felt there was a great deal more than that to know.

When I finally got up and was stumbling around waiting for

the water to boil for coffee, I saw the envelope on the floor near the door. It had my name on the front, in pencil, in a very un-formed hand. My first thought was: She's decided she talked too much last night and is saying she doesn't want to continue the acquaintance. The envelope, the long, white, plain kind you can buy in the grocery store, was sealed. I tore it open. Inside there was a penciled note from her on a sheet of loose-leaf notebook paper and, beneath it, three single-spaced typewritten pages which had been badly crumpled and then smoothed out again.

Dear Violet [said the note]: After talking to you last night I decided you should have the enclosed. Its your propperty now. The reason I witheld it this long is, well you'll see why when you read it. Not sure what it is but one thing I am sure of is it wouldn't have done us any good, Cheyenne and me. I found it on the floor beside his waste paper basket after he killed himself. I think he meant to drop it in and missed. I put it in my pocket fully intending to hand it over to the police. I don't really know why I picked it up at all. Human curiousity maybe. While Minerva was calling the troopers I went in her john and looked at it. I almost had decided to give it to them when I saw the part about us. I think it's us. Even if it isn't, others might think so. It isn't any of it true. He must have been sick or he wouldn't have used us that way. I just want to live up here in peace with my daughter. You seemed to understand and be someone I could trust, so I hope I won't have reason to re-gret giving you this. Also now I know you know the dates would be all wrong.

still your neighbor (hopefully)

The crumpled pages were Corrasable Bond and must have been balled up soon after being typed, because they were badly smudged. It took me some time to read them. And after I'd read them once I went back and read them again. And then again. On each rereading I had to revise conclusions I'd reached during the previous reading. Unlike Sam, I had known at first glance what it was: an outline, a plan for the great shape-shifting novel, *Capriccio*, which he'd talked about with me over our last lunch in New York. "Maybe in movements, like a piece of music," he had said. "Or mosaic-like. I want to have the freedom to skip around if I want . . . it would better suit the material of the book, which is that of a modern man awash in the flux of too many complexities and possibilities."

Capriccio, by Ambrose Clay

1. "Prelude." A woman sits in a large room playing a grand piano. Her fingers glide over the keys and wonderful sounds fill the room. The boy wants to do it so she buys him a toy piano and he sits in the room too and they have this game. He moves his fingers above the keys (she doesn't like it when he really touches them; bad sounds come out) and she pretends it is his wonderful music filling the room. "What have I just played?" he asks, after a particularly nice one. She tells him it's the last movement of a Bach partita and promises him when he's older she'll teach him to play it "on her piano." And eventually he does learn to read music and attempts to learn the piece. The process is slow and unrewarding. He can get the right hand and the left hand but can't make them work together. No longer does she exclaim, "A charming piece by a charming boy." When he goes to the "big piano," she smiles encouragingly but there is a pained look on her face. He gives up and forgets the whole thing, he even forgets the name of the movement. Years later in a foreign city when he is trying to salvage some of his life's wreckage in hopes of building some last minute edifice, the experience of this early failure comes back to him during a conversation with a woman. He has called her capricious and as soon as the word is out of his mouth he understands how he gave up on "Capriccio" because it no longer won him instant praise. He sees the early experience as a metaphor for what came after in his life. The question this book asks is, can he redeem himself? The title is symbolic because if he writes it he will have completed a real *Capriccio*.

2. "Variations on a Theme." Women, real and imagined, the growing difficulty in keeping them straight. How did this start? With his mother? With his brother's wife? Part of his problem stems from being a writer. When he came of age the "heroic" part of his life was already over and he began soon after to falsify

his first love into a more appealing, fictional woman. He leaves out the things that made him so guilty after her death. He makes his imagined woman as smooth and elusive and noble as the real one was unsure and clinging and deceitful. He will never know if she was lying or telling the truth about the pregnancy, as the coroner was a friend of the family and there was no autopsy. In a burst of remorse he confides in his mother. She tells him the dead are better buried with their secrets and confides to him how, as a small girl, she discovered her mother in bed with a lover and how she had never told. Later he makes a story out of this, substituting his own mother for the faithless one. He reads this story to various women and finds it has a magical effect: all of them became his mistresses (one even becomes his wife) after hearing it. The last woman to hear it tells him it would be more interesting if he changed the mother's lover to a woman. She relates the story of an aunt in Buenos Aires who had a lifetime affair with her best friend. He changes the lover to a woman and sends the story to his New York agent and is secretly relieved when the agent writes back to say it is lost. He begins dreaming about his own mother and her best friend and becomes convinced they actually were having a lesbian affair. A strange suspicion begins to grow in him: what if his old ghosts are starting to revenge themselves on him. He has falsified them past recognition in his fictions; now they will turn his life around backwards, impose these fictions on him. About this time everything begins to reverse for him. People don't say yes to him so quickly anymore. He contracts hepatitis. A tooth becomes abscessed. He notices his looks beginning to go. He returns to his own country and, lying in a cheap hotel on the night before his dentist will see him, he hallucinates in his fever. His mother is in the room with him, telling him how, in the Bach capriccio, "All the things that go up in the first half come down in the second, and that, my boy, is the law of life, wait and see!" He wakes shaken but determined to see the dream as a self-imposed warning for him to get on with it. He decides to leave the city at once, find a cabin in the woods, and begin his *Capriccio* in dead earnest. At the moment the dentist extracts his tooth, it comes back to him that his mother did actually say that about the last movement of the second Bach partita. Or is his memory playing tricks on him? Are his ghosts getting even again?

3. "Da Capo," or "Beginning Again." Now the time sequence will be complex here but not insurmountable. Think of *montage*, of Ford's brilliant time-shift in *The Good Soldier*. Present tense is the aging author in his cabin in the woods. (Vermont? Canada?) He settles in. Give convincing but not extensive details of local color, flora and fauna, etc. He becomes aware of his neighbors, an old lady in a big house who might be his mother and a young woman who lives alone with her little girl. One day as he sits in his cabin trying to make a plan for *Capriccio*, it strikes him *that fate has exactly reduplicated the setup in which he made his first bad mistakes.* There is Mother. There is the Widow and Child. Fate is offering him a chance to redeem himself. He should have married the other widow, the first one. He was obligated. If he had been an honorable man, he would have married her and helped her raise her fatherless child and any child they might have been going to have together. He becomes obsessed with this idea to the point that he cannot continue work on his novel. That is only a fiction. His whole life has been a fiction. Make good the real thing first, then the rest will follow. He decides this time to do it right. Win the child first (he is good with children) and then see if the mother comes round. The weeks pass, his precious time dwindles, and the mother shows no interest whatsoever. She is a strange woman. She reminds him a little of the goddess Diana. She appears to go out of her way to avoid him. As the summer progresses, he catches a fleeting, fugitive look about her when they meet. That face, where has he seen that face? And slowly he contrives a memory of where he might have seen that face. It was when he was driving west some years ago, on his way to get a Mexican divorce. He was also on his way to meet a woman who had pursued him since her childhood, a woman he met when she was a schoolgirl at a boarding school where he went to lecture about writing once. By chance he runs across her on Fifth Avenue when he was still married and, although nothing could happen between them in New York (her husband keeps a tight watch over her in the city), she will be visiting relatives in Mexico and has promised him a rendezvous if he can arrange to be in that

city at a specified time. He drives slowly west, as the specified time is not for four months. He picks up a girl hitchhiker and for one night they share a motel room. Next day their routes diverge and she goes her separate way. Now, alone for so many weeks in his cabin, his possibilities beginning to shrink on him, he becomes obsessed with a new idea. This woman *might have been the girl hitchhiker*. Their faces are not dissimilar. (The fact is, he cannot remember that earlier face very well.) And if so, then this child he is trying to woo in order to placate old ghosts turns out to be his biggest ghost. Now at this juncture a resounding *dénouement* is needed, a deep twist which would connect all the levels of his tale and free him from his dilemma. But he finds he is no longer interested in writing it. He is only interested in living it and ironically he lacks the means, the time, and alas the old charm which might have captivated this elusive woman, the most immune to him of all those lost faces. How to end such a tale of unaccomplished desires? You bankrupt rascal, this has been your biggest caprice of all.

The "outline" broke off at the bottom of the third page. Had he meant to go on with it? On the back of this page there followed some scribbled calculations having to do with expenses. And then, below the jumble, as elegant and flourishing as the other had been tentative and scribbled, the same leisurely hand in love with its own penmanship that I recognized from those old letters to his mother I had perused on Waverly Place:

A man of words and not of deeds
Is like a garden full of weeds.
And when the weeds begin to grow,
It's like a garden full of snow.
And when the snow begins to fall,
It's like a bird upon the wall.
And when the bird away does fly,
It's like an eagle in the sky.
And when the sky begins to roar,
It's like a lion at the door.
And when the door begins to crack,
It's like a stick across your back.

And when your back begins to smart,
It's like a penknife in your heart.
And when your heart begins to bleed,
You're dead, and dead, and dead, indeed.

Oh, Ambrose, your modern man was so awash in the flux of
all his complexities and possibilities that he drowned in them.
And you kept track of him even as he went down for the third
time.

Yet I couldn't help being disappointed that I had figured so
slightly in his chronicle. Surely I had been more to his imagination than a "fatherless child."

19

Sketches for a New Woman

It was a brilliant morning in mid-October, and Sam was lying
nude on two folded blankets in a warm and luminous area of
light on my cabin floor. We had arranged that any day she had
no job I would pay her three-fifty an hour to pose for me. She
was worth a lot more than that. Her body was supple and her
muscles trained so that she could easily maintain positions that
would have made other models tense or fidgety. But more remarkable was the range of human images her particular body
was capable of suggesting. Turn her three-quarters away and
have her bend as though to pick up something and you had the
rib cage and torso of a warrior; have her sit facing you, her shoulders in a relaxed position, and you had a fully mature woman
who had borne a child. Stretch her out lengthwise and see

tender angles counterposed against tough ones. She was like some hybrid woman, a composite of what had always been and what could be. Already I had dozens of sketches of her. Her shapes filled up the room in conté crayon, pencil both hard and rubbed, brush and ink, washes of oil thinned with turpentine, and combinations of these. Today I was beginning a prolonged oil sketch in which I wanted to try to capture her contours and the contours of the light which bathed them and gave them added dimensions.

It felt right to be working with a living human figure. It was that morning I began to suspect that for me this would always be the vital artistic subject.

In these sessions we talked or not, depending on our mood. Sometimes we listened to the classical music station from Albany on the radio I had bought; once or twice she rolled herself a homegrown weed and I declined in order to catch as sharply as I could a series of trancelike (and several wanton) poses. I knew her better now, she had opened up, though she was never to be chatty or anecdotal. She didn't go in much for fanciful dialogues and her humor was slow on the uptake. But the stolidness of her somehow lent itself to long posing sessions. You felt she was *there* as long as you needed her; she wouldn't fly away. Lately she had been bringing along a "test tutor" manual, which she studied when I was working up a background or when the pose allowed. She was doggedly plowing her way through the sections on which she'd eventually be tested in the high school equivalency exam.

I had rearranged my cabin space to accommodate the longer hours of indoor working, and the room was now my studio with a small corner where I ate and slept, and not my living space with a small corner where I painted. As I worked on more things at the same time, my materials sprawled in a wider and messier circumference around me. I had given up altogether on "tidying up" each evening in case Minerva dropped by on one of her infrequent but inevitable visits to see how I was getting on. She had squared her tiny shoulders sportingly the first time she saw her neat little rental property transformed by coffee cans stuffed with brushes, the unsightly makeshift shelf on which I spread out my jars and tubes, the newspapers and the plastic dropcloths on the floor. "You'll be sure to close anything inflammable, won't you, before you go to bed, dear?" she asked nervously, narrowing her eyes at the small print on a can of varnish. I assured her I would. I had also promised to patrol every room of her house at least three times a week while she was gone. Made bold by something (I know I did my best to talk her into seeing the world farther down than Cape May), she was at last taking up Sadie O'Halloran's annual invitation to spend the cold months in Florida. Mr. O'Halloran, the stay-at-home funeral director, had generously consented to store Minerva's furs and jewels as well as safeguard Mother's ashes in a special locked vault on his premises. The two ladies would depart in Sadie's cream-and-turquoise Le Mans next week. The geese had already gone. The colorful topping had blown off the trees and, oh yes, I had turned thirty-three.

I like to remember that October morning. I like to go back into it from the "future," where I now live, and retrospectively paint into it all the prescient signs of my belated emergence. For years of my life I developed my negative propensity for time travel. At a moment's notice I could plunge into some awful moment of the past (or some awfuler fantasy about the future) and come back with enough material to take a lugubrious bath in. Now I am becoming adept in making the positive trip as well. I send my mental spaceship to points past or future and it frequently comes back with old buds of present blossomings (like that October morning); or sometimes a bold design for fruits to come.

It is the quality of light I remember most intensely about that morning when it all started to happen, and how Sam's body seems to float in it. The light has simply bleached away all traces of blanket and floor and there she is, buoyed up by layers of fluid light. She appears to be crafted out of the light, so continuously and harmoniously do the parts of her body mesh with its contours. And yet I need her outline, too. Otherwise it will be just blobs of light. The linear plane of her individuality must be there so the light will have a special form to keep afloat.

She is lying on her back, the solid flank nearest me crossed at the peak of the other upraised knee. Her breasts slope away from each other and the strong, taut arms stretch above her head, obscuring the lower part of her face. She is studying, lying down. It is amazing how long she can keep her arms raised like that, holding the big orange-and-green manual which promises her the rest of her high school education.

I'll leave out the book, I think: just fade out suggestively at the top of the canvas and make it as if her hands are reaching for something, or perhaps examining something they already grasp. The main thing is to get the model sketched in and then, quickly, over the pencil outline, try to capture those fugitive contours of light. Yes, leave out the book. That's too particular.

At this point the Model speaks:

"What an asshole question. Christ, these bastards must think we're dumb."

"What are you on?"

" 'Interpretation of Literary Materials. Drama.' Listen to this: 'When Othello states "There lies your niece, whose breath, indeed, these hands have newly stopp'd," the reader knows Desdemona has died of (A) cancer, (B) stabbing, (C) old age, (D) strangulation.' If all the questions are this dumb, I'll pass with honors."

"I suppose if someone has skimmed that part of the play, they could mistake it for a stabbing," I say, putting the tiniest bit of shading under the triceps muscle of the raised arm nearest me.

"Hmph," she grunts. Her lips move lightly as she reads the next question to herself.

"Can you put your arm a little higher, like you had it before?" I don't want the mouth, it makes her too much Sam, and she is—I want her to be—just a woman suspended in light, her face half hidden, her arms reaching up, her eyes raised toward whatever it is she is reaching for or has got.

Sam will do all right on Interpretation of Literary Materials. You don't have to memorize things; you only have to read carefully and intelligently the passages they give you on the day of the test. If she had studied Ambrose's outline for "Capriccio" as closely as she studies these passages in the orange-and-green manual, she could have saved herself a lot of unnecessary anxiety. Even if that outline had found its way into the troopers' hands, and thence up to the BCI inspector at Saranac Lake, nobody would have made the false connection she was so afraid of. Even if the Bureau kept a highly specialized literary exegete on its staff, not all the minute rereadings in the world of "Capriccio" could have turned Cheyenne into Ambrose's daughter. And what harm would it have done if somebody had? There was no legacy involved except a name. But it would have narrowed Cheyenne's father down to one name and, strange as it sounds, that's what Sam resented most.

When she understood that I didn't intend to expose to the world those crumpled pages she had found balled up beside Ambrose's wastebasket on the night of his death, she relaxed her reticence and we talked more openly.

"Look," I said, "if you read it really carefully, it's clear that even the *character* in Ambrose's story knows he's contriving a fiction. It's a fiction compounded of attractive but lost possibilities; or . . . well, sometimes just alter stories . . . like people have alter egos. This character becomes obsessed by the *other* ways things could have gone in life. I mean, there were some things in there that bothered me, too, the first few times I read it. The part about my grandmother and my godmother, for example. But I went over it in my memory and I honestly couldn't come up with one bit of evidence that they'd been any more than deeply attached friends. Maybe he had different evidence. But maybe it was just a story somebody told him about some women in a Buenos Aires family." (The ubiquitous Pequeña again? But perhaps there had been many women in Mexico with stories of aunts in Buenos Aires.)

"But why would anybody want to write something like that about his own mother? Especially if it wasn't true?" said Sam. Adding, "Although he did throw it away. Or meant to."

"I think he only half meant to."

"You mean he really wanted somebody to find it?" She was alarmed again.

"I think he just wanted to leave some evidence that he had been serious. That he wasn't a phony but someone who had tried. You know that night you came and found me lying on the floor, that night? Well, say I had meant business, that the Luger had bullets in it and all that. What would I have done with all my sketches? I'd been working on sketches for a painting that didn't work out. I think before I killed myself I might have torn those sketches crosswise, but I don't think I would have destroyed them altogether. I would want people to know I had been up here trying. Also there's that secret hope-against-hope wish that later you'll be vindicated. Someone will come along years later and stick the pieces back together and say: 'What a tragedy she died before she knew she was great.' As for the other, why would he make up something about his own mother . . . or mine, for that matter? Well, making fiction is a little like making paintings. You put in what you see, but if the composition's still lacking, you put in what you don't see, too. I told you, his first book was this glorified version of my mother. The story is—I mean, the family version of the story is—he wanted to marry her after my father was killed. But she was too grief-stricken. Besides, Ambrose was only seventeen. Later, after he returned from the army, he sat down and wrote this version where the woman does accept. For some reason, in the book he never wrote, he was going to deglorify this figure based on my mother. I don't know why. Maybe they did have an affair and she was carrying his child when she drowned herself. God, after I read that outline, I even considered the possibility that maybe *I* was really his child. But that can't be because she was already pregnant when my father brought her home to meet the family. At least my grandmother said so. Oh, what does it all matter in the long run anyway, who is whose child? . . ." I stopped, afraid I'd trampled on Sam's tender area. "It's what we do with ourselves afterwards that counts."

"That's true," she agreed gruffly.

She didn't relate her whole story in a single extended monologue, as some people do when they find an interested listener; there was little of the raconteur about Sam. But as the weeks went by and she posed for me, bits and pieces surfaced while she lay naked on my floor in the sun, and we talked of ourselves and where we'd been and where we'd like to go. And by the time I left Plommet Falls, possessed of the painting that was her gift to me, the painting that was destined to bring me my first share of the long-wanted acknowledgment, I like to believe I gave her something in return. As she spread out the pieces of her adult life and looked at them for the first time in the company of a friend and saw what kind of picture they added up to, a confident pride grew in her. In spite of having been given some shoddy materials to work with, she had been gutsy enough to build all this? "I really think," I told her, "that the test of a person is, in the end, how well she's used what she was given to use. And, girl, you've used it." "Do you really think so?" she asked. I thought so, I told her.

I like to believe I held the mirror for her. While she modeled for me, so patient and generous with the planes and curves of her body and what she had made of them, I held the mirror for her and helped her put into words what an indomitable spirit, even when victimized, can achieve. And if you can do it once, you can do it again. Thus rises the indestructible edifice.

Sam's odyssey had begun eleven summers before in an ugly little housing development in Toledo, Ohio. Her mother had divorced the basically antisocial Captain De Vere, to the great relief of both, when Sam was twelve, and soon married a man much younger than herself. This man, Harry, to give him credit where probably little was due, agreed to take on the responsibilities of the overgrown daughter to get the mother. But as time passed and the "overgrowth" shaped itself into statuesque proportions, he started to entertain other ideas about their relationship. Sam began to go gray at sixteen, which made him feel less guilty about the discrepancy between their ages, although at the time he was not much more than thirty himself. Being a devious sort, he disguised his intentions at first under puritanical authority. He wouldn't let her close the door to her bedroom at night because young girls were known to indulge in unhealthy practices when given too much privacy. Then she would wake suddenly in the middle of the night to find him kneeling and panting in the dark beside her bed. "You were breathing funny," he would tell her. "I thought you might be sick, so I came to check."

For a long time, she actually believed she "breathed funny" in her sleep. That it was her fault that she had waked poor Harry.

Her mother became pregnant. Poor Harry was kept awake by her tossings and turnings, her ungainly spreadings about on their only average-sized double bed. He couldn't sleep on the couch and he needed his sleep because *he* had to go to work in the morning. He had to support the two women, didn't he? He persuaded Sam that she should let him share her bed. ("In the underprivileged countries, whole families have to sleep in one bed.") But no use to tell Mother about this. She would be upset and one didn't upset a pregnant woman; she might miscarry.

For several months, Sam lay ramrod straight, eyes wide open in the dark, waiting for him to inch closer, waiting to feel the repellent hard knot press against her buttocks. Then she'd cry out. "Shut up," he'd say. "Do you want your mother to miscarry?" Her mother miscarried anyway.

Sam told her mother what was going on. Her mother wept and called her a liar and said she was trying to ruin her marriage. "If he has made any advances, it's because you did something to encourage him."

Sam's mother told Harry and Harry told Sam that if she

didn't straighten up he would have to commit her to a mental institution. Harry told her she was "imagining things."

Sam actually wondered: was she imagining things?

She couldn't study and was held back at the end of her junior year. During the next year, when her friends were beginning their senior year, Harry picked her up at the high school and they went for a drive. He told her he was going to tell her something for her own good. The something was that Sam was, he thought, probably schizophrenic. "You manage to lead two lives and hide each one from the other. Do you know what I mean?" He was looking at her avidly. "Do you know what I'm referring to? You do know, don't you? If not, I'm afraid we'll have to get psychiatric help for you." Sam said no, she didn't know what he was referring to.

Harry told her that they had been having regular intercourse for a number of years, it had started when she was thirteen—she had been the first to make the advances when he came in to say good night one night. Now he was willing to continue with her, but she would have to be more honest about it and not worry her mother.

Sam thought she probably was going mad. She wrote to her father—they were not frequent correspondents—and suggested that she might come and live with him in Key West and finish high school down there. He didn't answer right away. When he did, it was to say he only had a small trailer and it wouldn't be proper for the two of them to share such close quarters. She ought to finish high school first and as a graduation present he would pay for her trip down to Key West for a visit. He added, perhaps as a consolation prize, that he intended to will her his land and shack in the Adirondacks so she would have a place of her own to go to when she was grown up.

Harry began wheedling Sam to let him kiss her breasts on the evenings her weekly allowance was due. "You've let me do a hell of a lot more than this, if only you'd remember."

Sam managed to get through her junior year with barely passing grades the second time round. She was on her way to the public swimming pool one Saturday morning when her mother was out shopping. Harry told her that her pubic hair was sticking out where everybody could see it and he couldn't let her go out to a public pool like that. "Okay, I'll go trim it," she said, starting into the bathroom. "You won't be able to reach the back parts. Better let me do it," he said, getting the look Sam hated on his face. She slammed the door on him and locked it and waited till her mother came back from the store. Harry told her mother she had been "acting crazy" and he forbade her to go swimming for a whole week.

One summer night a few days later, something "clicked" in Sam. She told her stepfather she was "beginning to remember some things," but he'd have to go slow. He could kiss her right nipple this week when she got her allowance—if he'd give her two weeks' allowance. "You little tease," he said, but he played her game. Something in him was even more aroused by it.

The following week, he was permitted access to the left nipple for another two weeks' allowance. "Why, you're turning into a regular old hand," he said. "But next week, I think it's time we stop being such a little tease."

The next week Sam was gone. She left the house one morning when both of them were out, with a few possessions and the allowance money in her gym bag, and hitchhiked to the interstate. She considered it her first piece of luck in years when three high-spirited, clean-cut blond college boys, on their way west to find summer jobs, picked her up.

They were very nice to her, flirted with her a little and even bought her dinner. They pretended not to believe her when she said she was eighteen. They were taking turns at the wheel, they told her, so as to drive straight through to California. Nobody bothered with last names. For some reason, they decided to camp out for the night when they reached the western side of South Dakota. Sam woke up to find herself being raped by one of them. She screamed, but the only people to hear her were the other two, who soon were on top of her themselves.

When it was all over, she began to cry hysterically. One of

them, cleaning himself up in the car, discovered blood on himself. He got word to the others fast and one of them comforted Sam, apologizing, telling her that they took her for some runaway divorcee out for a little adventure. Sam's gray hair, he explained. . . .

The others managed between them to pack everything up quietly and before Sam knew what had happened, she was sitting in the middle of nowhere, watching incredulously as the taillights of the car shot out of sight.

She began to walk. She walked for miles in a moonlit landscape whose contours were unlike anything she'd known in her life. She came to a river and took down her shorts and panties and splashed water up into herself. There was a lot of blood. She found herself absurdly gratified that she had been a virgin, that Harry had been lying, that she was not insane after all.

She walked along the river till it got light. So this was South Dakota. This was the West. She hadn't paid much attention to the scenery when she'd been wedged between whichever two of the clean-cut young men happened to be in the front seat while the third slept in the back.

It got light. She walked along, keeping to the river. She passed several farmhouses, not daring to go in and ask for help. She concentrated on walking as if she knew exactly where she was going.

In my life since Plommet Falls, there have been times when things did not go as I wished. I have been without enough money to provide myself with the sort of life I wanted. I have had to take jobs that took away valuable painting time and painting energies. I have been frequently alone, or without the kind of company I would prefer to my own. It was not until very recently that I got the kind of studio I wanted and had sold enough work to be able to stay home and paint in it. I have been robbed a couple of times (but the thief apparently did not consider my paintings good investments—he, or she, took Ambrose's Luger, however, and I often try to picture the circumstances in which that thief pulled the trigger for the first time). I have had more

"Violet in Blue" days, many more indeed, with false starts and sometimes no starts at all. I have had a couple of reviews so devastating that they could make me forget others that were discerning and laudatory. But never, since I heard Sam's story, have I been able to take my "Poor Little Me" moods seriously for very long. "Well, at least," I say humorously, "I'm not in the middle of South Dakota with nothing but the clothes on my back and a trio of rapists' seeds battling it out for ascendancy in my womb." And things begin to look quite bearable again.

Sam put me into proportion, as Ambrose put me into perspective.

About noon, Sam started to feel faint. She decided she would try the hospitality of the next human being she happened to meet if that person looked even vaguely friendly. She approached a run-down house with all its white paint either peeled or gray, and chickens running around the yard. There was an Indian woman with a long braid down her back, hoeing a vegetable garden. A black-and-white dog shot out from a barn with a roof half fallen in and ran in circles around Sam, barking viciously. Sam held her palm down to the dog as her father had taught her long ago and let the dog sniff her. The Indian woman stood up, as far as she could stand up with her arthritic back, and waited for Sam to make the first move.

Sam walked over, the dog following curiously now, and explained as calmly as she could that she had been hitchhiking west to look for a summer job and that the driver had abandoned her at a rest stop and gone off with all her clothes and money. Which was true. The boys had gone off with Sam's gym bag in their trunk. The other part she had decided to put as far back in her mind as she could. Maybe in time, she thought, she could succeed in forgetting it as completely as Harry told her she had "forgotten" his embraces.

Sam told the Indian woman that she was quite good with her hands and liked to work outdoors and there looked like there were a few things that might be fixed up here. She could paint the house. She could probably repair the barn. . . .

She had never painted a square foot of anything in her life. She had never hammered a nail into a piece of wood. But she suddenly felt she was capable of anything, if someone would give her the chance to work hard enough to forget all the things she wanted to forget.

The old woman was a Sioux and lived alone. Her husband had been a Swede. They had built this house by the Cheyenne River and farmed and now he had been dead fifteen years and she was just holding on. The house was mortgaged. She could barely keep the chickens alive and weed the garden with her arthritis.

"God was sure watching over me when he made me stop at Lila's house," Sam told me.

"It's too bad He wasn't watching over you the night before," I said.

"No, don't say that. I wouldn't have Cheyenne."

Ambrose's "fiction" about Sam had been intuitive in one sense. It was on the hitchhiking stretch of Sam's journey that Cheyenne had been conceived. Only his romantic imagination had turned it into a willing exchange on the clean sheets of a motel bed.

By the time Sam realized that she was pregnant, she and the old woman, Lila Swenson—whose maiden name had been Lila Singing Rock—had taken each other's measure. Both were strong women, not much given to talking, but susceptible to too much isolation. Lila had never had a child and Sam was very much in need of mothering. "Do you want to have this baby or you want me to give you something I know?" asked the old woman. "There's still time." It had been Lila who first confirmed Sam's condition.

Sam said she wanted the baby, but that she hoped for its sake it was a boy. She named it months before it was born after the river where she had washed herself and which also had led her to Lila.

Sam and Cheyenne stayed with the old woman till Cheyenne was seven and a half. Then Lila died and Sam mourned her like a real daughter. The house, much improved by Sam's self-taught course in carpentry, went to the bank, but Lila had left some savings to Sam. Sam bought a white jeep and when Cheyenne's school was out, she drove them east through the state along the same route the three boys had driven her west on eight and a half years before. At Sioux Falls they headed south toward Florida. As Sam drove, she imagined the reunion with her father. She had written him during her first weeks at Lila's, telling him she'd left home and why and asking him not to tell her mother where she was, just that she was safe and happy for a change. Several letters arrived from her mother, forwarded by her father. Sam threw them away without reading them. She told her father she did not read them and pretty soon the letters stopped. When Sam found out she was pregnant, she decided not to say anything about it in her letters to her father. She might miscarry and it would have been all for nothing. Then, when Cheyenne was safely delivered, Sam put it off again because her father had written a depressed note about how the doctor said he had to have an operation for cataracts before the year was out and it seemed wrong to tell him then. By the time he'd had his operation and was feeling better, it seemed too odd to write suddenly: "Oh, by the way, I have a daughter almost a year old now." Now she was simply going to drive to her father's place and surprise him with his granddaughter. Flesh would speak more eloquently than words.

But when she got to Key West, she found Captain De Vere lying in his trailer recovering from a stroke. The couple in a neighboring trailer were doing the best for him they could, but it was clear it couldn't go on like this on a permanent basis. The old man wept and wept, one side of his face grotesquely still, and begged Sam not to put him away in a nursing home. He "bribed" her: if she would stay and take care of him, he would make over the deed to his shack and the land in the Adirondacks immediately. That way she wouldn't have to pay inheritance tax. She said she'd stay as long as he needed her. But he had the lawyer come and made the grand gesture anyway, and thus began an uncomfortable time for everyone. There wasn't room for three of them to sleep in the trailer. Cheyenne slept in the jeep, as Sam had to be near her father in case he wanted anything. Cheyenne resented the querulous old man with the crooked face. He took all the attention her mother was used to giving her. To make matters worse, Captain De Vere had gotten off to a bad start with the child by calling her "he." The old man had looked at the slim little figure standing beside his bed in its T-shirt and shorts and sneakers, and its short pale kinky hair that sizzled round the critical little face, and asked, "Is he illegitimate?" Sam said she tried not to feel thankful when within a few weeks her father was so incapacitated by a second stroke that even he agreed he would be more comfortable in the home for retired seamen.

"How much does Cheyenne know about . . . about how she came to be in the world?" I asked.

"When we moved here I thought it was time to tell her everything. This was going to be her home. When we were in South Dakota, she went to this small school in an old railway depot. It was in a depressed area and many of the kids' fathers had left home to get work somewhere else. And there were some who were supposed to stay away so the wives could get welfare. So nobody felt like being too nosy, you know. I was Sam De Vere, who lived with Lila Swenson—maybe I was some relation, maybe not—and somewhere I guess everybody assumed there was a Mr. De Vere, who'd either deserted us or gone somewhere else to get work. But now we were coming to this new place where people might be more nosy and where somebody was sure to remember Cheyenne's grandfather's name was De Vere. So I asked her one day did she know what illegitimate meant, and she said yes, that's what she was, she knew that. These kids, they know more than we think they do. Then I told her she was almost eight years old now and had a right to ask me anything she wanted to about herself. I said I had kind of wondered why she hadn't asked sooner. She said Lila had told her I'd tell her when I was ready, so she had waited. 'What would you like to know?' I said. She was very calm; it was like she'd had these questions ready for years . . . Cheyenne can be so calm it's spooky. The first thing she wanted to know was did her father know about her. I said he didn't. Then she asked me did I think if he did know he would be pleased. I said I didn't think so. She took that in for a minute, then she asked was he an Indian. I said no, he was a nice-looking Anglo-Saxon, tall with light hair, like mine and hers. That was true. All three of them were. This description seemed to please her. Then she asked if I knew where he was now and I said I didn't, that I'd only seen him once in my life and didn't even know his last name. Then a weird thing happened. I was just getting ready to tell her the whole story—I figured the earlier she dealt with it, the better it would be for her. Also I didn't want to lie to her. My mother told me nothing but lies. Honest to God, I had my mouth open, ready to spill the whole story, and she looked at me in this peculiar way, and it was like she was the adult suddenly. She said, 'Wouldn't it be simplest, Mother, to tell people I don't have one and leave it at that? It isn't as if we've done anything wrong. Nobody can put us in jail because I don't have a father, can they?' I said no, they couldn't. 'Then let's forget it,' she said. And I got this weird feeling she knew I was going to tell her something she didn't want to hear and she was determined not to hear it. So I said, 'Okay, but remember you're free to ask me about it again.' She said she'd remember, but she thought she knew all that was necessary. Can you believe it? The funny thing is, it's never been a problem for us here. She was right, Cheyenne was right. She's managed to turn it to her advantage. Her friends look up to her and the way she carries her mystery. Can you believe a child could be so cool?"

I said I could, thinking of Cheyenne's cool little face with those large, demanding, critical eyes. Cheyenne suffered me because I guess she realized I was unavoidable, for a while anyway, but she made no attempt to hide her impatience if her mother spent a minute of time with me that Cheyenne wanted for herself. She liked her mother to go to work and come home to her. It was okay if she, Cheyenne, left her mother alone to go see a friend, but she didn't like it if her mother left her alone. Sam seemed to think this was perfectly natural; she laughed about it. She said once, "Even if that thing he wrote about us had been true—I just mean the part about him trying to woo me through her—it would never have worked. She wanted him for herself while I was away, but she wouldn't have accepted us as a couple. She probably wouldn't accept any third person. Even that time he came for dinner made her nervous. She liked it best when he stayed at his place. She commuted between us all summer."

I asked her if she didn't sometimes think about a man.

"Sometimes. More than I used to. I went for years thinking I never wanted one near me again. But I don't think about it enough yet to want to do anything about it. Not yet anyway." She shrugged. "Cheyenne'll probably be married before I get around to doing anything about it. I have some other things to catch up on first."

"The school?"

"Yeah. And I need to make more money. I think I'll have to have the school before I *can* make more money, because, let's face it, I'm a damn good carpenter but when people want the really expensive things done they still get a man. So I'll have to get the high school diploma and then see what can be done about the architect bit. We may have to move. Cheyenne wants a horse. I've thought about maybe going out west again. It's warmer and you can be outdoors more and I can somehow see it all happening better there. A university with a school of architecture for me and a horse for Cheyenne. Horses for Cheyenne if she wants them. Maybe I can get work on a ranch—I've thought of that, too. Only I've never ridden a horse in my life. Still, I've learned to do a lot of things I never did before. I can learn to do a few more."

"So you haven't ruled out men." I had been thinking about this subject a lot since I had received the first part of Milo's new novel, *Kaatje's Curse*, about the embittered man-hater who came into her patrimony too late.

"Men, yes," said Sam. "Maybe not one nice man." Then as an afterthought she added, "Ambrose was a nice man, in spite of what he wrote about us. But he was a little too old."

Kaatje is seduced by the Frenchman who comes to paint the portrait of herself she has commissioned. He abandons her and leaves her to have the child alone in her gaunt, expensive house. A young man passing by hears her cries and enters the forbidding house in spite of his fears and helps her deliver her child, as Milo had helped the woman in Greece. Kaatje threatens to kill the child and the young man takes it away and raises it himself. Two hundred years pass and a descendant of Kaatje, a bright young woman, falls under the spell of Kaatje's curse. She, too, has been jilted by a lover and she goes to live in her ancestress's house, seduced by the idea of punishing the world by refusing herself to it, as her ancestress had done. But Milo would get her out of that. In his novels people would continue to be saved through love from seductive eccentricities. Would someone do the same for Sam one day? For me? I hoped so.

"I haven't the least doubt you can do anything you want to do," I said to Sam, "when you've already done as much as you have." I thought to myself: You can probably even survive the adolescence and young womanhood of that superior, demanding little girl. Yet I could imagine Ambrose being drawn to her imperious ways. He probably did woo her. And she had a quick and precise mind; she was already quicker than her mother and unfortunately she knew it.

And I wondered, a little, what Ambrose would have found to do to avoid staring at the empty page if he had come here, as I had, in the fall and there was no imperious Cheyenne looking for daylight entertainment. Would he have found another diversion?

"I think I probably can," said Sam, "do pretty much of anything. If I have to."

"She looks almost mythical, your nude," a woman named Charlotte Nicholas would say to me, tilting her sleek head one way, then the other, narrowing her eyes, stepping forward three

cautious paces toward the canvas propped on the appraising easel, then retreating again, in the time-honored manner of gallery
owners who are taking their valuable time in making up their
valuable minds. I would be nervous, but not hopelessly so. For
I knew this painting had something to reveal and that someone
somewhere, sooner or later, would be able to see it. I was showing it first to Charlotte Nicholas, of the gallery of that name in
Wooster Street, because Carol Gruber, Ambrose's former wife,
had played tennis with her at their health club and learned that
she was assembling artwork for a traveling exhibition of women
painters. "This is your chance," Carol would telegraph to Plommet Falls, where I was staying through the spring at reduced
rates since I was now Minerva's caretaker. "Bring all you can
carry and get down here."

"No, she's not mythical; she's real, all right. She's my neighbor."

"Oh, Carol said you lived in a cabin in the woods," she said,
smiling. She spoke with a trace of an English accent.

"She lives in the next one." I was trying to assess her opinion
as I bantered. Her face was a smooth, cordial mask. But her eyes
were intelligent with good humor. "She's a remarkable person,
really."

"Mmm. I'm sure she is. Tell me, how did you prepare your
ground, to get that effect of layered translucency? Or am I asking for a trade secret?"

Since I had no trade yet, it was hardly a secret. "No. To be
honest, a lot of it evolved from trial and error. And just plain
fooling around. It's tempera and lead white and then gelatin and
damar varnish over that. It's the gelatin that gives it the
banded effect you can see through the layers of paint. I was
ready to try anything at that point. I had made so many wrong
starts I was getting desperate. Oh, I knew how I wanted it to
look, but what you see there is the last in a long line of frustrat-
ing attempts."

"There's nothing desperate about this painting. I like it immensely. Would you be willing to lease it to me for my show?

I can't offer a great deal of money, but I think you'll find the exposure some compensation. So far I've booked this show, if it materializes, for twelve major cities. I have every reason to believe it will materialize. The art world has just discovered women are a valuable commodity." She laughed. "We've known that for some time, haven't we? What do you say? Can you bear to part with your painting for half a year or more?"

I said I would try and bear it.

"What do you call it?"

"It hasn't got a name. But I think of her as a suspended woman. She's suspended in this light, she's suspended in . . . well, her own possibilities, what she might do. . . ."

"I shall let Carol win one tennis game next time we play. You've just given me a lovely idea. This is only a thought, I have to sleep on it—I always sleep on everything—but given the propitious parallel of where women are at the moment, why not call my traveling show 'Suspended Woman'? Furthermore . . . I don't know if you'll be agreeable to this—I don't actually know if you *should*, though color reproductions can be excellent these days—but what do you say to a poster of your suspended woman? It would be the poster for the show. Of course, no reproduction could reproduce these—what did you call them?— bands of light, but it would be awfully good exposure. Don't answer now. Sleep on it. You're staying at Carol's aren't you? You ring me and let me know how you feel about it in the morning."

And I would sleep on it, and ring her in the morning and tell her that, yes, it was okay if she leased my painting and named her show after it and put it on a poster and took it to what ended up being fourteen major cities, including a "Welcome Home" show at her gallery in Wooster Street.

But in the present time of my oil sketch, Sam is still lying in the October morning light, she is still suspended in her own present. As I am doing the area around her, she has dropped her arms and has them crossed over her breast. She rocks a little from side to side, her eyes closed, innocently enjoying the sun. The orange-and-green manual lies outside the range of my canvas.

Will she pass this exam, she is wondering, will she get that piece of paper that entitles her to (in the words of her manual) the "job, pay, prestige, and vocational opportunities previously denied you"?

And I'm wondering if my skills, as they are now, are up to the test of capturing the rich scene this October morning dazzles before me. Will I . . . oh, God, will I ever be able to put it down on one surface so that others will be dazzled, too?

"Could you stretch your arms up for one more minute?" I ask. "I need to make sure of these lines before I let you go."

Obligingly Sam stretches, her gesture all the answer I need.

"Good. Oh, good. Just a few seconds more."

And there she is, and will remain, securely netted in layers of light.

Meanwhile that limitless radiance which eludes us all spins on, taking our day with it, teasing and turning us for a time in its vibrant dimensions, continuing to spread its blind effulgence when we have gone.

*

A Note on the Type

The text of this book was set in the film version of
Caledonia, a face designed by W. A. Dwiggins. It
belongs to the family of printing types called "modern
face" by printers—a term used to mark the change in
style of type letters that occurred about 1800.
Caledonia borders on the general design of Scotch
Modern, but is more freely drawn than that letter.

Composed by Precision Typographers, Inc.,
New Hyde Park, New York

Printed and bound by
The Book Press, Inc., Brattleboro, Vermont

Designed by Gwen Townsend